IN PRAISE OF

M000199866

THIS BOOK PLUNGED ME INTO WWI...

"This book plunged me into WWI – the filthy conditions, the never-ending danger, the courageous, young fighters, the strongly bonded friendships – and the daily realities of war. But what stuck with me was the reception by the community and the government itself toward those who managed to return home alive." – KATHY CRETNEY

WHERE HISTORY AND FICTION MERGE...

"An incredible piece of historical fiction centered on Sam... a soldier, a Company First Sergeant, and finally a WWl vet who returns to an America that does little to support those who bravely fought on its behalf. Larry has created a riveting storyline with well-developed characters that traverse the war and the historical years beyond." – F. MICHELE JONES, RETIRED TEACHER OF CREATIVE WRITING

THIS STORY SEIZED MY RANGE OF EMOTIONS...

"Vivid descriptions of the horrors of World War I trench warfare combined with a tender love story seized my range of emotions! The Patriarch weaves a story of one man's indomitable spirit, leadership, and courage as a compelling introduction to the saga of the McCormick family." – SHAWN IRELAND

A WORTHY READ...

"The reader begins on the war front, experiencing the horrors of the fight as if in the bunkers himself. Eventually, he learns the hardships of transitioning to his 'new normal' life back home, after surviving the travesty of his war experience. An emotional and intellectual journey." – ALAN ZUBAY

EXCEPTIONAL STORY ON AMAZINGLY ACCURATE PIVOTAL EVENTS FROM OUR PAST...

"If the first book in the trilogy, Legacy of Honor by Larry Freeland is an accurate indicator, this series should be read by everyone. The descriptions of fighting in the trenches and the struggles of the soldiers in World War I is amazingly accurate. Almost nothing is overlooked with cars, baseball, steel mills, strikes, and the bonus army." – REGINA LOVERIDGE

EXCITING AND HISTORICALLY ACCURATE TALE OF WAR AND ROMANCE...

"Freeland weaves together an exciting, action-packed, and historically accurate tale of war and romance during and after World War 1." – JAMES HARVEY, AUTHOR OF GRAYTON BEACH AFFAIR

CAPTIVATING AND REALISTIC WW I EXPERIENCES...

"A captivating realistic story of one man's World War I experiences both on the battlefield and postwar; a powerful account of the strength, hope, and love that triumphs over the many obstacles soldiers and veterans endure." – PAULETTE J. BROWN

A MASTERFUL STORY...

"Once again, Larry Freeland tells a masterful story. Anxiously awaiting to read books two and three of "Legacy of Honor" trilogy." – L. MILLER

UNFORGETTABLE STORY...

"Crawl through the trenches of France with American infantrymen and experience the horrendous brutality of WWI warfare ... reminiscent of the carnage in Civil War battle scenes in The Red Badge of Courage. Then follow the "doughboys" as they assimilate back into American society, often with heartbreaking and unforgettable outcomes." – JAMESON GREGG, GOLD MEDAL WINNER, IBPA BENJAMIN FRANKLIN AWARD "GEORGIA AUTHOR OF THE YEAR"

FREELAND'S TRILOGY EXPLORE HOW THIS COUNTRY TREATS ITS WARRIORS AND VETERANS DURING AND AFTER OUR WARS.

"The Patriarch begins in early August 1918. Sgt. McCormick is in the trenches in Europe getting ready to lead his men over the top and engage Germans at the other end of a 300-yard killing field. Freeland does a good job painting the picture as we move from scene to scene in his new book. One example is the excellent transition McCormick goes through starting with a flirtation in the hospital, a few days of recuperation with baths and a clean uniform, a truck ride back to his unit, and then: "Jumping from the back of our truck, I land in mud almost up to the top of my trench boots." Freeland takes us immediately back to the front, and all that entails." – BILL MCCLOUD, VIETNAM VETERANS OF AMERICA-BOOKS IN REVIEW II

IN PRAISE OF LARRY A. FREELAND'S PREVIOUS
BOOK "CHARIOTS IN THE SKY"

"Impeccably faithful to historical events...a worthwhile peek into
the horrors of war." – KIRKUS REVIEWS

"A great book about men who control their fears and fly into
action knowing they need to be prepared to handle whatever
happens. – BILL MCCLOUD, REVIEWER FOR VIETNAM
VETERANS OF AMERICA

"There are more than enough harrowing flying scenes and
firefights on the ground that will keep readers of this genre inter-
ested." – THE VHPA AVIATOR, MAY/JUNE 2021

"A nicely written, exciting book. [The author] replays the feeling
of time and place extremely well. Well worth reading. – HELI-
COPTER LIFE, Spring 2021

"I was transported to Vietnam during the end of the war through
this book. The bravery and fear of the helicopter pilots
constantly facing death was palpable. I highly recommend
reading the book!" – KATHY CRETNEY

"Right up there with some of the best. I loved the book! [It] really
held my attention and let me visualize all of the various scenes as
they unfolded." – TONY MANCINI

"An eye-opening look into the world of American helicopter
aircrews at war in Vietnam." – RAY BROWN

LEGACY OF HONOR

THE PATRIARCH - A WW1 SAGA

LEGACY OF HONOR SERIES
BOOK ONE

LARRY A. FREELAND

Publish Authority

This book is a work of fiction. Names, characters, places, and incidents are products of the author's imagination or are used fictitiously. Any resemblance to actual events or locales or persons, living or dead, are entirely coincidental.

Copyright © 2022 Larry A. Freeland

Legacy of honor: The Patriarch
Larry A. Freeland
www.LarryFreeland.com

All rights reserved. No part of this book may be reproduced or used in any manner without written permission of the publisher except for the use of questions in a book review. For quantity purchases, address: Publish Authority, 300 Colonial Center Parkway, Suite 100, Roswell, GA 30076-4892. PublishAuthority.com

First paperback edition September 2022

Cover design lead: Raeghan Rebstock
Editor: Nancy Laning

Library of Congress Control Number: 2022916113

ISBN 978-1-954000-40-7 (Paperback)
ISBN 978-1-954000-41-4 (eBook)

Published by Publish Authority
Offices in Roswell (Atlanta) GA and Newport Beach, CA USA
www.PublishAuthority.com

Printed in the United States of America

*This novel is dedicated to my grandfather, Samuel H. Freeland, and the men who served with the **American Expeditionary Force** during the First World War. Only those who served in this war can truly know what they endured and the price paid by so many of their comrades-in-arms to bring the war to an end.*

"We never really let the Germans know who won the war. They are being told that their army was stabbed in the back, betrayed, that their army had not been defeated. The Germans never believed they were beaten. It will have to be done all over again...."

— GENERAL JOHN J. PERSHING

"The soldier above all others prays for peace, for it is the soldier who must suffer and bear the deepest wounds and scars of war."

— DOUGLAS MACARTHUR

"Wars may be fought with weapons, but they are won by men. It is the spirit of men who follow and of the man who leads that gains the victory."

— GEORGE S. PATTON

FOREWORD

The *Legacy of Honor* trilogy is a historical fiction story about three generations of men in one American family spanning a century of our Wars and Conflicts, beginning with World War I and progressing forward to present day. Each generation serves, experiences combat, and then must cope with how it affects them. The overarching theme deals with how this country treats its warriors and veterans during and after our wars and conflicts. The trilogy consists of three books: book 1-*The Patriarch*, book 2-*The Son*, and book 3-*The Descendants*.

The Patriarch begins with the protagonist serving in World War I—the war to end all wars. He participates in many battles culminating in the Meuse–Argonne offensive fought near Montfaucon, northwest of Verdun, France. This offensive was a major part of the final Allied operation of World War I that stretched along the entire Western Front. It was fought from September 26, 1918, until the Armistice of November 11, 1918. It was the largest and deadliest battle the American Expeditionary Force fought during the war and resulted in 26,277 Americans killed and 95,786 wounded.

During the Meuse-Argonne campaign, a temporary cemetery was established on October 14, 1918, on terrain captured by the American 32nd and 5th Divisions. This terrain ultimately became the Meuse-Argonne American Cemetery. The French government has granted the United States of America free use of the land on which it rests as a permanent burial ground in perpetuity without charge or taxation. The cemetery was created from several temporary cemeteries which lay scattered over the relevant battlefields of the Meuse-Argonne offensive. During the offensive, soldiers had to be buried within two to three days after death. With the reinterment of soldiers from temporary cemeteries to the Meuse-Argonne cemetery completed, it was finally dedicated on May 30, 1937. A brief description follows from the official Meuse-Argonne American Cemetery website (www. abmc.gov/Meuse-Argonne):

"Within the Meuse-Argonne American Cemetery and Memorial in France, which covers 130.5 acres, rest the largest number of our military dead in Europe, 14,246 in total. Most of those buried here lost their lives during the Meuse-Argonne Offensive of World War I. The immense array of headstones rises in long regular rows upward beyond a wide central pool to the chapel that crowns the ridge. A beautiful bronze screen separates the chapel foyer from the interior, which is decorated with stained-glass windows portraying American unit insignias; behind the altar are flags of the principal Allied nations."

PREFACE

A WAR TO END ALL WARS

On April 2, 1917, President Woodrow Wilson convened a joint session of Congress to request a declaration of war against Germany. President Wilson cited two main reasons for declaring war: Germany's violation of its pledge to suspend unrestricted submarine warfare in the North Atlantic, and its attempts to entice Mexico into an alliance against the United States. On April 4, 1917, the United States Senate voted in support of the measure to declare war on Germany, and two days later, the House concurred. On April 6, 1917, the United States declared war on Germany. Thus began a series of actions to mobilize. The Selective Service Act was enacted on May 18, 1917, which allowed for the conscription of men for military service. General Pershing was appointed commander in chief of the American Expeditionary Force (AEF). He landed in France on June 13th. The first American troops began arriving in Europe in late June 1917.

When America entered the war, there were only 127,500 men

in the United States Army. When the war ended, over four million men had served in the United States Army and over 800,000 in other military service branches.

INTRODUCTION

THE RAINBOW DIVISION

The 42nd Infantry Division was activated in August 1917, four months after America entered World War I. It was composed of National Guard units originating from twenty-six states and the District of Columbia. When the United States entered the war, the War Department wanted to send an Army Division over to France as soon as possible. The only divisions they believed were ready for deployment were the State National Guard Divisions. However, the War Department was concerned that if just one of these State National Guard Divisions went to France first, it would look like favoritism. Within the country, there was a growing desire and sentiment to go to Europe and fight the Huns (slang for Germans). Because of this, the War Department feared that selecting one state's division over another could anger many sections of the country. Therefore, the decision was made to select individual units within many of the State National Guard Divisions from across the country. The War Department's press person and originator of the idea, Major Douglas MacArthur, said the division would stretch across the United States "like a rainbow." So, the division quickly became known as "The Rainbow Division."

PROLOGUE

RMS LUSITANIA

During the First World War, Germany waged submarine warfare against the United Kingdom, implementing a naval blockade of Germany. On Friday, May 7, 1915, the Cunard Ocean liner RMS Lusitania, which had sailed from New York on May 1, 1915, was off the coast of southern Ireland on its way to Dublin. As the Lusitania came closer to Ireland, heavy fog engulfed the ship. The captain ordered depth soundings to be made, reduced the ship's speed, and called for the foghorn to be sounded. Some of the passengers on board were disturbed that the captain may be advertising their presence. By noon the fog had been replaced, as bright sunshine settled in over a clear, smooth sea, and the captain increased his ship's speed.

The German U-boat, U-20, was headed home on the surface when something was sighted, and the captain was summoned to the conning tower. At first, they believed they had sighted several ships, but it quickly became apparent that it was one large ocean liner appearing over the horizon. The U-boat submerged to periscope depth and set a course to intercept the liner. Having closed in on the liner, the captain ordered one gyroscopic torpedo to be fired, set to run at a depth of three meters. It was 2:10 on the afternoon of May 7, 1915. What happened next was recorded in the captain's own words in the log of the U-20:

> "Torpedo hit the starboard side right behind the bridge. An unusually heavy detonation takes place with a very strong explosive cloud. The explosion of the torpedo must have been followed by a second one, boiler or coal or powder? The ship stops immediately and heels over to starboard very quickly, immersing simultaneously at the bow...the name Lusitania becomes visible in golden letters."

Onboard the Lusitania, an eighteen-year-old lookout at the bow spotted the thin lines of foam racing toward the ship and shouted through his megaphone. "Torpedoes coming on the starboard side!"

The torpedo struck the Lusitania under the bridge, sending a plume of debris, steel plating, and water upward.

"It sounded like a million-ton hammer hitting a steam boiler," one passenger said. A second, more powerful explosion followed, sending a geyser of water, coal, dust, and debris high above the decks.

Based on testimony from surviving passengers and crew, the following briefly summarizes what occurred during the eighteen minutes it took for the Lusitania to sink.

> "There was panic and disorder on the decks. Ten minutes after the torpedoing, when Lusitania had slowed enough to start lowering boats into the water, the lifeboats on the starboard side swung out too far to step aboard safely. That only left lifeboats on the port side. Many of them overturned while

being loaded or lowering, spilling passengers into the sea; others were overturned by the ship's motion when they hit the water. Some crewmen lost their grip on ropes used to lower the lifeboats into the ocean. This caused the passengers to spill into the sea. Other lifeboats were tipped over as they launched because some panicking people jumped into the boats. The Lusitania had forty-eight lifeboats, more than enough for the crew and passengers, but only six were successfully lowered to the water. A few of the Lusitania's collapsible lifeboats washed off her decks as she sank and provided flotation for some survivors."

Despite being relatively close to shore, it took several hours for help to arrive from the Irish coast. Many of the passengers and crew members had succumbed to the cold in the 52 °F water when help finally arrived. By day's end, of the 1,959 passengers and crew aboard the Lusitania, 764 had been rescued and landed at Queenstown, 1,195 had been lost, including 123 Americans."

On her decks when the Lusitania was torpedoed was a middle-aged couple from the United States. They had just finished a light lunch and were taking a leisurely stroll around the promenade deck when the torpedo hit the liner. The American couple was sailing on the Lusitania to visit family and friends in England. They did not make it, and their bodies were never found.

1

WAITING TO ATTACK

Over the deafening noise, the raging sounds of battle, I hear myself yelling, "Come on, men! You can't live forever! Keep moving, men!" The appalling, nauseating smell of blood-soaked dirt and cordite is almost overpowering. Hundreds of us are charging forward with fixed bayonets, shouting, cursing, screaming, and dying. The Germans are dug in on the ridge line above us, throwing hand grenades and pouring murderous rifle and machine-gun fire into our ranks. Men are falling all around me as we close in on the German lines. Many Germans climb out of their trenches, leaving the relative security they are afforded and charge us. Some of our men yell out curses at the enemy, some call out for their mothers, and others just die in silence—their eyes glaze over and fade out. To my front, a German and American charge each other leading with their bayonets. They run head-on and impale each other through the chest. They stare into each other's eyes momentarily and die, standing up, heads hung down, as if to say, "I'm sorry for what I've done." We keep moving forward as our ranks continue to shrink. More Germans emerge from their trenches. They have us at a disadvantage and know it. We're fighting for our lives. We can't make our objective. Then we hear the call to retreat and begin the deadly hand-to-hand fight back to our trenches.

Two Germans to my right are slashing at one of my men. I rush them and thrust my bayonet into the closest soldier. The other man turns to attack me. I pull out my pistol and shoot him. He spins around and drops. But, it's too late for my comrade—they showed him no mercy.

Enraged, I try to rally what troops are left standing and fight a retreating action. As we move back, we're stepping over the dead bodies of hundreds of fellow Americans.

One of my men, a close friend, is being dragged back toward the German trenches by several soldiers trying to take him prisoner. My rifle and pistol are out of ammunition. I charge forward to rescue him. Two of the enemy turn to face me. I extend my rifle with the bayonet fixed, step into both and slash across their necks with all my might. The other Germans release my friend but club him to death with their rifle butts as he falls. They turn to charge me. Dropping my empty rifle, I desperately look around and grab another lying on the ground near me. Raising it barely in time, I fire, killing one as the other continues toward me with his bloody bayonet extended. Before he reaches me, an artillery shell goes off near us, and I'm thrown to the ground. The world around me goes dark.

I hear voices. "See that padre over there. He is busy picking up things to send back to their next of kin. Watch how carefully and reverently he is removing items from that soldier's pocket." Opening my eyes and looking toward the sounds of voices, I see a padre kneel and remove items from the chest pocket of a dead American soldier. Standing near the padre is a captain and private. The captain instructs the private to help the padre. The private kneels and removes some items from another dead soldier near him. He stands up, looks around at the field of dead and dying, and says, "God! I'm glad I'm not in the infantry. They haven't a chance, have they Captain?"

Suddenly I'm awakened from another nightmarish dream by one of my men.

I'T'S EARLY AUGUST 1918, and we're waiting on orders to go over the top of our trenches and attack the Huns to our front. My name is Sam McCormick. I'm a sergeant assigned to A Company as a squad leader in the First Platoon. We are part of the 166th Infantry Regiment, 83rd Infantry Brigade of the 42nd Infantry Division, The Rainbow Division.

I'm a little over six feet tall, with piercing green eyes, and have a natural wave to my reddish-brown hair. I'm often mistaken for a lumberjack from the northwestern part of the country. Born in Wellsville, Ohio, to a first-generation Irish father and English mother, I occasionally drink and play poker. Although I don't look for trouble, not running from it just comes naturally to me.

Before our National Guard unit was activated, I worked at a pottery factory in Wellsville as an unskilled common laborer. The work was backbreaking, menial, and mind-numbing, with long hours and little pay. In early 1916 some of the other fellows in the factory and I joined the National Guard to make some extra money. When we were called up for active duty, I became an American Infantryman, "doughboy," as they call us over here. I'm respected and well-liked by the men in my unit. They've followed me into many tough spots without hesitation since landing in France earlier this year.

Our unit occupies an old French trench system which we recaptured from the Germans last week. We are in the Champagne Region of France, several miles east of Château-Thierry and facing the German trenches to our front. In mid-July, we fought a fierce battle with the Germans to retake the city and push them back toward their border. Before the sun rises today, we will "go over the top," cross the open field in front of us and go straight at them again. When the sun sets tonight, many of the men around me will no longer walk among us, having spent their last day on earth.

It's pitch dark except for occasional flares lighting up the predawn sky. They produce an eerie light on the men nearest me as they float slowly down to earth. Moving among the men in my squad, I see the fear in their eyes and sense their anxiety. It's there, I know it, for I have it too. Every man is wondering if this will be his last day on earth. Will we "become a landowner," "be buzzed or huffed," "click it," or "draw our full issue?" All terms we use to cope with death and avoid saying "killed."

I fear this is going to be another terrible day for all of us.

Our company cooks have been moving up and down the trench line, pouring hot java and handing out our morning breakfast—warm biscuits. This is a morning favorite for many of us as we have one of the best cooks in the regiment. We call him Frenchie, and he can bake up enough hot, delicious biscuits to feed the division if they would allow him. The boys are enjoying them while making small talk.

Looking around at my squad of doughboys, I ask, "How's your java and biscuits?"

The usual responses: "Not bad!" "I could use a little sugar and cream for my java!" "What about getting us some bacon and eggs, Sergeant?" "When do we go, Sergeant?"

"I'll see what I can do." "No rush, soldier. Your day will start soon enough," I respond to them. Light humor helps to relieve some of the tension and anxiety we all feel, but only briefly. Humor is in short supply up here in the trenches, and we'll take whatever comes our way when we can.

Reaching the right side of my squad's position in the trench, I notice Sergeant Arthur Wilson—we call him Art—coming toward me. He yells out, "Good morning, Sam. It looks like another lovely morning to go over the top and get into another scrap with the Huns!"

Art and I have been together since we first met in training camp when our National Guard units were activated and brought together to form the regiment. Art is from Cleveland, Ohio, where he played professional baseball for the Cleveland Indians as a center fielder and power hitter. He's taller than I am, with muscular shoulders and upper arm strength. His years of playing baseball contributed to building his physical attributes. Art is a big man, strong, and fast. Like me, he enjoys a good card game and an occasional drink and doesn't run from trouble. We hit it off in training camp and have been close friends ever since.

"Good morning. If you say so!" I respond in a lighthearted manner. "Your men ready, Art? This is going to be another hellish morning of fighting."

Art replies, "How does one get ready to do what we're about to do? Damn, that sounds philosophical." A short pause. "To answer your question, Sam, yeah. The sooner we go, the better. The longer we wait, the more time I have to think about it."

"I know what you mean. It's the waiting that gets me. Once we're out there, I don't have time to think about it. I'm sure it won't be much longer before we go. How's your java and biscuits, Art? Frenchie outdid himself this morning on the biscuits."

"The java is good; the biscuit is great. I could do with a few more of those biscuits."

With a slight grin on my face and a little mischief in my voice, I respond. "Dream on Art. We're on the front lines. That only happens to the rear-echelon types."

Art looks over at me as he turns to go check on his men and says, "Good luck out there, Sam!"

"Thanks, Art, same to you. I'll see you over in the Huns trenches."

We both manage a weak salute and then go about the business of checking on our men.

The attack is set to jump off at 0500 hours before dawn begins to break over the open field in front of us. We are the first wave of infantrymen who will go over the top and into the killing fields. It's another massive assault against the German lines 300 yards to our front.

The Germans attacked our front-line trenches in wave after wave of men yesterday. It was our artillery that decimated their ranks. As shells fell among them, the ground rocked with explosions as dirt, debris, and body parts were thrown high into the air. The Huns closed to within a hundred feet of us when their lines finally crumbled. As they closed in on us, we could hear their screams and cries over the roar of battle. What a frightful sound. It's unnerving, impossible to block out, and I fear I'll never get over the sounds of dying men, should I live.

The whole area we fight over is flat open terrain as far as the eye can see. Before the war, it was open farmland with some pastures and small farmhouses. Now it's nothing more than a wasteland devoid of trees, vegetation, or any semblance of what it was. Peering out over the field after their attack yesterday, I could see what looked like hundreds of dead Germans littering the ground in front of us. They're the newest harvest of dead men whose bodies haven't begun to decompose or been attacked by rats that prowl the killing fields. Now it is our turn to go out there and add another layer of dead men. All this in the hope of taking the German's front-line trenches.

As the time approaches for our attack, men move about in the dark, busying themselves while waiting for the command to go. The relative calm is shattered when German whiz-bang shells begin exploding up and down our trench line system. A whiz-bang shell, when fired, travels at such a high speed the sound of its flight is heard, whiz, only for an instant, if at all, before the sound of its explosion, bang. These shells are followed by a massive bombardment using Jack Johnson shells, the largest the Huns have, and mortar shells. We are in for a grueling start to our day as they are tearing massive holes in our trenches, ripping up parapets (the protective wall or earth defense along the top of a trench), and collapsing our trench shelters. Men are dying up and down our trench line as their bodies are ripped open and shredded, with body parts severed by red hot shrapnel and propelled into the air.

I'm in Dante's seventh circle of hell: violence.

2

THE TRENCH SYSTEM

Our trench system zigzags as it runs its course for miles in each direction of the front line we defend. Within a trench system, there are never more than a dozen yards of a straight-line trench before the line zigs or zags in another direction. This design provides more protection for us in the trenches. Zigzagging the trench line reduces the kill zone, or blast radius, of artillery shells, bombs, rockets, or grenades that land in any section of our trenches. This unique feature is saving many doughboys' lives right now.

From the air looking down on a typical trench system, it appears as a large, quilted patchwork of interconnecting lines and cross-sections. They zigzag across open terrain in many directions, and all are interconnected. The front-line trench we occupy is the main line of resistance and faces the German trenches. Located over 100 yards behind us is a secondary trench, referred to as a support trench. This is garrisoned by a small number of infantrymen and other support personnel, such as litter barriers, runners, cooks, and medical personnel. Should our front trench come under heavy bombardment or be overrun, we can retreat to this trench. Behind the support trench and several hundred yards back is a third trench referred to as a reserve trench. This is where our reserve troops are located and amass for a counterattack when ordered.

Our trenches are normally seven to nine feet high, about six feet wide, and have firing platforms built into the front wall of the trenches. These provide us with firing positions so we can look over the top and shoot at the Germans. Trench walls are reinforced with sandbags, wooden planks, and, where possible, corrugated iron revetments. Reinforced bunkers, where we can take refuge when under artillery attack, and machine gun emplacements are strategically placed up and down our trench line systems. We live in reinforced shelters placed throughout the trench system.

Our home is the trench system when it's our turn on the front lines. They are nasty, smelly places where pools of water and mud collect and settle along the bottom of the trenches. Wooden platforms, called duckboards, are placed along the bottom. They are supposed to help keep us out of the water, mud, and filth which collects there. These platforms are built not only to help prevent trench foot—a common problem for those manning trench systems—but to make it easier for us to move faster through the trenches. However, most of the time, they are nothing more than repositories for disgustingly dirty water, mud, vomit, urine, feces, rotten food, and all other manner of filth that falls to the trench floor.

We are not the only inhabitants that live in trench systems. Rats, lice, and frogs live among us. Rats are a particular problem as they eat our food and nibble at our flesh when we sleep. Living in a trench system is akin to living in an open sewer system. The smell of cordite, the lingering odor of poison gas, rotting sand-bags, stagnant mud, toilets overflowing with waste, cigarette smoke, and cooking food are constant companions. Life in the trenches is very difficult. Lice spread a disease called trench fever, which makes a person itch terribly and causes fever, headache, and sore muscles, bones, and joints. Also, many of us living in the trenches suffer from trench foot. Even though we constantly apply foot powder to our feet, we can't escape the water and mud we live with daily.

All combatant nations in this war build similar trench systems and endure the same hardships. This is our world here on the front lines. We eat, sleep, tend to our very basic human needs, try to relax, and maintain some semblance of life and sanity in this environment while waiting for the next attack.

The space between the Germans and us is called "no man's land." It is a killing ground, devoid of vegetation, with large craters covering the landscape. These craters are the result of combatants' constantly raining down artillery barrages on "no man's land." Pools of water and mud, where a man could sink to his waist, have settled to the bottom of these craters. In various stages of decay, bodies of Americans and Germans lay scattered across this nightmarish landscape.

Barbed wire covers much of the entire area in "no man's land," separating us. This wire has proved to be another lethal weapon in trench warfare. Barbed wire is used to channel assaulting enemy forces into prepared kill zones covered either by machine guns or artillery target points. The wire is typically laid out in long zigzag belts running parallel to the trenches. There are often several rows, separated by dozens of feet, routinely placed well out into "no man's land." Both sides use barbed wire in front of their trenches.

Like ours, German machine gun emplacements can sow a grim harvest of death for hundreds of yards out in front of a trench system. These weapons of death can decimate the ranks of charging men. The machine gun is a deadly weapon, but they are not the most lethal weapon of this war. That distinction goes to the artillery. Both sides have the battlefield we fight over well zeroed in for artillery barrages that can rain death from the heavens indiscriminately. The previous day's attack by the Germans across the killing field in front of our trenches bears witness to that fact.

3

THE MARNE

OVER THE TOP BOYS

There is chaos in our trenches. The Germans are hitting us with everything possible. It's having a devastating effect; men are blown to the ground as shells land near them. The screams, cries, and cursing of those nearest me can be heard above the explosions. The air smells of cordite, urine, and feces as some men urinate and defecate in their pants uncontrollably; a natural reaction to fear that can overcome men in combat. Moving quickly among the men while hugging the front trench wall, I shout encouragement and commands as I move.

"Hang in there, boys; it'll be over in a few minutes. Keep down and hug the trench wall. Don't let the Hun bastards get to you. Our turn is coming!"

As our artillery units begin a massive barrage, I get an occasional thumbs-up from some of the boys. The sky above us whistles as large outgoing artillery shells fly over us, headed toward the German lines. We feel the ground shake in the distance as our shells land among the Germans. We hope this barrage reduces their ability and will to fight before we attack.

With all hell breaking loose around us, the word is passed down the line, "Jump off in five. We go on the green flares."

The noise is deafening. Our officers move up and down our trench, yelling out to us, "Wait for the whistles to go. Get ready!"

Let's get going and get the hell out of here.

When we hear the whistles, we will be the first wave of men to go over the top and into "no man's land." Waiting to go over the top is nerve-racking. It's like waiting your turn to die. German artillery shells continue to rain down among us from the sky above. We try to make ourselves invisible to them by hugging the trench walls and seeking cover in dugouts where available. We cling to the hope that the Huns' shells will fall short or fly well over our positions.

We can only hope.

Hearing our officer's command, I yell at my men, "Steady boys, we go in five. Fix bayonets!"

My squad of fourteen men obeys the command. Even over the noise, I can hear their steel bayonets clear the scabbards of the men closest to me. That distinct clicking sound follows as they fasten their long steel bayonets to the end of their rifles. We are now ready to attack and kill the Huns using our rifles and bayonets. Anxiety, fear, and apprehension over what is to follow are tempered, to some degree, by our excitement and adrenaline as we wait for the order to go over the top.

Moving among the men, I offer encouragement but sense their trepidation. Some are praying; others attempt to steady their nerves by puffing on cigarettes. Two men have just lost their breakfast and deposited it onto the duckboards below our feet. The sickening smell of our trenches and the pungent smell of cordite in the air has a terrible effect on us. I marvel at how the men keep their emotions in check as we await the order.

Over the past several days, the Germans have repeatedly attacked our front-line trenches, trying to break through. We have held the line and counterattacked at intervals to dislodge them from their front-line trench system. We are about to try again. It has been a costly duel of two armies to gain a lousy stretch of real estate. The area we fight over now was once open green pastureland with trees and other forms of vegetation. Now it's a ghostly, vast wasteland and the destination of many Americans and Germans who took their last breath on that field of death.

I wonder when and if this madness will ever end..

German artillery shells continue to explode within our ranks. The noise is deafening, and the ground shakes as their shells impact up and down our trench line. Mounds of dirt, debris, fragments of arms, legs, torsos, and heads from men directly hit by exploding shells fly into the air and land among us. Men who are hit by flying shrapnel and not killed outright scream in agony from their wounds. There is no place to hide; we must endure. What a ghastly place.

Give us the damn order to go over the top. They're killing us here. Give us a chance. Let's go!

Dawn is breaking as we see green flares in the sky above us and hear our officers blowing their whistles; it's time. I check my M-1903 Springfield rifle one more time to ensure the safety is off and yell out, "Follow me, men, let's go!" Up and down the line from our position, I can see hordes of men rising from the trench, going over the top, and flowing into "no man's land." As we move forward at a rapid pace and stay crouched low to the ground, men are getting hit and falling. I can't stop. We must cross this field and get into the Huns' trenches.

Shell holes and tree stumps become temporary cover as we close the distance. A man to my left is cut to pieces by a German

MG-08 machine gun, and chunks of his flesh splatter all over me and my gear. He was a new man who had just arrived yesterday. More men are hit by machine gun fire and exploding shells. They fall to the ground in droves, and many roll into shell holes. When they come to rest, their contorted bodies—or what's left of them—are a terrible fright to look upon.

How indiscriminate and random the taking of men's lives is out here on this killing field.

I must keep going. The men are following me, and if we don't get to the German trenches fast, we may all die out here. As we close in on the Huns, I can see that our ranks are thinning up and down our attack line. Hundreds may be dead; many are strung out like wreckage washed up to a high-water mark. Several have died on the enemy wire, like fish caught in a net. They hang there in grotesque postures. Some look as though they are praying—dying on their knees, the wire preventing their fall. From the way our dead and wounded are spread out, whether on the wire or lying on the ground, I can tell there are no gaps in the Huns' killing zones.

I believe to a man; we're determined to get into the Huns trenches and carry the day. We continue the charge through this living hell. My body aches and my feet feel like bricks as I struggle to lift them and keep moving forward. My lungs hurt from heavy breathing and exertion. My heart feels like it's ready to burst out of my chest. Continuing the advance, I give what encouragement I can to my men. "Keep going, boys. Don't stop. We're almost there."

I've endured enough. I just want revenge.

Every man knows the score out here. We can't turn back; we must keep up the attack. Although they can't hear me over the noise of battle, they see me out in front of them and press forward. At this moment, our little piece of the world is in front of us and beckons us on. If we don't keep going, we may never see the sunrise tomorrow.

I'm singularly focused on surviving, getting to the German trenches, and taking on the Huns. I find myself in another world. My senses are in overdrive. I've never felt this level of awareness of what is going on around me as I do now. Every fiber of my being is engaged in the moment. It's as if everything is happening in slow motion. I can see the bullets coming at me and smell the pungent odor of cordite that hangs in the air. I hear bullets whiz by—see men moving and falling all around me. The screaming, yelling, and moaning are almost muted to the point where I can see mouths moving but hear nothing.

We cross the 100-yard marker; I look back toward our lines and see the second wave emerging from the trenches we just left. These doughboys had occupied the trench line after we went over the top and are now joining us on the field of battle. Their places are taken by our third wave of doughboys, who are now moving into the trench line. When the second wave hits the 100-yard marker, they will "go over the top" and follow them onto the battlefield. Should our attack falter and be called off, the third wave will remain where they are in the trenches and provide covering fire as we fall back.

Moving forward, thousands of bullets come zooming past us. Rockets and flares flying in from all directions explode among us. Shrapnel bursts in the air above and rains down its deadly iron. Every minute as I'm moving forward, I feel as if I'm waiting to be called to the great beyond. I advance twenty yards at a time and look for cover. Stopping only for a minute to catch my breath. I wait for our artillery barrage to land in the Huns trenches in front of me, then I make another mad dash. There is death all around me as we leave some of our comrades cold to the touch on the field. Moving among this carnage is our chaplain trying to console the wounded and dying. What courage this man has and the faith he must possess! The field of the dead is a terrible sight. *I fear I'll never forget it, should I live to go home.*

Closing in on the Huns' trenches, I hear them screaming and taunting us. "Come on, Ami!" "You die, Ami!" "Fahr zur hölle, Ami!" Roughly translated as "go to hell, American!"

I can see them clearly now as they rise above their parapets to shoot at us. This is a grueling attack. Every ounce of strength I can bring to the attack is being drained from my body. My legs ache, my lungs ache, and it's hard to breathe as I gasp for air. Even though there is a chill in the air, I'm sweating profusely and could use some water. I can't stop. I must keep going.

The closer we get to the Huns' trench line, the more accurate their rifle and machine gun fire becomes. Our attack line slows down, and the order goes out to seek cover wherever we can find it. Shell craters, shredded tree trunks, and dead men's bodies serve as cover as we dive into or drop behind whatever is nearest. I fling myself into a shell crater landing on two other doughboys. We're still alive, but the crater has several other occupants—all dead. Crawling to the rim of the crater, I can see the Huns are less than forty yards from us. We trade rifle fire with them as they raise over their trench lines to fire at us. Looking around me, I see that my squad is down to nine men, from fourteen. Again, I marvel at how the men take steady aim and fire at our enemy with devastating effect.

The Huns' ranks are thinning. Their machine gun bunkers are slowly being silenced. Our artillery, and the accurate firing of our snipers up and down the attack line, are taking a toll on the Huns. Many of the troops from the second wave are starting to fill in the large gaps created from the loss of men in our first wave. We are gaining the initiative and must get going again if we are to take the trenches in front of us. The intensity of the battle raging around me is at a fevered pitch as I try to catch my breath and resume my forward movement.

Once again, I hear whistles blowing from our officers who made it this far and are signaling for the attack to continue. Our Company Commander (CO) is right next to my shell hole. As he stands up to charge forward, he's cut in half by a hail of bullets from a German machine gun. His lower torso falls forward, and his upper torso falls backward, twitching as if jolted by high voltage electricity. What a gruesome sight! He didn't know what hit him.

My god, what do I do? They are killing us out here. My whole body is trembling. I can't let the men see me. I'm scared to death and just want to burrow into the ground. My mind is telling me to stay here, lay low, and don't get up!

Our attack falters as men drop back down to the ground seeking cover. Realizing we must keep up the initiative, and without thinking, my body jumps up and makes a mad dash for the trench line in front of me. As I do, I scream at the men around me, "Get up, let's go, boys. We've got them now. Don't stop until we're in their trenches!"

I can't believe this is me. What is going on? One minute I'm frozen, and the next, I'm running like a tiger after my prey. What the hell am I doing?

The men in my squad jump up and start forward. Doughboys close to us see what we're doing and rise from their ground cover. This has a reassuring effect on the entire company up and down the line of attack. Our attack line reforms, and we continue forward.

I'm yelling, "Follow me, boys!" We're all screaming as we charge toward the enemy. This helps to control our fear and, to some extent, keep it from becoming overwhelming. We focus less on the noise and chaos around us by yelling and screaming as we charge. Supposedly this reduces our fear factor. At least that's the theory.

The men begin tossing grenades into the Huns' trenches as we close to within twenty yards of them. Fifteen yards, ten yards, five yards. We're now on top of the Huns' parapet. I jump into the trench with my rifle and bayonet extended in front of me as far as it will go. The whole time, I'm screaming like a mad man with an uncontrollable rage.

Landing upright in the trench, I impale one of the Huns. I hear his bones cracking as my steel bayonet goes completely through his body and bursts out of his back. Blood flows from his fatal wound as he gasps for air. His eyes glaze over as life slowly fades from his body. The look of fear I first saw in his eyes changes to a peaceful expression as he sighs a final weak breath. His body goes limp on the end of my bayonet as he dies. All he was or ever would have been is gone with his last heartbeat. My bayonet must have penetrated some of his bone structure and become lodged so deep that I can't pull it out. I push him to the ground with my rifle still sticking up from his chest.

Pulling out my 1911 Colt.45 pistol, I begin shooting every German near me and still in the fight. This weapon has incredible killing power in close quarters like we're engaged in now. I kill several more Germans. My men and I are almost overwhelmed as more Huns appear from a side bunker. We are in the fight of our lives as we shoot it out. Individual battles between foes occur using pistols, knives, rifle butts, trenching tools, and bare hands as life and death struggles ensue.

The experience of close-in combat is a horrific, terrifying trip into hell. Men yell, scream, cry, curse, fire their weapons, wield trench tools, and lunge at each other with their bayonets. These are some of the tools of death we use as we try to kill each other. Men we don't know, have never met, and maybe would have considered friends in another time and place, we now viciously fight to kill.

As our life and death struggle continues in the German trenches, artillery shells explode all around us. Our supporting artillery doesn't realize we have entered the Huns' trenches, and they continue their barrage.

What the hell are our guys doing? Can't they see we're in the trenches now?.

The Germans see their men jumping out of the trenches and running to the rear. They immediately redirect their artillery fire onto the trench system we are fighting over. They're shelling their own trenches, hoping that we don't continue toward their last trench line after taking this one.

I think to myself as I fend off more Huns, *what a hell of a situation to find ourselves in; everyone is trying to kill us. Even our own men!*

Another Hun lunges at me, and I instinctively pull the trigger on my pistol, but it doesn't fire. I'm out of ammunition. No time to reload as I grab an entrenching spade, like a small shovel, lying on the ground next to me and attack my adversary. He thrusts at me with his rifle and fixed bayonet. I parry his thrust with the entrenching spade and hit him in the back of the head with a crushing blow. His helmet flies off, and I finish him with repeated blows to the head. He was probably dead with my first blow, but rage has overtaken my actions. I feel no remorse, pity, or sorrow for him; he was trying to do the same to me.

Looking around, I realize our situation has become dire.

When will our second wave get here? This isn't good!.

Then I hear yelling and screaming behind me. Looking up, I see our men pouring over the top, jumping into the trenches, and joining in the fight.

The second wave. Thank you, God!

The Germans immediately sense the futility of continuing

the fight and surrender. There is momentary silence in the trenches. Also missing is the whistling of artillery shells going over our heads. There is an eerie quiet settling across the battlefield. Both sides are reassessing the situation and regrouping.

It's almost noon, and we have been fighting for several hours. I'm exhausted, sweating profusely, and craving some water. My mouth is dry, my heart races, and my eyes are irritated. They are tearing up from all the smoke and dust of combat. I just want to lay down and rest. As the squad leader, I can't take a time out and must go about my duties. We need to secure the Germans that surrendered and send them back to our rear with some guards. We also need to begin fortifying our new position and prepare for the possibility of a German counterattack at any moment.

Taking the canteen from my weapons belt, I drink some water as I move among the men checking their status. I'm elated to see there are still nine men standing in my squad and able to fight. Although bloody and exhausted, we're alive and determined to carry on.

Moving among them, I engage by making small talk.

"Good job, boys."

"Glad to see you made it."

"How are you?"

"Anybody wounded?"

They are slow to respond and do so in subdued tones.

"No, Sergeant, I'm okay."

"I got some scratches, but I'm still here."

"I think I made it!"

"I'll let you know in the morning after I have room service, a hot meal, and a good night's sleep."

This response from Jim, the squad comedian, provides some humor and much-needed light laughter.

I respond to their comments. "Good, there's still a lot of

daylight, and it's going to be a long night. Check your weapons, stay at the ready and see to your duties. We should be getting some chow brought up soon. I'll give you an update after I meet with whomever our new CO is."

I select two men and send them back to the rear with the Huns we captured in our section of the trench. I then turn my attention to coordinating with the second wave troops that filtered into our section. My good friend Henry Miller, a sergeant and squad leader in B Company, part of the second wave, has joined his squad with mine. It's good to see another friend.

"Henry, glad to see you made it. Did you lose any men?"

In a low-key voice, Henry replies, " I started across the field with thirteen men, and I'm down to eight. I think two were wounded, but we couldn't stop to help them. What about you?"

I respond, "I started with fourteen and now have nine men left. I did see my new guy go down. Damn, he just joined us yesterday. I'm sure he was killed instantly. At this moment, I have no idea about the fate of the other four men. I can only hope they survived our attack across that damn killing field. I can only hope!"

"Yeah, me too," Henry replies.

Henry is from Canton, Ohio, where he worked in a local steel mill as an ironworker in the hot sections. Those sections include blast furnaces for iron making, converters for steel making, and ladles for transporting and pouring hot molten metals. All these areas produce terrific heat; hence they are called hot sections. Henry's National Guard unit was activated at the same time as mine. Henry is also a big, strong fellow, having worked hard labor in the steel mill for several years. He's not a big drinker, plays a good poker game, and enjoys boxing. In fact, he is very good at boxing and is our current Regimental Champion.

Henry, Art, and I met at training camp, where we were assigned to the same training company. After completing our training, we shipped out together. We've been together since arriving in France and have become close friends.

Art, who has been leading the squad to my right, approaches us and joins the conversation. "Hey boys, looks like you made it. That was one hell of a shelling we took crossing that field. I'm surprised we didn't lose more men than we did. We've been at this back and forth attacking and counterattacking for weeks now, and all for the same lousy piece of ground. This has got to end soon!"

I respond, "Let's hope so. How'd you fare out there, Art? How many men did you lose?"

Shaking some and in a remorseful tone, Art responds. "I started with fifteen; I'm down to ten. I lost five men in one shell crater they took cover in. Damn, of all the luck! It took a direct hit from a Hun artillery shell. In an instant, all five men were gone in a groundswell of dirt and a cloud of smoke, just like that. All gone. Damnedest thing!"

"Sorry to hear that, Art. It's a damn shame." Henry responds in a compassionate, soft-spoken manner.

I respond, "Art, that's got to be a hell of a thing to see. It's too damn bad, all those men at one time." After a short pause, I continue. "Fellows, I think we better get back to the job at hand. Henry, would you take the left side of my squad's position and reinforce it with the rest of your men until we get further orders?"

"Yeah, no problem, Sam. We'll shore up the trench wall facing the Germans and take up firing positions to our front. I'll check in with you later. See you, Art."

Art replies to both of us as he looks our way. "I best get back to my squad. Glad we all made it. Be careful."

We all agree and tap each other on the shoulder as we return to the business at hand.

With a brief respite from the action, my mind wanders off

and replays what, on many occasions, has given me pause to reflect.

We have been at this back and forth attacking for weeks now, and it's had a terrible effect on the men's morale. It seems so futile to go over the top and charge across open fields into the Huns' machine guns and artillery shells that so meticulously cut us down without mercy. How does a man deal with this? What can you do? Surely there must be another way to end all this madness.

4

THE NEW CAPTAIN

It's been a calm afternoon as the day fades into early evening. The light rain that started our day became heavier, slowed down, and has now subsided. The sun, which broke through the overcast skies for a brief appearance, has now settled below the horizon to our west. The early night's twilight takes over as a heavy mist and chilly air settles over the battlefield. There is occasional artillery fire coming from both sides, which is no more than the usual harassing fire we endure almost every night. Using a captured German "Rabbit Ears Trench Binoculars Periscope," I can look across the ground separating us from the German's new defensive line about 300 yards to our front. With this periscope, I'm able to stay below the top of the trench line and not expose myself to German sniper fire. The ground in front of us looks eerily like what we fought over earlier today, a wasteland! It is our new "no man's land."

Moving to the back of the trench, I look out over the killing field we crossed early today. I can barely make out our men in the ambulance company clearing the field of our wounded and dead. They have been at it since noon. They also remove any wounded

Germans they find and take them to our first aid stations for medical care. With some exceptions, both sides show mercy to their wounded enemy and provide some level of medical care.

After doing what I can to ensure my squad is settled in for the evening, I take a short break and sit on what's left of some firing platforms built into the trench. With the day coming to an end, it dawns on me that I'm soaked to the bone. It has been another rainy, wind-chilled day. Our temporary trench line is a mess, and there is no place to take shelter from the weather. American artillery units did a good job of destroying large sections of it. There are very few reinforced bunkers left to take shelter in, and the trench walls in many places have collapsed or been reduced to dirt. Without sandbags or wooden planks to reinforce the walls, the dirt turns to mud and collapses in on us. As the walls collapse, the mud just rolls down, filling up the bottom of our trenches.

Just another day on the front lines..

Resigned to our situation, I pull out my pipe, pack it with stale tobacco and try to light it with a match. This proves to be a daunting task as everything I have is either wet or damp. One of the men nearest me sees my predicament and lends me his lighter—I finally succeed. Drawing the tobacco smoke in and exhaling slowly, I casually look down the line on both sides of me. We are exhausted, soaked, muddy, cold, need some rest and hot chow. I'm not in charge and can only respond to orders. So here I sit in silence, smoking my pipe while trying to obtain a little warmth from the burning tobacco.

While enjoying my pipe, our new CO's runner approaches me. A runner is a soldier responsible for carrying messages between and within units in the trenches and on the battlefield. Being a runner is considered the hardest and most dangerous of the many jobs an infantryman could have. For a runner, it's only a matter of time before they are wounded or killed.

"Sergeant McCormick, you're needed at a briefing with our new CO. We need to find Sergeants Miller and Wilson and bring them along."

"Sure. Henry's over there on my left, and Art is on my right. Let's get them and go."

The runner guides Henry, Art, and me to the new CO's commandeered bunker. When we enter the dimly lit bunker, it's cramped and crowded with our company's surviving platoon officers and sergeants. At least it's dry, and we're temporarily out of the misty, chilly air outside. Our new CO is an Infantry Captain. He's been assigned command of what's left of our company since our last CO was killed earlier today as we closed in on the Huns. Our new captain begins his briefing.

"Gentleman, it's been one hell of a day. I'm glad to see all of you made it. I'm Captain Charles Glazebrook. I've been assigned command of A Company. The remnants of B Company have been assigned to A Company. You, gentlemen, are the designated leaders of your platoons and squads. Each of you should have been notified earlier by the Company First Sergeant of your responsibilities. If not, speak up before I begin this briefing."

No one speaks up.

Captain Glazebrook is from upstate New York and was an Investment Banker in New York City with JP Morgan & Company. He was one of the senior officers responsible for handling their major relationship with the U.S. Steel Corporation. When war was declared, his National Guard unit was called up to join the Rainbow Division. He is well-groomed, rather stocky, distinguished-looking, and has a matter-of-fact business tone to his speech. Occasionally his New York accent comes through.

He looks around at the faces of the men in his new command. As he does, I get the sense he's pleased with what he sees. After a long pause and hearing no questions from the men, he proceeds.

"You did a good job out there today. We've been trying to cover that ground for weeks now. We've finally succeeded. Well, done!"

After another brief pause, he continues. "Fellows, I'm afraid we'll be going at it again tomorrow. We're launching a major attack in the morning, supported by tanks. We'll be crossing the last piece of territory in front of us. By sunset tomorrow, we hope to have finally routed the Germans out of this sector. According to Division Headquarters, we've managed to push them back to their last trench line system. They're exhausted, low on men, and in a general state of disarray. Any questions?"

Looking at Henry and Art, I sense from their facial expressions we're all thinking the same thing. The men are exhausted, hungry, and need some water and rest. I speak up. "Captain, when will they bring us up some hot chow? We also need ammunition, grenades, some water, and a little rest. Sir!"

He looks over at me and says in a friendly manner. "It's Sergeant McCormick, isn't it?"

I responded, "Yes, sir."

He continues. "You did a good job out there today, Sergeant. Our attack may have failed if you had not stood up and led your squad forward when you did. Your leadership inspired your men and the rest of the company to continue the attack and carry the day. Well, done!"

"Thank you, sir," I respond in a low-key, almost embarrassed tone. "But there were several other men out there with me."

Turning to look me in the eyes and in a matter-of-fact voice, he responds. "Yes, Sergeant, there were. They were following you!" I have no verbal response and just nod my appreciation.

Captain Glazebrook continues. "Well, Sergeant, back to your questions. Hot chow, water, and resupply of ammunition should be here within the hour. Make sure your men get fed and resupplied when it gets here. You, gentlemen, know the drill for rotating guard shifts during the night. Also, I want each platoon to send out a listening post, but not too far from our trenches. I want our men to get all the rest they can. Tomorrow will be another tough one."

Although he directed his comments at all of us, I speak up first. "I will, Sir, and thank you!"

The other leaders in the briefing also acknowledge his orders. "Yes, sir!" "Will do!"

Captain Glazebrook looks around the bunker at us and asks if there are any other questions. Henry speaks up. "Sir, when will we go in the morning? How many tanks will be assigned to our sector?"

Looking over at Henry, he responds. "We'll go at 0600 hours on the green flares. As for tanks, there will be none in our sector. It's my understanding they'll be on our regiment's flanks. A few will be in the middle of our attack formation, acting as a wedge. We'll have the usual artillery barrages for our immediate support in this sector."

I don't say anything. It's a big disappointment that we will not have any tanks in front of us during the attack tomorrow. Tanks have recently been introduced to American forces and are proving very valuable on the battlefield. For now, it looks like we'll have to wait our turn before we can take advantage of the protection and added firepower tanks provide. I see in my comrades' eyes that I am not the only man disappointed.

Captain Glazebrook concludes his briefing with a summary of the last few weeks and what to expect tomorrow. "Gentleman, as you're aware, we have been fighting the Huns since their offensive began back in early July. They punched a big bulge into the French lines and were winning the day. Had we not been thrown into the battle early on, they may well have broken through to Paris. All of you helped in blunting their offensive. We now have them on the run."

He pauses, takes out a cigarette, lights it, and continues with his summary. "If successful tomorrow, we'll have pushed them back to where they started at the beginning of this battle. Which, if you haven't heard yet, is now being referred to as the 'Second Battle of The Marne.' If we carry the day tomorrow, this could be the beginning of the end for the Germans. I just thought I would share that with you. Any questions?"

Looking around at his cadre of leaders' facial expressions, he can tell we are ready for some good news. I take hope from his comments that we may well be on the downside of this war.

There being no questions, he concludes his remarks. "Alright then, see that your men are taken care of and get some rest. We're going back to work early in the morning. That is all!"

Henry, Art, and I head back to our squads in silence. We are lost in our thoughts as we contemplate what we just heard.

Could it be the beginning of the end? Will we carry the day tomorrow? Can I take much more of this constant combat?

Questions with answers that have yet to be determined..

Reaching our section of the line, we bid each other a good night's rest and proceed to check on the needs of our squads. Dawn comes early, and we have another day of hard fighting ahead. After ensuring my men have been fed, given fresh water, and resupplied with ammunition, I settle in for a long night of waiting, wondering, worrying, and another frightful, restless sleep.

5

LET'S FINISH THIS

The morning dawns early, and we find ourselves shrouded in a light fog with a mild breeze blowing in from the German side. Our company's mess cooks have been passing out biscuits and pouring hot coffee into our cups as they work their way down the trench line. Knowing it was going to be another terrible day, I didn't sleep well during the night. I fear many more of us will not live to see the end of this day. As I sip my coffee and take in the smell of its weak aroma, I also detect the distinct odor of sulfur—chlorine gas—making its presence known. Instinctively I realize we are under a chlorine gas attack by the Huns. They have released the gas into the morning fog from their side, allowing it to slowly drift with the breeze across "no man's land" toward our trenches.

Chlorine gas is one of a group of chemical weapons used by both sides. It causes vomiting and, although short-term, very intense respiratory distress. It is intended to temporarily disable and terrify enemy troops. It is generally believed that Germany was the first combatant of the war to begin using gas attacks in early 1915. However, the French used some chemicals against the Germans in August 1914 with little effect. Following the German's successful use of gas in 1915, the French and British developed their own chemical weapons inventories and began using them.

This is not our first time under chemical attack. We've experienced this truly terrifying weapon of war before. Acting fast, and before it's too late, I yell out, "Boys, it's a gas attack. Get your mask on now. Hurry!" I throw my cup down and yank out my gas mask while holding my breath. Slipping it on proves daunting, as I'm slow to react and struggle to adjust the straps and securely fasten the mask to my face. Having done so, I move rapidly among the men ensuring they are responding to my command. No one has panicked. I hear cursing and complaining while the boys don their masks and check each other over. With our gas masks on and standing close to the trench wall, waiting to go over the top, we look like a long line of goblins. To a man, I believe we hate these masks. They are bulky, hard to wear, harder to see out of, and often prove inadequate as gas penetrates the filters and mask housing.

As if the initial onslaught of chlorine gas wasn't enough, German artillery canisters begin crashing all around us, releasing their deadly mustard gas. This gas can cause large blisters on exposed skin and a man's lungs when inhaled. It is often fatal if a soldier is exposed to large concentrations of this gas.

If I had any doubts that this was going to be a bad day—they vanished with this gas attack.

We are in for another terrible day of fighting and dying.

The Huns have struck first. I stand on the firing platform and look out across "no man's land." I see no Germans crossing the open terrain in front of us.

I guess they just want to kill us with their chemical weapons.

Our platoon leader moves among the squad leaders, checking on us and yelling out. "The attack is still on. We go at 0600 hours on the green flares."

I pass the word among my squad and have them check their equipment. The Huns have continued to shell us with chemical canisters. Their deadly fumes shroud us in smoke as it slowly settles to the ground covering it in thick, low-hanging clouds. Some of the gas in the air is gradually seeping through the corner of my mask. I try to adjust it further with some success. My eyes have become irritated and begin welling up with tears. It's not bad yet and reminds me of our training exercises back in the States when they subjected us to tear gas.

I'm lucky. I secure the gas mask to my face and prevent myself from inhaling any poisonous gas. However, some men didn't react fast enough and are vomiting up their biscuits and struggling to breathe. Some roll around on the ground, coughing and gasping for breath. These gases are deadly, and we have no place to hide. The men around me and I do what we can to help those struggling. There is nothing more we can do for those overcome by gas and who are in no condition to fight. It's now up to the medical teams to get them back to the rear area as soon as possible. We can't spare any men to take them back to the nearest aid stations. We're going over the top any minute. These poor fellows are going to have to wait for further help.

The air is full of German chemical shells crashing in our midst. Mustard gas bites into our lungs like a consuming fire, and chlorine gas with its deadly poison, fills the air. These chemicals cause such agony that our surgeons, hardened by the carnage they deal with every day, turn away from the anguish and torment of its victims.

We thought we had the initiative, but this gas attack has a terrible, disorienting effect on the boys. As if a gift from heaven just arrived, our artillery has begun a massive barrage on the German trenches. We hear our outgoing shells whistle as they fly overhead, and the ground shakes when they crash into the Huns' trenches to our front. Our officers, my fellow sergeants, and I move among the men trying to restore calm and a sense of order. With some patience and luck, we manage to reduce their fear. We regain some control over the "panic beast" that dwells within all of us and wait for the signal.

Nothing like a good outgoing artillery barrage to gain back some initiative and restore some confidence in your men!

The word passes down the line, "Five minutes. We go on the green flares. Keep your mask on and be careful of the low-lying gas fumes out there."

Running across "no man's land" with bullets coming at you in torrents, mortar and artillery shells crashing all around, is terrifying enough. When you add gas to the equation and these damn gas masks, it's downright horrific!

Once again, I yell at my squad through the gas mask, "Fix bayonets, check your rifles and keep your mask on."

With speed and purpose, they move as one and come to the ready. The sky is lit up with green flares, and the command comes.

"Over the top, boys."

This is followed by the sound of whistles blown by our officers, who led us out of the trenches. Here we go again into the killing fields. I'm out and over the top of the trench, running as fast as I can and keeping a low profile. Yelling as I go, "Follow me, boys!"

The noise is deafening, and our visibility is severely limited by the smoke from exploding shells and poisonous gas fumes. Even if we could go without our masks on, it would be hard to see what's in front of us. These gas masks make it almost impossible. I have the urge to rip it off, but that would prove fatal. I must stay low and keep going. Looking around, I see the men closest to me are following and keeping up a healthy pace. Although I can't see them, Henry's squad is on my left flank, and Art's squad is on my right.

We cross the ground in front of us, moving as fast as we can, staying as low as possible. We're still shrouded in smoke and gas fumes which are helping us to move forward faster than we could if the field was clear. The Germans are having difficulty seeing and firing into our ranks with accuracy. It's the artillery and mortar rounds crashing all around us that are taking a toll. Our ranks are thinning, and I fear our attack may falter. As we continue to advance, men fall over dead into shell holes, slump over mangled tree stumps, and collapse on barbed wire, hanging there like rag dolls. They've given their last full measure.

The smoke and poisonous gas fumes have started to dissipate across the battlefield as the Germans stopped shelling us with gas canisters. Their artillery and mortar fire has also tapered off considerably. Mother nature takes over and slowly cleanses the air around us. Once again, I have the urge to remove my mask, but that can't happen. Poison gas fumes still linger in the air and slowly settle to the ground. As they do, large pools of white and yellow gas accumulate in the lower-lying areas of the ground. If one of us were to fall into any of those gas pools, we could easily be overcome by the fumes.

As we close in on the German trenches to our front, I can see some of them with their distinctive spiked top helmets, called Pickelhelms, as they raise up to shoot at us. This helmet was replaced beginning in 1917 by the Stahlhelm, which means steel helmet in German. It provides more head protection, but some Huns still prefer to wear the spiked helmet. I would like to see all of them wear spiked helmets. It makes it easier to spot them as they rise from a concealed position.

As our visibility improves, so does that of the Huns. They

have the advantage of being protected by the trench; we are out here in the killing fields with no place to hide. We're easy targets for the Huns, who are well-trained marksmen. For them, it's like shooting fish in a barrel, and they are taking full advantage of that fact.

The Huns are pouring their machine guns and rifle fire into our ranks with deadly accuracy. Bullets, thousands of them, fill the air around us as they whiz by, sounding like bees swarming over a honeysuckle bush for its nectar. Some find their mark as we hear the inevitable thud when a bullet hits a man, and he falls to the ground. They say you never hear the bullet that hits you. If that's true, then I might just make it through the day—I feel like I can hear every damn bullet out here coming directly at me.

That gives me no peace of mind since I'm in "no man's land!"

I signal my men to take cover and begin returning fire. We are now less than fifty yards from the Huns' trenches. Although we are caught in another firestorm, the volume of fire directed at us seems to be tapering off. Hopefully, we have put them on their heels.

Trying to catch my breath and control the "panicked beast" within me from emerging, I look at the men on my right and left. They're still with me, but the faces I can see through their gas masks reflect concern and anxiety. I'm sure mine does. Looking back across the field we just crossed, I see the second wave emerging from the haze of smoke and poisonous gas, slowly clearing. Our boys are a welcome sight. Again, our officers blow their whistles. We rise from our protective ground cover and rejoin the attack. My body takes over, and fear momentarily recedes into my subconscious. I move rapidly forward, keeping low, crouched over, firing, and yelling as we close in on the Huns. Our artillery has been steadily pounding the German's trench lines during the attack. Now they shift their shelling to the terrain behind the Huns' lines as we close in on their trenches. The Huns have nowhere to hide as some of them start retreating to their rear through our artillery barrage.

Reinforced by the second wave, we overwhelm the Germans and jump into their trenches, landing among them. Fierce fighting erupts as men struggle for their lives. But it is hopeless for them. They drop their weapons in mass surrender. Just like that, it's over.

There is no time to relax or rejoice; we instruct them to raise their hands and keep them up. Our men start checking each German for hidden weapons and line them up.

Art approaches me from the right and says, "Sam, you, okay?"

"Yeah, but I'm exhausted. How about you?"

"The same. I wish we could take these damn gas masks off!" Art responds as he tries adjusting his mask, so it feels more comfortable.

Looking around at the men nearest me, I see we are all trying to adjust them. The air around us seems clear, but we haven't received the command from our officers to remove them yet. I look at Art and yell through my mask. "Art, let's get some of the men to take these prisoners back and then organize our defenses for a possible counterattack."

Art agrees, grabs some of his men, and details them to take the captured Huns to the rear. I walk up and down our section of the captured German trench and yell at the boys. "The Huns will be coming back. Prepare for a counterattack. Move all the sandbags you can from the side of the trench facing our lines over to the other side facing the Germans. Be quick about it, boys!"

The men move with a sense of urgency as they prepare their new trench line to face another possible German onslaught.

Art yells over to me, "We have the Hun prisoners ready. We're going to take them back to the rear now."

"Sounds good. Get them out of here." Just as I speak, a German oberleutnant (1st Lieutenant) steps out from behind the line of Huns standing in front of me with their hands up and fires his P08 Parabellum pistol, commonly called a German Luger, at me. A bullet hits me in the left shoulder, and another grazes my left cheek as it passes through my gas mask. The bullet feels hot as it penetrates my flesh and knocks me to the ground. I can feel blood running down my face from the wound on my cheek, and my gas mask has a hole in it. As I fall, I'm trying to plug the hole in my mask with a finger, so gas doesn't seep in.

Lying there on the ground, in severe pain, I struggle to keep from breathing in the toxic gas pooled at the bottom of the trench. The sound of gunfire shatters the relative calm as I hear several of my men firing their rifles at the oberleutnant. It's a short distance between the Hun and me. As bullets tear into his body, his blood and flesh splatter me and the men closest to him. He falls dead to the ground in a hail of bullets. Two of the Germans standing nearest him have also been killed by the frenzied firing of my men.

By the rules of war, this act of treachery by the oberleutnant would result in a firing squad for him had my men not killed him first. Supposedly, by the rules of war, if you surrender to your enemy, you give up your right to continue the fight. With few exceptions, all sides tend to behave in this manner. Some don't. I was the unfortunate doughboy to be in the line of fire when this Hun chose his fate.

Henry heard the shots and came running over to my position. Seeing me on the ground, he kneels and lifts my head above the gas cloud on the trench floor. Another man leans over and gives him a gas mask he removed from one of the dead Germans. They both work to replace mine. Their quick action saves me from becoming another toxic gas casualty.

While Henry is comforting me and doing what he can to tend to my shoulder, Art sends for Captain Glazebrook and some litter bearers. My shoulder is throbbing, and I'm growing faint. I remain conscious enough to be aware of the activity around me as men go about moving sandbags to reinforce the trench wall facing the Germans and prepare for a counterattack. Art has his detail move the Huns out of the trench and back toward the rear. Even though they have their gas masks on, I can see the fear in the Huns' eyes. They surrendered and didn't participate in this treacherous act; however, they are tarnished by it and could be subject to retribution. They may well be wondering if they'll make it back alive to our rear area.

Their oberleutnant placed them all in the same category by his action. I could almost feel sorry for Fritz, the sympathetic nickname we use for German soldiers, but not at this moment.

My litter bearers arrive with Captain Glazebrook, who directs his questions at Art. "What happened here, Sergeant? Is that Sergeant McCormick? How is he?"

Art responds, "Yes, sir! It is Sergeant McCormick, and that dead German lieutenant shot him. After he and his remaining men surrendered, the lieutenant pushed through the men in front of him and opened up on Sam."

Captain Glazebrook responds as he looks over at the dead German, "Damn Boche treachery! What about the other two dead Huns? Did they fire too?"

"No, sir, they were just standing next to him when our boys started shooting at the lieutenant."

Kneeling down next to me and in a low, concerned voice, Captain Glazebrook says, "Sam, how are you doing? Hold on. These litter bearers will get you back to the rear and into an ambulance company. Then you're off to a dressing station. I believe your wounds warrant some long-term care. You'll be well back from the front lines for a while, which will give you some time to rest and recover."

I'm exhausted, weary, in severe pain, and feel like I might pass out any minute. However, I manage to respond in a calm, low whisper, "Thanks, sir, sounds good to me. Maybe I'll meet one of those famous French nurses."

While grinning, he responds in a low-key, lighthearted manner, "You just might, Sam!" Looking over at the litter bearer team, he instructs them to get me to the rear fast.

They place me on the litter, lift me up, and we begin our journey back toward the rear area. Weaving our way through the trench and passing by my men, many place a hand on my good shoulder and offer words of encouragement.

"Good luck Sam."

"See you soon, Sam."

"Be careful back there, Sergeant, with all those rear-echelon types."

"Give the nurses some kisses for us, Sergeant."

I'm too weak to respond, so I just wave my hand slowly to acknowledge their good wishes. Emerging from the trench system, I become aware of the eerie silence which has settled over the area. No artillery shells are flying overhead from either direction. I hear no rifles or machine guns firing. The air around and above me seems to be clearing of poisonous gases released on us early in the battle.

As we clear the German trench system, I hear the all-clear being given to our boys in the trenches. The air is okay to breathe again, and we can take off our gas masks. Although I'm on my way back to a dressing station and out of harm's way, I'm elated for our men to have a respite from the fighting. Hopefully, we have taken the day, and this battle is over.

My litter bearer team moves rapidly across "no man's land"

to a waiting ambulance company. The field we just crossed is littered with dead and wounded doughboys. Once again, our chaplains are moving among the wounded, offering comfort and praying over our dead. I'm saddened by what I see but thankful I'm not one of the dead.

Arriving at an ambulance company, the litter bearers place me on the ground next to an ambulance wagon and remove my mask. One of the medics cleanses the blood from my face and tells me it's just a flesh wound and not bad. I didn't think it was, but I'm relieved to get confirmation and thank him.

The ambulance wagon is hitched to several mules. It's common to use wagons pulled by mules because of the terrain's poor conditions at and near the front lines. Painted on the wagon's side is the "330th Ambulance Company." I've heard from other men that they have a good reputation. Although in considerable pain, I feel some degree of comfort knowing that I'm in good hands.

Several other ambulance wagons make up the 330th Ambulance Company, and they are members of the 308th Sanitary Train. An ambulance company is part of a sanitary train. The word "train" is unique and identifies the support units assigned to an infantry division. There are four trains: ammunition, supply, engineer, and sanitary. All use horse or mule-drawn wagons or motor vehicles in order to be mobile and provide support to division personnel. The purpose of the sanitary train is to provide medical care to the division. They include ambulance companies, field hospitals, camp infirmaries, and a divisional medical supply unit.

These ambulance wagons will transport us from the front lines back to field stations for care. The men of this ambulance company are very busy helping the wounded from our morning attack. We all need medical attention, and except for a few of the boys, we suffer in silence.

From the litters lying on the ground closest to mine, I notice several men appear to be casualties of the gas attack. Their eyes are bandaged, they have blisters on their face and hands, and many are coughing and having a rough time breathing. While I wait for my turn to be placed in a wagon, I feel sorry for the fellows suffering from the Huns' poisonous gas. There is no "humane weapon of war." The purpose of weapons of war is simple-to kill or maim your enemy. However, poisonous gas is a heinous way to die. If you survive the attack, in many cases, you are severely maimed for life. At best, you may only have visible scarring on your body from the severity of burns sustained from mustard gas that penetrated your skin. The less fortunate among those who have inhaled poisonous gas will suffer from severe scarring of their lungs. Depending on the degree of scarring, a man could be subjected to a lifetime of severe respiratory issues.

I've seen my share of death on the battlefields but lying here among the wounded and dying men. I feel a particular sense of sadness. Not all these men are going to survive. Many who do will live their remaining years dealing with complications from the wounds they survived.

The pain I'm enduring is quite intense. My wounds are not critical, but I need medical attention as soon as possible. Up until this point, all that has been done for me includes sprinkling a yellow sulfa powder on my shoulder and facial wounds. In addition, heavy gauze bandages have been placed over my wounds. Both actions have the intended purpose of protecting the wounds from infection and further blood loss. Any additional medical care will be administered at the dressing station by doctors and nurses. From my perspective, we can't get to the aid station fast enough.

Finally, I'm placed into a wagon with several other men. Once settled in, the wagon begins moving. We follow several other wagons in what amounts to a wagon train, like the old west. The wagons move slowly, leaving the front and heading to the rear with their precious cargo of wounded and dying men. Our ride is not comfortable. We bounce up and down as the wagons hit holes in the dirt road we travel over. This only adds to our misery, and my pain becomes too much to bear. My vision and awareness slowly fade away until I pass out. No dreams, no nightmares. Just total darkness and emptiness.

6

CHÂTEAU-THIERRY FIELD HOSPITAL

It's late afternoon, and I'm jolted awake by litter bearers removing me from the ambulance wagon and placing me on the ground. Slowly awakening from my unconscious state, I notice the place is a beehive of activity. There is a large two-story building near us that appears to have been some form of a warehouse complex. The building is in terrible condition, having been bombed and shelled in earlier battles fought around this area. However, with some effort, it's been converted into a field hospital that can accommodate hundreds of wounded men, American and French.

Doctors move among the wounded, instructing their Red Cross nurses where to send us. They are performing triage. The term comes from the French word trier, meaning to separate, sort or shift.

Modern medical triage was invented by Dominique Jean Larrey, a French surgeon during the Napoleonic Wars. He organized and treated wounded men according to the severity of their wounds regardless of rank or nationality. Triage is a standard practice used by French doctors treating battlefield wounded at aid stations behind the front. The United States quickly recognized this technique as an effective way for front-line medical personnel to sort, classify and distribute the sick and wounded and adopted the practice.

After being triaged, I'm moved to a group that is deemed critical but not urgent. In other words, I must wait for some time before a medical team will attend to my wounds.

The sky above me is clear, and the air has a freshness to it that I've not had the pleasure of experiencing in a long time. There is no stink in the air—always present in the trenches or the smell of cordite in the air. It's quiet. There's no sound of gunfire or artillery shells flying overhead or exploding nearby. There is a certain tranquility to the area. I have a momentary thought that I might be dead and have crossed over the river. No, that can't be. I still feel the pain in my shoulder and the general discomfort from what I've been through.

Lying here looking up into the heavens, I reflect on my experience of living in the trenches. It is not an easy life. Sanitation conditions are terrible. There is the constant disgusting aroma of our latrine stations, the smell of men who haven't bathed in weeks, and the odor of dead and decaying men left out in "no man's land," which drifts over our trenches. Our food is a constant source of complaints. Diarrhea and dysentery regularly nag at our stomachs. Water is brought up regularly, but the source of our water and any purification treatments it might be given before we receive it is questionable. It's generally foul-smelling and dirty.

These thoughts don't help my attitude as I slowly begin to take stock of how I feel since regaining consciousness. My head aches from the bullet that grazed me, and my shoulder pains me greatly. These wounds don't concern me too much, as I believe they will heal quickly. What concerns me is my breathing. Although it seems normal, I notice it burns when I take a deep breath and exhale. My first reaction is panic as I try to breathe normally and still notice some irritation in my lungs.

My god, did I inhale mustard gas?

Red Cross nurses, many of whom are French, are moving among the wounded. They are doing what they can to make everyone comfortable and reassure us that we'll be okay. I'm not convinced, and apparently, it doesn't go unnoticed by one of the nurses working her way toward me.

Noticing my agitation, which is bordering on a mild panic, she moves quickly toward me. She is French. Oh my god, what a beautiful woman. She moves with the grace and presence of an accomplished ballerina. She cuts a very handsome figure in her nursing uniform. Slim and graceful, with long brown hair pulled up into a bun and beautiful, penetrating hazel green eyes. I'm overtaken by her beauty. I feel safe and relaxed and forget about my wounds and the war momentarily in her presence.

She reaches me, kneels, and clasps her hands over one of mine. She is a goddess! Her skin is soft with a beautiful texture and color that is mesmerizing.

How does a woman this beautiful handle the carnage she lives with and works around every day?

Still clasping my hand in hers and looking into my eyes, she says in a soft voice, "Bonjour, Monsieur!" "Je m'appelle Marie Petit.". "Quel est votre nom?"

I'm overtaken by her presence; this is a woman with whom I could spend eternity. I know almost no words in French and struggle to communicate.

"Bonjour Madame Marie Petit! Je m'appelle Sam McCormick. Parlez-vous Anglais?"

I'm trying my best to impress her, but from the smile on her face, I suspect I'm butchering her French language.

Oh well! It's the thought that counts. I hope.

She responds, "Oui, I do!"

"C'est Bon! What a stroke of luck. Where am I, and what happens next, if you don't mind my asking?"

In almost perfect English, she responds. "You are at a field hospital in Château-Thierry. Your wounds will be attended to shortly. You'll then be moved to another location nearby to recuperate. May I call you Sam?"

"S'il vous plait. May I call you Marie?"

"S'il vous plait, Sam. Is there anything you need right now? You should be moved inside very soon." She releases my hand and slowly stands up, never taking her eyes off me. "I must continue to move around and check the other men, but I'll come by later and visit."

"I understand. Merci beaucoup, Marie! Thank you. Marie, I'm counting on you to keep your promise. Until then, au revoir!"

"Oui, au revoir, Sam!"

My goodness, what an incredible woman. I can't take my eyes off her as she moves gracefully around the field of wounded men and eventually disappears from my view. I desperately hope our paths cross again. And soon.

As Marie fades from my view, two litter bearers pick me up and carry me inside the building. The place is crowded with people moving in all directions. It's a scene of utter chaos. The sounds of wounded men screaming in pain and moaning can be heard above the chatter of doctors and Red Cross nurses trying to save their lives. The place smells of death. Blood-stained clothes and bandages are strewn everywhere you look. It's not heaven on earth for sure and may well be Dante's first level of hell.

My litter bearers place me on an old tabletop laid across two barrels. This serves as my operating table. There is a doctor and two Red Cross nurses assisting him. He looks down at me and says, "Son, where are you hit, and how long has it been since you were wounded? Can you tell me?"

Looking up at him, I struggle to respond. "I was shot in my

shoulder; a bullet grazed my face, and I think I inhaled some mustard gas. Not sure how long ago, but maybe ten or twelve hours."

He looks at me while instructing his nurses on what he'll need. "Son, you're going to be fine; we'll have you patched up soon. With a few days' rest, you'll be able to rejoin your unit! Okay with you?"

I nod yes as they place a mask over my nose and mouth. I'm given anesthesia as the doctor is talking. I hear gas flowing into the mask and slowly pass out. I fade off into a blackened space, with no dreaming, no nightmares, no light in the distance, nothing.

Slowly regaining consciousness later that evening, I look around me. I'm lying on a cot in an old church, surrounded by wounded men and Red Cross nurses. The church has sustained battle damage, but not as severely as the warehouse complex where I was first taken.

The Red Cross nurses move among us, tending to our needs as best they can. My shoulder is sore but not too painful and is covered in a thick bandage. My left cheek is dressed in a cloth that wraps around my face. The fabric does not cover my eyes, nose, or mouth. I look at myself and check to ensure I still have all my God-given body parts. Thank goodness they're still intact.

Wounds to your legs or arms can result in amputations as an expeditious way to treat soldiers and save their lives. But the feeling among some of us fighting is that there may be too much of a rush to amputate a limb and move on to the next man. Not being a doctor, I'm in no position to judge. As a doughboy doing the fighting, I prefer to believe they take every precaution to save our limbs while treating us. We're young and have our entire lives ahead of us if we survive this place.

Feeling better about my situation, I close my eyes and lie there, wondering what happens next. Without any sense of movement near me, I suddenly feel the soft touch of a woman on my hand and look up to see the angelic face of Marie. My heart races, my breath quickens, and I struggle to come up with something to say.

Marie takes care of that as she leans down next to me and takes a seat. "Bonjour, Monsieur Sam, how are you?"

I try raising myself to speak but lack the strength to do so. Marie instinctively stands, walks away, and returns quickly with two small pillows. She lifts my head slightly, places the pillows behind it, and adjusts them to make me more comfortable. Once again, she clasps my hand in hers. "Now, how is that Sam?"

Looking up into her beautiful hazel green eyes, I respond, "Merci beaucoup, Marie! It's very comfortable. Can you stay and visit? I want to get to know you better."

Marie nods and says, "Oui Sam, but only for a few minutes. It's my shift, and there are many of you to attend."

"Terrific! Tell me a little about yourself. Where are you from? How long have you been a Red Cross Nurse? Where did you learn to speak such good English? What did you do....?" She stops me in mid-sentence.

"So many questions, so little time, let me try and answer a few before I continue my rounds."

I respond, "Sorry, please, whatever time you can spend with me."

Looking at me with those adorable eyes and a smile on her face, Marie begins sharing some of her story with me. She tells me she was born in Versailles, France, in September 1897. She was trained by British Red Cross nurses in Paris and assigned to work at British hospitals. When we entered the war, she was reassigned to American field hospitals. Because of her bilingual abilities, she is considered a very valuable addition to the American medical staff. Marie is one of the interpreters for the French and Americans as they work together to help wounded soldiers.

She also interacts with the local French population to help secure their cooperation and support.

Marie became fluent in English before being trained as a nurse. She studied English for many years while in school. Whenever an opportunity presented itself to interact with Americans, she would jump at the chance. Visiting the Montmartre neighborhood became a particular favorite when time permitted. Americans living in or visiting Paris frequented this area because of its many activities.

Montmartre, situated on Paris's highest hill, is known for its cabaret nightlife, high-kicking cancan girls, and a very active jazz scene. Many quaint cafés surrounding the main square are a frequent location for struggling artists, poets, and dreamers to gather. Marie confesses that she had to be careful not to mix with the wrong crowd while there but found most Americans very friendly, outgoing, and a joy to be around. Lastly, Marie mentioned that someday she would love to visit America and perhaps live there.

So little time and it passes so quickly. Marie stands up, releases my hand, and says, "Sam, I have to go now. I promise I'll continue to check in on you while you're with us. Maybe we can spend a little time together before you have to return to your unit."

In a low melancholy voice, I respond, "Marie, Je t'aime! I love you!"

I just subconsciously blurt that out. Her reaction is beyond my ability to read; as she just smiles, there is no sign of a blush. Maybe, just maybe, she feels something too.

I continue, "I'm holding you to your promise. Please, your hand."

She extends it to me, and I pull it toward me ever so gently and kiss the top of her hand.

"I'll be thinking of you."

"Au revoir, Sam."

I release her hand slowly as she turns to resume her duties. As Marie moves gracefully around the church, tending to the wounded, she is angelic in her behavior. She often stops, kneels next to a man who reaches out to her, and tries to comfort him in his hour of need. She has a tranquil and reassuring nature about her, and the men can sense it. I feel safe and secure knowing she is moving among us tonight and slowly fade off into a deep, restful sleep.

7

MARIE

While recovering from my wounds at the 308th Sanitary Train facilities, they continue to repair and improve all their buildings. The old church I'm in is not home, but it's certainly much better than the trenches. Here the food is hot, has a distinctive French taste, and is served regularly. We occasionally get clean sheets and a bath. I soon begin to relax in this environment, feel less stressed, and recover quickly from my wounds.

I'm fortunate. My shoulder is healing, and there is no damage to the bone or surrounding tissue where the bullet entered. My cheek has healed, but I might have a little scar to show my grandchildren someday. As for the mustard gas, according to the doctors, they have detected no discernible damage to my lungs. This is good news. Although I'm in no hurry to return to the front, I am looking forward to rejoining the men. However, leaving Marie behind is another matter. I dread the day we have to say goodbye and part company. She is a pure delight to be with, and I feel at total peace while in her company.

Marie and I have some time together almost every day

during my recovery. When together, our time is spent outside where we can enjoy the fresh air and a little privacy. She always manages to bring some local wine and cheese. We return each time to a small, secluded spot near the church we found on our first day together. Our brief time is spent talking about little things such as the weather, news from the front, how her family is doing, and her plans after the war. I do not discuss my family, and she does not bring up the subject.

While talking, we sip wine and nibble on small slices of cheese. French wine and cheeses are beyond anything I've ever tasted before arriving in this country. Although, according to Marie, what she manages to bring is not their best. It's better than any I've ever enjoyed. I'm rapidly developing a taste for these simple pleasures of life and look forward to enjoying them well into the future.

One afternoon while we're outside together, a German plane buzzes overhead as he lines up for a bomb run. Hearing the sound and instinctively reacting to it, Marie dropped to the ground and landed in some mud. I've grown numb to this kind of harassment by the Huns and remain standing, although in a somewhat crouched position. Luckily, it was just one Fokker Triplane. This plane has a very distinctive airframe and is considered the most famous plane that flies in the skies above us. The German ace Von Richthofen, called the Red Baron, flies one. This is not him.

Whoever is flying this plane swoops down close to the ground, drops his bombs near our location, and flies back into the clouds. The area is clearly designated as a hospital zone with large red crosses on building tops and tent structures. The sky above us is overcast. Maybe the Hun didn't notice the red crosses when lining up for his attack. That, or he just doesn't give a damn about following the rules of war.

His bombs impact harmlessly in a pasture not far from our

location with a muted roar. The ground shakes mildly beneath our feet as a slight shock wave and wind blow past. Marie is a little distraught. Kneeling next to her, I place my arms on her shoulders, attempting to comfort her. Helping her up, I instinctively pull her close to me for the first time. I sense her hesitation and feel her trembling. Although shaken by the near-miss, she recovers quickly and draws back from me.

We're both a little muddy and share a moment of laughter at our appearance. I'm used to being muddy; Marie is not. Nurses are expected to remain as clean as possible when on duty in the Field Hospital. Brushing what mud we can off ourselves, Marie and I head back inside the church, where she helps me get settled in. After tending to me, Marie heads for the Nurses Quarters to change into a clean garment. When she returns, she looks very presentable and attractive as always. As I watch her move about, I cannot believe I will ever find another woman that has captured my heart as Marie has. I've grown very fond of her over these past several days. I will miss our visitations, conversations, and her company when I'm sent back to the front.

The next day dawns early. I'm awakened by a nurse and taken to a doctor's office. The doctor informs me I'm being released to return to my unit. The day I've dreaded for some time now has arrived. I would be lying to myself if I said I wasn't afraid to go back to the front. I am! But my feelings for Marie make going back more difficult to accept and harder to control my emotions as they begin overpowering me. I turn from facing the doctor to hide my face and wipe away the tears. The time I've spent with Marie has been precious. I'll look back on those times with cherished memories of her, this place, and our time together.

The doctor's comments strike me like a sledgehammer. I knew this time was coming, but the suddenness, finality, and total lack of empathy he displays in telling me, hit hard. Without any emotion, he instructs me to pack my gear, grab some breakfast and be back here in an hour. Transportation back to the front will be here then. He hands me my release papers, shakes my hand, and wishes me good luck. Combat hardens infantrymen, and we can grow numb to its horrific violence and the death it spawns. Until now, I never really thought about how it may affect doctors and nurses.

We're all casualties of this war!

I return to the church, pack my bags, and locate Marie. She joins me for a quick breakfast, and then we walk over to the doctor's office. We wait outside the building and stand under an extended roof overhang to stay out of the weather. We spend our last moments together before I leave. I'm still unsure of her feelings toward me. However, I suspect and hope she has found a place in her heart for me. We have yet to show any real affection toward each other, but I know the desire is there. As we share our last moments, I pull her close to me and kiss her on the cheek. She momentarily draws back, looks deeply into my eyes, and then pulls me to her tightly. We embrace and kiss passionately until a sergeant taps me on the shoulder.

"Sergeant McCormick, your ride is here."

"Okay, I'll be right there," I respond in a low, melancholy voice.

Marie and I separate, promising to write and see each other again as soon as circumstances allow. After climbing onto the truck, I grip her hand and don't let go until the last second. As we drive off, my gaze stays fixated on her. To my pure delight, Marie gazes back at me until we can no longer see each other.

I don't know how this happened, call it destiny, fate, luck, whatever, but Marie has come into my life, and I want her to stay. In the middle of this war, what happens to us now is in God's hands.

8

BACK TO MY REGIMENT

Like many preceding it, this day dawned with overcast skies, light rain, and a chill in the air. If that wasn't depressing enough, I had to leave the woman who came into my life that I fell in love with and now may never see again.

We're riding in an old 1911 Latil French truck that can carry up to ten doughboys in full combat gear. We sit spaced out from each other because of all the equipment we're carrying back to the front. With our equipment and the simple fact that the average American soldier is bigger than the average French soldier, we are limited in the number of men this truck can carry. The cargo space in the back of the truck has running boards attached to each side. They serve as our seats. A partially rolled-up tarp covers the top of the back cargo space giving us some protection from the weather. The running boards we're sitting on are very uncomfortable. We feel every pothole on the road. Looking around at the men and their solemn faces as we head back to the front lines, I try to lighten the mood and offer them a wager.

"I'll bet any of you that some of us will be bounced off the bench and thrown to the floor of the truck before we get to where we're going. Any takers?"

Granted, it was a weak attempt at humor and only drew a few responses with a chuckle or two. "No thanks, Sergeant!"

"Are you kidding?"

"I've almost fallen twice now!"

"Not even Fritz would take that bet!"

I draw no takers, but I do get a few smiles.

Resigned to the fact that it will be an unpleasant trip back to the front, I do my best to get comfortable. I tighten the trench coat belt around my waist and pull up the collar, so it touches the rim of my steel combat M1917 helmet. Our helmets are called by many names: the shrapnel helmet, battle bowler, tin hat, and by Americans, the doughboy helmet. Realizing that I'm as comfortable as my current circumstances will allow, I pull out my pipe, tobacco pouch, and lighter. Packing the tobacco into my pipe chamber is a slow, methodical process. It takes three or four small batches of tobacco to reach the level I prefer to smoke. I press each batch down with my thumb until the mixture is uniform in thickness. This allows for good airflow. Once satisfied, I light up, draw deeply from the pipe and exhale. It's certainly not the best tobacco I've had, but it helps relax me on the trip back.

My uniform and equipment are all new, having been issued just before being discharged from the hospital. My rifle, pistol belt, Colt.45, and gas mask should be returned to me when I arrive back at the company. While in the hospital recovering, I was able to bathe, wear clean medical garments, dine on hot food, and drink clean water. I almost feel like a new man. That won't last long when I return to the trenches.

The drive back to the front where my unit is located is a long, slow trip. We must weave our way over dirt roads potted with large shell holes, pools of water, and mud everywhere from recent rains. Destroyed vehicles are scattered all over the land-scape we traverse. We are continually slowing down or stopping to allow troops walking on both sides of the road to continue their journey. The men on one side are headed up to the front. They look relatively clean and rested. Their weapons are slung over their shoulders, and their web belts and shoulder packs are full to overflowing with ammunition and supplies. Their faces reflect the stress and anxiety of heading to the front-line trenches. With few exceptions, the men don't talk or look in our direction. When they do, some tease us with their comments.

"Hey Mack, how'd you rate a truck ride?"

"Where are you going in that lorry?"

"You boys in the Cavalry?"

"Where are your horses?"

Those of us in the truck rate a ride to the front since we were wounded and are still recovering from our wounds. I, for one, feel we deserve this truck ride back to the front lines.

The men on the other side of our truck are heading toward the rear. They're filthy, worn out, battle fatigued, in need of some hot decent food, and above all, time away from the hell they just left. They are too tired to express any feelings of joy and relief at heading to the rear for some much-needed rest and recupera-tion. Occasionally some of these men look up at us with an expression of empathy, knowing we are headed back into hell, the place they just left.

While in Château-Thierry waiting for my transportation, a Red Cross volunteer handed me a cup of coffee, a doughnut, and a copy of the latest Stars and Stripes newspaper. The Stars and Stripes is an American newspaper published in France by the American Expeditionary Forces of the United States Army. It was first published on February 8, 1918. It has become the main source of news about what is going on over here and how we are doing. While sipping coffee and nibbling on my doughnut, I unfold the newspaper. The story on the front page is an article about the battle we just fought against the Germans.

It reads in part:

The Americans proved their mettle at the Second Battle of the Marne, and General Pershing got his wish. He has been assigned to lead an independent American fighting force for the remainder of the war. Under French command, the Americans were thrust into combat during this battle. The United States Army's 3rd Infantry Division fought so ferociously that it earned the enduring nickname "Rock of the Marne." National Guardsmen from across the United States fought together in the 42nd Infantry Division, the "Rainbow Division." They will forever be remembered for their valor and fighting spirit in the trenches.

This battle could well be the last major German offensive on the western front. The battle began on July 15, 1918, near the Marne River in the Champagne region of France. The Germans launched a massive attack across a wide front and managed to penetrate deep into the French lines and create a large bulge. Attacks and counterattacks by both sides ensued over several weeks resulting in massive casualties for the Germans and, to a lesser extent, the Allies. Ultimately the German offensive failed when the Allies counterattacked, and the Germans began a major retreat toward their border in early August. This defeat marked the beginning of relentless Allied advances against the German front lines. The Allies' new initiative and their ongoing offensive attacks may well culminate in defeating the Germans and bringing an end to this war.

THIS IS ENCOURAGING NEWS. I hope we're nearing the end of this horrific conflict and orgy of death. After finishing my coffee and pitching my unfinished doughnut out the back of the truck, I shift my body to get some relief from the constant bouncing around. It's no use. I just resign myself to the discomfort and accept my situation. We should almost be there. Looking around at the men with me, none of whom I know, it's apparent we're not a happy bunch of fellows on our way back to the front. We're a solemn bunch, lost in our own thoughts.

Reflecting on what I just read and the combat I've endured since arriving in France gives me hope but cause for concern. There is still much fighting to be done before the Huns seek an armistice. With no guarantees of survival on the battlefield, I cannot dwell on the prospects of going home until it's over!

During my short time on the line, I've participated in ferocious combat and witnessed gruesome deaths. I've seen mangled bodies of men who survived their wounds but will be crippled and maimed for the rest of their lives. Whether you're an American or German, your fate on the battlefield can be sealed in a single moment in time. Once sealed, you don't get it back. It is forever.

Millions of men from several countries have been killed and many more wounded since this war began in 1914. It's now late August 1918, and we're still at war. The sooner it ends, the sooner we can all return home and rejoin our families and friends. These thoughts and reflections are not improving my mental outlook as I'm becoming a very despondent doughboy. To refocus on more pleasant thoughts, I notice another article in the newspaper which piques my interest. Having just met Marie and fallen for her, I believe this article about French nurses may prove enlightening.

Repacking my pipe with fresh tobacco, I light it, settle back in, and proceed to read it.

Observers of home life in France must have been struck by the lack of an organized system of trained nursing such as we are accustomed to finding in America, Great Britain, and the countries of Northern Europe. Before the separation of the Roman Catholic Church from the French State, nursing was almost entirely in the hands of nuns. Although their knowledge of the science of nursing did not always measure up to twentieth-century requirements, they were not looked down upon, and their importance was not minimized the way many women workers are.

The separation of the Roman Catholic Church from the French State occurred before qualified nurses had been trained to replace them. Excellent nursing colleges were started, but, unfortunately, very few women would entertain nursing as a profession until the outbreak of war. Up till now, women relied on the protection of the Roman Catholic Church to shield them from criticism and disrespect if they practiced nursing. But because of the separation of church and state, this protection was no longer available to them. Thus, few women sought out nursing as a vocation. It all changed after the first battle of the Marne—fought in early September 1914. Wounded, sick, and dying men were hurried into the cities, towns, and villages. Hospitals were improvised in station waiting rooms, halls, schoolhouses, and churches. French women came flocking forward to work as Red Cross nurses and give a helping hand.

The British had a well-established nursing cadre and helped train French women to become nurses. Their efforts resulted in large numbers of French women becoming professional, well-trained, and highly praised Red Cross nurses. The French Flag Nursing Corps was established in late 1914 to provide a band of certified British nurses for service in French Military Hospitals and was placed under the authority of the French War Office.

INTERESTING ARTICLE. I had no idea about the short history of the French Nursing Corps. Many of the Red Cross nurses at the field hospital were French. My care and that of my comrades was nothing short of excellent. Every man was well cared for and treated with the utmost respect, and whenever we lost one of our boys due to their wounds, the nurses took it very hard. It was as if they had lost one of their family members. I will never forget what they did for me, and I'm sure the other boys feel the same way about the treatment we received. As for my French nurse, Marie, she is the woman I hope to spend the rest of my life with should I survive this war.

I haven't been paying any attention to where we are or what we've passed on our way to the front when the truck abruptly stops. We're at Regimental Headquarters, which is well behind the front lines. An officer approaches the back of our truck and yells at us to disembark and report to the duty officer for reassignment to our units. The weather is lousy, it's raining hard, and the wind has a distinct chill to it.

Welcome back to the front!

Jumping from the back of our truck, I land in mud almost up to the top of my trench boots. Our trench boots, sometimes known as the "Pershing boot," are American combat boots made for the cold mud of trench warfare. They are designed to prevent trench foot. Walking toward the partially bombed-out building serving as Regimental Headquarters, I need to be careful where I step for fear of slipping into a mud hole filled with water. It is not an easy task as some other fellows are learning. Two go down and are covered in mud up to their waist, and we just got here.

Entering the building, I'm confronted with organized chaos. Something is afoot! There are men everywhere talking, looking over maps, and studying documents.

I'm met by Captain Glazebrook. With a hardy handshake and pat on the back, he says, "Welcome back, Sam. It's good to see you. The men have missed you. They will certainly be glad to have you back."

"Thanks, Captain. I'm looking forward to rejoining the boys."

He continues, "Did they treat you well back there? How are your wounds? I'm assuming you've recovered enough to get back into action?"

"They did. They're healed. And I'm ready, Sir!"

He nods his approval and directs me over to a secluded and quiet spot. "Sergeant, we've been resting and replenishing our ranks with new men just arriving from the States. They're green but eager, from what I can tell. We'll be moving to another sector shortly and back into the front lines. I fully expect we'll see more heavy action soon. I'm placing you in charge of my first platoon, which includes your old second squad. I've assigned Henry to take over your second squad, and Art has been assigned to your platoon's first squad. This places both of your friends in the first platoon, and you should feel confident in their abilities."

He pauses, looks directly at me with a seriousness I've not seen since being wounded, and continues.

"You'll need to get your platoon battle-ready. When we move back on the line, I'll be counting on you and your platoon to carry the company. I'm certain we'll be challenged beyond anything we've seen so far. Henry, Art, and you are battle-tested and fine soldiers. Our new men will be looking to you three men for leadership, and I'm counting on that. Any questions, Sam?"

It can't be worse than what we have seen so far? How is that possible?

My response is, "No, sir, no questions! We'll give it our best."

"I know you will—one other item. You've been recommended for the Distinguished Service Cross and an Army Wound

Ribbon for your actions in leading your squad in our last two attacks against the German trenches. Congratulations, Sam."

"Thank you, Captain."

After a long pause, "But what are they for?" I ask in a quizzical, matter-of-fact tone.

"They're new awards established by General Pershing. The Distinguished Service Cross is awarded for exceptional bravery. It is second only to the Medal of Honor. The Army Wound Ribbon is in recognition of individual soldiers who are wounded in action."

"Sir, what about the other boys who jumped into the trenches with me? They all put up one hell of a fight. It wasn't a one-man show."

"Sergeant, those are the men who approached me and requested I recommend you to Division for some recognition."

I'm humbled and honored by the fact that my men felt compelled to do what they did. At the same time, I don't feel any more worthy of this recognition than the other men who were with me. I believe my whole squad deserves similar recognition for their bravery in action.

My facial expression must have betrayed my inner thoughts, as Captain Glazebrook says. "Sam, your men, followed your leadership, and they know it. They're all good men, but they may not have performed as well as they did without a good leader they trust. Whether you realize it or not, you were that leader." He pauses and waits for a response.

I have none. The captain shakes my hand, congratulates me, and says he's proud to be my CO. He then concludes with, "See those two men over there in the corner who rode up here with you? They're joining our company. Go ahead and round them up. Wait for me outside, and we'll head back to our company area shortly."

Responding with "Yes, sir!" I salute him as I come to attention, then head over to the new men—Private John Smith and his brother Alex, also a private. They hail from Western North Carolina. Before being drafted, they were moonshiners. I believe they'll fit very nicely into our company——since we have a lot of fellows who enjoy drinking, having two brothers who can make moonshine should make them very popular. Securing liquor can be difficult while serving on or close to the front lines. After introducing myself, we head outside to the captain's truck.

I'm back in the war!

9

166TH INFANTRY REGIMENT

REAR AREA

Saint-Mihiel is a town in the Meuse Department in northwestern France. French Departments are the mid-level, of three levels, under the French national government. They are like a county in the United States and generally encompass about three times the land area of a county in America. Our Regimental Headquarters is in a rear area near Beaumont, a small village about thirty miles east of Saint-Mihiel and several miles behind our trench lines. The area around here is relatively flat and consists of farmland with some rolling hills. The salient, a bulge in the French lines, which the Germans created earlier during the battle for Saint-Mihiel, did not make it this far. There was heavy shelling and bombing, but the area remained under French control. Our division has responsibility for this whole sector in preparation for another offensive against the Germans.

While waiting on the captain, I light my pipe and visit some of the boys around the immediate vicinity of our Regimental HQ.

They tell me this area is relatively quiet and only occasionally shelled by German long-range artillery. Since we are far removed from the battlefield, the Huns' artillery rounds are not very accurate and only amount to harassing fire. Apparently, a greater threat is the occasional air raid by German fighters or bombers. In this sector, it is believed we have air superiority which prevents the Germans from getting through to us. If the Huns do make it through, their bombing and machine gun strafing are accurate and deadly. I'm told that I had better head for the nearest bunker if we do have an air raid or the Germans begin to shell us, just in case.

While I was circulating, John and Alex met two men from our company, Rick and Chet. They had accompanied the captain to the HQ and were running errands for him while he was in meetings. The men were having a conversation about the lack of good liquor available in camp when I walked up on them. Rick and Chet recognize me and head my way as I approach them.

In an excited voice, Chet yells, "Hey, look, it's Sergeant McCormick! How have you been, Sergeant? We've sure missed you around here."

Walking up to them, I extend my hand and exchange greetings with both men. "I'm doing well, thank you. And you boys, how's it going for you?"

Rick responds, "Not bad, can't complain! We've been getting a little rest, some recreation, hot food, an occasional bath, and some letters from home. You could say it's been a regular paradise around here."

"Well, I'm glad to hear that. I hope it'll continue for a few more days." Looking over at the brothers and back at Chet and Rick, I inquired. "Have you gotten acquainted with our new men yet?"

"Yep, they're going to fit right in, Sergeant!" Chet responds with some mischief in his voice.

The Smith brothers, who have been silent, speak up with some trepidation in their voices. Alex, the older brother, speaks first. "Y'all looking to have us make some moonshine? Can we do that over here?"

"Well, I reckon so. You just let me know what you need, and I'll go about procuring it." Chet says in a matter-of-fact voice.

John looks over at me with a quizzical expression and says, "Sergeant, we're law-abiding boys and don't want no trouble with revenuers."

His comment sparks some light laughter as I respond. "Don't worry, boys; you'll be fine."

Our conversation abruptly ends as Captain Glazebrook walks out of Regimental HQs toward the truck. Approaching us at a quick step and in a hurry, he walks right past us and motions for us to follow.

He doesn't slow down, and no customary hand salutes are exchanged. He is a fine officer and treats his men with respect and dignity. He sometimes dispenses with strict military protocol, such as a hand salute, and goes about the task at hand. Climbing into the truck on the driver's side and sliding in behind the wheel, he says in a command voice. "Let's go, gentlemen. It's getting late. I need to get back to the company."

I join the captain up front as the other four men climb onto the back of the truck. We're in a Jeffery Quad, also known as the Nash Quad or Quad. The Quad has four-wheel drive, four-wheel brakes, and a four-wheel steering system. This unique approach to steering allows the rear wheels to track the front wheels around turns preventing the rear wheels from having to dig new "ruts" on muddy curves. A great feature to have over here in France with all the rain and mud we encounter.

The engine is slow to crank, and the captain must nurse it. After several attempts, the Quad's engine comes to life, and we head for the company area. It's a short distance back to the company, and since the Quad only has a 28-horsepower engine, it's a slow drive over. Once there, Captain Glazebrook drives us around for a quick tour of the area.

The company area consists of several squad tents which can house up to ten men each. They serve as temporary quarters while we're here. Our personal gear is stored under the army-issued cot we sleep on, and our rifles are placed on gun racks set up inside the tent. Several small slit trenches are built near our tents. These are shallow, narrow trenches designed to provide us with some protection when we're being shelled or bombed.

There are several small wooden structures—shacks, which serve various purposes. They are primarily used for storing items such as food, fuel, and unassigned military gear, including clothing, blankets, pistol belts, backpacks, and boots. Our ammunition and larger weapons, such as machine guns and mortars, are placed in reinforced bunkers. There is a small shack dedicated to handling our mail. The largest structure in the area is the cook's kitchen and our mess hall. It's nothing more than a large canvas tent set up over an elevated wooden platform designed to keep us out of the mud and water. It looks like a small circus tent. In fact, some of the company's artists took it upon themselves to inject a little hometown feeling. They painted "Barnum & Bailey Circus " on the top of the tent. The fellows refer to it as the BBC!

After finishing our brief tour, we pull up to the Company HQ tent, and the captain shuts off the Quad. Looking over at me, he says, "Again, Sam, it's good to have you back. The new men, the brothers, are yours. Take them back with you to the platoon area and get them settled. I'll be briefing our officers and sergeants here at HQ tonight at 2000 hours. I'll see you then."

Stepping out of the Quad, I salute him and say, "Yes, sir, see you at 2000 hours."

Chet and Rick are part of another platoon and leave us as they head off in the direction of their squad tent. Captain Glazebrook pointed out my platoon area and squad tent during our brief tour. With the brothers following, we head for the platoon area. Approaching my tent, Henry, and Art, who share the tent with me, see us coming their way and hustle over.

Henry approaches with his hand extended and says, "Damn Art, look who's decided to come back. Damn, I would have thought you had enough of this war and got yourself shipped home. Great to have you back, Sam!"

Before I can say anything, Henry grabs me, puts me in a bear hug, squeezes hard, and lifts me off my feet. Henry is a strong man and, in his zest to welcome me back, is overzealous in his greeting. Grimacing in pain and trying to say something, Henry realizes what he's done and releases his grip. What a relief, since my wounded shoulder hasn't fully healed.

He steps back and, with a sheepish grin, offers an apology. "Sorry old man, I sometimes get carried away..." Before he can finish, I respond, "That's alright. I missed you fellows, too."

Thank goodness Art is more reserved and just welcomes me back with a hardy handshake. He takes my equipment and places it in our squad tent. After returning, I introduce the two brothers to Art and Henry. I ask Art which of our squads needs two men the most.

He replies, "Henry could use them."

Looking over at Henry, I say, "They're yours. See that they get settled. I'm going to stow my gear and then get some chow. Anyone want to join me?"

They all nod yes. "Good. One more item. Henry, Art, we have a briefing with the captain at 2000 hours up at his HQ tent."

Art responds, "Got it. Any idea what it's about, Sam?"

"Nope, I have no idea!"

10

PLANNING BRIEFING

Later that evening, after dinner, the A Company officers and sergeants are present in Captain Glazebrook's HQ tent. It's evening, and we have endured another rainy, windy, and generally miserable day. There appears to be no end in sight to this weather. We are headed into the fall and winter season over here, and I fear this will be the norm. Apparently, I'm not alone in this assumption, as it was a topic of discussion over dinner. This is followed by speculation as to what this meeting is about and what awaits us next.

The HQ tent is dimly lit, but we can see each other with little difficulty. It's a tight fit in the tent with over sixteen of us crammed inside. With a steady beating of raindrops hitting the top of the tent, I get a little jittery, thinking we're taking German fire.

Damn, I hope the other fellows don't notice my reaction or the concern my facial expression might be conveying at this time.

Looking around at the faces of the men closest to me, I can see I'm not alone in my reaction to the constant pounding of rain on the tent. Captain Glazebrook begins his briefing in a low-key, matter-of-fact voice. "Gentleman, welcome. I trust you all enjoyed a good, hot meal?"

He pauses, looking for some confirmation. He gets it in the form of nods and several responses of "Yes, sir!"

"Good. Now onto the business at hand. We'll be going back on the front lines in four days. Another major offensive is scheduled to kick off on September 12th, "D-Day," and "H-Hour" is yet to be established. We are intent on pushing the Huns back into Germany and hopefully bring about an armistice." Noticing the quizzical looks on our faces, he pauses, "Why the looks?"

I respond instinctively, "Sir, what does "D-Day" and "H-Hour" mean?"

"Oh yes, my apologies, gentlemen. I just heard the new terms myself earlier today. At General Pershing's direction, the army adopted " D-Day " to designate the day a combat attack or operation is scheduled to begin. The term "H-Hour" designates the time of the attack. Any questions about this?"

There are none, and he continues his briefing.

"General Pershing has planned a massive assault to take place across the entire Saint-Mihiel salient. We are going straight at the German front lines. More than fifty miles wide. He hopes to break through and ultimately capture the fortified city of Metz. This will be the United States Army's first large-scale offensive operation since we arrived here."

He pauses, "Any questions?"

No one speaks, as many of us react to the news with nervous gestures, a shuffling of feet, and muted comments. He looks around the tent at us while making eye contact with his reassuring facial expression, for which he's known. It has the intended effect of calming us down.

This is going to be one hell of a battle. Thinking back to what the captain told me when I first reported to him earlier today. "Sam, I'm certain we'll be tested beyond anything we've seen so far!"

Captain Glazebrook takes a few steps over to the side of his HQ tent, where a large map of our area is hanging. "We are one of nine American infantry divisions that is being thrown into this offensive."

Using a pointer, he continues speaking while showing us on the map. "Our sector stretches from Limey west toward Marvoisin. On our left flank is the 89th Division and on our right is the 1st Division. As you can see, our division is in the middle. Our objective is simple. We are to attack aggressively and capture the German-held village of Essey.

Stepping back from the map, he looks around at us and continues in a more authoritative, command voice. "Now for the bad news. The Germans have installed a series of in-depth trenches, wire obstacles, and machine gun nests. Our weather people tell us we're in for several days of rain and heavy winds. The battlefield will be very muddy. Nothing new there."

Taking a moment to sip his coffee and light up a cigarette, he continues the briefing. "Gentleman, here is some good news. That long-awaited tank support we all wanted—well, it will be in front of us for our attack on Essey. General Pershing's plan calls for several tank units to support the offensive. A fellow named Lieutenant Colonel George Patton has recently finished training two tank battalions. They consist of 144 French-built Renault FT light tanks organized as the 344th and 345th Battalions of the United States Tank Corps. His tanks will lead the attack on the village of Essey. Our regiment will be his infantry support."

This brings smiles to everyone's faces and several comments.

"That is good news."

"Hooray for Pershing!"

"About time!"

"Who is this fellow Patton? I want to shake his hand."

The captain cuts in on the celebration. "Okay, gentlemen. It's getting late. We need to bring this to an end for the night. Over the next four days, ensure all your men check their equipment and weapons carefully. If any of your men need more target practice, see that they get it. Schedule some light training patrols to get the men out of camp and start thinking about infantry tactics again. Also, give them some time off for recreation and letter writing and ensure their insurance paperwork is current. That's all for now. Let's get some rest."

The customary hand salutes are exchanged between Captain Glazebrook and his men as we depart the HQ tent for our tents. Henry, Art, and I walk back together without conversing. We're each lost in our own thoughts.

Another furious battle and a fresh harvest of dead men are just over the horizon!

11

THE CALM BEFORE THE FURY

GETTING READY

The next day dawns with a light mist, a slight chill in the air and overcast skies—an improvement over the last few days since there is no heavy rain. We're all thankful for the change. After enjoying a hot breakfast with some of our cook's famous biscuits at the BBC, I have the men fall out in full gear and weapons. The squad leaders and I spend the next hour inspecting equipment and weapons.

We'll be going back to the front lines, where we'll once again find ourselves fighting to survive in a living hell. That survival could well depend on our weapons and combat gear functioning as intended.

They're a good bunch of soldiers. Everything is in order. With just a few exceptions, their rifles and Colt .45 pistols are well cleaned, oiled, and ready for combat. I then give them three hours of personal time for leisurely pursuits. This makes for a happy group of doughboys. Before dismissing the platoon, I instruct them to return here by 1300 hours in full combat gear with their weapons.

When I return at 1300 hours, I find everyone present and standing at attention in platoon formation. I give the command to stand at rest. In unison, they go to parade rest and look at me in anticipation of what to expect this afternoon. Using my best command voice as I walk back and forth in front of the platoon, I go over our afternoon training activities with the men.

"Fellows, we're going on a practice combat patrol. You will be issued ammunition, but do not load your weapons. This is a training exercise only and will be conducted within our regiment's sector. According to HQ, our sector is quiet with no reported activity. They consider it generally secured. We're going about five miles out and five miles back. We'll be taking a different route each way."

Looking around to see if everyone is listening, I ask, "Any questions, fellows?" There are none, and by their expressions, I surmise they are looking forward to getting out of camp for the afternoon.

"We'll head out in two columns. Art, your first squad, and Henry, your second squad, will take the lead, followed by squads three and four. When we clear camp, Art and Henry, your squads will fan out into a V formation with squad one on the left and squad two on the right. Keep your spacing between men at about ten yards."

Glancing in their direction, I see their nods of approval. I then proceed, "Squad three, you'll form the next V formation about twenty yards behind them. Spread your men out a similar distance. Squad four, you'll be the last V formation about twenty yards behind squad three. Keep your men about ten yards apart. I'll be with squad three."

This formation would look like a large flock of birds flying low to the ground in three waves if looking down from above.

The first wave forms a large V, followed by a second, smaller V, and behind them, a third V of similar size. This type of combat patrol formation provides considerable maneuverability and protection for the men on patrol.

It's a standard combat patrol formation to use when moving over flat land, and according to Captain Glazebrook, once we break through the German front lines, much of the terrain we'll be fighting over is flat. By spreading the men out, we cover a much larger area and increase our chances of not being surprised by the enemy. Also, the more distance between the men, the fewer men we would lose when engaged by the Huns' machine guns, mortars, and artillery.

I give the men a chance to let what I said sink in. Then, in a matter-of-fact command voice, I say, "Any of you fellas have a question? Speak up!"

There are none, so I continue, "Okay, attention, shoulder arms, left face, forward march!"

We march out of the rest area at a leisurely pace in two columns of thirty men each. I'm at the front of the platoon and setting the pace. Once we clear the rest area, I give the command to go into our patrol formation. The men respond, and we move at a measured pace with weapons at the ready.

Usually, there would be no talking, only hand signals and whispers to the men nearest you, if needed. Since this is friendly territory, I have given the men some leeway for limited conversation.

I hear comments like, "Good to get out of camp for some light duty." "How's your girl doing?" "How's the family?" "Sure wish this damn war would end!" "I could use a good month's rest." All typical doughboy talk, whenever they're in groups on maneuvers.

About four miles outside of our camp and moving across open pastureland, we see a French house and barn in the distance. Our point man at the head of the first V formation suddenly disappears from our view. The two men nearest him rush to his aide. They disappear from our view. It's like the earth just swallowed them up.

I yell out to the platoon, "Halt, take a knee. Lock and load your weapons. Stay alert!"

To a man, they drop to one knee. I hear ammo clips being inserted into rifles and the rustle of equipment being adjusted for more ease of firing if necessary. I rush forward to where the men were. I hear their conversations coming from underground and notice an opening in the earth. Watching my step as I move forward, I ease up on a hole in the ground about six feet in diameter.

Taking a knee, I peer into the hole, looking for my men.

"Hey fellows, everyone all right down there? What is this?"

It takes a moment, then Chet appears, looking up at me and grinning from ear to ear. "Sergeant, it's our lucky day; we fell into a hidden wine cellar. There must be over 100 bottles down here. Hot damn!"

Responding, I say, "Chet, you and the fellows grab twenty-five bottles, and I'll get you some help."

"Yes, sir, Sergeant!" he responds in a loud, excited voice.

All the rain we've had lately has weakened the roof of this underground wine cellar. The weight of our boys caused it to collapse, and it took them with it. I stand up, step back and turn to the platoon and yell out, "They're alright. Fellows, we'll be enjoying some French wine later this evening. They fell into a hidden wine cellar."

This brings some laughter and cheers from the boys. I direct three of the men from the first squad to help bring up the wine and then assist the men in climbing out of the wine cellar. We are not supposed to requisition supplies from local French inhabitants, but in some cases, it's permissible. I'm not sure this is one of them, but I, for one, could use some wine. To give it some legitimacy, I send Henry with two men over to the French farmhouse to inform them of our requisition. They're also to tell them their wine cellar roof is weakened and needs repair.

While waiting for Henry to return and the men to retrieve the wine and clear the wine cellar, I call my other squad leaders to join me for a moment.

"Gentlemen, we've had the good fortune to come across twenty-five bottles of French wine. Unless any of you have an objection, I'm planning on taking them back. Each squad will be given six bottles to do with as they please. I'll be keeping one for myself."

After a long pause, I repeat, "Does anyone have any objections?"

Looking around, I discern nothing but broad smiles on their faces and no comments.

"Okay then. Pick five men from each of your squads that you can trust with this stuff and have them come up here. We'll hand the wine bottles out to them. When Henry returns, we'll finish the patrol and head back to camp."

They return to their squads, select their men, and send them forward. Within minutes, the boys appear, select their bottles, and return to their places in the formation.

Henry returns with his two men.

"Henry, is everything good with the French farmer?"

"Not a problem, Sam. His two boys are off fighting the Germans somewhere north of here, and it's just him and his wife. He fears his sons may be dead and says to take what we want, as he'll never use all of it."

"Sorry about his boys. My god, how the French people have suffered, and it's not over yet!" Thoughts of Marie momentarily come to the forefront. Returning to the situation at hand, I inform Henry about what we're doing. Not surprisingly, he has no objections. After Henry's squad secures their allotment of wine, we move back out on patrol and finish our training for the day.

That evening in camp, after dinner, the boys of my platoon and I enjoy some good French wine, compliments of a French farmer. Our practice combat patrol became known as "The Best Combat Patrol Ever" among the men. Over time, it became legendary within the regiment as the word spread.

The rain returned later into the evening following our training patrol. We are once again inundated with water and mud. Having no choice, I drill the platoon in basic tactics over the next three days. We are in mud and water up to the top of our Pershing boots during this time. When we are not cleaning the mud off our boots and equipment, I give the boys time off for recreation, rest, and letter writing. Once the wine is gone, the Smith brothers become very popular among the boys. Somehow, with a bit of help, they procure the necessary equipment and ingredients to make a small supply of moonshine for the platoon. Doughboys can't keep a secret when it comes to liquor, gambling, or local ladies. The platoon's moonshine activities spread quickly throughout our company, and the popularity of the Smith brothers keeps growing.

D-Day is only two days away. Tonight, is our last night in camp. We're returning to the front sometime tomorrow evening. I haven't found the time to write my first letter to Marie since leaving her and returning to my unit. With rain steadily pelting the top of my tent and using a dimly lit field lamp, I take a seat on my cot and settle in. Pulling an old ammo box that I use for a nightstand close to me, I take out some writing paper, pack my pipe, light it, and begin to write.

∽

Dearest Marie,

It's early evening. I want to write you a few lines to let you know I am alright. I trust and hope you are the same. At present, we are in a rear area and will be moving back up to the front shortly. The weather has been simply awful. It's been raining almost every day since I got here and hasn't let up. To tell you the truth, while writing this letter, I am damp and chilled to the bone, having just returned from some routine field exercises earlier. I'm sitting as close as I can next to our wood-burning stove, trying to dry out and warm up as I write you this letter.

We've been given our winter coats now, but they cause more curses than you can imagine. They are made of a thick woolen material that is heavy, very bulky, and becomes more so when soaked by the rain and caked with mud. They make maneuvering around much more difficult for us. For instance, last night, I was "sergeant-of-the-guard" and walked through our company area for a routine check. We are required to do them every forty-five minutes while we are on duty. It was pitch dark. There are no lights allowed outside of our tents and shacks. We use black-out sheets at night to keep the light from showing outside our structures. Well, honestly, while doing my rounds, I tripped over that damn coat and fell over multiple times. I was covered in mud up to my beltline, and mud seeped into my Pershing boots. What a mess I was from the waist down. It brought back thoughts of you and me when we were together that time and got a little muddy. I would much rather take that mud over what I'm dealing with here and now.

Our days here in camp have gone by quickly as we've been busy with routine tasks. We've had a few highlights during this period. Remember me telling you about Henry Miller, the boxer? He's our regimental boxing champ and has been practicing when possible during the last few days. Henry will be going up against the champ from the 328th Infantry Regiment in a few weeks. Henry is a terrific boxer. I would not get in a ring with him. We understand that the champ from the opposing regiment is also quite good. Should be a great match. Art and I will be in Henry's corner for the fight when it occurs. I look forward to the event.

On another note, it seems like every other home near our rest camp is an *Estaminet* (small French café) where they sell what they call "beer." As much as I like a good beer, I just can't bring myself to drink it. It's too thick, hard to swallow, has no taste, and I've yet to feel any buzz from alcohol. Oh, how I miss your wines! And speaking of wine. I took the men out on a practice patrol the other day, and we came across a wine cellar. The French farmer who owns the wine cellar very graciously gave us some of his wine. His generosity made a large group of doughboys very happy that night!

Time to stop. I've got to check on the men and get some rest. I hope this letter finds you healthy and doing well. I'm so looking forward to seeing you again and holding you in my arms.

Marie, you mean a great deal to me, and I've grown very fond of you. In fact, I've fallen in love with you. I hope to see you again soon, and we can spend more time together and see where this leads us. For now, I must sign off. Take care of yourself and stay safe.

Je t'aime!
        Yours always,
        Sam

12

BACK TO THE FRONT LINES

We're back in the front-line trenches and once again facing the Huns. Our regiment will be part of the first wave of doughboys from the Rainbow Division to go over the top on D-Day.

We departed our camp in Beaumont early this afternoon and arrived here as the sun set in the west. We slogged five miles to get up here through mud and water. It was a challenge. Our feet would be sucked into the mud up to our knees with every step we took. It's a real struggle as you fight to pull them out so you can take the next step forward. I'm exhausted, muddy, and damp to the bone from the forced march up here, as are all the men.

It's starting to get dark, and occasionally rockets and flares explode above us, lighting up the sky. Some belong to us; the others belong to the Huns. With the light they provide, we're able to look around at our trenches. I'm not impressed, and it's very easy to become despondent. They're in a sorry state and need considerable repair. Captain Glazebrook told us earlier they would be a mess, but this is beyond anything I would have suspected. The walls are collapsing in, many of the firing steps are gone or broken, the bunkers and shelters are of limited value. With few exceptions, they're falling in on themselves and have gaping holes in their roofs. There has been no effort to repair them since planning began for this offensive a week or so back. Apparently, we're expected to route the Germans from this area, and we'll have no further need for them after that.

Arriving in our section of the trenches, I was surprised to see they were thinly manned. The men assigned to this sector have been here about two weeks and have seen little action. With our arrival, they are sent back to the rear area for a few days of rest. The Germans we face now have settled on a defensive posture and are content with the status quo. Except for occasional artillery and mortar fire and a few casualties, this area is considered quiet. I think that's going to change within the next two days.

My platoon occupies a section about fifty yards long that has two machine gun emplacements and four bunkers. They're all in a sorry state and do not afford much protection from the weather. I bring my squad leaders together for a quick briefing.

"Art, I want you on my left flank taking up about twenty-five yards, and Henry, place your squad on my right for the other twenty-five yards. Squads three and four, you are the reserves. I want you to settle in behind squads one and two."

I stop and take a moment to gauge their reactions. They're exhausted, and like me, just want to take shelter from this lousy weather and rest. There are no complaints; we've been here too many times before. They just nod their understanding.

I continue, "You men work it out among yourselves as to guard duty assignments for your squads. I want ten men manning our section of this trench line on two-hour shifts the rest of the night. Your men should do their best to stay out of the weather and rest when they're not on guard duty."

Art looks at me and speaks up. "What about us? What shifts do you want us to take?"

"Each of us will take our turn on duty tonight as the sergeant-of-the-guard, starting with me. We'll keep it simple, starting with you, Art. You'll relieve me. Then Henry will relieve you, and so forth. Any questions?"

Henry, always hungry and looking for some food, blurts out. "What about some chow? I'm hungry. I need some food. Surely, I'm not the only bloke here that's hungry?"

He looked around for a response from the rest of us. Not getting one, he says in a low, dejected voice. "I guess I am the only one!"

Art speaks up, "Hell, Henry, you're always hungry. I don't think the chow wagons and cooks are even close to us up here yet. Our supply columns are all bogged down in the mud, stretched out for miles, and it could be a while before they catch up to us here in the trenches."

"How do you know that, Mr. Baseball?"

"Well, Henry, you big bloke, I paid attention to what was going on around us on our way up here. That's how."

The other two squad leaders look on in amusement as Art and Henry continue their back and forth. This is one way they blow off some steam. Before it goes too far, I cut in on them.

"Fellows, we should have some hot coffee and biscuits for breakfast early in the morning. Tonight, do your best and eat whatever you brought up here with you."

That quiets them down, and I continue, "See to your men. I've got the first watch. See you in two hours, Art."

As they disperse, I take my equipment to the bunker I'll be sharing with my squad leaders and drop it off. After reporting our status to Captain Glazebrook, I return to my section and take up a position on the front trench firing platform. Checking the time, 2000 hours, it dawns on me I've got some time before I get a break and some rest—my whole body aches. I'm hungry, exhausted, and just want to curl up and go to sleep. But that's not an option; this is going to be a rough two hours.

While on duty, I'll need to stay awake and keep a sharp lookout. I do not care to keep lifting my head above the trench to look over at the Huns. However, it must be done. There are no periscope binoculars, so I must raise my head above the parapet to peer out over "no man's land." It's always eerie to watch the enemy trench at night. To me, it appears somewhat like a black wave in the distance slowly coming at us. Their trench system is only about a hundred yards to my front.

Suddenly I see the flash from some of their rifles and machine guns. Immediately after, nasty thuds of their bullets impact the sandbags that I'm leaning against, resting. I fire several shots at their flashes, the only target available, and their reply is more bullets. Their rounds lodge in the parapet on either side of my head. There are only inches between me and certain death. I thought this area was supposed to be quiet. But maybe, just maybe, I've lost the edge. I've been off the firing line for several weeks and grown used to being in relatively safe areas. There are many advantages to being off the firing line. One of them is that there is no lead flying around looking for a man to kill.

I'm at the front again, get your head in the game, or you could "become a landowner" up here.

After that close call, I pay considerably more attention to how I go about looking over the top of our trench. The rest of my shift goes without incident and comes to an end. As it does, Art approaches me.

"Go get some rest, Sam. It's my turn. I got it."

He turns to spit out some chewing tobacco and continues, "What a shitty night!"

"You got that right, Art. Keep your head down. They almost "topped me off" with their sniper and machine gun fire earlier. Be careful, Art."

"Thanks, I got this, old buddy."

With that, I turn my post over to Art and work my way slowly through the trench, looking for our bunker. It's a daunting task because of the darkness and the mud and water, which cause me to slip and fall several times. Reaching the opening, I crawl into our bunker, find a corner, and collapse.

The night passes quickly, and I'm awakened by Henry. "Come on, old man, we need to check on the men and see how our trench really looks. From what little I've seen, it's not pretty!"

I slowly bring myself to a sitting position, shaking my head, stretching my legs and arms in a feeble attempt to wake up. Responding to Henry while yawning, "We shouldn't be here very long, but let's go and look. First, I need some hot java. Have you seen anybody with a bucket of coffee?"

"Our supply trains still haven't made it up here. I did see some of the fellows brewing up a weak pot of java just outside the bunker," Henry replies as we crawl out of the bunker.

The men with the java are just around the corner from the bunker, and they're very generous about sharing some with us. Thanking them, we move on to check the condition of our trench sector.

Taking my first sip, I look over at Henry, "Damn, I wouldn't call it coffee, but it'll have to do for now!"

With the first ray of light in the morning, the full extent of our trench situation becomes painfully apparent. We inhabit a muddy, filthy, full of water up to our Pershing boots trench system that smells of human waste, dirty bodies, rotting sand-bags, stagnant mud, and cigarette smoke. There is also the lingering odor of poison gas. To make matters worse, our supply trains are strung out for miles and struggling with the muddy roads as they make their way to the front. We may not have any hot food until way into the late afternoon or evening.

I hope this day gets better and we get the hell out of here soon. Such is the life of a front-line doughboy.

13

BATTLE FOR SAINT-MIHIEL

DAY ONE

The supply trains finally caught up with our regiment, and we were served some hot chow for dinner this evening. This helped improve the men's morale somewhat, but the offensive starts tomorrow, the long-awaited D-Day. It's hard to feel good when you're going back into battle with the Huns in less than twenty-four hours. The mood of the men is tempered by what is to come.

Captain Glazebrook calls his leaders together after dinner for a status briefing. With all present in his dimly lit bunker, he begins his briefing. We all intently listen as he speaks in a reassuring, calm, and commanding voice.

"Gentlemen, good evening. Tomorrow's the start of our long-awaited offensive. H-Hour is set for 0600. Artillery barrages will start two hours before we go over the top. Our regiment will lead the attack and support Colonel Patton's 327th Tank Battalion. Our objective tomorrow is to capture the German-held village of Essey. Lieutenant Colonel Patton's tanks will spread out across the battlefield after breaking through the Huns' last trench lines and head for the village. Once we clear the German trenches, it's open ground. We can expect some artillery and mortar barrages. There's also a possibility German aircraft will strafe us and drop bombs as we close in on Essey."

He pauses for a moment and scans our faces. His facial expression reflects a calm, reassuring look and I, for one, am glad he is our CO. He continues, "According to reports received by Division HQ, the Germans may know many of the details about our offensive campaign. A Swiss newspaper has published the date, time, and duration of our preparatory artillery barrages. So much for being a neutral country!"

Noticing this information doesn't sit well with me or any of the men, Captain Glazebrook takes a long pause, lights up a cigarette, and proceeds to give us a brief history lesson.

"Fellows, allow me to share this with you. Following Napoleon's defeat at Waterloo, many European powers agreed it was in their best interest to allow Switzerland to remain a neutral country. Although most of the country seems to favor the Axis powers, they have managed to stay neutral and out of this war. Because of its neutrality, Switzerland has become a haven for many foreign politicians, artists, pacifists, and thinkers. Oh, and I might add, their banking system has also flourished."

Knowing the captain worked for JP Morgan & Company, he would know something about the banking industry and a little of its history.

Some men still have a problem with the Swiss newspaper, and one speaks up.

"Sir, that doesn't give them the right to publish that kind of information and place our lives at risk!"

"I can't agree with you more. It doesn't." Looking around at his men as a smile crosses his face, he continues. "All we can do is hope the Huns don't read Swiss newspapers."

This brings a few smiles and chuckles, and the captain continues.

"The Swiss article is not good news and may well contribute to more casualties than we might have suffered if they hadn't run the article. There is nothing we can do about that, but there is some good news. The Huns lack sufficient manpower, firepower, and effective leadership to mount an offensive operation or put up a strong defense. They're beginning to fall back toward Germany and consolidate their forces near the Hindenburg Line."

Drawing deeply on his cigarette and looking around at the men with him, Captain Glazebrook brings his meeting to a close.

"Okay, fellows, you know the score. You know what's expected tomorrow. Brief your men, get them ready, grab some rest and let's get this thing done in the morning. Dismissed!"

DAY TWO

Morning

Morning for us begins early. It's 0400 hours when I'm awakened by noise in the trenches created by men stirring about as they get ready for the day. Our cooks are working their way through the trenches handing out warm biscuits and pouring hot coffee into whatever container a doughboy holds up. The rain has slowed down considerably, turning into a slight drizzle with the ever-present chill in the air. Hopefully, this will make our task of moving through the terrain in front of us a little less difficult. However, I fear the damage has already been done. The killing fields in front of us are pockmarked with large shell holes full of stagnant water and mud. We must go through or around them as we move forward. It's going to be a tough slog to cross those hundred yards and get at the Huns. Our tanks must traverse this same terrain before breaking through the Huns' trenches. Once we're on the other side of the German trenches, we'll be on open, relatively flat land and able to maneuver much better and faster.

That's how it's supposed to unfold. Time will tell!

Moving through my sector of the trench, checking on the men, I hear the muffled firing of our artillery behind us as they begin their barrage. The sound starts as a low rumble and rapidly builds to a thundering crescendo as all our field artillery pieces engage the Huns. The shells whistle overhead as they seek out their pre-designated targets along the German trenches. It's always a more comforting sound when it's outgoing toward the Huns and not incoming from them.

Our preparatory barrages are scheduled to last two hours before we go over the top. I take a moment to light my pipe, seek out some coffee and continue moving among the men. Then, I hear the all too familiar sounds of German artillery responding to our barrage attack in the distance. We are now on the receiving end as German artillery shells explode up and down our trench line positions and mostly behind us.

Seeking protection close to the trench wall, I clear my pipe of tobacco and place it in my trench overcoat. With all the excitement, I spill my remaining coffee all over my rifle. Not to worry, the damn thing is all wet anyway. Yelling at the men as I hug the trench wall, "Boys, here we go again, keep close to the wall. Stay down."

What a hell of a way to start your morning.

The Huns initially fire most of their rounds over our heads and some at a distance behind us. They're now firing their artillery in a slow, methodical manner such that exploding shells creep forward, landing ever closer to us. This has the intended effect of creating fear and a realization that we can't run back to the support trench. We are trapped here and have nowhere to go.

It's a terrible feeling of despair and foreboding. We all struggle to control our inner fears, but some just can't. Some among us succumb to being "shell shocked." If they survive the artillery attack, they'll have to be taken off the line.

Shells crash into our trench lines with a thunderous effect. A terrible feeling of helplessness overtakes me. There is nowhere to hide. I must take it and hope my name is not on one of those shells. Continuing to move through my sector, I hear the whistling of shells headed straight for me. I move to seek some protection against the wall, but I'm too late. A shell lands close to me with a horrific explosion throwing me forcibly back and to the muddy ground. Two men closest to me are blown to pieces. Two human beings, in a flash, are reduced to body pieces flying in all directions.

Everything I witness is moving in slow motion. The noise is deafening. Looking to my left, I see another man go down as his head is severed at the neck from flying shrapnel. His skull and helmet are thrown through the air and land on the trench floor. They slowly sink into the mud and water accumulated there. His torso twitches, and blood squirts from the neck as his heart beats for the last time. Slowly falling to the trench floor, the torso moves as if looking for its head and then goes stiff.

God, what a ghastly sight. No man should have to endure this. I struggle to control my emotions and get back on my feet. The shelling is relentless, but I must get up and rally my men. Over the roar of battle, I hear Captain Glazebrook yelling as he moves along the trench line. "Stay at your post, boys. Hang in there. Stay calm. We'll get our turn!" His voice fades as he continues moving down the trench line.

Regaining some sense of where I am and what's going on, I continue moving among the men in my platoon. As I do, I marvel at their courage and stamina in this horrific bombardment. This was supposed to be our offensive attack. It seems the Germans have turned the tables on us for the moment.

Locating Henry, I'm relieved to see he is alright, and I yell over the noise, "Henry, what's your squad's status?"

"Sam, we're catching hell. The boys are hanging in there. Two of my men are down, and the rest of us just want to get the hell out of this trench and take the bastards on."

"I'm with you. Hang in there. I'm going to check on the rest of the platoon."

Henry gives me a thumbs-up. I turn and continue moving down the trench line, yelling out encouragement. "Hang in there, men. It won't be long now. We'll get the bastards!"

Moving through the trench and staying as close to the wall as possible, I locate Art. I'm relieved to see he's still with us. His squad is taking a hell of a beating too.

"Art, good to see you're still with us. What's your status?"

"Sam, damn, what a hell of a way to start our morning. I thought we were supposed to be the guys doing the attacking. It looks like someone forgot to tell Fritz!"

A slight grin works its way across my face as I react to Art's attempt at some humor during all this chaos. I respond, "When we take their trenches, I'll see that you get a chance to lodge your complaints with the Kaiser. How's that?"

He gives me a thumbs-up as I continue, "How are your boys doing, Art?"

"Sam, we're still in this fight, but I've lost three men. They were killed outright with one shell burst. We need to get out of these damn trenches and on with our attack!"

"Agreed! I'm going to find the captain and see what's going on. Hang in there, Art."

"I'm not going anywhere. Besides, I didn't have any other plans for this morning!" Art—always trying to inject some levity into a tough situation.

I wonder if he learned that playing professional baseball?

Working my way through the trench line looking for Captain Glazebrook, a sudden, eerie silence settles over our position. No more German shells are landing in our trenches and dealing out death. Their artillery barrage has stopped. Looking at my watch, it's now 0515 hours. They have been shelling us for an hour. Overhead, the only sounds we hear are the sounds of our outgoing rounds headed for the Huns' trenches. Although a comforting sound, I fear we've already sustained several losses and have yet to go on the attack.

Locating Captain Glazebrook, he motions for me to join him and some of his officers who have taken shelter in what's left of a bunker.

"Sam, we've just received new orders. Our attack has been moved up; we go in ten minutes—the usual, green flares and whistles. Return to your men, get them ready. We have to get out of these trenches and go on the attack."

"Yes, sir!" Turning to leave, he adds, "Sam, be careful out there." Saluting him, I respond, "You too, Sir," and head back to my platoon.

Moving at a fast clip back to my platoon, I pass litter bearers already at work removing wounded and dead men to the rear. Our losses could have been worse. The stagnant mud and water filling our trench system reduced the killing zone of artillery shells landing among us. Many of the shots impacting the ground penetrated deep into the mud and wet ground before exploding, reducing their killing radius. Looking at the carnage around me, I'm emotionally shaken. My hands begin to quiver, tears slowly flow down my cheeks, my stomach aches—not from hunger but fear. I just want to sit down and cry.

God, how I hate this place, I yearn to be home away from it all, and most of all with Marie, holding her in my arms in a loving embrace. No time to dwell on my emotions. I have a responsibility to my men and the unit. I must hold it together and get the job done.

Returning to the platoon, I call the squad leaders together and brief them on our situation and pending attack. After wishing them luck, I send them back to their squads. The men are now busy preparing themselves to go over the top and back into "no man's land."

John and Alex, the new brothers, already have a look of terror on their faces and that "hundred-yard stare" in their eyes. It is one of the signs that "shell shock" may be setting in. Henry, realizing this, pulls them aside and close to him.

"Fellows, I want you to stay with me when we go over the top —John on my left and Alex on my right. Keep behind me and stay spaced out. Keep low to the ground and move with a purpose. Don't bunch up. Follow my lead. Whatever I do, you do. You boys got that?"

With apprehension and fear in their voices, they respond,

"Yes, Sergeant."

"Yes, Sergeant."

Henry looks them dead in the eyes and, in a matter-of-fact, serious tone, says, "Boys, one more thing. When we go over the top, and we're out there in the killing fields, remember this."

"What's that, Sergeant?" Says Alex.

"Never look back. Just keep going, or you're a dead man!"

I witness this exchange and can only feel pity for them. We've all been there. They'll just have to endure, persevere, and move forward with the other men. Looking at the brothers, I try to reassure them as a father would his sons. "Boys, follow your sergeant. We'll see you in the Huns' trenches. Good luck out there!"

Returning to my place in the trench line, I adjust my equipment, load my rifle, and yell out to the men, "Fix bayonets." They move in unison as if on the drill field, pulling bayonets from their sheaths and attaching them to the end of their rifles. Standing on what's left of one of the firing platforms, I carefully look out into "no man's land." Our artillery has been relentless in the bombardment of the Huns' trenches. They also took on the German artillery batteries in their rear area. They must have been successful, as we're now only receiving sporadic artillery fire from the Huns.

With only a few minutes to go before going over the top, our artillery shifts their fire to about fifty yards in front of us. Shells are landing in the middle of "no man's land." They continue to adjust their fire by inching it closer to the Huns' trenches, then on top of them, and then shifting behind the German lines. The purpose here is to instill fear in the Huns, blow holes in their barbed wire, create new shell holes for us to use as cover, and take out any new landmines the Germans may have placed in front of their trenches.

We can only hope and pray this works. We'll know in a moment!

Green flares light up the early morning misty, dreary sky above. Now the whistles. It's over the top for us. Once again, we're the first wave. We'll be joined by the second wave when we reach the halfway point out there. Climbing up and over, I yell out, "Let's go, boys, follow me!" Men pour out of the trenches and charge forward, trying to maintain a low profile, while yelling as we attack the Huns.

Although we're not receiving German artillery fire, they have started firing heavy mortar rounds. They're dropping randomly across the terrain in front of us. One lands just to my right, killing the man next to me, blowing me off my feet and into a shell hole. I'm momentarily stunned and can't hear anything but ringing in my ears. Two of my men jump into the shell hole to check on me. Seeing I'm alright, they help me to my feet, and we move forward up and out of the hole. Just as we clear the top of the shell hole, both men are cut down by German machine guns.

They must have died instantly, not murmuring a sound, as they gave their last full measure. Their shredded bodies fall to the ground and slowly roll back into the shell hole we were just in.

These Boche bastards are murdering us out here. I'll show no mercy when I get into their trenches.

Approaching the middle of "no man's land," I signal the men following me to take cover. Taking cover behind a tree stump, I look to my left, right, and back toward our trenches. From the carnage I see around me, it's apparent we have taken a beating getting this far, but we're still in the fight. Rising and maintaining a low profile, I yell out to the men. "Let's go; follow me!" As one, we rise and charge straight at the German trenches. There is fire in our eyes, revenge in our hearts, and mercy has just taken the day off.

I would not want to be a Hun when we get in their trenches.

The ferocity of our attack has shaken the German defenders, and many start running out the back of their trenches. We cover the ground quickly as our men jump into the trenches and take on the Huns. I lunge forward and jump down into the trench, shooting my rifle at a German staring up at me. He drops to the ground like a rag doll without making a sound. He quickly dies as I shoot him in the head, turning his face to jelly as blood splattered his trench coat, helmet, and rifle. We are now engaged in fierce combat, and the winners will take all.

Hearing a loud yell from one of my men, I look to my left and catch the crazed look of a Hun closing in on me for the kill. His rifle and bayonet are extended to the fullest in anticipation of running it clean through my body. It's not to be—the man who yelled fires his rifle almost point-blank into the back of the charging Hun. Yelling out in pain and staggering from his wound, he continues toward me. I'm quick enough to step back and turn to face him as he closes in on me. Slashing my bayonet across his face and cutting deep into his eyes, he falls to his knees, clutching his face. Blood gushes from between his fingers and clenched hands as I bring my rifle up to my shoulder, aim, and shoot him in the head.

The Huns that remain in the trench are putting up a hell of a fight, but we're steadily overpowering them. Working my way to the left, killing Germans as I go, a German flamethrower squad emerges from a hidden bunker. They ignite their weapon and disperse its lethal flame gel out onto a group of men fighting near them. They are Americans and Germans. Both are now covered in flames, screaming in agonizing pain as they fall to the ground and roll around trying to put out the fire. It doesn't help. The lethal gel sticks to their bodies and consumes them in flame. Their burning flesh has a sickening smell, and I struggle not to vomit. Men in the immediate vicinity of this brutal attack, both American and German, stop fighting each other.

Everyone looks on in horror as these men burn to death. Watching them die in horrific pain and suffering infuriates both the Germans and Americans. The combatants, who stopped fighting, turned their weapons on the German flamethrower squad and shoot them dead. There is nothing that can be done for the men burning to death. Out of mercy, we shoot them. The Germans in our sector of the trench stop fighting and immediately surrender. This act of butchery has taken the fight out of them.

Who in the hell kills their own men just to kill some of the enemy?

The second wave arrives, jumps into the trenches, and for now, the brutal fighting ends. The Germans surrender en masse.

Afternoon

With the German trench system captured, the first and second wave troops assume a defensive posture, secure the Germans that surrendered and begin moving them to the rear area. Litter bearers are at work clearing the field behind us of wounded and dead and those in the captured trenches we now occupy. The third wave of fresh troops has just passed through us, gone over the top and out into the open terrain to our front. As far as I can see, from one end of the trench line to the other, our boys charge forward in massive numbers as they continue to pursue demoralized, retreating Germans. Wave two will follow them after regrouping. Since we were the first wave, we are given a short rest before rejoining them on the field to continue our attack.

My heart rate slows down as I take a moment to rest, my breathing returns to normal, and the adrenaline rush begins to ease off. All the men around me, including myself, are covered in mud and splattered with blood from the close combat with the Huns. Our faces reflect exhaustion, fear, and the strain of what we just endured. Many of us struggle to control our inner emotions and keep them from bursting out for all to see.

These men are warriors. They fight for their brothers—the men around them. Not for glory but to prove themselves worthy of their comrades. Most would sacrifice themselves for the men around them. How do you speak of such courage, self-sacrifice, and feats of daring by men who before this war were anything but warriors? But that's what they are, warriors, who will never be able to truly speak openly about what they've done over here except to the men who have endured this living hell with them.

Having regrouped, the second wave goes over the top and rejoins the attack. There is a general stillness and peacefulness in the immediate area we now find ourselves. The sound of battle has shifted out to the front as our troops advance rapidly in the open terrain. While taking a brief respite, I'm brought back to reality when one of Captain Glazebrooks' runners finds me.

"Sergeant, you're wanted by the captain for a quick meeting. Follow me."

"Okay, let's go." Following the runner, I yell over to Art as we pass him. "I'll be back momentarily. Take charge and check on the status of the platoon. When you get it, join me at the captain's briefing, be quick!"

He responds with a thumbs-up and moves out with a sense of purpose. I didn't have a chance to move among my platoon and check everyone's status before this briefing. I fear we have sustained heavy losses taking this damn trench, and the captain will want our status.

Arriving, I'm directed to an uncovered side trench where Captain Glazebrook, two lieutenants, and five other non-commissioned officers (NCOs) are standing. All are covered in mud and dried blood. They look tired and drawn. Most smoke cigarettes to relieve some of the tension and get a nicotine rush.

Since entering this war, cigarette use has increased dramatically among American military personnel as tobacco companies target them. These companies promote cigarettes as a way for soldiers to psychologically escape from their current circumstances and boost overall troop morale. Because of their ease of use, cigarettes have supplanted pipes as the most popular means of tobacco consumption. Those of us who smoke pipes must keep our loose tobacco dry, take time to fill our pipes, and relight them frequently. I've found this very acceptable, more calming, and choose not to switch to cigarettes.

Captain Glazebrook begins, "Fellows, we took a beating getting here this morning. Two platoons lost their lieutenants, and three lost their platoon sergeants. Except for Sergeant McCormick, you other sergeants are their replacements, and you've been told your assignments. You gentlemen will take us the rest of the way today. Now, I need the status of your platoons."

Looking around at the group of men, it's clear my platoon is the only one that didn't lose our lieutenant or me, the platoon sergeant. I'm not looking for a bullet or artillery shell; however, I can't help but think about the prospects of a bullet or shell having my name on one of them eventually. The law of probability must catch up with me at some point over here. How random can death be?

Captain Glazebrook receives a report from the other platoon sergeants and then glances over at me. "Sam, what's your status?"

"Sir, I'm waiting on Sergeant Wilson to bring it to me. He should be here any minute. I didn't get a chance to take it before coming here, but I fear we have sustained heavy losses. Sorry, sir!"

"That's okay, Sam. I'll go ahead and start. Our company is being shifted to the right and will provide some additional support for Lieutenant Colonel Patton's 327th Tank Battalion. We'll be temporarily attached to the 84th Infantry Brigade as Patton continues his attack toward Essey. Patton needs more infantry support because units supporting him suffered heavy casualties breaking through the German trenches. They are now in open country and gearing up for a full-scale tank assault over muddy terrain. Our support will be critical to Patton's remaining tanks."

He pauses, gives us a chance to process what he said, and then continues in a calm, reassuring voice. "Any questions, fellows?"

I ask, "When do we go, and how far is it to the tank units we'll be supporting?"

Continuing in his command voice and matter-of-fact tone, he responds. "We jump off in ten minutes. We'll be moving across open terrain and through other supporting infantry companies to get there. I want a V-shaped formation, spread out, with the first platoon followed by second and so on. We have about six hundred yards to cover before we link up with Patton's trailing tank units."

He pauses and lights up another cigarette while he looks around at us. At that moment, Art joins us and informs him of our platoon's status.

"Sir, the first platoon has forty-four men left out of the sixty we started with, and we're still able to fight. Nine were killed and seven wounded."

Noting the report, the captain closes the briefing with, "Gentlemen, rejoin your platoons, get them ready and join me over at the first platoon's position in ten minutes. We'll jump off from there."

After rejoining the men, ensuring they are ready to jump off, and giving them a quick overview of what we're about to do, we wait for the rest of the company's platoons to join us.

Captain Glazebrook joins our platoon and, with the other three platoons assembled, leads us out of the trench system. Once in the open field, we move into our combat formation and proceed forward across a large area. Moving quickly, we come upon some of Patton's tanks destroyed earlier as they crossed open terrain. They look like death traps to me. They are not very big or heavily armored. Passing by the tanks, we see several dead crew members still in them. Many are horribly burned and mutilated from direct hits by artillery shells. Some of the bodies hang partially out of their tanks in a last futile attempt to escape the death traps they fought in.

These Renault FT light tanks only have two-man crews and are lightly armed with a 37mm M1916 gun or a Marlin Rockwell M1917 machine gun. When we entered the war, the U.S. Army had no tanks and was forced to scramble to obtain sufficient tanks for use on the battlefield. Heavier tanks, like the Mark Is and Mark Vs, are built by the British and used by them and the French. We do not have any heavy tanks and are dependent on our Allies for support when it comes to using heavier tanks on the battlefield.

Moving across the open terrain, we pass dead Germans, horses, smashed artillery pieces, and other debris of war. The landscape we cross has not seen much war up to this point. There are no trenches. There is no massive devastation of the land which would have occurred from constant artillery barrages, nor is there the stench of death in the air from dead and decaying bodies lying in the open for weeks. There is a newness to the destruction laid before us and scattered across the fields we cross. The carnage we see results from just a few hours of combat. Just a few hours!

Is there a difference? Not to the men who fought and died here, not to those of us who walk through these fields on our way to the next battle, nor to the French people who call this place home.

Reaching Patton's rear tank elements without incident, Captain Glazebrook halts the company and has us take covering positions. He motions for my platoon lieutenant and me to join him. The three of us then move forward to contact the officer in charge of the tank units in front of us.

Captain Glazebrook works his way through the tanks until he locates a major commanding the tank unit. They exchange salutes and greetings, and then he motions for the lieutenant and me to join them. The major informs us they're in a holding position waiting for Lieutenant Colonel Patton to call them forward. He continues with an overview of what has occurred so far.

In a command voice and matter-of-fact tone, he gives us an overview. "With reports coming in that some of his tanks were bogged down on the battlefield, Patton began moving northwest toward Essey. General MacArthur was making his way north through the Sonnard Woods to the same place. Patton spotted MacArthur on a small hill and walked over to him. The two stood and talked in the middle of an artillery barrage while everyone else apparently ran for cover. We don't know what they talked about."

Pausing to light a cigarette, he then continues. "Patton returned to his lead tank units and resumed his attack on the Germans who were retreating from Essey. As they neared town, Patton encountered five of his tanks, reluctant to advance for fear of shelling. He then got off the tank he was riding and led the tanks into town on foot. Some of the tankers stopped again, refusing to cross the only bridge to pursue the fleeing Germans. They believed the bridge was mined. Patton walked across the bridge and noticed some explosives under the bridge, but the wires had been cut. He then ordered his tanks to proceed. Patton is now conferring with MacArthur again, seeking permission to continue his advance against the Germans and attack the town of Pannes to the north."

After the tank unit commander's status report, Captain Glazebrook says, "This Patton sounds like one hell of a combat leader!"

"Yes, he is, Captain. He believes in leading from the front, always attacking, never retreating or stopping to defend a position. When we get the word to move up, you'll see what I mean."

"Yes, sir, I'm going to bring my company up and deploy them around your tanks."

"Sounds good, Captain. I would be quick about it. I'm expecting to hear from Patton any minute now, wanting us to advance and continue the attack."

The two officers salute each other, and Captain Glazebrook instructs his lieutenant to go back and bring the company forward. He and I then move around the tanks to check on the terrain and the tank formation to see how we may best deploy the men to protect them.

When the lieutenant returns with the company, Captain

Glazebrook calls us together and gives us our orders. He instructs us to stay spread out and cover each other's flanks as we move in on the town. Each platoon is assigned to cover ten tanks. We're ready.

Patton's order reaches us. We're moving out and joining the attack on Pannes. The village of Essey was taken, and several thousand Germans have been captured.

My god, how many Germans are left? Surely this next village should be easy to capture.

The monotonous hum of tank engines fills the air as their motors roar back to life and tune up. Once online and ready, the tanks begin moving forward to join Patton's lead tank elements and join in on the attack. We fall in around them to provide protection and move forward with them.

Even to friendly eyes, watching these tanks move forward in mass formation is frightful and, at the same time, mesmerizing. It is as if they are monsters from a prehistoric age that had long since gone extinct. Yet here, as we move among them and provide infantry support, they seem to have taken on a life of their own. These metal monsters are ready to deal out death with impunity from rifle and machine gun fire from the Huns.

Finally, we have some tank support!

It's late into the afternoon, and the sky is overcast with the same light mist we have endured most of the day. Much of the terrain we cover is soaked, and the roads and paths are muddy. It's not too bad, as we manage to slog our way through. In some cases, the tanks have a rough go of making it through or around mud holes and craters.

We move quickly over the terrain and cover the distance needed to form up behind Patton's tanks. With Patton sitting on the lead tank, they have already started to close in on Pannes. I marvel at how our light tanks tear and grind away at barbed wire entanglements and roll over small trench lines and German firing positions.

Approaching Pannes with tanks in front and us following, some Germans rise from their fighting positions and attack us. They come charging and yelling like crazed animals. This is not "no man's land" terrain, pitted with shell holes and places to hide. It's virgin open terrain—not many shell holes to dive into and hide from our tanks.

What are these Huns thinking? Surely, they can hear our tanks, if not see them.

The Huns are about a hundred yards out and closing in on us when from above, we hear, then see, several German Fokker D.VII fighter aircraft come streaking out of the overcast sky, followed by several German AEG G.IV medium bombers. Both are some of Germany's best aircraft. They begin strafing our attack lines and dropping bombs on our tank formations. Their fighters swarm over our line of attack like bees to honey. Several men are hit by German aircraft machine gun fire, and some of our tanks take direct hits from bombs. Those that blow up create giant fireballs with smoke billowing up into the air. Our tank crews don't have a chance when they take a direct hit. If not killed outright, they will burn to death before anyone can save them.

Now I know what they were thinking. It's a coordinated air and ground attack. A new strategy is being deployed along the front lines by the Americans and Germans. But, in this case, not all the Germans left their fortified positions to join in on the attack across open terrain. The ones who did begin losing their courage as our tanks bore in on them with their guns, mowing them down in droves.

As fast as the German aircraft descended on us, our boys, flying in their British Sopwith Camels and French Spad XIII fighters, emerged from the clouds and take on the Huns.

When America entered the war, there were very few aircraft in the United States Army's inventory. Aircraft from Britain and France had to be procured in large numbers, resulting in a formidable American presence in the air war. The British Sopwith Camels have shot down more German warplanes than any other aircraft from the Allied force in the war so far. The French Spad XIII is highly regarded as one of the most successful fighter planes in the Allies' inventory. Americans flying these aircraft have racked up impressive victories in the sky above the battlefields.

Aerial dogfights ensue between the American and German pilots flying above us. They maneuver their aircraft like well-trained ballerinas. Pushing their aircraft to its limits as they climb, dive, spiral, perform loops and barrel rolls, trying to get behind their enemy for a clean kill shot. If successful, the pilot who is the target will be riddled with machine gunfire. If not killed outright, he is doomed, for there is no escape. He will have to ride his aircraft to the ground. These men fly without parachutes. Several of our fighters also take on the German bombers and shoot many of them down before they can seek protection back in the clouds. The remaining German fighters, being much faster, break off their attack and head for the clouds.

The Huns' air attack inflicts several casualties among our ranks and knocks out some tanks, but not enough to stop us. At the beginning of their coordinated attacks, our company takes a defensive position around the tanks we're assigned to protect. We seek cover behind anything that can provide some protection —new shell holes, ditches, and the remains of buildings. We then take aim at the Huns attacking ground troops and pour lead into their dwindling ranks.

Before departing, two of the German Fokker fighter planes dive down on us one last time, firing their machine guns. The lead plane is followed by the second plane, about fifty yards behind. They make their strafing run at treetop level, firing as they fly over us. The first plane catches the brothers from North Carolina in the open and knocks them both to the ground, severely wounding them. John partially stands up and staggers toward his brother, Alex, to help him. The second plane continues his attack on the brothers firing his machine gun into their already dying bodies. John is hit several more times, keels over dead, and lands next to his brother with one arm extended over his brother's dead body. Having dealt out death from above, the planes disappear into the cloud cover as they rock their wings back and forth. This gesture is usually a display of support for the troops on the ground. In this case, it's just a taunting, a despicable act of disrespect for the men they just killed.

Once again, the Hun shows his inclination for butchery. Some of the men rush over to the brothers. I realize it's a futile gesture but an instinctive one. They are both gone; not even their mother could recognize them from all the damage the German machine guns did to their bodies.

We will exact revenge!

With the sky clear of German planes and the Huns' ground attack falling apart, I rally my men. "The brothers are dead. Let's move out. Follow me, and let's get on with the business of killing these bastards!"

The men respond. They rise from their protective cover and resume our frontal attack. Rifles at the ready, bayonets attached, we fall in behind the tanks and move forward at a brisk pace. Seeing us move forward inspires the units on our left and right. Doughboys, up and down our line of attack, rise from the ground and join in the attack. The tanks supported by our infantry begin a massive advance on the now retreating Germans. The first few minutes are an awful slaughter as we engage the Huns in close combat.

Closing in on them, we reap a terrible harvest of wounded

and dead Germans. Firing our rifles as we move forward, bayoneting any German that dares to challenge us. All the while, our tanks spit withering fire into their retreating and dwindling ranks without mercy. Many Huns seek cover wherever they can as our onslaught continues. But they are not safe from our tanks as they lumber over trenches, fallen trees, stone walls, firing as they roll on, leaving devastation in their wake. Some of the Huns hold their ground and make a defiant stand against us in hand-to-hand combat.

Moving forward, firing my rifle as I go and yelling at the men around me to keep up the attack, I find myself face to face with two charging Huns. They're attacking me with bayonets extended and closing in for the kill. Pulling the trigger on my rifle, one round spirals down the barrel, exits the rifle, and finds its mark. The Hun closest to me falls back, withering in pain from the impact of my bullet as it smashes into his stomach.

Aiming at the other Hun, slamming the bolt forward to insert another round in the chamber, and pulling the trigger, nothing happens. I'm out of ammunition, have no time to reload, and instantly rush toward the other Hun with my bayonet extended. He is a big German and shows no fear, only rage as we close in for a death duel. Extending his rifle and bayonet at full length and lunging at me, he trips. His fate is sealed as I drive my bayonet with such force through his throat that it bursts out the back of his neck. He drops like a rock to his knees as blood splatters everywhere. His eyes go cold, he moans as I put my foot on his chest and strain to pull the bayonet out. What a ghastly sight. It makes my stomach sick.

When will they quit? I fear I'll never get over all the carnage I've witnessed and the deaths I've caused in this terrible war.

We have shaken the Germans to their core. Not even their officers can inspire them to stand and fight now. They yell and curse at them, but the bonds of discipline, the core of the

German army, cannot be regained, and completely collapses. Germans run to their rear, drop their weapons and surrender by the hundreds.

The whole German front line in this area collapses under the weight and ferocity of our attack. They retreat in a panic heading back toward their own country. We have captured Pannes and the entire area around the village. There are signs everywhere of a panicky German retreat: the musical instruments of a regimental band laid out near the village square; a battery of guns left behind still stand their station; and, in a nearby barn, a horse, already saddled, waits for a German officer.

Evening

With the battle for this area over, our company is assigned a sector to defend while we await new orders. Once again, our company has sustained several losses, and we're down to half strength. Later in the evening, Captain Glazebrook calls his leaders together and conveys the latest news and orders.

"Gentleman, glad to see we all made it through the day. It's been another bad one, but I do have some good news. We're staying here for a few days. We are responsible for this section of our new front lines. We'll be pulled off the line in two or three days and moved back to a rear area. It's further north of here and somewhere west of Verdun at a village called Lemmes. We'll be given several days of rest, receive new replacements, some training, and then back to the front. General Pershing has halted further advances in this area so that Americans can be withdrawn for the coming offensive in the Meuse-Argonne sector. This offensive will be the largest we've ever fought—with over one million American troops participating. The goal is simple: Capture the railway hub at Sedan, which could break the railway network supporting the

German army in France. If successful, this could help bring about an end to this war."

We've heard this before, but coming from Captain Glazebrook, planned by the capable leadership of General Pershing, with over a million American Doughboys fighting in it, maybe, just maybe, it will end the war.

He pauses, lights up a cigarette, and motions for us to relax and take out a smoke. Miraculously, both lieutenants and all six sergeants made it through the day. We're exhausted, hungry, and need some rest. I don't know about the other fellows, but my arms are weak and sore from fighting the Huns all day. They give out as I try to assume a relaxed position on the ground, using my arms to stabilize me, and I fall unceremoniously to the ground. No damage done, but it elicits some light laughter from the group assembled.

Captain Glazebrook looks over at me with his reassuring smile and says, "You alright over there, Sam?"

Pulling out my pipe, calmly packing it, lighting it up, and slowly taking in a few draws of smoke from my pipe, I respond in a lighthearted manner. "Yes, sir, doing just fine! Nothing wrong with me that several days in the rear can't fix!"

He grins, "Well, Sam, I'm coming to that. When we break up here in a few minutes, I want all of you to see to the needs of your men. Hot chow is on the way, along with freshwater and ammunition resupplies. We don't expect any action from the Germans in this area for several days. They're still in a total state of disarray and retreat. We could get some long-distance artillery shelling from them occasionally, so keep your men well dispersed. Set out your guard details during the night and keep them quiet. With daybreak tomorrow, we'll go about the business of reinforcing our defensive lines just in case the Huns turn around and take another stab at us."

Taking a minute to let that settle in, he continues. "While in the rest area, we'll be taking time off for some recreational activities. Regimental HQ is trying to set up a few baseball games. They have also scheduled a boxing match. Our regimental boxing champ will fight the champ of the 82nd Division's 328th Infantry Regiment."

He stops, looks over at me, and says, "You know what that means, Sam. Make sure Sergeants Miller and Wilson are rested and ready."

With excitement in my voice, I respond, "Yes, sir! This is good news. They'll like it, and I'm sure they'll be ready." He nods and then disperses us.

We return to our platoons, see to the feeding and re-arming of the men, and settle in for the night.

One more battle down, with an unknown number to follow.

14

REST AND RECREATION - LEMMES

DAY ONE

After three uneventful days on the front lines, we are relieved by another American unit just in from the States. Those of us who survived the battle and had not been sent to the rear area earlier due to injuries are loaded into several Nash Quad trucks. Our long line of trucks is strung out for several miles as we travel over French country roads to our next rest area. Lousy weather continues with intermittent rain or mist, the sky above is overcast, and the countryside we drive over, as always, is muddy. Even with our Quad trucks, the trip to Lemmes is a long, slow slog through mud holes. We must exit our trucks on several occasions and help push them through the mud. Many of the French civilians we encounter greet us with waves as we drive through the countryside. They give us French bread, cheese, and their local wine at some rest stops. The hospitality shown to us is most welcome and makes our trip a little more bearable.

The men of the regiment and our equipment travel most of the day to arrive at Lemmes. Finally arriving at our destination, Art, Henry, and I are ordered to report to Captain Glazebrook after settling our men into their assigned squad tents. We accomplish this order with due haste, as the men are anxious to get settled in and begin to unwind. We then report to the captain. Entering his tent, we render the customary hand salute as we come to attention. He starts with, "At ease, gentlemen. I trust you had a comfortable road trip here?"

That elicits a few grins and chuckles from us as the captain adds to the levity with a grin. "Yeah, me too!" He pulls out a cigarette, lights it, and continues. "Feel free to smoke. Welcome to Camp Lemmes. This will be our home for at least a week or more. Here we should be able to get some much-needed rest. How does that sound?"

Neither Henry nor Art smoke. They both believe it's bad for their athletic endeavors. Art pulls out his chewing tobacco, places some in his mouth, and starts chewing on it. I pull out my pipe, stuff it with tobacco, and light up as we all respond similarly. "Sounds good, thank you, sir."

Captain Glazebrook continues, "This area has been built up to serve as a large staging camp to prepare for our upcoming offensive in the Meuse-Argonne sector. While here, we'll enjoy some rest and recreation, continue training, and bring the regiment back to full strength with new stateside replacements."

Taking a moment as he looks around at his men, he slowly continues in a subdued, low-key voice. "I've been told that our regiment sustained many casualties and deaths during the battle for Essey and Pannes. We're currently at about 60 percent of our designated strength level. It will take time to rebuild the regiment, train the new men, and give us veterans some time to relax and recuperate. General Pershing believes we performed admirably during the battle around Saint-Mihiel, and so do I. Having said that, we have much to do to get ready for the big offensive in the Argonne. I'll be looking to each of you fellows to help me get it done," he says, drawing in deeply on his cigarette as he looks at each of us. "Sam, you're being promoted to Company First Sergeant. You'll report directly to me. I'm looking to you to provide strong leadership and help me see that our men get what they need when they need it. Art, you're taking over the first platoon, and Henry, you now have the second platoon. These assignments are effective immediately. Any questions, men?"

Looking over at Art and Henry, I respond while taking the pipe out of my mouth. "No, sir, I don't. What about you fellows?"

Art responds first, "No sir, no questions on my new assignment. But is there any news on us possibly playing some baseball while we're here?"

Henry speaks up before the captain can respond, "Only one, sir. Any news on my fight with the champ of the 328th Infantry Regiment, sir?"

With a smile on his face and some pride in his voice, he calmly responds. "The skies are clearing up, and we're supposed to enjoy some dry weather for several days. This is good news. We'll know more later tomorrow about both your sports-related questions. But, I have it on good authority your fight is on for later in the week."

This brings smiles to our faces, and I, for one, am already looking forward to some downtime and a chance to relax. With this news, the captain mentions he'll have a planning meeting mid-morning tomorrow to prepare our schedule for the week. He then dismisses us. The walk back to our area is cheerful, and thoughts of celebrating later into the evening cross our minds. However, we are dog tired, need the rest, and with the loss of the brothers from North Carolina, we have no moonshine to help us celebrate. It's dinner, then sleep for us tonight.

After dinner and upon returning to my tent, I find a letter on my cot from Marie. What a terrific surprise. I settle in, lay back on my cot, open her letter, and commence reading using my Beacon army light.

My dearest Sam,

I hope and pray this letter finds you and your friends all doing well. I miss you terribly and wish this war would end. The misery and suffering of so many people for all these years are more than one can bear to think about. I don't want to dwell on the past, but how will we ever put all this behind us when it is over?

I wonder how any of us will ever forget what we've seen and all the suffering, death, and destruction we've endured? The sooner this war ends, the sooner we can start down the road to recovery. We can hope!

Since you left, we have been very busy, with many wounded men constantly arriving from the front. We usually see American, French, and English, but occasionally we receive some Germans. Since we only receive severely wounded men, the types of wounds we're dealing with are horrific. I fear many of these men's lives will never be the same again for them. In many cases, I fear, they will be condemned to a life of misery. God forbid.

I'm doing well and maintaining my health as well as I can under the circumstances. We work seven days a week with long hours. More nurses and doctors have been stationed here recently, so our situation is not dire.

My precious Sam, how I miss you! I wish we were together again so very much. I didn't fully realize, appreciate, or comprehend how much you have become a part of my heart, life, and soul. I care for you very much and believe I'm falling in love with you. I find myself dreaming of us spending our lives together after the war ends. We shared much about ourselves, our dreams, and our desires when we were together. I would like to know more about your family. You avoided talking about them whenever we were together, and I chose not to pursue the subject at the time. I ask you now, if you're more comfortable with my feelings toward you and my desire for you, that you share some of your family background. Your family certainly played a role in your upbringing and helped to shape the man you became. You are a good, honorable, and courageous man. You will make a fine husband for some woman.

I'm not prying, and if you're not comfortable sharing this information, please do not hold me in any disrespect for asking.

I must go now. Another large number of wounded men have just arrived from the front, and I'm needed at the hospital. Take care of yourself and say hello to Art and Henry, oh and Captain Glazebrook too. Even though I haven't met them yet, I feel as if I know them all.

Until we meet again,

Je t'aime, your loving Marie.

WHAT A LETTER! Marie has given me new life, hope, and another reason to survive this war. I must survive, reunite with her, hold her in my arms and take her back with me to America. I turn my light off, roll over on my side, and fall into a deep sleep, which I haven't had for a long time.

DAY TWO

With the sound of réveille, I'm awakened from a deep sleep. "Réveille," called in French "Le Réveil," is a bugle call and is chiefly used to wake military personnel at sunrise. The name comes from réveille, the French word for "wake up." Slowly getting up from my cot and rejoining the rest of the world that's awake, it dawns on me I didn't have any flashbacks, dreams, or nightmares—what a great feeling. I had forgotten just how rested one could become with a good night's sleep.

Art, Henry, and I head over to the mess tent for breakfast after dressing. Approaching the massive, circus-looking tent, we can't help but notice the artists that walk among us in the regiment have struck again. Some of our fellow doughboys have taken it upon themselves to paint the top of the tent with the "Barnum and Bailey Circus" logo. The BBC is back in town. At the front entrance, the cooks have placed a menu on the bulletin board listing what we can expect daily for our meals. Several of us crowd around. Henry takes it upon himself to read it out loud.

Daily Menu

Breakfast: oatmeal, pork sausages, fried potatoes, biscuits, bread and butter, jam, and coffee.

Lunch: roast beef, baked potatoes, bread and butter, cornstarch pudding, and coffee.

Dinner: beef stew, corn bread, soups and custards, prunes, and tea.

Note: Subject to change, based on availability and supply deliveries.

Enjoy Your Meals!

Compliments of the 166th Regimental Chefs

TRYING to contain his amusement with the last two comments, Henry blurts out. "Damn fellows, that looks pretty good. I will need all that and more to get back in shape for my big fight. I hope they meet their commitments, or else."

Art says, "Or else what, big guy?"

Henry responds in a cool, calm, and matter-of-fact voice. "I'll be up here and express my displeasure to the head chef, and maybe I'll just get in a few bouts before the big event."

This brings on some laughter among the group as we escort Henry inside. The place is full of doughboys enjoying a real breakfast for the first time in several weeks. We go through the chow line, load up on food, grab a tin cup of coffee and settle in at the first open table we find, and enjoy our breakfast.

After breakfast, we head over to Captain Glazebrook's HQ tent for a meeting to lay out the plans and schedules for the next week. The men present are the new executive officer, a new first lieutenant who just arrived, our four platoon leaders who are all first lieutenants—two having just arrived—our four platoon sergeants, and myself. I've all but given up trying to remember their names or where they're from. We have lost so many officers and platoon sergeants every time we have engaged the Germans.

All military personnel must display their rank somewhere on the uniform they wear. Enlisted men and non-commissioned officers wear our rank insignia patches on the upper sleeves of our shirts and jackets. Officers place their rank on the collars of shirts they wear and display rank on the shoulders of their jackets. This keeps it simple, totally impersonal, and makes it easy to address a man without remembering or using his name.

Getting close to new men assigned to our company is tough. It makes it harder to deal with if they're killed. Men like Art and Henry, with whom I shipped over and grew to know and respect and consider good friends, fall under a special category. When you train together, deploy together, and fight alongside each other, over time, you develop a special bond, one that can only be broken by death. Losing men in this category is heart-wrenching, devastating, and becomes even more difficult over time with the more you lose. Circumstances draw us closer together, and you think of them as brothers, as family. Unfortunately, we have no choice and learn to deal with whatever fate comes our way. As for new men, we can try and control how close we let them in. That doesn't mean the loss of a new man doesn't bother you. It does! But not as much as the loss of a close friend.

Captain Glazebrook holds a short meeting with us and lays out the general schedule of activities for the next seven days. They include basic physical training followed by rifle practice every morning. After lunch, our afternoons will consist of organized recreational activities and free time to pursue personal endeavors. The regimental boxing match between Henry, our regiment's champion, and the 328th Infantry Regiment's champion will take place on day seven, a Saturday. Over the next five days, baseball games will be organized and played between each company. A playoff game between the two teams with the most wins will be played on day six, a Friday. Each day we're subject to receive replacements from the States and will process them as they arrive. Finally, all men are instructed to clean, repair, and draw new equipment if needed. There will be a regimental inspection on day eight, followed by a full-dress review formation and parade in front of the Rainbow Division's senior commanding officers.

Following the meeting, we're all energized and looking forward to the days ahead. The remainder of this day is spent organizing the activities, including picking baseball players for each company's team. Our company's team is built around Art, who is acting like a kid turned loose in a candy store full of sweets. He approached his duties of picking a team with the fervor of a professional baseball team manager and has already held a practice session.

Henry has laid out an afternoon workout routine beginning tomorrow. He asked Art and me to be in his corner for the fight. We both accepted, and since I don't play baseball, I'll be working with Henry to get him ready. Regimental pride will ride on his shoulders the day of the fight, and I'm sure many wagers will be made.

Later in the evening, after dinner, I return to my tent and settle in to write Marie a letter. After pulling a box next to my cot, securing some writing paper, preparing, and lighting my pipe, I begin writing.

Dearest Marie,

We are now in a rest area and will be here for several days, we hope. I can't tell you where, but we are well behind the front and should be relatively safe here. This is a good thing since we all need the peace and quiet it brings. This should give us rest and a chance to recover some of our sanity. At least, I hope so.

Your letter was waiting for me when I arrived at camp. I must say, it was a delightful surprise and I've already read it several times. Your words of love and wanting to be together was what I've been waiting to hear from you. It's exactly how I have felt since I first saw you back at the field hospital. I have hoped for some time that you have those feelings for me. You've made me a very happy man. I live for the day we are together again and can start creating a life for ourselves as a family.

Marie, you asked me about my parents, who they are and why don't I talk about them. You also sensed a real bitterness in me toward the Germans. I didn't feel comfortable sharing this period in my life with you at the time. However, my feelings for you grow stronger every passing day. I hope to survive this war, marry you and spend the rest of my life with you by my side. Having said that, I will attempt to share my parents' story with you briefly. Here it goes.

My father's first name is Somhairlin, which is Irish for Sam, and my mother's name is Corrine O'Connor McCormick. O'Connor was my mother's maiden name. Dad was the son of an Irish father and English mother, who immigrated to America shortly after they married in England. When they arrived in this country, they settled in Wellsville, Ohio.

My mother is English and was born in Manchester, England. Her family moved to Liverpool, Ohio, a few years after she was born. Both towns in Ohio are very close to each other. In their senior year, my parents met at a school dance at the Liverpool High School, dated, and eventually married. They purchased a small home and settled into a good life in Wellsville. My father was a partial investor and worked as a senior-level manager with Knowles, Taylor, and Knowles (K.T.&K.) Pottery Company in Liverpool, Ohio.

I was their only child and graduated from Wellsville High School in June 1914. After graduating, my dad secured a job for me in the pottery mill as a common laborer. He wanted me to learn the business from the ground up and hoped that someday I would ascend to a senior position within K.T.&K. On May 1, 1915, my parents boarded the Lusitania in New York. They were sailing to Liverpool, England, to visit my mother's family in Manchester, England. I was told later by someone they met on board that they were standing on the promenade deck when the Lusitania was torpedoed. My father and mother did not survive the attack, and their bodies were never found.

With the loss of my parents, I inherited their small home and continued to work as a common laborer at the mill. The pay was not good, and like many of the fellows at the mill, I joined the Ohio National Guard in late 1916. I did so for two reasons. One for the extra money and the other, well, that's more personal. I wanted to come over here to kill Germans and exact my revenge for my parents' death. It was clear to me at the time that America would eventually get into this war and send many of us over here to fight.

It seems like I've been in this war for an eternity and have certainly taken the lives of many Germans. Revenge, what is it? I don't know any more. There's a good chance I may never comprehend the meaning of it. I didn't know the men I've killed and had no idea what they believed in, cared about, or their life's ambitions. Unless they served on the U-boat that sank the Lusitania, they weren't directly responsible for my parents' death. I guess what I'm trying to say is that the hatred that I carried for the Germans has faded. I fight because I must, and I take the lives of Germans to save those of my men and my own life. I pray this madness ends soon. I'm exhausted, I've had a bellyful of killing other men, and I'm sick and tired of seeing our men getting killed and wounded. If only it would end, and we could all go home.

I've carried on too long and will stop for now. I hope this gives you a better idea of my family and the man you have come to love. I certainly love you and can't wait to hold you in my arms again. It's getting late, and I must stop for now. Taps just sounded, and that means lights out. I'll write to you again before we leave here.

> For now, Je t'aime!
>
> Yours always,
>
> Sam

~

DAYS THREE - FIVE

THE REGIMENT CARRIED on with our planned activities for the next three days without fail. Each day we received new replacements, and by day five, we were back at full strength. The new men seem eager to take on the Germans and are well trained. These new men are a welcome sight and have been a real morale booster for the rest of us who've been at this for some time now. I can remember how I felt when we first arrived. It was much like their attitude. However, somewhere along the way, I must have lost it. Now, I just want the fighting to stop.

Our afternoon recreational activities have been an absolute joy for all of us. I feel more relaxed, have grown more rested, enjoy the chow we get at the BBC mess tent, and delight in the esprit de corps of the men around me. We could almost forget we're going back to the front lines within a week. That's then, this is now, and my morale, attitude, and general well-being improve with each new day.

Although some of us may not have fully comprehended what was going on these past several days, I know our senior officers are trying to prepare us mentally for what is to come. It's a tough job for any commanding officer to tackle. Each man must deal with his fears, anxieties, and thoughts of mortality and come to grips with it. Combat commanders can only do so much in this regard; then, it's up to their men. I, for one, have accepted my circumstances and will continue to do the best I can to lead my men, survive this war and return home with Marie by my side.

Every evening I write a short letter to Marie and send it off. I haven't received any new letters from her as our mail deliveries are very erratic and delayed. With the buildup of our forces all around this area in preparation for the Argonne Offensive, several more logistical complications must be worked out before the mail situation is resolved. I hope it gets fixed soon, as I go through each day looking for another letter from Marie.

DAY SIX

The big day is here. Our company, A Company, won all four of their games and will play D Company, who came in second with three wins. Art chose his team well, managed it well, and he's performed flawlessly. While playing center field, he threw players out who tried to run for home plate. His power-hitting drove in many runs over the four games. Art loves the game, and he can't see himself, nor can I, doing anything else but playing professional baseball when we return home.

At game time, the weather is pleasant, the players are ready, and most of the regiment has turned out for the big game. Henry and I walk over to the ball field with Art while engaging him in conversion.

"Art, are you and your boys ready for this? I've got some money riding on you today." Henry says in a quizzical manner.

With a confident voice and calm manner, Art responds. "Don't worry, Henry, I've got it all planned out, and we're going to carry the day! You just get a good seat. Then watch and enjoy the game. It'll be one for the record books."

I join the conversation with, "You know Art, D Company has

two of its own professional ballplayers, and I understand they're good."

"They are! I played against both when I was with the Cleveland Indians. I know a few of their batting weaknesses and have passed that on to our pitcher. This should be fun."

Arriving at the field, Art leaves us and runs over to his team's sideline. We seek out a good location to watch the game. The whole area is full of doughboys. With the teams assembled and standing on their respective baselines, we are called to attention as the regimental bugler plays our National Anthem, and several fellows sing it. With the opening ceremony complete, the game announcer yells out over his megaphone, "Play ball!"

The game is on.

It's a seven-inning game, and through six innings, it has been an almost perfect game, with both teams making very few errors. Art has played a terrific game making several plays from center field, and his batting has been superb. It's the bottom of the seventh inning, and the score is tied three to three. Our company is at bat, with a man on first base, another on second base, and we have two outs.

The batter at the plate now has a full count; three balls, and two strikes. His next two swings result in ground foul balls down the left field base line. On the next pitch, he hits a high fly ball over the shortstop's head, who just misses catching it. Our players advance another base, and the hitter makes it to first base. Big Art grabs his bat and moves toward home plate to bat next. Bases are loaded, there are two outs, and the game hangs in the balance.

Art, who can be somewhat of a showman, takes his time walking to the plate. The noise level is almost deafening as doughboys yell and cheer for their teams. As Art approaches the plate, he stops, kneels, rubs his hands in the dirt, grips his bat, stands up, and continues toward the plate. Stepping into the batter's box, he adjusts his stance, swings his bat a few times, and steps back from the plate. The crowd noise subsides as everyone wonders what he's doing. Just then, he raises his bat and points it out at center field as if to say that's where the ball is going.

Although there is still cheering, it has lessened as the dough-boys await the first pitch to see what happens. Art steps back into the batter's box, takes his stance, and stares right into the eyes of the pitcher. Here it comes, a fast ball is thrown waist high and to the outside of the plate. Apparently, the pitcher didn't do his homework as that's Art's favorite pitch. Art swings and connects with the ball driving it high into the air, over the center fielder's head. The ball travels through the air well beyond the outer markers set to highlight the outfield boundaries. He has hit a grand slam home run. Game over, the crowd goes wild, and even D Company men cheer him. What a feat. He chose his own shot and made it. That night, money changed hands, and the boys of Company A celebrated with some local French wine. At day's end, I'm richer by one hundred dollars.

DAY SEVEN

Today dawns with the hope in the air that Henry will be the winner of this afternoon's boxing match. The weather continues to cooperate. It's only partially overcast, with a cool breeze and no rain in the forecast for the afternoon. This is good since over a thousand men from the two regiments will be here today to watch the boxing event.

When the United States declared war on Germany, the Commission on Training Camp Activities established training programs unique to the American war effort. Included in these programs was boxing which became a mandatory activity in military training camps. It was believed that boxing would help condition troops for hand-to-hand combat, lead to success with the bayonet and boost overall confidence. Therefore, each major training camp in the United States established a boxing program to train combat troops in the basics of boxing. A natural extension of the program was holding boxing matches between training units. This practice has been carried over to France, where boxing matches are held whenever possible in rear areas and rest camps like ours.

As the hour approaches for the big fight, Art and I work with Henry to help him get ready as we talk about strategy. Boxing is akin to a game of chess since each boxer needs to be thinking ahead of his opponent. The one who does has an advantage over the one who doesn't. There is no such thing as taking turns hitting each other. Each boxer can throw or block as many punches as they are physically capable of doing. The more punches a boxer throws, the harder it becomes to throw the next one. We don't have to discuss this aspect with Henry; he is fully aware of it and has accumulated quite a record becoming the regimental champion. He's had sixteen boxing matches to his credit since reporting to the Rainbow Division, and all were KOs (knockouts). His strategy is simple, start slowly by probing his opponent's moves, look for his weaknesses and then take the fight to him.

Henry is ready. His boxing wardrobe consists of an army-issue dark sleeveless tee-shirt, long knee-length black shorts, high wool socks, and black standard boxing shoes. Draped over his shoulders is a full-length boxing robe made especially for him by our supply unit. It has the Rainbow Division insignia sewn onto the back. Henry cuts quite an impressive figure as we work our way over to the boxing ring set up for the match.

The boxing ring has been built to standard size and elevated about six feet off the ground. This height provides better visibility and can accommodate more men standing further from the ring. The setup is certainly justified as well over a thousand men are gathered around the ring today. We must work our way through them to get to our corner. As we do, Henry is cheered on by our boys in the regiment. We can hear cheering for his opponent as he approaches the ring from the other side.

Henry's adrenaline is pumping as he's bobbing, weaving, and throwing fake punches while making his way to the ring. Once there, he grasps the ropes, pulls them apart, and slips between them into the ring. Inside the ring, he continues bobbing and weaving to the delight of the crowd. Always the showman. His opponent enters the ring from the other side. At first glance, he appears to outweigh Henry and towers over him in height. He, too, starts his own show, bobbing and weaving, not looking at Henry. He appears very confident. This is going to be a tough fight. The doughboys close in around the ring, and the noise level rises as they are whooping, cheering, and yelling. They're ready for a good fight. I'm sure there's a considerable amount of money riding on the outcome of this fight. I know; I placed a hefty sum of money on Henry.

The moment arrives as the announcer and referee step to the center of the ring. With his megaphone, the announcer yells out to the boys to quiet down. As they do, he points to our corner and announces, "In this corner is Sergeant Henry Miller, the reigning champion of the Rainbow Division's 166th Infantry Regiment. With him in his corner is Company First Sergeant Sam McCormick and Sergeant Arthur Wilson." Our boys go wild, and it takes some time for the announcer to regain control.

As the noise level subsides, he looks over to the other side. He announces, "And in this corner is Sergeant Bill O'Connell, the reigning champion of the 82nd Division's 328th Infantry Regiment. He's assisted by Corporal Alvin York and Sergeant Jim Davis." Their boys go wild, and once again, it takes some time to quiet them down.

The announcer motions for us to come to the center of the ring, where he gives each boxer the rules for the fight. We exchange handshakes and return to our corners to wait for the bell. It's a seven-round fight with three-minute rounds. Henry takes off his robe as we climb out of the ring and take our places behind him on the ground, resting our arms on the boxing ring's floormat.

The bell rings, and round one is on. The two men rush to the center of the ring. They waste no time throwing punches, blocking them and testing each other. They are both in good shape and clearly know how to box. I feel that we're in for a long battle.

The first four rounds fly by as neither man lands a devastating blow to their opponent. They both seem to be made of steel, and if tired, they don't show it. The judges' point counting currently has the fight even. Sitting on his stool waiting for the bell to ring for round five, Henry is relaxed and looks confident. Wiping Henry's face and giving him some water to swish around in his mouth, I offer some advice in an authoritative manner. "Henry, this guy is good, but he has a weak spot. Every time he throws a hard right punch, he tends to drop his left. Have you picked that up?"

Henry nods yes. I continue, "You need to block that right punch with your left and crush him in the jaw with your right. A few of those will take him out!" Henry looks at me with a grin and, through his mouthpiece, gurgles, "We got him."

The bell rings, and they close to the center of the ring as round five begins. Again, they spar, looking for opportunities to end it. They test each other with jabs and blocks. Bill feinted a swing and landed a good blow on Henry's ribs. He winces as the impact penetrates his rib cage. Henry's follow-up, a right hook to Bill's jaw, caught air as Bill pulled his head back, and Henry's punch missed its target. Bill counter-attacks, throwing a flurry of punches with reckless abandonment. Big mistake. Henry sees his opportunity and lands a cruising blow to Bill's head with his right. Bill falls back, staggering, and looks dazed. The referee steps in and checks Bill's condition. Blood trickles down his face from the cut on his eye that Henry just gave him. His lips puff up, and blood seeps from his mouth.

After a brief respite, the referee resumes the fight. Once again, Bill goes on the offensive, throwing multiple punches that land harmlessly on Henry's boxing gloves. Bill is tiring as the bell rings, ending the round. The crowd of doughboys is yelling for their man, "Finish him!" "Knock the bum out!" "Let's end it!" "Take it home!" "Floor him!"

A minute into the sixth round, Bill makes a mistake. His first big mistake. His arms have grown weak from all the punches he's thrown, causing him to let his guard down. Henry moves in on him, throwing left jabs to the head, followed by right hooks to the rib cage. Bill falls back, trying to get some relief from the relentless attack. Bill then throws a weak right, drops his left, and Henry sees his opening. Henry blocks Bill's right-hand punch, closes in, and lands a powerful right hook to Bill's jaw. He staggers and collapses to the mat. The 82nd Division's 328th Infantry Regiment's Boxing Champion is not knocked out, but he's not going to get back up. It's over. The medical team rushes in, takes out his mouth guard, starts stuffing cotton up his nose, and presses some against his upper lip to stem the bleeding.

Once Bill is back on his feet, the referee calls all of us to the center of the ring. He holds Henry's arm up, proclaiming him the winner. Our guys yell it up. Bill extends his hand to Henry, and they shake. He then turns to shake Art's and my hand. With that gesture, we all shake hands and try to chat briefly above the noise.

I find Corporal Alvin York an interesting fellow. He has a history of drinking and fighting, attends church regularly, and enjoys leading the singing of hymns. Except for hymn singing, we are in some ways alike. I like the man right off. I wish him the best of luck in the upcoming Argonne Offensive when we part. He does the same for me.

The large gathering of doughboys at the fight was quite a sight. We all seemed to relish the action, and for a while, it was like being back home. I'm sure there are many doughboys disappointed in the outcome, but I would have to say we all got our money's worth. As for me, I'm another two hundred dollars richer.

That evening was another joyous one for the men of our regiment. Particularly for Henry and A Company. With some of their winnings from the match, the fellows threw Henry a little party with lots of wine and some French beer. I heard that Rick and Chet placed considerable money on the fight and did quite well. It was their idea to throw Henry a big party for which they contributed some of their winnings. I still can't bring myself to drink French beer. But their wine, that's another story. That evening I consumed my share of local wine provided by the villagers near our rest camp.

DAY EIGHT

Morning

It's mid-morning on our eighth day. I'm standing at parade rest in front of A Company. In front of me and a little to my right is Captain Glazebrook, also standing at parade rest. Beside him is our company flag bearer carrying the company banner. To our left is B Company, to their left is C Company, and so forth down the line. Each company is arranged as we are. Our regiment consists of a regimental headquarters company, a machine gun company, a supply company, and twelve rifle companies. The entire regiment of fifteen companies, comprising 3,700 men, is aligned across the field, standing at parade rest, waiting for the command to begin our regimental parade review.

Standing in front of the regimental formation and looking up at the review stands to their front is our senior staff and Color Guard. They carry the American flag, and our Rainbow Division colors. Riflemen flank each side of the flag bearers. We must be a splendid formation to behold from the review stand. We'll be marching by the review stand in front of General Douglas MacArthur, the Rainbow Division's Chief of Staff, his senior staff members, and our regimental commander.

The regiment is at our authorized troop strength, fully equipped, rested, and hopefully ready for what awaits us on the battlefield. The upcoming Argonne Offensive weighs heavily on my mind, as I'm sure it does on the other combat veterans in the regiment. The new boys appear anxious to get into a scrap, as they now call it, with the Huns. Give them a few days on the front lines, and if they survive, I think they'll wish they were back on this parade field just marching.

The weather is brisk and chilly but comfortable as the sun peeks through a light overcast. It's a good day for a parade. The regiment is called to attention. Up and down the line of dough-boys, I hear heels clicking together and rifles being raised to shoulder arms, all in unison. This is followed by the command to do a right face. With the regiment formed and ready, we are given the command to forward march. We step out smartly as the regimental band plays John Philip Sousa's "The Washington Post." I feel a tremendous sense of pride knowing I'm part of a magnificent group of men who are resolved to see this war through to the end and help achieve victory.

. . .

Afternoon

Later in the afternoon, Captain Glazebrook calls his company leaders together for a briefing. Henry, Art, and I enter his HQ tent and are the last to arrive. Customary hand salutes are exchanged. The captain begins with, "Gentlemen, please make yourselves comfortable and feel free to light up."

Several men share their cigarettes and help each other light them. I pull out my pipe, take my time placing several layers of tobacco into it, slowly pack each layer, and then light up. I find my first draw of tobacco very enjoyable and soothing. While in camp, I was able to procure a can of "Bull Durham Smoking Tobacco, " a much sought-after tobacco. Now all I must do is keep it dry and secure.

One can hope!

Captain Glazebrook continues, "General MacArthur was very impressed with our regiment's performance this morning. He was quite generous with his comments concerning the parade review and praised us for our record on the battlefield. This comes from a man who has accumulated quite a battlefield record of his own, in case you didn't know. His awards include two Distinguished Service Crosses, Six Silver Citation Stars, the Distinguished Service Medal, and two Croix de Guerre French medals. I only share this with you to give you some appreciation for the caliber of the man we'll follow into battle."

I am impressed by the man's record, and from the expressions on many of the fellows present, it's clear I'm not alone. Captain Glazebrook continues, "I'm going to keep this short and to the point. The entire regiment is leaving tomorrow morning and going back to the front lines. We'll be taking up positions about eight miles south of Cheppy. Once again, we'll be supported by Patton's tanks as we move on the German front lines near this village. Another unit is assigned to protect his tanks. We'll be behind them in the order of attack. We'll receive further orders when we arrive there tomorrow and take up our positions. At this point, that's about all I know."

He gives us time to ponder what he just said, then asks, "Any questions, men?"

There are none, and he continues. "Fellows, this major offensive has been in the planning stages for some time now. Hopefully, it will bring the Germans to the negotiating table. Time will tell. In the meantime, you know what to do. Use the rest of this day to prepare for tomorrow. Make sure your men have their legal paperwork in order. If they've written any letters and want them mailed, they'll need to get them out this evening. It'll be some time before we can send or receive mail."

In closing and in a very uncharacteristic manner, he struggles to keep his emotions in check. "Gentlemen, these last eight days have provided us with opportunities to enjoy our time together, and I've come to know more about each of you personally. The performance of our baseball team and Henry's boxing match are both one for the books. Well, done to all of you! I'm proud of you men, you're a fine group of soldiers, and it's an honor to serve with you. Dismissed!"

Evening

After checking on the men, the status of their equipment, reminding them to ensure their legal affairs are in order, and enjoying a good dinner with Art, Henry, and some other fellows at our table, I retire to my tent to write a short letter to Marie.

Dearest Marie,
      I trust this letter will find you doing well and maintaining

hope that we are closing in on the end of this war. I'm doing fine and have gained a few pounds from all the food provided during our rest here. The regiment is back to full strength and ready to return to the front. Earlier today, we held a full regimental parade review in front of General MacArthur and his top staff. It was a grand showing, and we are all proud of our performance.

I'm happy to convey that my mental state has improved, and I feel much more rested. It took several days to reach this state. I guess that is to be expected since we've been enduring almost constant combat before arriving here for an extended rest.

Tomorrow we head back to the front lines. I can't talk about what we're doing or what comes next. However, I firmly believe we are at a critical moment in this war, and what we do next could turn the tide. My god, I hope so. The killing and suffering we have both seen and been forced, by circumstances, to endure are beyond anything heretofore imaginable in my mind. I'm sure you are of a similar mindset.

I long to be with you again, hold you tightly, and make plans for our future together. I must go now and will leave you with these thoughts. Marie, I love you very much, there is no other woman for me, and I'm looking forward to spending the rest of our lives together. Should anything happen to me, always remember that.

Je t'aime,

Your loving Sam

After finishing the letter, I seal it, walk over to our regimental mail post office, and drop it in the box. It's a beautiful night with a clear sky, bright stars shining above, and a three-quarter moon visible to the west. There's a comfortable breeze blowing gently across the open field. The air has a sweet, clean aroma which reminds me of fall weather back home. I take my time walking back as I wish to savor this peaceful moment in time, for I know it's short-lived. We're going back to the front lines where more hellish fighting awaits us, and more men will die. Of this, I am sure.

15

BATTLE OF THE MEUSE-ARGONNE

BACKGROUND

The monumental battle of the Meuse-Argonne begins with a shouting match between General John J. Pershing and his immediate commander, French Field Marshal Ferdinand Foch.

Field Marshall Foch met with General Pershing at his headquarters for the new American First Army in Ligny-en-Barrois, twenty-five miles southeast of St. Mihiel, on August 30, 1918. General Pershing and his staff officers had just completed operational plans for wiping out the German salient that bulged into the Allied lines north and south of St. Mihiel that Field Marshall Foch had ordered him to prepare.

Field Marshall Foch informed General Pershing he had changed his mind. Field Marshal Douglas Haig, the British commander, convinced him it was time to launch a massive assault on the entire German front lines in France. They were planning to attack the Germans across the entire front. Field Marshall Foch wanted General Pershing to reduce his planned offensive in St. Mihiel to nothing more than a limited show of force in the area. He wanted General Pershing to give him two-thirds of the First Army's troops so he could redistribute them across the front to Field Marshal Haig and several French generals.

General Pershing refused to comply with the order, whereupon a heated exchange occurred between the two men. Field Marshal Foch relented and agreed to let General Pershing retain total control over his army and go ahead with the St. Mihiel attack. However, General Pershing had to commit his American First Army to support the Argonne Offensive. General Pershing agreed and stated he would finish St. Mihiel and then commit his army to an assault in the valley of the Argonne.

Unfortunately for the doughboys of the American First Army, neither general was thinking very clearly. American soldiers had fought well up to this time as individual units in various sectors on the front under French and British commanders. However, they had not fought together as one army under American command. General Pershing had committed the American First Army to fight two major battles sixty miles apart within fifteen days. He had also accepted responsibility for attacking the huge, tunnel-like Argonne Valley. This entire area was bounded on the west by a dense forest and on the east by the Meuse River. The terrain consisted of many natural barriers that favored the German defenders, such as high ridgelines, towering hills, ravines, and steep slopes.

General Pershing's commitments would be a tough nut to crack for any army. With a command staff that had limited experience and was untested in major offensive operations to this point in the war, it would prove particularly difficult and costly. The Meuse-Argonne would become the largest and bloodiest operation the American Expeditionary Force (AEF) would fight during the war.

16

BATTLE OF THE MEUSE-ARGONNE

ARRIVAL

The journey from Lemmes is long, tiring, and thankfully, uneventful. The areas we travel through have seen their share of war over the past few years. Buildings in rubble, farmland destroyed, vegetation minimal or gone, bridges partially or fully destroyed and replaced with makeshift overpasses. Roads, in many cases, have been so severely shelled they make traveling over them a real challenge for our best drivers and their trucks. The weather is chilly, damp and a low overcast hangs above us, which doesn't help our spirits.

Upon arriving, we're assigned a section of an old French trench system on the front lines about eight miles south of Cheppy. Although it's not the best trench system we've occupied, the French have maintained it well. It's considerably better than the last trench system we inhabited. Once again, we have no plans to stay long since we're going on the offensive within twenty-four to forty-eight hours. This area has been quiet for a few days, with most of the fighting off to our left in the French sector of the front. Hopefully, this will continue so we can have a restful night's sleep before going into action.

After disembarking the trucks and filing into our positions in the trench system, we are given some warm chow, fresh water, and time to settle into our new positions. Using this time, I work with my platoon sergeants to inspect the area, make overnight guard duty assignments, and see to the needs of our men. With night approaching and the weather turning to a cold rain, I make a hasty retreat to my bunker after completing my tasks. Moving quickly through the small hole serving as an entrance, I find the inside damp, stuffy, with the usual unpleasant odors and very little room for the eight men sharing this space. There are two bunk beds which are small and stacked four beds high. Since I'm the Company First Sergeant, I get my choice of either of the two lower bunks. I drop my gear at the foot of one and sit down on what serves as a mattress, some hay covered with a soiled wool blanket.

The men sharing this bunker with me are now outside performing their assigned duties. I have the place to myself, so I pull out my pipe and tobacco pouch, pack my pipe, and light up. Before leaving Lemmes, we were given our mail which finally caught up with us. Eight days in a rest camp, and they give us our mail the morning we leave for the front. Included in the delivery were three letters from Marie. Settling onto my bunk, I pull one of Marie's letters from my army backpack and using a small Beacon army flashlight, I read it.

My Dearest Sam,

I hope and trust this letter finds you in good health, far back from the front, and in no danger. I've received three of your letters so far. I surmise from them that you're in a rest area of some kind and doing well. This is good. I wish you were here with me, and we could spend time together enjoying each other's company.

Darling, I miss you terribly. I find it becomes more unbearable with each passing day, as all I do is wonder when I'll see you again. I take some comfort in knowing the war seems to be going badly for Germany, and we may be approaching the end. I live for this and take solace in knowing every night brings a new dawn and you closer to me.

We were moved out of Château Thierry recently and relocated to a field hospital camp on the outskirts of Verdun. It is very large and includes many tents, hastily constructed wooden barracks, and various buildings that have been pressed into service. The number of wounded has increased considerably. French, British, and many more Americans among them. Clearly, you doughboys are in the thick of the fighting now. When a new group arrives, I dread approaching them for fear of finding you lying there on a litter.

I have written to my parents telling them all about you. They are looking forward to meeting you and are quite excited for that opportunity. My papa is particularly anxious to share some of his special wine and pipe tobacco with you. This is a rare occurrence as he's very particular about who he shares his wine and tobacco with, so you are special to him. Both mama and papa are happy for me, knowing how I feel about you.

Sam, I must go back to work now. Be careful, take care of yourself, and stay safe. I love you very much, miss you more than words can convey, and live every day waiting for you to come back to me.

Je t'aime,

Love, Marie

～

I SET this one aside and read the other two letters. Reading Marie's letters is very comforting for me but incredibly difficult. I yearn to be by her side, yet I realize that is not possible. Going through the hell of combat as we do up here on the front is tough enough. Loving someone, like I love Marie, makes it damn near impossible to endure.

We have no choice. Accept your fate, deal with what comes your way, rely on your training, believe in your fellow soldiers, and do your best. If fate is on your side, you will see Marie again when this is over.

Taking one last draw of tobacco smoke, I empty my pipe onto the bunker floor and stomp out the ashes that still glimmer. I'm not hungry and skip going through the chow line. Securing my gear and rifle, I lay down on the bunk, pull a blanket over my head, and drift off to sleep while thinking of Marie.

The next morning dawns early as both Art and Henry jostle me awake from a light sleep. Henry is the most animated in his efforts to wake me. In a lighthearted and calm voice, Henry says, "Sam, Sam, wake up! Breakfast is being served on the front porch. We need to get out there before the rest of the boys clean it out."

Art just says, "Get up, Sam, I'm hungry."

Sitting up and looking around our cramped, dimly lit bunker, my eyes slowly adjust as their faces come into focus. "Okay, fellows, I'm coming. What's the weather like out there? Was it a quiet night? I didn't hear anything alarming during the night."

Henry has already exited the bunker in his quest for food, no doubt. Art replies, "It was a quiet night around here, and the weather is lousy. It's raining again, but not very hard. There's a cold wind blowing out there. Get your mess kit, and let's get some breakfast before it's gone."

Grabbing my kit, I move over to the exit and crawl through the hole with Art following. We emerge into a world all too familiar to us, and it's not very welcoming. Men are lined up behind two small mess kitchens that are set up on each side of our bunker exit and about fifty yards apart. The cooks are passing out biscuits, coffee, and some canned corned beef referred to as bully beef. As we approach the nearest kitchen, we find Henry leaning against the trench wall under a shelter with several other men. They look very angry and a far cry from being content as they eat their food while trying to prevent it from getting soaked.

As we approach, Henry, in an angry voice, says, "Don't get the damn biscuits. They're made of foot powder!" The other fellows standing around him blurt out the same warning.

I stop in front of Henry, looking over at Art and then back at Henry, and say agitatedly. "What the hell are you talking about, Henry? Foot powder! Is this a joke? If it is, I'm in no mood for it today."

"No, it's no joke!" Henry replies.

Art jumps in with, "What the hell happened then?"

Henry shares the story he was told. "Well, you see, it's like this. Last night, a couple of fellows in our supply train mixed up some flour barrels with barrels containing foot powder. It was dark, and they made a mistake. Earlier this morning, while it was still dark, our cooks were trying to bake the biscuits and were having a difficult time. It seems that our foot powder doesn't have the same consistency that flour does, and their biscuits were not rising much or holding together well."

Art interrupts him and asks, "Why didn't they realize the problem?"

Henry continues, "When asked that question, our cooks said they were working with very little light, under stress, and just tired as hell. They chalked it up to a poor batch of flour and continued well as they could. It wasn't until we started eating their biscuits this morning and complaining about the taste that the realization of what happened settled in."

Trench foot is a serious condition that results from our feet being wet for too long. We use foot powder to absorb and help control moisture that builds up on our feet, socks, and inside our boots. On the other hand, flour will not help in this regard and can create a sticky mess when it meets moisture and water.

Trying to find a little humor in our situation, I chuckle as I respond to Henry's comments. "Well, boys, at least we're not the company who ended up with barrels of flour to put on our feet and inside our Pershing boots. Anybody who uses that flour on their feet is going to have one hell of a mess!"

That brings on some laughter among the men, and the mood lightens. This situation is not a good way to start the day as biscuits are always a favorite of the men. We settle for warm coffee and bully beef for breakfast.

After breakfast, our day progresses slowly with occasional harassing artillery fire from the Germans and the ever-present rain and cold winds. The men of the regiment spend the day cleaning their weapons, sharpening their bayonets, checking their gear, and drawing full loads of ammunition and grenades. Evening brings some relief from the weather, and the Huns, as the artillery shelling has ceased for now.

Captain Glazebrook called us into his command bunker for a briefing. With his leaders present, he begins. "Gentlemen, welcome. I trust all of you have spent the day working with your men to ensure they're ready. Tomorrow morning at 0600 hours, we go over the top and join the Argonne Offensive!"

He looks around, trying to gauge our reaction. The men present are silent and serious. We knew this moment was coming since our early days back in the rest camp. Rest and recreation are over. We are going back into battle, fighting will be ferocious, and many men will die.

Realizing he has our full attention, he continues. "At 0400 hours, our artillery will commence a massive bombardment of the entire German front lines facing us. When we go over the top, they will shift their fire and start walking it back further behind the German lines. The goal is to cut off their retreat to the rear. Our entire regiment will advance in two waves. We'll be in the first wave consisting of six companies. The other six companies will join us on the field when we're close to the Huns' first trench system. Any questions?"

I'm sure he is going to mention it, but I speak up anyway. "Captain, will we have any tank support in front of us?"

He looks over at me with that reassuring grin on his face and responds. "Sam, we'll be supporting Lieutenant Colonel Patton's tanks again. He'll be leading them on a frontal assault into the town of Cheppy. This is our first objective. It's heavily defended by the Germans. Patton's tanks will be on our left, and we'll be providing infantry protection for his right flank. Although his tanks will not be out in front of us, they will be the center of attention for the Germans once we begin our attack. This should relieve some of the pressure on us."

Looking around the bunker at his men and then focusing on me, he continues. "That's the situation with our tank support, men. Any questions?" I look around at the other fellows and, sensing there are no questions, respond for the group. "No, sir!"

Captain Glazebrook continues, "When we capture Cheppy, we'll take up defensive positions around the town to hold it while another regiment passes through and presses forward with the attack. Men, the strategy is simple. We'll continue attacking until the Argonne region is secured. General Pershing has committed his entire First Army to the offensive. This campaign could last a few months, and I fear it will be very costly."

He takes a moment to let what he said sink in. We're silent. We know our situation and that many doughboys will die before this offensive operation is over.

"Okay, gentlemen, see that your men are well fed tonight. Oh, I understand they baked us some fresh biscuits using flour this time!"

His last comment elicits some laughter and a much-needed moment of levity. He continues, "Are there any questions?" No one speaks up. "All right then, see to your men, get some rest, and I'll see you in the morning. Dismissed!"

17

BATTLE OF THE MEUSE-ARGONNE

PATTON'S RESCUE

Our artillery has been shelling the Germans for two hours now as 0600, H-Hour, approaches. It's early morning, September 26, 1918, and the sky is just beginning to show glimmers of light. We go over the top in five minutes. The Germans have uncharacteristically refrained from or are incapable of returning artillery fire. I don't believe it's the latter and fear they'll unload on us once we're in the middle of "no man's land." The rain has stopped, but it's damp, chilly, and a thick fog hangs over us. The men are ready with weapons loaded, bayonets fixed, and a grim determination to get on with the business of killing Huns.

The sky above us is full of artillery shells headed toward the German trenches. They make long, loud, piercing noises as they stream overhead, making it almost impossible to communicate verbally. I strain to hear the command to jump off, followed by our officers' whistles. Looking out over the terrain in front of us, all I can see is fog; our visibility is limited, as it is for the

Germans. I know it's time to go, but I can't see the green flares. Captain Glazebrook is to my left. Although I can't hear his command or his whistle blowing, I see him climb the ladder and step out into "no man's land."

I go over the top, stand on the parapet and direct my men to follow me. Rising from the trenches, we charge forward through the fog in a human wave. We do not yell as we move forward, trying to keep the noise to a minimum. We do this hoping the Huns will not hear us until we're right on top of them.

We gain considerable ground before German artillery shells start raining down on us, exploding among the men. The fog has helped cover our initial advance, but as we close in on the German trenches, they now hear our movements and realize we're attacking in force. Since their artillery units have pre-sighted targets on the terrain we're crossing, they unleash hell on us with their artillery.

We cover the ground quickly, staying low to the ground and moving with a sense of purpose. But at a cost. Men around me fall to the ground as artillery shells explode on impact, sending deadly fragments into their bodies. Machine gun fire is methodically cutting across our ranks. For the Huns, it's too late to stop our attack. Hordes of doughboys emerge from the fog and descend on them in their trenches. Vicious hand-to-hand combat ensues as individual duels to the death occur up and down the trench line. Their resistance is short-lived as we overwhelm and quickly subdue them. I believe they're losing the will to keep up the fight, and like us, they just want the war to end. The Huns we capture look exhausted and malnourished, many are sporting bandages from earlier wounds, and their eyes betray them. There is a look of despair, despondency, and defeat in them.

Having captured the trench line, I set about organizing our defenses, rounding up captured Germans to send to the rear, and

I see to our wounded. From what I can surmise, our casualties are lighter than expected. The speed of our attack, which was helped by the ground fog, has contributed to our low casualties. The Germans' artillery shifts away from us and toward Patton's tank attack as we enter the Huns' trenches. This undoubtedly helps us, but I know the men with Patton are now bearing the brunt of the Huns' artillery.

The second wave of our infantry companies passes through the trenches we hold and continues attacking the retreating Germans. The fog is lifting, and the sky above is clearing. We now hear a faint sound of plane motors in the distance that is continuously growing in volume.

The combination of the sky clearing, the sound of planes flying over, and the momentary stillness on the ground around us has drawn our attention toward the heavens. It becomes full of planes from both sides fighting aerial duels. They are fighting in single combat and squadrons as they maneuver their planes to gain an advantage over their enemy. The noise from their motors and machine gun fire grows louder and becomes continuous. We're witnessing major aerial combat above us, the likes of which I have never seen before. First, one goes, and then another falls from the heavens and spirals toward the ground in flames. As the battle rages above us, the sight of planes crashing to earth becomes almost common. Our curiosity and fascination with the aerial war raging above doesn't last long. Our attention is redirected back to the ground battles, which continue to rage across a wide area before us.

Captain Glazebrook finds me, pulls me with him into a side trench, and briefs me on Patton's tank attack status. "Sam, what's our company status?"

"Sir, I believe casualties are minimal. I have the platoon sergeants checking their status now. We should hear from them shortly."

"Good! We have a new mission. I just came from a briefing with the colonel."

I respond, "Yes, sir. What's next?"

"Patton led his men to a crossroads on the edge of Cheppy. When the fog began to lift, Patton discovered he advanced beyond his own tanks. Many of them got entangled in a trench barrier well to his rear. As the protective shield of fog lifted, Patton and his men were subjected to withering fire from all directions. The Germans built several machine gun emplacements to protect the town."

Stopping to pull out a cigarette and light it, he continues.

"Patton, with some of his men, were successful in getting five tanks across the breach and within several hundred yards of Cheppy. About a hundred and fifty doughboys from one of our companies followed him. When they arrived, the onslaught of machine gun fire and heavy artillery shelling forced them to the ground, halting their attack. They suffered heavy casualties and are unable to move forward to support Patton."

He pauses, wipes the sweat from his forehead using a shirt sleeve, and takes a few draws on his cigarette.

"Patton moved forward with one tank, a partial squad of men, and continued attacking some machine gun emplacements. As he came close to the German lines, Patton was hit. An enemy machine gun bullet tore through his body, knocking him to the ground. His orderly, Private Joe Angelo, dragged him to a shallow crater where both men are now caught in German crossfire. The company supporting Patton is pinned down, has too many casualties, and cannot attempt a rescue."

I interject, "I guess that's where we come in, right?"

Captain Glazebrook, in a matter-of-fact tone, responds. "Yes, Sam, we have been ordered to move over to Patton's position and relieve the pressure on him and the men supporting him. Time is of the essence!"

Our company platoon sergeants and three platoon leaders report to the captain as he finishes. We lost the first platoon leader when he was struck by a mortar round and killed instantly. Even with his loss, our status is considered good. Up to this point, we've only had a few casualties. The men are ready to continue the fight, and their morale is high. Captain Glazebrook gathers us around him and informs the men of our new mission.

He closes the meeting with his final orders. "Gentlemen, we will be moving out in ten minutes. We'll move diagonally across the terrain to our front using our V formations. Ensure the men keep their distance. The town of Cheppy has several well-placed machine gun emplacements, and they are wreaking havoc. Sam, you'll lead the first platoon. I'll be with the third platoon. We should be able to reach their position within the hour. Be sure your men load up on ammo and grenades."

He stops, looks around at each of us, again with his reassuring smile, takes a last puff on his cigarette, and asks if there are any questions. We have none.

"Okay, fellows, we'll form up and depart from this area. Go get your men and let's get back to work!"

With our company assembled and ready, we move out from the relative safety of the German trenches we had just captured. I lead the first platoon across the open terrain passing through other American units as they continue to press forward in their sectors. The ground is littered with dead and wounded men. Litter bearers move among the wounded as they work to clear them from the field and take them back to aid stations. Chaplains are busy moving among the dead and dying, providing last rites, and praying over them. They try comforting the wounded while waiting for litter bearers to reach them. It's a ghastly sight the German artillery barrages have created out here in these open killing fields. Men who started the day alive, hoping they would make it home, now lie scattered across this terrain. Their bodies are testament to the horror of war, lying where they died, contorted, blown apart, and in many cases unrecognizable to their commanders and fellow doughboys.

Rapidly closing the distance to Patton's position, we hear heavy artillery and machine gun fire. I see artillery shells exploding among the doughboys supporting Patton as we close in. Machine gun fire is intense. Tracer rounds are coming from all directions and heading directly at them. Seeking protection, they have taken shelter wherever they can find it in shell holes, destroyed tanks, behind crumbling walls and buildings. What a damn mess. I halt the platoon and motion for them to take cover. The platoons to my rear do the same. I move back to find Captain Glazebrook.

Reporting to the captain, I share my observations and plan with him. "Sir, we have the forward element of Patton's men in sight. They are pinned down by heavy machine gun fire and some artillery. They're scattered about the area and have sought cover. I have a plan that will give us a chance to relieve the pressure on Patton's men."

"What's your plan, Sam?"

"I'm going to take Art and what's left of his first squad and work our way to Patton's position to see if we can't take out some of those machine gun nests. We could try to move the company closer to the action, but not too close yet. I would suggest waiting until I knock out some of their gun emplacements before charging into Cheppy!"

Captain Glazebrook stares at me with an intensity I've not seen from him before. Pausing to reflect, he responds. "Sam, that's a bold idea and damn risky. Go ahead, give it a try. Do you want to take more men out there with you?"

"No, sir, I don't want to risk any more men than necessary. Besides, I think too many might attract more attention from the

Huns. Hopefully, we can get close to them before they realize what we're doing."

"Okay, Sam. Good luck and godspeed!" With that, he extends his hand, shakes mine, and renders me a hand salute.

I return his salute and head back to the first platoon.

By his reaction, the captain must view this as a suicide mission from which I won't return. My god, what have I just done?

Returning to the platoon, I seek out Art and his first squad. There are seven men left in the squad. I brief them on what we are going to do and then turn the remaining men in the first platoon over to my senior squad leader. I direct him to wait until the second platoon moves up, at which time he will fall under the command of Henry. With everyone clear on their orders, I move out, with Art and his first squad following me as we head for Patton's position.

The Huns have retreated into Cheppy and are ferociously defending the town. They have the attacking units pinned down and have been pouring deadly fire into their ranks. Tracer rounds fill the air just above our heads, and artillery and mortar rounds crash into the ground we advance over. There is no pattern to their targeting as it seems to be totally random, intermittent, and thank goodness, not very effective. But it's still unnerving.

Staying low to the ground, moving forward slowly and very cautiously, using any cover available, we manage to reach some of the men supporting Patton. They have taken cover in a massive shell crater where we join them. I seek out the senior man present and ask him to point out Patton's location to me, along with the German defenses. To our immediate front, about fifty yards out, three machine gun nests are pinning us down with continuous firing and preventing our forward movement. Patton's supporting troops are being murdered by those Hun bastards. The distance from our position to where Patton sought cover in a shell crater is not more than thirty yards to our front.

That's not very far, but under these conditions, we aren't going anywhere just yet.

Scanning the terrain to my front, I see two large barrels stamped "flour," which have not yet been opened. They fell from a Hun truck as they retreated earlier toward Cheppy. The barrels are only a few yards out from the crater we're in. The ground in front of us is relatively flat. Closer to Patton's position, it seems to slope down toward the shell hole in which he has taken refuge. I have an idea and crawl over to Art to explain it. As I do, a smile spreads across his face. He clearly likes it.

I grab a runner to send back to Captain Glazebrook with an order to brief him on what we're going to attempt. Nodding that he understands, I finish with, "Corporal, we're going to need the company to provide us with all the covering fire possible. We'll wait until I see the captain fire off a green flare giving us the okay before we move out. Understand?" He nods yes. Looking at him with a slight grin on my face, I yell, "Go!"

As he heads for the captain, Art and I check our ammunition situation, grab some grenades from the men nearest us, and check our rifles and .45 pistols to ensure they're loaded. Looking back toward the captain's location, we wait for the green flare. It takes a few minutes before the captain raises up and fires the green flare. Looking over at Art, I yell, "You ready?"

He responds, "I'm ready. Let's get at the bastards!"

We crawl forward toward the two big barrels with our rifles resting on top of our arms and several grenades in each of our satchel bags. Crawling forward on our bellies and staying as low as possible, we reach the barrels, tip them over on their sides and get behind them. Using the barrels as cover, we slowly roll them forward, inching our way toward Patton. The men behind us and in our company realize what we are attempting to do and begin cheering us on.

The Huns who are manning the machine gun we are closing

in on look with disbelief. When they comprehend what we are attempting to do, they turn their weapons on us, and a sheet of hot lead comes flying our way. Their rounds are whizzing by and overhead. Many hit the barrels, making a loud bang as if a hammer had struck them. It's very unnerving, and I can't help but fear some might penetrate the barrel, exit the other side, and hit us. However, it isn't to be, as the barrels absorb the lead, and none reaches us. Although the flour makes the barrels very heavy and hard to push forward, they certainly keep us safe.

The men in our company begin pouring heavy fire into the German positions, which is reassuring and reduces the hot lead coming our way. It's a slow, exhausting effort to push the barrels forward and cover the distance to the crater. Reaching the edge of the crater where Patton is, we manage to slide down the side of it and into the hole untouched.

What a relief!

In front of us is Lieutenant Colonel Patton and a private tending to him. Patton has been wounded in the upper leg, but it has been bandaged. His bandages are soaked in blood, giving me the impression that his wound is serious. He strikes me as a tall man with distinguishing features and a commanding presence, even in his current state. Crawling over to him, he looks directly into my eyes and yells over the noise at me.

"What's your name, son?"

Responding, I say, "Company First Sergeant Sam McCormick, sir! We're with A Company of the 166th Regiment."

"And the man with you?"

"Sir, that's Sergeant Arthur Wilson."

Looking over at the private next to him, he says, "This is my aide, Private Joe Angelo. He saved my life out here, and I'm going to give him a goddamn medal for it. You fellows get me out of here, and you'll get one too."

"We'll see what we can do about that, Colonel!" I respond as

Art, and I crawl up the side of the crater to peer out to our front. The Germans are traversing their machine guns back and forth across a wide area. They have us in a crossfire and at a distinct disadvantage.

Bullets whiz over our heads as others impact the top of the crater, kicking up dirt. It is becoming intolerable. I've had enough. I raise my head above the top, peer out, and locate three machine gun emplacements spread out about thirty yards in front of us. Sliding back down next to Art, I tell him the situation and where the gun emplacements are located.

Grinning as he looks at me, he barks out, "I can handle this, Sam. A few well-placed grenades on each gun should quiet them down some. What do you think?"

"Sounds good, Art. With your baseball arm, it should be easy. Just like throwing a man out at home plate. Don't you think?"

Art, with a grin, responds. "Yep, not a problem!"

"Okay then. I'll throw some of my grenades out first as a distraction. Then you go with yours!"

Art gives me a thumbs up as we reach into our satchel bags, pulling out several grenades each. We're ready. I pull the pin on my first grenade and throw it. I follow with two more grenades in rapid succession. Three explosions are heard, one after the other.

Art pulls the pin on his first grenade, rears back, and hurls it skyward. In quick succession, he does this repeatedly, throwing two grenades at each location. With the sound of his grenades exploding, the noise from the machine guns stops. What an arm! The whole area in front of us is quiet now. Three machine gun nests have been taken out of action. Art and I slide over the top of the crater and crawl over to the nearest gun emplacement. All the Germans inside are dead. Working our way to the other two emplacements, we find the same outcome, all dead.

Captain Glazebrook witnesses our action and now brings his

company forward. The few surviving doughboys, who have been supporting Patton, rise from their hiding places as our company moves forward and through their positions. They join the ranks of our company as it continues the attack on Cheppy. Returning to the crater where we left Patton, we find him receiving medical attention as he's being carried out of the crater by some litter bearers. He stops them and motions for us to come over to him.

"Boys, that was some damn fine fighting and a hell of a display of courage. Well done. I'm going to see that you get some medals. You've earned my respect and gratitude. Stay safe, and I'll see you down the road!"

We thank him and render a hand salute as he is carried off to a waiting ambulance truck.

18

BATTLE OF THE MEUSE-ARGONNE

AN ACT OF TREACHERY

Sitting on the side of the crater from which we just rescued Patton, Art, the men in the first squad, and I take a break. I remove my pipe and tobacco pouch, pack the pipe with tobacco, light my pipe and take pleasure in the moment. Art places some chewing tobacco in his mouth while some of the other fellows enjoy their cigarettes. Captain Glazebrook walks up to us. My first inclination is to stand up, but he motions for us to remain seated.

"Fellows, that was a handy piece of work! Sam, where did you come up with the idea to use those barrels as cover?"

In a low-key, calm voice, I respond. "I'm not sure. It just seemed like the right thing to do at the time. Those damn machine guns were killing a lot of doughboys. We needed to stop them!"

"Sam, Art, and you other men, well done. Take a few minutes and then rejoin the company. I'll place the first platoon at the back of our company, and you can hook up with them. We're moving through Cheppy now and should push the Germans out before long. When we do, we'll take up defensive positions somewhere on the other side of town."

"Yes, sir, Captain!" After my response, Captain Glazebrook rejoins his men at the head of the column as they move through our position and continue into Cheppy.

After a brief rest, I spread the men out in the squad, and we cautiously move forward into Cheppy. We are not under direct fire from German artillery or machine guns. The combination of American artillery and Allied air superiority gained over the battlefield has eliminated these German threats for now. Catching up with the first platoon, I take charge again and continue sweeping through the town. Moving forward, we encounter heavy resistance from small, isolated pockets of Germans, who refuse to surrender. Hand-to-hand, close combat ensues. Using rifle bayonets, pistols, and grenades, we engage the Huns, eliminate the threat, and continue to move forward, slowly clearing the town.

Approaching a corner café on the other side of town, we are hit with a vicious crossfire from well-placed German riflemen. They are hiding in the second-story windows of two adjacent buildings. They rain accurate death down on us as three of my men keel over from being shot in the head. They drop like sacks of flour, not knowing what hit them. The rest of us take cover and return fire. We have superior firepower and unleash it on the second-story windows. Gaping holes are torn into the buildings. The Germans stop firing, throw their weapons out the windows and show themselves with arms held high. We move forward with our rifles at the ready and tell them to come down.

As they exit the front entrances of both buildings, a German emerges from one of the top windows and hurls a grenade into our group down on the street. Art, who is close to me, reacts instantly. Running to the grenade, he picks it up and throws it back at the German in the window. The grenade explodes almost immediately after leaving his hand. Pieces of hot shrapnel rip into the right side of Art's body as he's thrown violently backward and to the street. His right arm is mangled and hangs limply at his side as he falls.

This act of treachery by the Hun is met with swift revenge as the men around me fire their rifles at the Germans emerging from the buildings, cutting them down where they stand. Others unload their rifles on the German in the window. He seeks refuge behind the wall upstairs. I rush into the building, followed by some of the men, and head for the stairs. As I do, another grenade comes rolling down the stairs toward me. I yell, "Grenade!"

We drop to the floor, taking cover behind furniture scattered around the first floor. The grenade explodes, but we are unharmed. Moving cautiously to the stairwell, I direct the men to keep up a steady volume of fire on the top of the stairs. I throw one of my grenades up onto the second-floor hallway. The loud explosion is followed by the German screaming in pain. I rush up the stairs with my .45 pistol drawn and no mercy in my heart. Rounding the corner at the top of the stairs, I find him rolling around on the floor, screaming in pain from his wounds. Without hesitating, I aim my .45 pistol at his head and pull the trigger. His rolling stops when the bullet enters the front of his head and explodes out the back spraying gray matter on the floor. I feel nothing for him. It's over.

Rushing back down to my friend, I find him unconscious and bleeding badly from several shrapnel wounds. His right arm is a mess, and I fear the doctors may have to amputate it. Kneeling beside him, I cradle his head while the medics work to stop the bleeding and bandage him. Looking at Art, tears begin to well up in my eyes as I strain to control my emotions. Art is a good man, a good friend, and I don't want to lose him. It's out of my hands, and I can only pray that he makes it.

Captain Glazebrook approaches the scene, looks around at the dead Germans, sees Art lying there fighting for his life, and knows without asking what happened. Before he gets a chance to ask, one of the doughboys blurts out. "The dead Huns on the street surrendered. One of them stayed upstairs and tossed a grenade at us from the second-story window up there. They tried to murder us, so we shot them!" No remorse, no pity, no sense of glee in his voice, only pure hatred is conveyed in a matter-of-fact tone.

His burning eyes convey Captain Glazebrook's disgust as he looks over the scene before him. He speaks emotionally but with a calm demeanor. "These damn Boche bastards and their treachery. Will it ever end? What the hell is wrong with them? When this is over, we better ensure they never start another war. I fear there are many men among them, like these, very capable of unspeakable horrors and atrocities."

The captain kneels next to me, placing a hand on my shoulder, and says, "Sam, you stay here until Art is stabilized and moved back to the aid station. I will leave a man here to accompany Art and stay with him until they know his status. When they do, he's to rejoin the company and give us a report on Art's condition."

I've kept my head down to conceal the tears. But his act of kindness, knowing the friendship Art and I have, compels me to look over at him and nod my appreciation. I fear if I speak now, my emotions will overtake the moment.

He then says, "When he's sent back, come forward and rejoin the company. I need you with me."

Again, I nod yes. He concludes with, "See you soon, Sam." Standing up and squeezing my shoulder as he does, I feel a sense of comradeship and total respect for this man. He is definitely a leader.

As the company moves on, I'm asked by the medics to release Art from my grip as they're ready to lift him onto a litter. They've done all they can for him and must rush him back to an aid station. Art is not conscious; his wounds are bandaged, and the bleeding has stopped. I fear the wounds to his right arm are very serious. They lift him onto the litter and carry him to a waiting ambulance while I follow them. After the litter bearers place him in the ambulance wagon, I bid him farewell. This is where I leave Art and remind the runner accompanying him to report back to me as soon as he knows something definite.

As the ambulance wagon heads back toward the rear area aid station, I'm left standing there by myself, totally alone and lost in my thoughts. I don't believe I can bear the loss of a good friend. A feeling of hopelessness takes over, and there's nothing I can do. It's out of my hands. His fate is now in God's hands. I move out at a brisk pace to rejoin my unit.

Several hundred yards on the other side of Cheppy, I catch up with the second platoon of our company and locate Henry. It's good to see him and his friendly face. As we approach each other, he rushes forward, grabs me, and gives me a bear hug. At least this time, I'm not nursing a shoulder wound.

We just stand there, joined together in our moment of grief as we try to console each other over the seriousness of Art's wounds. Henry releases me, steps back, and says, "Captain Glazebrook placed my platoon at the rear of the company so I could lag behind and keep an eye open for you. Damn shame. I understand it's serious. Those bastards, they're going to pay for this. Are you okay?"

"Yeah, I think so. It's good to see you, Henry." I take a long pause and continue. "Those damn Boche! We just can't trust some of them. Where did they learn to be so damn treacherous?"

Henry replies, "I don't know, but I can tell you one thing. Many of the men are having second thoughts about Germans surrendering to them. We're going to have to address that concern with the captain." A pause, then he continues, "How is Art? Is he going to make it?"

I respond in a low-key melancholy voice. "I don't know, Henry, but it doesn't look good. His right arm is in bad shape, and the right side of his body took a lot of shrapnel from the grenade. I just don't know. The captain sent a runner back to the aid station with him and ordered him to wait until they knew his condition. He'll report back to us when he knows Art's condition."

After a short pause, I continue in a calm, matter-of-fact voice, "What's our status, and where's the captain?"

Henry responds, "Captain Glazebrook joined the first platoon, took them to the front of our column, and is leading the attack. We've gained considerable ground from the Germans. We should be settling into some defensive positions before too long. It's late. The sun will be setting soon."

"I've got to find the captain and get back in the fight. Take care, Henry. I'll see you soon." He responds, "You do the same, Sam." We part company as I head out to find Captain Glazebrook.

Moving forward, I pass through the fourth platoon, then the third platoon's attack lines, and now see the first platoon at the front of the company. The company has been moving at a brisk pace as the Germans are in full retreat. We're not receiving any Hun artillery shelling or heavy weapons fire. We are getting shot at by German snipers and their rear-guard troops. It's not very accurate and mostly just harassing fire. The Germans are currently in a state of panic and totally disorganized.

Catching up with Captain Glazebrook, I see he has halted the company's advance at a shallow German trench line. The trench line appears to have been recently and hurriedly constructed. He ordered the company to stop all forward movement and take cover in these abandoned German trenches. I acknowledge him without rendering a hand salute as I approach his position. That would signal to any Hun snipers in the area that he's an officer, thus making him a high-value target.

"Sir, what are your orders?" I ask in a calm, matter-of-fact manner. He responds, "Sam, are you okay? Did you get Art sent back to the aid station?"

"Yes, sir! Art is on his way to the rear. He's in bad shape, but I think he might pull through. As for me, I've been better. I could use a little rest and some food. It's been a long, damn day!"

The captain takes out a cigarette, lights it, and looks directly at me. "Sam, I hope Art pulls through and that we'll know his status soon. Right now, I need you in the fight and your help in organizing the company along this shallow German trench line. In a nutshell, we've been ordered to stop here for the night and take up defensive positions. We'll have a company briefing later this evening after I meet with the battalion CO. For now, let's get the men settled in, resupplied with ammo, and see what we can do about some chow!"

I respond, "Yes, sir!" Over the next few hours, I organize our section of the trenches and see to the needs of the men. The shallow trench system we're in was hastily dug and not well fortified. There are no bunkers with overhead protection to seek shelter if the Huns shell us. A few sections in the trench line have some overhead cover designed to provide a little relief from the weather. It looks like most of us will be sleeping in the open, subject to the whims of Mother Nature.

Since we don't know if we'll be staying here a few days or continuing the attack in the morning, I have the men settle into whatever shelter is available. If we're ordered to stay here for a few days, we'll set about reinforcing our position at first light.

After sunset, some cold chow and freshwater are provided. I do not find our meal very appealing, but at least we are not being shelled, gassed, or counterattacked by the Huns. In addition, the weather is pleasantly cool, with no rain.

Later in the evening, Captain Glazebrook calls us together for a short briefing with his leaders. He informs us we will remain in this location for a few days and be held in reserve for the regiment. The battle for the Argonne kicked off in earnest but is not going well for us. He gives us a quick summary of the situation, as explained to him earlier. The meeting ends on a positive note. Our runner just returned and conveyed good news. Art will survive his wounds. His right arm was saved but will require several surgeries. However, the doctors do not believe he'll have full use of his right arm when he recovers. He's being sent to an American hospital unit in Paris for a long recovery before being shipped home.

With the meeting over, I retire to my section of the trench line and find a little cover from the elements. I spend much of the night thinking about Art. He's alive and will be going home. That's great news, but will he accept his situation? His baseball career is over, his dreams and aspirations to set records in professional baseball are shattered, and his life is forever changed.

How will he deal with it? What will he do with the rest of his life? What can a man like Art be expected to do when he returns home and tries to start a new life for himself? I ponder these questions and feel for Art. I'm in for a long sleepless night with much tossing and turning, with little rest.

How would I deal with a life-changing situation such as this if it were me? I have no idea, and pray, I won't have to.

19

BATTLE OF THE MEUSE-ARGONNE - CÔTE DE CHÂTILLON

OVERVIEW

The Meuse-Argonne Offensive opens with coordination between the American First Army and the French Fourth and Fifth Armies. The newly formed American Second Army will join the offensive late into October. American troops will advance through successive lines of German strongpoints with the aid of French tanks, aircraft, and artillery support.

The Germans have proven themselves masters in the art of defensive fighting at this time in the war. Lieutenant General Robert Lee Bullard, Commander of the newly formed Second American Army, described the German defenses in the Meuse-Argonne area as follows:

"The way out is forward, through the eastern section of the Hindenburg Line. Not a line, but a net, four kilometers deep with a dense network of prepared killing grounds the Germans have created. Wire, interlaced knee-high in grass. Wire, tangled devilishly in forests. Pill boxes, in succession, each one covering another. No fox hole cover for German gunners here, but concrete bunkers from which to fight. Bits of trenches. More wire. A few light guns. Defense in depth. Eventually, coming to the main trenches—many of them, in baffling irregularity, the attacker never knows when he has mopped up. Farther back, again defense-in-depth, and a wide band of artillery emplacements."

General Pershing launched this offensive on September 26, 1918, not fully aware of what his doughboys would face and must fight through. It did not go well. His attacking forces walked into a buzz saw. Lacking experienced commanders and staff personnel, fighting in a narrow twenty-five-mile front and through prepared killing grounds the Germans had created between the Meuse River and the Argonne Forest, we, the Americans, made little progress. All Pershing thought to do was push more men into the fight, take even heavier losses, and hope something would break his way. General Pershing noted in his diary, "There is no course except to fight it out."

An example of the difficulties we faced took place early in the offensive, when what would become known as the "Lost Battalion" occurred. The Lost Battalion is the name given to nine companies of roughly 554 men who moved well beyond the rest of the American line and found themselves surrounded by German forces. For six days, suffering heavy losses, the men of the "Lost Battalion" and the American units desperate to relieve them would fight an intense battle in the Argonne Forest.

The battalion suffered many hardships. Food was scarce, and water was available only by crawling, under fire, to a nearby stream. Communications were also a problem, and at times they were bombarded by shells from our own artillery. Attempts to resupply the battalion by air failed. All the supplies being delivered would go off target. They would get lost in the woods or land among the German attackers. Every runner dispatched either became lost or ran into German patrols. Carrier pigeons became the only method of communicating. Despite all these hardships, they were able to hold their ground until American units broke through the German lines and rescued the battalion that had been labeled as lost.

The Americans launched a series of costly frontal assaults early in the offensive, trying to break through the main German defenses. Missouri and Kansas National Guard units were the first American troops who attempted to break through the stronghold of the Hindenburg Line at Côte de Châtillon. They were held off and beaten back due to poor leadership. The elite First Infantry Division tried and failed after suffering catastrophic casualties.

This was the ominous situation confronting Brigadier General MacArthur's Rainbow Division when it relieved the exhausted First Division. The Germans wasted no time in welcoming the Rainbow Division to the fight. According to one American officer: "Late on the first night of our arrival, General MacArthur went over to the First Division's headquarters on an inspection tour. While we were talking, the Germans were constantly shelling the valley with gas shells, mostly mustard and tear gas. I remember well that both the general, myself, and others present consumed so much of the gas we could hardly see or talk because of the effect of the fumes."

The Rainbow Division is in a pivotal spot since the key to this entire section of the Argonne front lines is a low hill mass known as the Côte de Châtillon. The Rainbow Division has two main objectives in this phase of the Meuse-Argonne Offensive: take the two dominant hills in the area, Hill 288 and Côte de Châtillon. Then drive the enemy north of the nearby towns and establish a new front-line on the high ground there.

My company, A Company, 166th Infantry Regiment, 83rd Infantry Brigade of the 42nd Infantry Division (Rainbow Division), will be in the middle of the battle.

20

BATTLE OF THE MEUSE-ARGONNE - CÔTE DE CHÂTILLON

A HEAVY PRICE TO PAY

DAY ONE

The following day dawns with light rain, an overcast sky, and chilly winds—just another day in France on the front lines. The Germans have been harassing us this morning with light artillery barrages. Fortunately for us, but not so for the rear-guard, they have been going well over our heads and hitting far behind us. Sometime during the night, Frenchie and his cooks arrived and set up their equipment in an area just behind our trenches. We are now enjoying some hot coffee and his legendary warm biscuits.

I managed to find a couple of empty ammunition boxes and set them up as stools under my shelter. I'm sitting here enjoying my breakfast when Henry walks up on me. He grabs one of the boxes, moves it closer to me, and sits himself down. He's carrying a small sack with him, a tin cup full of coffee, and his rifle slung over his shoulder.

He places the sack on his lap, puts his coffee down, removes the rifle from his shoulder, and settles it against the trench wall. He then pulls out a fresh biscuit from the sack and says in a friendly voice. "Good morning, Sam. How was your night? Did you sleep well? How about another fresh biscuit?"

I look at Henry with amusement. He has a childlike grin of mischief on his face, and I respond. "Henry, you always manage to get more food out of our cooks than any other man I know? How do you do it? Do you threaten them?"

"What, me? Of course not! I might give them an occasional menacing stare, but just as a last resort. I hold my mess kit out until they fill it to my satisfaction. Of course, it probably helps that I'm the regimental boxing champ right now." Henry responds with a bit of humor in his voice.

"You know, Henry, it could be that the cooks figure they owe you something. I understand they bet heavily on you in the fight and did quite well."

"Really, Sam? I didn't know that. Well, I'll be damned!"

Our breakfast and conversation are interrupted when the captain's runner joins us. "First Sergeant, Sergeant Miller, the captain has called a briefing and wants you to join him at his shelter. If you'll follow me, I'll take you there."

We gulp down our coffee, drop the unfinished biscuits we're eating, grab our rifles and follow the runner. We trudge through ankle-deep mud having to be careful not to slip and fall into any mud holes.

These damn trenches, I'm not going to miss them when I get back home. When I leave France, I'll do my darndest to purge them from my memory. But I doubt I'll ever be able to forget them!

We arrive without incident and join the other platoon sergeants and officers in the captain's shelter. The shelter is covered with wood and tarps giving us protection from the weather. Surprisingly it can accommodate all of us. The customary greetings and salutes are rendered, and Captain Glazebrook begins his briefing.

"Good morning, gentlemen. I trust everyone has had some breakfast." He takes a moment as he looks around at us for some form of acknowledgment. The other men and I respond with a "Yes, sir" or an affirmative head nod. He then asks, "How about rest? Did everyone get a chance to rest? We're going to need it before this day is done."

The responses to this question are not very positive. "Some!" "Not very much!" "Could have been better!" "Lousy accommodations!" "No room service and the sleeping arrangements could be improved!" "I've had better!" This light exchange brings on some much-needed levity for a moment as we all smile or manage a little laughter, including the captain.

We settle down. Captain Glazebrook's manner becomes serious as he continues with the briefing. "Okay, fellows, here is the situation. Our division has been tasked with taking two dominant hills in the area a few miles to the northeast of our current location. Hill 288 and Côte de Châtillon. These key positions must be taken to move forward and secure the Argonne area. Unfortunately, initial reconnaissance of the area revealed it to be very well defended. Fellows, it's going to be a tough nut to crack."

He scans the faces of the men around him as we digest his comments and react with sighs, moans, and faint whispers among ourselves. "My god!" "Here we go again!" "Will this ever end?" Looks of dread, fear, and anxiety begin to spread across some of the men's faces. Captain Glazebrook senses our trepidation and responds with his legendary cool, calm, businesslike manner.

"We've been here before, men, so this is nothing new. The

entire division will be in on this fight, so there will be plenty of doughboys in the field with us."

He lets that sink in for a minute, then continues in a matter-of-fact tone, "We'll be moving out around 1400 hours and taking up abandoned German trenches about a mile to our front. When we secure them, we will dig in for the night. From there, we'll be attacking our main objectives until they are taken. Ensure your men are briefed, fed some lunch, and well supplied with ammunition and fresh water. Also, if you have any man who has not signed his life insurance papers yet, make sure they do. I don't want any man "buying the farm" up here and then find out they haven't completed their insurance forms."

"Buying the farm" is synonymous with dying. We are given life insurance policies worth $5,000, but the paperwork must be properly completed and signed. This amount of money is about the price of an average farm, so if a soldier dies, he bought the farm for his survivors.

With his last comments, he asks if there are any questions. There are none, and he dismisses us. As I turn to leave, he pulls me aside. When the men have left, he informs me that Lieutenant Colonel Patton has recommended me, Art, and the squad members for some medals. I've been recommended for my second American Distinguished Service Cross and Art for his first. Art will receive an Army Wound Ribbon for his wounds. The other men in the squad have been recommended for a Military Medal for bravery under fire.

He concludes, "With Patton's recommendations, it's a sure thing they will be awarded to you and your men. Well, done and well deserved."

"Thank you, sir!" I salute him, turn toward the opening in his shelter and head back toward my position.

It's an honor to be recognized once again with this medal. It's also very gratifying for me to know that Patton recognized it was a team effort, not just one man. Recommending all the men for recognition was the right thing to do.

After lunch, the men are resupplied, briefed; and ready to move out as a regiment toward our objectives. Our company is one of four placed in the first wave. *We're always in the first wave.* A second wave of four companies will follow us. The remaining five companies will stay in our current trench system as a reserve force and eventually be brought up for the main assault on Côte de Châtillon.

The distance between attacking waves is set at one hundred yards. If one were to look down on our formation from above when we move forward, our regiment would be an incredible fighting force to behold. But we are only men. When the Huns open on us with artillery shelling, gas attacks, and machine guns, I'm sure they'll create massive gaps in our battle line formation.

At the set time, green flares shoot into the air, and our officers' whistles signal the attack is on. We go over the top and onto the battlefield as our grand attack begins. Charging forward, we are immediately hit with a heavy barrage of fire coming from the Huns. Shells are exploding all around, and intense machine gun fire causes us to flatten ourselves on the ground to avoid being hit. All the incoming fire directed at us is coming from fortifications built into the hills behind the trench line to our front that we're attacking. We rise and continue moving forward. Without warning, several Hun planes fly out of the overcast sky, swoop down on us at low level and drop bombs on our company. They look like vultures attacking a dying animal. The attack is swift and deadly. There is no time to react. Three of our men are killed and four wounded.

Their air attack momentarily disrupts our momentum, but we recover quickly and continue moving steadily forward under heavy machine gun fire and artillery shelling. Our artillery is having trouble finding and then pounding the German's rear area artillery pieces and hidden pill boxes in the hills to our front. This is not helping us as the Huns' resistance is stiffening.

With the trench lines now visible to our front, we pick up the pace and charge forward with rifles at the ready and yelling at the top of our lungs. The ground we move over has been plowed and churned into a sickening mud-covered field. Not a blade of grass remains. Reaching the trenches, we jump into them with great caution and move through them. To our surprise, no Huns are waiting to challenge us. The trenches are abandoned! What a relief. No one says anything, but I think many of us believe the Huns have abandoned them for a reason.

The second wave catches up to us and filters into the trenches. With their arrival, we secure the abandoned Hun trenches and set about the task of organizing our defenses for the night. I've been so focused on the attack with my adrenaline running high that I didn't realize the Germans had stopped shelling us, and their machine gun firing had tapered off. This is good; however, I can't help but feel uneasy and believe they have something planned for us. But what?

This trench system is worse than what we left earlier today and needs considerable repair. I move among the men, directing them to dig in, prepare firing positions, and build protective overhead shelter where possible. We still have some daylight, and there is much to do to make this trench line more defensible.

As the men and I dig down into the trenches to give us more depth and clear out some locations for firing positions, we begin uncovering a ghastly site. Not only is dirt and mud dug up, but decaying parts of human remains, legs, arms, and skulls. As we dig further down, all manner of debris from several years of fighting over this entire area is unearthed. They include helmets, shell casings, live ammunition, rifle parts, bayonets, and all types of entrenching tools.

Obviously, this area has seen many years of heavy fighting, and these trench lines started out much deeper than they are now.

How tragic! Fighting over the same piece of real estate and going nowhere!

We work well into the night to shore up our defensive positions, and as midnight approaches, our officers direct us to settle in for a long night. Once again, I am bone tired, ache all over, covered in mud, and fighting nausea from the stink of everything we uncovered while digging. Sitting in my firing position, under a small tarp set up as a shelter from the weather, I take a break. The small pleasures of life up here on the front lines, such as smoking my pipe and sipping some warm coffee, are a brief respite from the horrors of it all.

As I sit there enjoying the moment, a terrible thought crosses my mind. What if the Boche bastards allowed us to be drawn into this trench system. Our attack earlier to secure these trenches was met with little resistance from the Huns, and we only sustained light casualties. They may well want us here and could have the area underneath us mined. I shudder to think of that possibility. There is no doubt they have this entire area pre-sighted and targeted by their big guns set well back to the rear. Our regiment is exposed here, and we have no place to go but forward into their established kill zones.

Just before midnight, I get my answer. The Huns unleash a massive artillery barrage, and a solid sheet of flame lights up the horizon well behind us. They're hitting our reserve and support troops in the rear area. Off to my left, a horrific explosion occurs as a portion of the German trench line we hold goes up in a massive displacement of dirt, mud, and body parts from my fellow doughboys. The Germans set off an underground mine they dug under the trenches. There goes another explosion!

My god, they have placed underground mines up and down their abandoned trenches. No wonder we were able to take them with little trouble.

Several men in the regiment holding those sections of the trench system just "bought the farm." Meanwhile, the men in our rear area are catching hell from the massive artillery shelling by the Huns.

O God, O God, the poor souls on the other end of all this death! Care for them, God, and watch over the families back home of those of us who die tonight.

DAY TWO

It's approaching 0100 hours of day two. We still have about five hours until sunrise, and the Germans are continuing their massive artillery barrage on our rear area. We are watching an incredible show of firepower, the likes of which I haven't seen before. The ground shakes beneath us as large explosions in our rear area light up the sky. If we were having a thunderstorm, this would be one hell of a lightning show to behold. But it's not! Many men are dying as death comes crashing down on them from the heavens.

I fear the Germans have brought into play their heavy artillery to include "Big Bertha." It is the German's largest and most powerful piece of mobile artillery. It can fire a projectile weighing up to 1,785 pounds over five miles. Supposedly the Huns only have a few of these weapons, but it appears they brought up at least one to use against us.

Our artillery units to the rear area, both American and French, finally join the battle and unleash their massive firepower on the German lines to our front. We are now in the middle and witness to this titanic artillery duel as shells fly overhead in both directions. The noise from shells whistling overhead on their way to targets and their subsequent explosions when they impact the ground is deafening.

No one sleeps the rest of this night!

The titanic artillery duel between the Huns and us is relentless and continues through the night. As dawn approaches, it begins to taper off. The trench lines we occupy were not shelled during the night. It was all directed at our rear areas, and the first reports are that it was pretty devasting with multiple casualties. As for us, we suffered heavy losses from the detonation of three separate large underground mines. Both sides have long employed underground mining of our adversary's trenches, but what they did to us last night must be a record.

The Huns know we are here to fight, and we'll attack when given the command to do so. When we take the field to our front and move forward, they will have the upper hand. Their defensive fortifications are seemingly impenetrable. They simply expect to kill or maim all of us as we go over the top and advance. Their artillery barrage was designed to diminish our morale, fighting spirit, and capacity to resupply the front lines with more men, weapons, and ammunition to continue the fight. The underground mining of our trench lines was simply designed to kill as many of us as possible and spread fear through our ranks.

The last six hours have been nerve-racking. The weather has deteriorated as a steady rain settles over the battlefield. If I were ever to get shell-shocked, last night would have been the time for it. I'm lucky! I made it through the night. I'm still standing and have escaped any wounds. The day is just starting. Hopefully, my luck will continue. I move slowly through the company trench line, checking on the condition of the men. They are a great bunch of fellows who have withstood the onslaught and are itching to get at the Huns for some payback.

I find Henry, with Rick and Chet, leaning against the trench wall nibbling on some canned corned beef while sipping cold, weak coffee and chatting among themselves. Our cooks didn't make it up to our new positions, so we must rely on the food rations we carried with us. I approach them and strike up a conversation.

"Hey fellows, everyone all right here? How's the corned beef?"

Henry speaks first as the other two men acknowledge my presence with head nods. "Sam, damn, what a night! We're good. My platoon didn't lose any boys yet. As for the corned beef —I miss my biscuits and could surely use a cup of hot java."

Looking at Henry and then over at Rick and Chet, I respond. "Yeah, me too, Henry. Look, I'm going to find the captain and see what's going on. I'm sure he'll have a briefing shortly. I'll send for you and the other platoon sergeants when I know something. You boys enjoy your breakfast."

My last comment about breakfast elicited a few smirks. "Thanks, Sam, we will!" Henry blurts out, followed by Rick and Chet letting out a few grunts. Turning to leave, I respond, "See you later, fellows."

Moving through our trench line, I'm met by Captain Glazebrook's runner, who is looking for me. He takes me to the captain.

As I approach him, he dispenses with saluting and gets right to the point. "Sam, you, okay? Are the men ready for a fight?"

"I'm good, and they're ready. How are you, sir?"

"I'm doing all right, thanks for asking."

I nod and continue emotionally and firmly. "The men want to go; they're itching for some payback. I sense several long for just one German to take apart piece by piece and then feed to the animals. They've had enough of us getting pounded like this."

"Let's hope so. We're going over the top to attack in thirty minutes. I've sent runners to get our other company leaders for a quick briefing."

Within minutes everyone is gathered around the captain, and he briefs us. "Men, we go over the top at 0700 and onto the field. The regiment to our left will be attacking Hill 288, and our regiment will be taking on Côte de Châtillon. From the high ground they hold, the Germans can pour machine gun fire and small arms fire down on our attacking waves with almost complete impunity. We can also expect heavy artillery and gas. Any questions?"

Looking around and hearing none, he continues. "The regiment to our left lost many men during the night from those damn Boche trench mines. Our rear area also took quite a beating from the German artillery barrages. When we advance, what's left of our reserve companies will file into these trenches and give us some support. More reinforcements are being brought in and will take up positions to our rear."

Captain Glazebrook stops, lights a cigarette, and closes his briefing in a soft, calm voice. "Fellows, we have another American Army joining the fight. The newly formed Second Army commanded by Lieutenant General Robert Bullard. He has been pouring his troops into the lines behind us. General Pershing now commands the First and Second American Armies. These two Armies now make up the AEF. Lieutenant General Hunter Liggett has assumed command of the First Army from General Pershing. We now have close to a million men committed to this offensive. I want you to know, a hell of a lot of doughboys are now in this fight until the end."

I, for one, find it comforting that many more Americans are in the fight. However, if the truth be known, I would rather they take the lead in today's assault and let us stay back as reserve troops.

The captain concludes, "When we get onto the field, we are to advance as far as possible and hold the ground we take—no exceptions to this order. We'll be reinforced on the field with another wave of doughboys as the attack unfolds. After we secure a defensible position, more men will be brought up to help us hold that position. That's it! Get your men ready. Godspeed and good luck out there, gentlemen."

Our whole company is going over at once. Captain Glazebrook is placing himself with the third platoon, and he wants me with the first platoon. After briefing the men, I assume my place in the trench and wait for the order to go. Looking up and down the long line of doughboys ready to go with their bayonets fixed and gas masks ready, I feel a sense of pride to serve with and walk among them.

The green flares shoot into the air, followed by the whistles. Up and over we go. Standing on top of the trench parapet, I yell encouragement to the men as they climb over the top and onto the field. We charge forward. There are thousands of us charging over this killing field toward Côte de Châtillon. Our objective comes into full view. It is a formidable obstacle rising 820 feet high and dominates this entire sector. There is no way around it; we must take it from the Huns.

What happens next as we move forward is a slow-motion, unbearably distressing, excruciatingly noisy, and intensely chaotic trip through hell. When our regiment takes the field, charging forward, the Germans unleash their firepower on us with mortars, artillery, and gas canisters. There is the acrid odor of gas as shells explode above our heads, creating beautiful little puff balls dispersing gas which slowly settles to the ground. There's the continuous whine of bullets and above all, the terrible cries from our comrades that are hit and fall, dying on the muddy field. Their bodies roll, twitch, or convulse as some give their last full measure.

I wonder, how did I get this far? I feel confident I'm the one man in the world out here who can escape being wounded or dying. That will never happen to me! Or will it? I believe we all think this way. How else can one deal with this insanity called war?

We advance over terrain under high explosive shells crashing among us, spreading their hot metal shrapnel and machine gun fire mixed plentifully with gas. When gas canisters start exploding around us, I drop to the ground on one knee and put on my gas mask. The men follow my lead and struggle to get their masks on quickly. The smoke and gas are so thick that it doesn't take long to lose my bearings. Since the men depend on me to lead them forward, I slow down and struggle to see where I'm going. Thank goodness the gas starts to dissipate, so I take off my gas mask to see better. Somehow, I get us through it. Looking around for the rest of the company, I don't see them. The realization that I've led the first platoon way out in front of the rest of the company is immediate and frightening. We have no option but to continue forward with our attack.

A high concentration of German machine gun fire is directed our way since we are the only Americans visible to them at this moment. We are close to the base of Côte de Châtillon. The Huns are hitting us from our right flank and out to our front about 200 yards. To charge at them across this open field and up the ridge will be suicide. To stay here is worse. We need better protection.

I'm not about to pull any hero stuff since I figure we are lucky to have gotten this far. I order a withdrawal of about 100 paces back to a more defensible position with some ground cover. As we turn and start back, several more of the Huns' machine gun emplacements located above the base of Côte de Châtillon lay down a catastrophic field of fire. Bullets are coming at us as thick as bees churning around their hives. "Get down, stay low!" I yell out over the noise of battle. Then all the bells in the land break loose. I'm hit. I grab my head with my hand as blood pours down my face and into my eyes. I lay there for several moments, wondering whether I'm dead or alive.

A bullet has gone through the top right side of my doughboy helmet. Clearing the blood from my eyes and realizing it isn't a serious wound, I turn to the man on my left, Chet. He sure seems to be hugging the ground. I hit him with a stone. He doesn't move. He is dead. I turned to the man on my right, Rick. He's lying on his side, and I see him get hit twice more. He is dead. Two men I've served with for many months and good friends have just perished next to me in a hail of bullets. No time to mourn now. I must get a message back to Captain Glazebrook and set up a firing line with the men around me who are still alive.

Realizing we're well ahead of the rest of the company and maybe even the regiment, I motion for the men to follow me. I begin crawling back toward a more defensible location with the men following and staying as low to the ground as possible. All the time, bullets are whizzing just above our heads. German artillery is still raining down around us, but the gassing has stopped. The real threat out here is those damn Hun machine gun emplacements that seem to be everywhere to our front.

After an eternity of crawling over thirty yards through the mud, we manage to find cover behind a long bank of elevated ground. It stretches in both directions to our left and right flanks for some distance. Henry joins me along with some of the other fellows. I can discern a look of surprise on their faces as they stare at my helmet. Seeing the hole in my helmet and the blood on my face and hands, they are surely wondering why I'm not dead. My helmet deflected the bullet over my right ear, giving me a scalp wound. Without a doubt, this helmet saved my life. I will take it home with me as a souvenir to remember this day.

It's not surprising we lost contact with our company given all the confusion of battle raging around us and smoke covering the ground across which we just charged. As I scan the area to our rear and flanks, I don't see our company or other elements from the regiment. Surveying the terrain around me, seeking to locate a defensible position, I decide to stay where we are. The bank of earth we're hiding behind is about three feet in height. It stretches for a considerable distance on both our flanks and parallels the base of Côte de Châtillon about 200 yards to our front. It will provide us with significant defilade protection from the Huns. This is protection from hostile observation and fire provided by an obstacle such as a hill, ridge, or bank.

Looking directly at Henry and in a loud, authoritative voice, I say, "We need to dig in here, wait for the rest of the company and see what we're going to do. What do you think?"

He responds, "I agree. Let's get busy. I'll send a runner to locate the captain and let him know what we're doing up here!"

Before I can respond to Henry, the rest of our company comes charging through the smoke. They run up on our position, seek cover along the terrain features we're in, and form a firing line over a hundred yards long. Thank God we have some support. Just as they are settling in, more companies from our regiment emerge from the smoke and continue to fill in our ranks and spread out on both flanks. What a glorious sight! I don't know how many doughboys have made it to this point, but it sure looks to me like a small army of them. The men form a long-staggered firing line and dig in while being shelled and shot at by the Huns holding the high ground to our front.

Looking at Henry and grinning, I say to him, "What a glorious sight; maybe we'll survive the day yet." He nods affirmatively and says, "Agreed!"

I lean over to him and yell above the noise, "Take charge of this section! I'm going to find the captain and see what we're going to do!"

He responds, "I got it. Stay low and be careful, Sam."

I respond with a head nod and move down the firing line looking for the captain. Men from several companies in our regiment have been filling in where needed in what is rapidly becoming our new defensive position. I see so many new faces that I don't recognize as I work my way through them. I find Captain Glazebrook with two other company officers from our regiment talking over the situation. Seeing me approach, the captain moves away from them and over to me. The look on his face tells me he sees the dried blood and bullet hole in my helmet. With concern in his voice, he says, "What the hell happened to you, Sam?"

His concern is genuine and caring. I respond, "I ran into a Hun's machine gun bullet. It's only a flesh wound to the side of my head. I'm okay."

He moves closer to check out my wound for himself. Satisfied that I'm still fit to fight, he pulls me over to the other officers and introduces me. Their conversation continues as Captain Glazebrook details our current situation and orders. With evening setting in, the entire regiment has been brought up to this location with orders to dig in for the night. We are to hold this sector and will resume our attack early in the morning. Reconnaissance patrols from several companies are to be sent out later tonight. They will be charged with looking for gaps in the wire, and terrain features we can use to our advantage during tomorrow's attack. He further indicates that another regiment has taken over the trench line system, where we began our attack from earlier this morning. They're our new reserves, who will join us out here in the killing fields when ordered.

A new harvest of men for the Huns to slaughter.

Finally, he indicates that American and French artillery units will start a massive barrage after our patrols return later tonight. Their barrage will continue through the night and be lifted when we attack at dawn. He dismisses the group to return to their units and carry out his orders. He grabs my arm holding me back. When the other men leave, he speaks softly and in a matter-of-fact tone.

"Sam, I don't want you to lead any patrols out there tonight. Assign some of our capable sergeants to take a few men with them. I think two patrols going out should do it. You take care of making the assignments. Then see to your wound and get some rest. I'm going to need you out there tomorrow when we attack. Do you understand?"

I wasn't planning on leading any patrols tonight, as I'm exhausted, and my head throbs from my wound. It feels like a hammer hit me in the head. It is reassuring to know that the captain cares enough about me to cut me some slack.

I respond, "Yes, sir, thank you. I'll see what we can do about gathering valuable information concerning what's in front of us!"

Looking squarely into my eyes, trying to read my inner thoughts, he responds. "Good, go get it done. I'll check in with you later tonight."

As the sun sets and the evening progresses, I move up and down our sector of the line, checking on the men and ensuring they have fortified their positions as well as they can under the circumstances. Then I find a medic and have my wound cleaned and bandaged. Next, I assign two sergeants, Henry and the second platoon sergeant, Jim, to lead patrols out to our front and scout out the area. With my work complete for the moment, I stop to nibble on some dried biscuits and a few bites of canned corned beef. Settling in to wait for the patrols to return, I take some time to enjoy smoking my pipe. Thank goodness the throbbing in my head has subsided, and it's only sore to the touch.

The Germans lift their artillery and machine gun fire as dusk settles over us. I suspect the Huns feel confident they'll begin killing us again in large numbers when we resume our attack tomorrow. The night progresses quietly.

With midnight approaching, I hear noise to our front. It's our night patrols returning. They whisper out the password, and we respond with the counter password. They are cleared to crawl forward and join us in the firing line. Good news is they all made it and have some valuable information to share with our commanders.

The patrols found gaps in the wire to our front and defilade positions near some of the machine gun emplacements we'll have to destroy when we attack at dawn. After debriefing Captain Glazebrook on what they discover, we return to our positions on the firing line to wait out the rest of the night. We have no overhead cover, just fighting positions dug into the side of the embankment. For the remainder of the night, we'll be at the mercy of a rainy sky, with chilly winds and occasional harassing fire from the Huns. Settling back into my foxhole and adjusting my trench coat for maximum protection from the weather, I try to rest as thoughts of Marie overwhelm me.

Where is she now? How is she doing? God, I would love to be holding her in my arms right now! Will I ever see her again?

DAY THREE

Upon return of our patrols, their information is analyzed by regimental staff officers, and an attack plan devised. Captain Glazebrook summons us to his shelter at 0300 hours for a briefing. With his company leaders present, he begins.

"Gentleman, H-Hour is 0600. Our attack will be preceded by a massive artillery barrage. From the information gathered by our patrols, it looks like there are some clear avenues of approach we can use to cover the distance between us and the base of Côte de Châtillon."

He pulls out a small map depicting the terrain to our front and a sheet of paper with notes on it. Using an ammo crate as a tabletop, he spreads the map out and motions for us to gather around. Using a small trench torch flashlight, he proceeds with his briefing. He reads from his notes and points out areas on the map as he speaks.

"These are specific areas to our front that need to be avoided." Pausing as he points them out on the map. "These over here are areas we should pour through as rapidly as possible until we reach the base of Côte de Châtillon." Pausing again, he points to them on his map.

"We'll be crossing about 200 yards of open ground, which is relatively flat and covered in barbed wire. There are multiple machine gun nests at the base of the hill and layered up its slopes."

Taking a moment to light up a cigarette, he motions for us to join him. Several men pull out cigarettes and light them while I prepare and light my pipe. Taking his time, the captain scans our faces, looking for any reactions. I guess we're too damn tired and numb to display any real emotion. It's clear to me it's going to be a bloodbath out there, and I, for one, just want to get on with it. Observing no visible reaction, he continues in a calm, low-key voice.

"All the machine gun nests have clear fields of fire over the open ground we'll be crossing. After we take the Huns' trench line at the base of the hill, we'll be fighting blind from there on. We don't know where they placed their defensive positions on the slopes going up Côte de Châtillon. When we take their trench line, we'll pause to reorganize, catch our breath, then continue the attack up the slopes. Our advances from then on will be extremely dangerous and deadly."

Taking a long drag on his cigarette, as if this would be his last, he continues. "You need to remain alert and react instantly to every situation that confronts us out there as we fight our way to their trenches and then up the slopes. Don't stop for any man who falls. We must continue our attack. Our wounded will be the responsibility of the medics. Any questions about that order?" There are none. We know what the score is once we get out there on the battlefield.

As rain continues to fall from a low hanging overcast sky, Captain Glazebrook makes his closing point. "The ground is muddy, soggy, and will be difficult to move through as we attack the base of Côte de Châtillon. Once at the base, it will be even more difficult for us to traverse the terrain and work our way up the slopes to reach the top. Men, I don't have to mention this. We've all been there before. But the sooner we secure the trenches at the base, the more time we'll have to rest before launching our attack up the hill. Any questions?"

What can we say? What can we ask that we don't already know the answer? It's clear what we're facing and what needs to be done. There are no questions. The captain dismisses us, and we return to our post. I try to relax and rest for the remaining few hours before the attack.

An eerie silence has settled over the battlefield to our front and throughout the firing line as dawn breaks. Doughboys are preparing for the deadly work that awaits us this day and do so in unusual silence. The Germans defending the slopes of Côte de Châtillon are also quiet. We can see smoke rising from several of their locations along the slopes. They are clearly confident in their defensive positions and believe they're impregnable. A light breeze carries some of the smoke our way. By this time in the war, the Huns' food rations are meager and limited in variety. To me, it smells like they're boiling potatoes and turnips, and warming up coffee. On the other hand, we are eating hard biscuits and bully beef out of small tin cans. To reduce the chances of Germans spotting our exact locations along the firing line, we refrain from building any fires and endure the cold food with no coffee.

Staying low to the ground in a crouched position, I make my way along the company's firing line, encouraging the men and checking their readiness. While doing so, I stuff my pipe with damp tobacco and light it. I slowly and purposely draw in tobacco smoke, savor the aroma, and then exhale as I move among my comrades. My nerves are on edge. I fear what lies ahead of us this day. Hopefully, smoking this pipe conveys a mood to the men that I'm calm, confident, and in control.

That's my hope.

As H-Hour, 0600 hours, approaches, I assume my place in the firing line and prepare. With this attack, we will follow our artillery barrages as they lay down a heavy volume of shells to our front. They will systematically walk them forward through the battlefield, blasting large holes in the wire out there, and continue lobbing shells up the slopes. They will begin firing a few minutes before we get the signal to attack. In theory, this will give the Huns less time to get organized and react to our initial onslaught.

That's the theory.

Massive artillery firing is heard to our rear. It is followed by a crescendo of shells whistling overhead, landing not more than thirty yards to our front. The noise is deafening. The ground shakes beneath us as the shells explode on impact. As they do, massive amounts of mud, dirt and barbed wire fly into the air. Smoke covers the area in front. Looking around at the men nearest me, I'm once again amazed at the courage shown by them. Some are obviously having a difficult time as they soil their pants, lose their breakfast, and curse the situation in which we find ourselves. I'm certainly not immune to the terror unfolding around me, but I must control the emotions of fear dwelling within. These men depend on me, and I can't let them down.

As always, my good friend, Henry, is on my right with his platoon. We make eye contact and trade abbreviated hand salutes. The Huns haven't begun to retaliate with their artillery when the signal to attack is given. Green flares in the sky, followed by our officers blowing their whistles, call us forward. I spring to my feet, climb up the bank and yell above the noise. "Let's go, men. Follow me!" They rise and charge forward. To my left and down the line, I see Captain Glazebrook leading the way for the men around him. As we enter the thick smoke bank created by our artillery barrages, I lose sight of him. I set a slow, deliberate pace, trying to ensure I don't lose my footing on this muddy ground and continue leading the men forward. Our artillery created many gaps in the wire, which aids our progress. Trying to remember the avenues of approach pointed out to us in the briefing is all but impossible out here. The artillery barrages have changed the landscape around me, and the smoke hides much of it. I just continue forward and react to my immediate surroundings.

We haven't received any incoming fire at this point in our attack. Our artillery is continuing to walk their barrages forward toward the base of the hill. The thick, towering smoke offers us some cover and makes it difficult for the Germans to target us accurately.

Oh, but how fortunes of war can change!

As our artillery shells continue to whistle overhead, the Huns open with their artillery. We hear it coming our way. Suddenly it crashes around us. Men are blown into the air, their bodies shredded and torn. Near me, a large piece of a Hun shell struck a man in the webbing of his military backpack, where his pack strap crossed his shoulder and turned him over twice before he hit the ground. I'm so used to seeing men die. I knew he was dead and didn't even look his way.

We're getting closer to the base of the hill and encounter no difficulty traversing huge gaps in the wire obstacles. As we close in on the Huns, they increase their machine gun fire and send volumes of bullets whizzing all around us. They methodically traverse their weapons across the field using their pre-established kill zones. Red hot lead cuts more men down. Our ranks are thinning. Henry is still to my right and moving forward with what's left of his platoon. To my left, I don't see the captain. He is shrouded in smoke and too far down the line to see from here. We keep advancing and finally break out of the smoke. Our artillery has shifted their fire to the ridgeline and top of the hill. They're not going to risk hitting us as we close in on the Huns' trenches to our front. We're on our own; it's now up to us to engage and destroy the enemy.

We're visible to the Huns defending Côte de Châtillon as we emerge from the smoke. Their machine gun fortresses on the heights and slopes fire on us mercilessly, raining lead down on us. There are a few 7.7cm Hun light field cannons, relatively small and very mobile, on the summit of the hill. They add to our misery and pour down their deadly messages. I hit the ground seeking cover from this firestorm as the men follow my lead. Slowly we crawl forward, closing the distance to the first German line of resistance at the base of the hill. We face massive fire from machine guns and rifles, along with shrapnel from exploding artillery shells and hand grenades. It's deadly work we go about this day. Many men are dying out here, and our ranks have sustained severe losses.

Rising enough to look behind me and back across the field we crossed, I see a massive wave of doughboys rushing forward. To my left, I now see Captain Glazebrook, who's leading the men around him in a mad dash toward the Huns.

I'm exhausted, need water, and feel like I can't move anymore. Crossing that field and running through deep mud has drained my strength. Adrenaline takes over and moves me forward. I jump up, yelling. "Let's go, boys. Follow me. If we stay here, we die. Come on!"

The men get up and move forward, bayonets at the ready and

tossing grenades into the Hun defenders' positions as we advance. Twenty, fifteen, ten, five yards, and we're almost on top of them. As we close the distance, the Huns jump out of their protective cover and charge us. It's now man against man, in the open, with cold steel and bullets.

Henry has closed the distance between us, and we're standing close together as we take on several charging Huns. Henry shoots one in the chest and bayonets another as I drop one with my rifle and lunge at another with my bayonet. He's bigger than me, and stronger. His bayonet thrust pierces my left shoulder. I'm in the fight of my life and may not survive. Without hesitation, Henry draws his.45 pistol and shoots the Hun. He drops like a boxer hit with a knockout punch and falls dead to the ground. Panting, straining, and gasping for air, we both struggle to speak. "Thanks, Henry!"

Henry responds, "That was too close, Sam, but you're welcome." He takes a long pause and struggles for more air, then continues. "Sam, is your arm all right? It's bleeding, but the cut doesn't look too deep."

I simply respond, "I'm all right. Let's finish these bastards."

My adrenaline is in overdrive. I'm mad as hell and oblivious to the bayonet wound to my shoulder. Although some blood is flowing from the wound, it doesn't hurt and seems superficial— no time to stop. We're still engaging the enemy. We kill the Huns who charged us and jump into and overtake their trenches. We're now fighting the few Huns who stayed in them. To my rear, I hear the yelling of doughboys as they close the distance and join us in the trenches. With new reinforcements, we overwhelm the few defenders still in the fight. They drop their weapons, raise their arms, and surrender. This trench system at the base of the hill is ours. We now turn our attention to the slopes.

While catching my breath and surveying the slopes to our

front, I have a medic bandage my shoulder. Captain Glazebrook worked his way over to Henry and me. Seeing the medic working on me, he asks. "Sam, what happened this time? I'm beginning to think these Huns just don't like you!"

A moment of humor is cut short before I can respond. The Germans manning their fortifications to our front directed a new round of shelling and machine gun fire at us. They had ceased firing momentarily, giving their men a chance to retreat and pull back up the slopes. We are now under heavy fire again. Doughboys up and down the new trench line that we just captured turn their attention upward to the slopes. Securing whatever fighting positions available, we begin returning fire on the Germans above.

Once again, the Germans have the advantage since they hold the high ground. They're looking down on us, making it harder for us to rise and shoot back. The captain and I manage to peer over the top of the trench and what we see is not good. Trees are wired together up the entire slope, making it an impossible barrier to breach. Their machine guns are laying down a carpet of lead across the ground leading up to the first tree line on the slope. Going across this space and up the slope will be more difficult because of the rain and mud. We drop back down into the trench and discuss our situation.

"Sam, this is a sticky wicket! We're going to need volunteers to face the Huns' fire and cut lanes through those belts of barbed wire. Your thoughts?"

I respond. "It's going to be deadly work. We can't call on our artillery to open lanes for us through the wire. The tree line is too close to us for them to take a chance. They could hit us." *Friendly fire!*

I have a thought. "Captain, let's have some Stokes mortars brought up and turn them on the Germans."

He likes the idea and sends two runners back to have several

Stokes mortar teams brought up here. He then sends runners to our left flank and the other to our right, instructing them to tell the other officers that mortar teams are on the way. The Stokes mortar is a British trench mortar issued and widely used by the American Expeditionary Force. We've heard the Rainbow Division has over forty of them in use. The Stokes mortar is a smooth-bore, muzzle-loading, 3-inch trench mortar weapon used for high angles of fire. It is quite effective in helping to clear paths through barbed wire fortifications and on machine gun emplacements.

Captain Glazebrook settles back against the trench wall, pulls out a cigarette, and lights it. Henry settles in, puts a wad of chewing tobacco in his mouth, and sets about gnawing on it. I lean back against the wall, take out my canteen and gulp water down like a man who's come in from the desert and gone without water for a long time. Then I settle in for a few minutes rest and enjoy my pipe while waiting on the mortar teams.

The Huns continue their relentless shelling and high volume of machine gun and rifle fire into our positions. Staying low and close to the trench wall is keeping our casualties down. But we can't stay here for long. We need to attack, get into the trees, and start working our way up the slopes.

Taking the last draw from my pipe, I see three Stokes mortar teams working their way to our location. The senior sergeant in the group approaches Captain Glazebrook and reports to him. The captain directs him to set up one team here and concentrate on blowing large gaps in the wire and then hit their bunkers. He instructs me to take the other two teams and disperse them further down the trench line, about fifty yards apart.

We work our way down the trench line, with the two teams following me. Approaching a good spot to set up a team about fifty yards from where we started, I stop, deploy a team, and continue down the line. The other team follows me another fifty yards down the trench line, where we stop and set up their mortar. These men are well trained and efficient. They set up immediately, adjust their aim, and begin lobbing mortar shells into the wire and gun emplacements to our front. As I work my way back toward the captain, I hear our deployed mortar teams firing their 10-pound, 11-ounce high explosive shells.

The sweet sound of outgoing rounds.

These mortar teams methodically go about their business and are very effective. They silence several of the gun emplacements, create huge gaps in the wire obstacles to our front and clear the way for us to continue the attack.

The order to attack begins with officers blowing their whistles. Once again, we rise from the trench line and charge forward. A line of doughboys stretches out on both my flanks as far as I can see from my position. With our rifles, fixed bayonets, and grenades, we set upon the Hun defenders. The resulting close combat between the Huns and us is horrific, ghastly, and as vicious as I've experienced. Americans and Germans are slashing, cutting, stabbing, shooting, and blowing each other up with grenades in a life and death struggle. We Americans want the hill; the Germans want to keep it. The resulting carnage is sickening to my sight and senses. Yet we continue, yard by yard, struggling through the mud and over the slippery slopes as we gain ground on them, but at a terrible cost to us. As dusk approaches, the wire has been penetrated, and the greater part of the slopes are captured.

One last charge to the top of Côte de Châtillon, and it's ours. We have stopped to regroup, take a quick breather, and reload our weapons. Looking at Captain Glazebrook on my left and Henry on my right, I see the grim determination on their faces. Their eyes are intense, piercing, fixated on the terrain in front of us, and burn fiercely with hatred. I can't see my face, but I know I have the same look. I feel it. The whistles blow again. Rising, the three of us take a moment to look at each other, knowing this could be the last time we're together alive. Only men in this situation can fully grasp the helplessness you feel, the sudden realization this could be your final moment on earth. All you were, and are at this moment in time, could come to an end. There is no "what will you become!"

Our bayonets extended, charging forward, and showing no mercy, we set upon the Hun defenders. These Germans are brave men. Many stand their ground, fight us savagely, and die at our hands. As I clear the summit of the hill, I feel sharp, burning sensations and hear the thuds of bullets impacting my body on the right side. I fall backward, hit the ground hard, and start rolling back down the hill several yards before my body comes to rest after hitting a tree trunk. I'm conscious but in considerable pain as I yell out for help. Men closest to me rush to my side, try to make me comfortable as they check my wounds and yell for a medic.

Has my luck run out? This is bad. I can feel it. Oh, my god, will I ever see Marie Petit again? Will I go back home to America? Will I die over here and be placed in some military cemetery, yet to be built, so future generations can walk through it and wonder who we were? When this war ends, will anybody even give a damn about the men who fought it?

I feel blood flowing from my chest and down my right leg. I think I've been hit by several bullets as my comrades try to stop the bleeding while waiting on the medics. The pain is excruciating and overwhelms me. It is then that I pass out.

I'm awakened by medics working on me as Captain Glazebrook and Henry talk to me in loud voices, trying to keep me awake. The medics don't want me to go into shock and try to keep me from fading out on them again. Seeing that I've joined the living, for now, the captain kneels, leans over me, and speaks in his reassuring voice.

"Sam, you've been hit in the chest and thigh by a machine gun. The medics have stopped the bleeding, and you're being moved down the hill to a waiting Ambulance Company. You'll be taken to a field hospital in Verdun. The medics believe you'll be all right, but you'll probably be in recovery for some time."

The captain places his right hand on my shoulder, struggles to contain his emotions, and continues. "Sam, you did damn good here today. I'm going to miss you being by my side. You're one hell of a fine man and soldier."

Before I can say anything, the captain stands up, looks down at me, nods his appreciation, turns, and heads back up the hill to rejoin his company. Henry kneels next to me. He's wounded in the arm, has it wrapped in gauze, and fights to control his emotions. But his face betrays him as he speaks to me in a low, melancholy manner. Tears start to form in the corners of his eyes. "Sam, good buddy. I'm going to miss seeing you around and counting on you when the chips are down. You've been there for me so many times. Who the hell am I going to count on now to be there?"

Cutting him off and because it's difficult to breathe, I say in a soft shallow voice, "Henry, you'll be fine. There are a lot of good men in the company. We'll see each other soon; this war is going to end any day now."

I struggle to say those words and can't continue to speak. The medics tell me to stop and save my strength as I'm going to need it for the trip to Verdun. Henry stands up and looks down at me as I look up at him. We both struggle to contain our emotions as we bid each other farewell for now. As the litter bearers lift me onto the litter and pick me up, Henry turns and heads back up the hill.

Captain Glazebrook, Henry, and Art are fine men, good soldiers, and I know we'll be good friends for life when we return home.

21

FIELD STATION - BASE OF CÔTE DE CHÂTILLON

My litter bearers move slowly as they work their way down the slopes, avoiding muddy, slippery ground as they go. The trip down is made more difficult as the sun sets and darkness closes in. As we progress down the slope, we pass endless wounded and dead doughboys. The sheer number of litter bearers making their way down to the base of the hill forms an endless line of misery. My wounds have stopped bleeding but pain me greatly. I find myself fading in and out of consciousness from the trauma of my injuries. I desperately want someone to ease my pain and tend my wounds. There's no use screaming out. Until I reach the field station, no one can make a difference in my situation. These fellows carrying me have done what they could. It's now up to the doctors.

It seems like an eternity before we clear the hill, reach its base, and travel the distance to a field station. The field station has several tents set up to receive wounded men. The area is near the trench line where we started our attack earlier today. It is a beehive of activity. Men move in all directions as they shuffle the wounded around while carrying lanterns to light their way. The area looks like a field covered with lightning bugs flying around in all directions.

As feared, we have suffered significantly to take Côte de Châtillon. There are wounded doughboys on litters scattered all over the ground, waiting for doctors to help them. Many moan, some scream out, and others suffer in silence. This close to the front, there are no nurses to assist the medical staff, just medics and litter bearers who have some training in first aid. Observing the scene before me, I fear they may be overwhelmed. There are just too many of us. It could be a long wait.

The wounded are being laid on the ground forming long lines of stretchers. Medics circulate among us, doing what they can to ease our suffering while waiting on doctors to help us. My litter bearers place me on the ground in one of the endless lines, wish me luck, and head back toward the hill for more wounded.

Our army is no different in general respects from any other army. You always find some men who are cowards sneaking to the rear on some trivial excuse. Shell shock and gas have become the main excuse for being pulled off the line. For a man to come off the line, he must have a good dose of gas or a severe case of shell shock to get admitted. Discerning between those men who are faking it and those who are genuinely suffering falls to the medical staff.

One young doctor at the field station, a captain, whose apparent business it is to perform triage and ferret out these cases, is walking up and down the lines. As he moves among us, he identifies the severely wounded men and directs litter bearers to relocate them to another area for immediate attention. As he approaches my location, he stops, looks down at a lieutenant sitting on a stretcher next to me, and confronts him in a contentious manner.

"And what's the matter with you, buddy?" he demands.

"Well, I guess I've got a little gas."

"You do? Are you sure? Don't try to pull that bluff. There wasn't any gas shot today."

The doctor motions for an armed soldier to come over and escort this officer to another location. He doesn't resist; he just gets up and follows him. The doctor then kneels next to me and checks on my wounds.

Looking at me, he says compassionately, "Sergeant, you need immediate attention."

He stands up, turns to some litter bearers, orders them to take me directly to the nearest field station tent and see that I'm tended to immediately. Finished with me, the doctor continues walking down the endless line of wounded men performing his duty. The litter bearers pick me up, carry me to the nearest field station tent and place my litter on two wooden sawhorses. This configuration serves as the doctor's examination table.

They locate two doctors who turn their attention to me. I'm filthy, covered in mud, blood, and I have terrible body odor. I don't see how they can do their jobs in all this filth, carnage, chaos, and suffering surrounding them as they work. Indeed, these are men who believe in their Hippocratic Oath.

The doctors struggle to remove my clothing so they can examine my wounds. Their task is not easy, but they have considerable experience and remove what they need to proceed with their examination. The older doctor removes the gauze from my shoulder, chest, and thigh wounds. While he is checking on my injuries, a younger doctor administers morphine by injection. The pain I've endured up to this point fades from my body as the morphine takes effect. The medical staff can't operate, only stabilize patients—so they do what they can for me.

Feeling no pain and fading in and out of consciousness, I sense they have cleansed my wounds with water or saline, used sodium hypochlorite, and applied sulfa powder to them. This is standard procedure. New gauze is then applied and held in place by tying long cloth strips around the wounds. I'm now ready to make the trip back to Verdun for proper care.

The field jacket and field trousers removed from me earlier are discarded. The night air is cold, and the younger doctor covers me with a wool blanket. Litter bearers then carry me out of the tent to a large clearing where many wounded men lay on their litters. They gently place me on the ground, among my comrades, where we await transportation back to Verdun. Thank God the rain has stopped. It's damp and chilly, but with the morphine, I'm feeling no discomfort. Still drifting in and out of consciousness, I overhear one of the medics talking to the other medics near him.

"They are saying that the entire Rainbow Division suffered over 3,000 casualties in five days of fighting in this sector. Well over half of them were on the slopes of Côte de Châtillon."

I'm exhausted, have lost blood, have no strength or energy to draw on, and feel no pain. I close my eyes and pass out—no dreams, nightmares, or thoughts of Marie—just total darkness and silence.

22

VERDUN FIELD HOSPITAL

ARRIVAL

A severe jolt awakens me as two medics lift me out of a mule-drawn ambulance wagon. I'm groggy and disoriented, and the wounds to my chest and thigh are painful. The morphine must be wearing off. Looking around at my surroundings, I recognize some familiar structures and military units. We're on the outskirts of Cheppy, and I'm among old friends. The 308th Sanitary Train handles this sector, and I was brought here by the 330th Ambulance Company. I know they're a good unit from my previous experience with them. Although they treated me well the last time, I would rather this be a visit among old friends and not a patient again.

It's still dark, light rain is falling, and a cold wind blows as the medics carry me into a partially bombed-out warehouse converted to an aid station. They set me on the floor, and one kneels next to me.

In a low, compassionate voice, he says, "Sergeant, you're in Cheppy. You'll be here a few hours before we continue the trip to

Verdun. You'll be given some food, and a doctor will be by shortly to check on you. How do you feel? Can I get you anything?"

My mouth feels like cotton is stuffed in it, my tongue feels twice its normal size, and my veins feel as though fire runs through them instead of blood. I'm weak and groggy, and my reply is almost unintelligible. "I could use some water. More morphine. Pain is worse..."

Without responding, he hurries away and returns with a cup of water. Kneeling next to me, he lifts my head gently and tips it forward as he helps me sip some water. A moment later, a doctor arrives, kneels, and gives me another morphine injection. Without saying a word, he stands up and moves on to the next wounded man needing relief from pain.

Still kneeling and helping me with the water, the medic asked, "There. How's that, Sergeant?"

"Better, thanks...how long before we reach Verdun?"

After I finish the water in the cup, he stands up, looks down at me, and responds. "We're transferring you to a motorized ambulance for the trip to Verdun. Depending on the roads and traffic, it should only take a few hours."

I feel no pain as the morphine takes over, and I slowly drift into unconsciousness as I try to respond. "Thanks again. I have a French nurse waiting for me there if they...."

Several hours later, I'm awakened by a multitude of sounds coming from every direction. My first observation is of my surroundings in the truck. There must be sixteen of us in this truck. We're stacked up, one on top of the other, four high, like a bunk bed, with eight of us on each side of the truck. Some of the fellows are awake and looking around as I'm now doing. I hear no moaning or complaining among those of us who are awake; we're all quiet. I'm uncomfortable but not in much pain and assume the morphine is still working. I could use a sip of water, but I'll have to wait. I sense and hope we are close to our destination.

The tarp covering the side of our truck has been tied down, but the back has been rolled up. We can see what's happening outside the truck as we drive by. It's early morning with no rain. The sun is starting to rise as some light rays reflect off vehicle windshields as they drive past us, headed toward the front. I feel some relief knowing we are headed back from the front, and maybe my part in this war will finally end.

I don't want to leave the men or my closest friends to carry on without me, but I'm exhausted, drained, tired of fighting and killing. I just want it to end so we can all go home together with heads held high, pride in our hearts, and the remainder of our lives ahead of us without facing the insanity of war every day.

Leaning my head to one side and resting it on my good upper arm and shoulder, I strain to observe all the noise and activity going on around us. It is beautiful. Military equipment is everywhere; trucks, tanks, and artillery pieces are all headed toward the front. War supplies are stacked up in large quantities waiting to be transported forward. We pass large groups of German prisoners being held in pens awaiting their fate. This is a mighty army moving forward. There are also large groups of wounded and dead doughboys being treated with the respect and dignity they deserve.

What strikes me the most is the large columns of doughboys moving toward the front lines. The infantry—always flowing forward as far as the eye can see—the infantry. Often called the Queen of Battle. An unwavering line of men advancing toward an unknown fate with courage, resolve, and dedication. It gives me a sense of gratification and pride to be associated with men of this caliber, my fellow brothers in arms.

Our truck slows down, makes a few turns, pulls up to a building, and stops. We are at the field hospital in Verdun. This area is well behind the front lines and is considered safe from any form of German harassment.

PROCESSING

Litter bearers unload the wounded from our ambulance train. My turn comes as they lift me off the hooks supporting my litter, slide me off the back of the truck, and carry me to an area lined with wounded soldiers lying on the ground. Always the ground! They place me next to some fellows from my battalion who are badly wounded and appear to be semi-conscious. I recognize their unit patch but do not know them. Lying there in silence, on the ground, waiting for my turn to see a doctor, I feel pity for these fellows. They're moaning in pain and struggling to breathe. Why doesn't someone come and take care of them or take me away? But that is not possible since a doctor must evaluate us all to determine our level of need and priority.

If I survive this war, I'll never allow myself to be forced to wait in lines again.

Looking around at the scene before me, I see hundreds of men scattered about on the ground in an organized fashion. Many appear to be suffering badly from shell shock. It's sad to see them. They look and talk like old men trapped in young bodies. They talk about their buddies who were blown to bits or were wounded and never brought in. One young, freckled-faced doughboy next to me grumbled and said his job was to carry ammunition boxes and mortar shells up to the front lines. While going through the trenches, he had to push past men with their arms blown off, legs shattered, and all manner of wounds. They would yell at him, "Don't touch me," but he had to get past to deliver his supply of ammunition. Many times, he would stand on something wobbly and nearly fall only to see it was a dying or dead man, half covered in mud.

I feel for the young lad, but his experiences mirror those of his fellow front-line doughboys. Why do some men crack under the strain, and others seem to endure what they face? I've come close to being shell-shocked but have yet to cross over into that world.

I wonder—is there going to be a day of reckoning for all of us who survive and go home? Will we suffer shell shock someday in the future? What will it be called then? Who will care? How will our fellow Americans treat us? Questions that can only be answered by the passage of time.

A middle-aged, bespectacled, unshaven, exhausted doctor comes over, looks down at me, and asks in a low, tired, sympathetic voice. "Sergeant. Sergeant, when were you wounded? How many days ago?"

I haven't spoken in some time. My mouth is dry and sore, and I'm drained of strength. My response is weak and shallow. "I think it's been two days now. Am I going to make it?"

He kneels and looks at the medical tag they placed on me, which lists the basics—wounds, medicine, morphine shots administered. All of which give the doctor a brief history of my situation up to this point. He then pulls back the wool blanket and inspects my wounds. His facial expression is neutral. I can't discern any emotion or reaction from him about what he sees or what he saw noted on my tag. Pulling the wool blanket back over me, he stands and tells the medics to move me to the surgical building for immediate attention. He looks down and says, "Son, I think you'll make it." He then turns his attention to the young boy next to me, that is mumbling and appears shell-shocked.

The medics move me to a large building that surprisingly has sustained minimal war damage and is now a fully functioning surgical facility. There are multiple surgical tables set up. Doctors, nurses, and medics move and function as if they're working on a factory production line. One big difference, here they are trying to save lives, not manufacture guns, trucks, tanks, and other weapons of war. They are trying to save the men who use the weapons of war.

Carrying me to one of the empty tables, they set me on it, and as they leave, they both wish me good luck. I raise my hand in a gesture of appreciation and turn my attention to what happens next. This all seems like "Déjà vu," I've been here before. One, then two doctors join me at the table, remove the wool blanket and begin their assessment. I've not had a bath in weeks. I'm filthy, and I smell. I have a hard time living with myself and don't see how these doctors deal with what we, the wounded dough-boys, present.

One of the doctors motions for a nurse to move over to the table and assist them. She is hidden from my view, but I immediately recognize her voice as she responds. "Doctor, I'm going off duty now. I've been at it all night, and other nurses are coming on duty. I can start with you, but I'll be relieved shortly. Is that all right with you?"

Before the doctor can respond, Marie steps next to the table and looks down at me. Her face betrays the emotions she feels as she recognizes me. Marie's exhausted facial expression slowly melts away and becomes one of concern, dread, relief, and calm. She looks into my eyes. We stare at each other, oblivious to the sounds and voices around us, as she clasps her hands around my good hand. We both show emotion as tears flow from her eyes, as do mine.

Marie responds to the doctors in a strong, assertive, and almost demanding voice. "I'm staying and will assist. I know this man. Please do whatever it takes to save his life!"

The doctors acknowledge her response with head nods as they remove my clothing, clean my wounds, and prepare me for surgery. Still holding my hand, Marie lowers herself to whisper in my ear. "Sam, these doctors will take good care of you. Please stay with me, don't die! I love you. Je t'aime." She gives me a small kiss on the forehead and begins assisting the doctors.

I'm in good hands, feel confident, and look forward to getting through this surgery and beginning my recovery. One of the doctors places a mask over my nose and mouth and administers chloroform gas. Looking up at Marie's face and beautiful eyes, I slowly drift off as she fades from view. My senses are dull. Everything goes dark and silent. I drift off into unconsciousness.

REUNITED

War nursing's most frequent hazards include infected fingers, sickness, and physical strain. Some of the more common complaints and comments by nurses are: "My back is busted in two tonight." "I'm tired of moving through wards, doing the dressings, and making the beds." "Will this ever end? I'm ready to go home." "I never want to see another bedpan when this war is over."

A simple truth is that without nurses and their devotion to duty, many soldiers would die and suffer more egregiously. They are truly the angels of mercy. Their work is demanding, grueling, horrific, and full of disappointment as they watch men suffer and die from their wounds as they labor to save them. Their frequent changing of dressings and application of antiseptic, though physically exhausting, serves a critical medical function. It is the most effective method for healing infected war wounds and preventing many limb amputations. In this everyday working environment, nurses seek out close friendships. They become indispensable, romances serve as welcome distractions, and some lead to engagements.

It's been two days since I arrived at the field hospital in Verdun. I've been unconscious most of the time, only occasionally awakening to mumble incoherently. On the morning of the third day, my eyes slowly open, and I begin to focus on my surroundings. I hear movement, voices, and the sounds of activity all around. As I regain sight, I try to sit up, but I'm too weak and have no leverage to lift myself. My chest, left shoulder, and right leg are all wrapped in bandages. My leg is elevated, suspended, and supported by a rope hanging down from a wooden stand over my bed. It reminds me of a hangman's gallows. I'm thirsty, hungry, anxious to know my condition, and just want to get up and get the hell out of here.

A mild panic begins to overtake me. How wounded am I? Where is a doctor? Where is Marie? The area I'm in is massive and appears to house over a hundred men. It is well ventilated, with lights and supply stations close to the wounded. There are nurses everywhere attending to the needs of the men. We are in beds. Yes, beds with clean sheets. It just occurred to me that I'm also clean. Someone must have given me a sponge bath. This is all good, but what is my state of health and recovery?

Where is Marie?

I hear a familiar voice. It's her! Walking up from behind me, Marie says, "Bonjour, good morning, Sam. Welcome back. You've been unconscious for two days. Let me check you first, and then I'll feed you some soup and give you fresh water."

Kneeling next to me, she leans over and kisses me on the forehead. She then checks my bandages, takes my temperature, and tilts my head up so I can sip some water. I feel better already and believe I'll make a full recovery eventually. Looking into Marie's eyes, I slowly and lovingly speak in a soft voice. "Marie, I missed you very much. There wasn't a day that went by that I would not have come back to you if I could have. Give me your hand!"

She extends her hand; I grab it and gently caress it. She takes her other hand, brushes my hair back, and runs her hand around my face ever so gently while looking at me with love in her eyes.

We share an intimate moment that will last me a lifetime. I've never known a woman like Marie. She's intriguing, elegant, confident, caring, loving, and beautiful. This is a lady I could spend the rest of my life with! She makes me want to be a better man.

"Sam, the doctor will be by shortly to look you over and answer all your questions. I can tell you this. You will recover. Your two bullet wounds were through and through, as they say. Just bullet holes, no bone or organ damage. One bullet hit your right thigh and exited your buttocks. There is some muscle damage to your thigh, but you will recover. Your bayonet wound is already starting to heal."

I listen intently while never taking my eyes off her adoring face. She continues. "Sam, if I can have my hand back for a moment, I'll go get some soup and feed you."

Reluctantly releasing her hand and saying nothing, I follow her movements until she disappears out of sight. Two doctors approach me as one pulls the medical chart hanging from the end of my bed off its hook. They look it over and then direct their attention to me. The older doctor checks my bandages and then begins a calm, matter-of-fact conversation.

"Sergeant, you're a lucky fellow."

Without hesitating, I blurt out, "Lucky; I don't feel lucky, sir!"

He responds very calmly. "I understand your feelings, Sergeant. Maybe that was the wrong choice of words. Your wounds are not life-threatening and will heal over time. The wound to your thigh will take longer to heal. You'll require some extended rest and recovery, which could take at least a month. We're sending you to the American Field Hospital Number 57 in Paris when you are released from here. There you'll continue to receive medical attention as your recovery progresses. In the meantime, enjoy your stay with us for the next two weeks. This should give you time to regain some of your strength before the trip to Paris."

He turns to leave, and I direct my gaze over to the younger doctor, who speaks to me more authoritatively and directly.

"Sergeant, this war has produced medical issues largely unknown in civilian life. The most common are wound infections. When you men are riddled by machine gun bullets, bits of uniform and the polluted mud from the trenches are driven into your wounds. Most notably, abdomens and internal organs. You are very fortunate. None of your wounds impacted vital organs. Your wounds are less severe and more easily treated, but we must be careful to keep them clean, so they don't get infected. We'll do everything to ensure that yours do not become infected. We'll need your cooperation and active participation in your ongoing medical care. This is where your nurse comes in. Follow every direction she gives you, and you'll do fine. Any questions?"

"Just one, sir. Who is my nurse?'

"That would be Marie Petit."

The assignment of Marie to be my guardian angel for the next two weeks is a godsend. I slowly drift off into a deep sleep, knowing I am in good hands and will be watched over carefully.

TWO WEEK STAY

The following day arrives early as I'm gently shaken awake by Marie. She leans in close and, with a soft voice, says, "Bonjour Sam, you must wake up. It's time for your breakfast."

Slowly waking up from the first long, uninterrupted sleep I've had in several weeks, I feel refreshed. I look into Marie's loving eyes and angelic face. "Marie, how long have I been out?"

"You slept soundly for twenty-four hours. How do you feel this morning? Do you have any pain or discomfort?"

As I respond, my voice is weak but feels stronger than it did yesterday. "Marie, give me your hand, s'il vous plaît." She clasps her two hands around my good hand as I continue. "I feel okay. I'm relaxed. I feel very little pain or discomfort right now."

"Très bien, très bien. This is very good. Sam, let me feed you breakfast while I give you an overview of what your daily routine will be for the next two weeks. Okay?"

"Oui, Marie."

Marie takes her time explaining what I can expect as she feeds me a breakfast of oatmeal, one biscuit, and some coffee. My routine will consist of three meals a day, multiple checks by her daily, a sponge bath every three days with a change of dressing for my wounds, doctors will check with me daily, and finally, if I make good progress, Marie can take me outside for some fresh air in a wheelchair.

I am in paradise!

Time seems to pass quickly, with the daily routine keeping me occupied. My wounds are beginning to heal. I'm regaining some strength and looking forward to Paris. It's now my tenth day here, and the doctors just removed my leg from that damn suspension contraption. I sure feel better with my leg resting on the bed. They tell me my thigh is healing nicely, and I should be able to go outside in another day or two for some fresh air. Up to this point, Marie has spent a considerable amount of time each day taking care of me. I relish our time together and live for the moment I'll be able to stand up, hold her tightly in my arms and feel her body next to mine. Hopefully soon!

After removing my leg from its suspension and finishing their routine check-up on me, one of the doctors hands me a copy of The Stars and Stripes American newspaper dated today, October 30, 1918. I thank him as they turn and move on to another doughboy. Looking at the newsletter, I notice the main story on the front page is an article about the Meuse-Argonne Offensive. It reads in part:

The Rainbow Division under Brigadier General Douglas MacArthur was finally able to take Côte de Châtillon after exposing a gap in the German defenses that was discovered by MacArthur's soldiers. This victory at Côte de Châtillon is considered a decisive turning point for the Meuse-Argonne Offensive. American doughboys have advanced ten miles and cleared the Argonne Forest. On their left, the French have advanced twenty miles, reaching the Aisne River. There were numerous acts of personal bravery; it is perhaps the Rainbow Division's greatest achievement so far in this war. The division was too decimated to press their advantage, but the tide has turned with the taking of Châtillon.

This is good news. We're a tough outfit, and I am proud to be a member of the Rainbow Division. The men I served with, living and dead. I shall always remember, respect, and mourn those who will not return home.

Turning the page, another article catches my eye. Corporal Alvin York was one of the assistants for Sergeant Bill O'Connell, the boxing champion of the 82nd Division's 328th Infantry Regiment. Bill was the boxer that Henry defeated back in Lemmes during our rest and recreation stand down. It reads:

Corporal Alvin York was promoted to Sergeant and was awarded the Distinguished Service Medal (DSM) for leading an attack on German machine gun nests where he took thirty-five machine guns, killed at least twenty-five enemy soldiers, and captured 132 prisoners. Senior Military Command is reviewing his actions for possible elevation to the Medal of Honor.

In an October 8, 1918, attack that occurred during the Meuse-Argonne Offensive, York's battalion aimed to capture

German positions near Hill 223. His actions that day earned him the DSM. He later recalled:

"The Germans got us, and they got us right smart. They just stopped us dead in our tracks. Their machine guns were up there on the heights overlooking us and well hidden, and we couldn't tell for certain where the terrible heavy fire was coming from. And I'm telling you, they were shooting straight. Our boys just went down like the long grass before the mowing machine at home. Our attack just faded out. And there we were, lying down, about halfway across the valley, and those German machine guns and big shells getting us hard."

Under the command of Sergeant Bernard Early, four non-commissioned officers, including recently promoted Corporal York and thirteen privates, were ordered to infiltrate the German lines to take out German machine gun nests. The group worked their way behind the Germans and overran the headquarters of a German unit, capturing a large group of German soldiers. Early's men were contending with the prisoners when German machine gun fire suddenly peppered the area, killing six Americans and wounding three others. The loss of the nine killed and wounded put York in charge of the seven remaining soldiers. As his men remained under cover, guarding the prisoners, York worked his way into position to silence the German machine guns. York said:

"And those machine guns were spitting fire and cutting down the undergrowth all around me, something awful. And the Germans were yelling orders. You never heard such a racket in all your life. I didn't have time to dodge behind a tree or dive into the brush. As soon as the machine guns opened fire on me, I began to exchange shots with them. There were over thirty of them in continuous action, and all I could do was touch the Germans off just as fast as I could. I was sharpshooting. All the time, I kept yelling at them to come down. I didn't want to kill any more than I had to. But it was them or me. And I was giving them the best I had."

Resting the paper on my chest, I think back to the day I met this man. He made an impression on me then, and now I have a better idea why. He was big, quiet, respectful, carried himself well, and was rather unassuming. But he impressed me as being a self-assured, confident, and God-fearing man with a warrior streak hiding within. In other words, he was not a man to trifle with; he had his limits. Apparently, the Huns learned that the hard way.

The day passes slowly for Marie and me as we spend it talking about our future together while she cares for me. Marie mentions she has requested a transfer to Field Hospital 57 in Paris and hopes it will be approved before I'm moved there in a few days. Her transfer, if approved, would be fantastic. My feelings for her have reached the pinnacle of one's ability to love another. I want to ask her to marry me. But now is not the time. We need to spend time together away from this war to develop a romantic relationship, especially with a view toward marriage. Marie needs to be sure. It's going to be a tough road for me to travel while always wanting to know her answer.

Over the remaining two days before I'm moved to Paris, Marie secures a wheelchair and takes me outside for short periods. The fresh air is invigorating. It lifts my spirits significantly. We talk about everything and nothing. We just want to be together. My love for her grows. I sense she feels the same, but it's still hard to gauge exactly how she feels. Our surroundings are such that we have no privacy. We can't show real affection or enjoy our limited time together without being interrupted by all the activity.

It's the morning of my fourteenth day; time to go. I'm sitting in a wheelchair outside the building where I've been housed for the last two weeks. Marie and I are spending what little time we have left before I must board an ambulance truck for transport to the train station south of Verdun. I'm being released from here and sent to Paris for an extended recovery period. While waiting, Marie looks at me in a way that makes the world fade away. No soldiers, medics, doctors, trucks, or wounded men, just the two of us, together on a cobblestone sidewalk in a dreary morning mist.

In her soft, elegant French accent, Marie says, "Sam, I love you. I want to be with you and spend the rest of our lives together. I hope you don't think of me as being too forward, but you are my world." Tears well up in her eyes as she brushes them aside with her sleeves.

Looking up from my wheelchair, gazing into her beautiful green eyes, I simply say, "Marie, I love you. I desperately want to ask for your hand in marriage but feel I must wait."

I couldn't help myself. The words just flowed from my mouth. Marie kneels, hugs me as tightly as possible without crushing my arm or chest, and we kiss. Our awkward embrace becomes a passionate kiss. We're now the center of attention for those around us. We are brought back to reality as one of the medics assisting me interrupts our moment.

"Sergeant, I'm sorry, but we have to place you into the ambulance truck. It's time to go."

I draw back from Marie. A smile spreads across her angelic face as she says, "Oui, Sam. Yes, I will marry you. We don't have to wait."

It's my turn to get misty-eyed as I respond. "You've made me the happiest man on earth. I love you."

The medics lift me out of the wheelchair, place me on a stretcher and slide the stretcher into the ambulance. Marie holds my hand until the last second and has the look of a little girl ready to explode if she doesn't tell her secret. Looking into each other's eyes before they close the door on us, she flips the bangs back from her forehead and says with excitement in her voice,

"Sam, one more thing. I'll see you in Paris in a few days. I've been transferred to Field Hospital 57! Au revoir, mon amour."

The doors close.

My god, can this day get any better?

23
FIELD HOSPITAL NUMBER 57 - PARIS

SERGEANT ARTHUR WILSON-REUNITED

I've been here at the American Field Hospital Number 57 for several days now and have grown comfortable with my new surroundings. We are on a strict schedule of three meals a day, daily visits by doctors who manage our progress, Red Cross nurses to see to our daily needs, change our sheets, and sponge bathe us every three days. In my case, I'm fortunate enough to be taken outside daily in a wheelchair, weather permitting, to enjoy fresh air, sun, and the local scenery. Although I still occasionally feel pain, I've been taken off morphine as my wounds continue to mend. However, the doctors informed me I could be here for at least another month. I have no qualms about that. This is better than being back on the front lines.

This Paris field hospital was set up on August 21, 1918. The medical team took over the large school building in which we're currently housed, installing over 1,800 beds. I share a hospital ward with fifty other men, all of whom are recovering from their wounds. Our wounds include amputations of arms and legs, bullet holes, severe bayonet slashes, infections, and excessive exposure to deadly gases resulting in severe burns and lung damage so extreme that each breath is a struggle. I don't see how they will survive. I've been told by the doctors that my lungs sustained some mild scarring from gas which could give me trouble later in life. It's no surprise that this would be my fate, given all the gas attacks I endured while on the front lines.

The trip from Verdun to Paris was by train, consisting of thirty rail cars built to carry wounded soldiers. Each rail car could carry up to forty men—so we were told. With one exception, the trip from Verdun to the hospital was uneventful and pleasant. Most of the men in my train car were gas attack survivors, well cared for by medical personnel during our trip. Unfortunately, before we reached Paris, one of the men succumbed to his gas attack wounds. He struggled and labored to breathe until he could not. His last breath was like a sigh of relief, it was over, and he was going home—what a horrible way to die. The use of chemicals in warfare should never be allowed. When this war ends, it should be banned forever.

Much of the French countryside we traveled through is still scarred by years of war. However, the closer we got to Paris, the less visible the scars. Traveling through the outskirts of Central Paris to the Gare du Nord, North Station, was a real experience for me. I've heard many things about Paris and the Parisians but seeing it for myself was mesmerizing.

Paris is one of the most beautiful cities in the world, the capital of France, art, and fashion. Over the course of the war, the Germans have, on many occasions, attacked the city with their Deutsche Luftstreitkräfte—German Air Force. We saw the damage caused by German bombers and large artillery shells to parts of the city as we passed through. For several months beginning in July 1918, German bombardments of the city intensified.

The Paris Gun, the name given to Germany's long-range siege gun by the Parisians, the largest used in the war, was used on Paris. Works of art were evacuated from the Louvre; sandbags were placed around monuments, and the streetlights were turned off at ten in the evening to hide the city from German night bombers. Why would anyone want to destroy such a lovely, historical, and culturally diverse city as Paris?

It's the morning of my seventh day here at the hospital, and I inquire about the status of Sergeant Arthur Wilson. My doctor informs me that Art is in another hospital ward and has been here for some time. He arranges for us to meet and spend some time together after lunch.

I'm anxious to see Art, and like a kid, I practically inhale my lunch. My nurse pushes my wheelchair through the corridors and onto a large, tree-shaded terrace. Art is waiting for me, slumped over in his wheelchair, looking dejected, withdrawn, and depressed. He does not look like the same man I fought alongside since arriving in France. As I'm wheeled close to him, he raises his head, sees me, and manages a slight smile. I'm wheeled up next to him. Our emotions take over as I wrap my two arms around his neck, and he wraps his good arm around mine. We pull each other close, touching heads. Tears stream from our eyes. As our emotions flow out, we struggle to keep them bottled up and try to muffle our sobbing. People near us sense the love, respect, and sadness we both display, and everyone on the terrace becomes quiet out of respect for these two broken warriors.

Pulling back from our embrace, regaining some control over our emotions, and settling in, we engage in some conversation.

"Art, my god, it's good to be back together with you. How long have you been here, and how's your recovery going?"

He responds in a low-key, melancholy voice, looking into my eyes with a sense of profound sadness reflected in his. "Sam, it is good to see you too. It's been too long. My shrapnel wounds are severe. They've been slowly healing. My right arm was shattered and will be of little use to me. The doctors wanted to amputate above the elbow, but I won't allow it. They managed to save my arm but had to perform several surgeries to do so. I may need some more surgeries when I get home." He pauses and starts to choke up as he speaks. "I'll never play baseball again."

Art stops, begins sobbing again, and struggles to regain his composure. His reactions are hard for me to witness as I feel his pain and wish there was something I could do. It's gut-wrenching to see one of your closest friends going through this emotional distress. I reach out, embrace him, and try to console him. Slowly regaining his composure, he pulls back from me, raises his head to look at me, and continues in a more calm and controlled voice. "Sam, what about you? How are you doing?"

As I respond, I think—*another man's dreams were shattered by this war!*

"Art, I'm pretty lucky. All I got in the last battle was a couple of bullet holes and a bayonet slash to my shoulder. My thigh wound is taking a while, but the other wounds are healing pretty fast." I pause, looking for a response. Getting none, I continue. "Art, have you seen any of the other fellows from our outfit since you got here?"

"No, I haven't. They've kept me isolated. What about you? Did Henry and Captain Glazebrook make it?"

"As far as I know, they did. We all made it through the last battle, where I got wounded. I haven't seen any of the other fellows yet. But if you haven't heard, the Rainbow Division sustained massive casualties in our battle for Côte de Châtillon. Taking that damn hill was a bloody mess. We lost a lot of good men. According to a Stars and Stripes article, it was considered a victory and decisive turning point for the whole Meuse-Argonne offensive."

Art looks at me with an outburst of passion and responds angrily. "At what cost? At what cost, Sam?"

After a long pause, I respond in a soft, calm, and somewhat emotional voice. "I can't answer that. I don't know how to answer you, Art. Trading men's lives to gain real estate is a nasty business. I, for one, don't want any more to do with it!"

Art nods his approval as we both slip back into silence, settle into our wheelchairs, and enjoy each other's company for the rest of the afternoon on the terrace.

Over the next several days, we visit each other and share stories. I begin to see a glimmer of the old Art shine through as we interact and rekindle our close relationship. The day we all look forward to finally arrives for Art. Discharge Day! Art was given his discharge papers and is being sent home on the next ship departing for America. He'll return to Cleveland, Ohio, where he plans to live with his parents until he can settle back into civilian life. We exchange hometown addresses and promise to stay in touch upon our return home. Art's future is uncertain, and, as we all do, he fears the unknown. Art believes returning veterans will be neglected shortly after the war is over, if not outright abandoned. Particularly after the parades and speeches —which are sure to follow—fade quickly from the American public's consciousness.

I hope he is wrong!

MARIE PETIT RETURNS

It's November 9th, and I'm anxious to reunite with Marie. One of the French Red Cross nurses told me last night that Marie was transferring in today and should be here by noon. The excitement and anticipation of reuniting with Marie made for a long night of tossing and turning. I got very little sleep waiting for today to begin. I gulped down my breakfast earlier and sit here on my bed anxiously watching for her. The door to our ward opens, and there she is. Our eyes meet as she heads straight for me—what a beautiful woman. I want to get up, rush to her, pick her up, spin her around and hold her body next to mine. Given my current condition, that is not possible. I'll have to be satisfied just thinking about it for now.

Her pace quickens, but not enough to draw attention to herself. Marie approaches, reaches out and embraces me tightly as we savor the moment. Reluctantly and slowly, pulling back, she grabs a chair and sits next to me. Whereupon we begin a lively and joyful conversion.

"Bonjour Sam, happy to see me?"

"Delirious is more like it. Marie, you look terrific!"

"Merci, Monsieur Sam! I have great news; I'm assigned to work in your ward. We'll be together until you're discharged. I have my other duties, but you are my top patient."

"Great. When do you start?"

"Tomorrow officially, so we have the rest of today to spend together. What would you like to do?"

"After the doctors make their rounds will you take me outside in a wheelchair, and we can have some alone time while I enjoy the fresh air?"

Marie stands up, lifts my medical chart off the hook, and begins reading it. As she's looking it over, she proceeds, "Sam, we'll do just that. But first, please tell me how you're feeling. Are your wounds healing?"

"Yes, I'm doing well. I've been told within a day or two, I'll be given some crutches so I can get around here on my own. I'm looking forward to that."

Looking at me while placing the chart back, she continues. "Sam, darling, your chart looks good. You seem to be recovering very nicely. Let me get a wheelchair, and we'll go outside for a while."

For the remainder of this day and the next, Marie and I spend what time we can together.

I'm beginning to believe I'll survive this war.

THE ARMISTICE

It's mid-morning on November 11th, and Marie is sitting by my side, feeding me some oatmeal while we share a cup of coffee. The ward is full of Red Cross nurses tending to the men and doctors making their morning rounds. The sounds and voices of normal daily activities fill the air as we go about our business. It's just the start of another quiet and peaceful day. The doors to our ward fly open and slam against the walls. Our morning tranquility is shattered as an orderly bursts into the ward, yelling in an excited and joyous voice.

"The war is over! The war is over! The Germans surrendered. They signed an Armistice early this morning. The fighting stops at 11:00 this morning."

He exits the ward as fast as he ran in, headed for the next ward. The room is silent. Everyone is momentarily stunned by the news as we process what we heard. What starts out as a low murmur of comments grows to a crescendo of cheers, yelling, and jubilation as we all react in our own way. Hugging, shedding tears, and crying soon follow as celebrating the end of the war begins in earnest. I hear noise from other wards in the school as they are informed. The entire building complex seems to be shaking from the sounds of joy and celebration.

As the doctors and Red Cross nurses flow out of the wards and into the hallways, we, the doughboys, are left alone. Many of the men in this ward are bed-bound, immobile, or otherwise in no condition to celebrate. The room slowly settles into a deathly silence as people in the hallway empty out of the building and into the streets. Many of us look around the ward at the faces of our comrades, making eye contact as if to say, what now? The fighting men, who helped bring about this Armistice, are left alone to ponder our fates. Surely, they're not going to forget this quickly.

Thank God for Marie. She stays, moves among the men, sees to their needs, and comforts those she can. While circulating within the ward, she congratulates and thanks each man personally for their sacrifices and help in saving France. I sit up in my bed, mesmerized as I watch her amazing display of grace, class, kindness, and concern for these men.

My god, I'm a lucky man!

THE END IS NEAR

Over the next several days, the people of Paris continue their wild celebrations over the end of the war. People shout, kiss, play their trumpets, and blow the horns of trucks surrounded by crowds. Any soldier encountered is embraced and carried in triumph. The lights come back on during the evening, and buses begin running again. Parisians sing, dance, and parade all over Paris.

Neither I nor any of the men in this ward witness the wild celebrations. Our medical staff tells us about them as they perform their daily duties. After the first day of the Armistice, things began to settle down in the ward, but it isn't business as usual. As the days progress, there is a discernible change in the overall attitude of many staff members toward us. I sense an attitude emerging from some staff that we are becoming a burden. The war is over. The Allies won, the Germans lost, and there is no reason to worry about the Huns taking Paris. I believe everyone just wants to go home and get on with their lives. For the men in this ward and all the hospitals filled with wounded soldiers, our plight is more difficult and uncertain. Many men will need long-term medical care and attention. I can only hope our leaders don't turn their attention away too quickly from the needs of the men who helped win the peace.

A disturbing rumor has been making its way through the hospital wards concerning the Armistice. The Armistice was signed very early on the morning of November 11th, well before the 11:00 a.m. time for hostilities to cease. With the war set to end by 11:00 a.m., there would have been no need to continue fighting over ground that by 11:01 a.m., men could casually walk over while smoking a cigarette or their pipes.

Apparently, several Allied units were ordered to make full-frontal assaults right up to the time set for the Armistice to begin. Between signing the treaty and its implementation, several hours later, men were killed and wounded. What a tragedy! Surely this can't be true. If so, some men in power couldn't even wait for the war to officially end before they started to forget about the men who fought it.

On a much brighter note, thank goodness for Marie. We have spent considerable time together, and I've enjoyed every minute. I continue to make progress and was issued a set of crutches. With some training, I'm able to maneuver around the building with relative ease. How liberating it is to move freely on my own and take care of myself. My thigh is the only wound still being covered with gauze. If I continue to make progress, I'll be given daily furloughs to spend time visiting various sites around Paris. The end of the tunnel is near for the process they call recovery.

THE STARS AND STRIPES - LATEST EDITION

Marie wakes me up from a sound sleep. She is leaning down and caressing my face as she looks into my eyes with her beautiful green eyes—not a bad way to wake up, with such a lovely, angelic lady looking over me. With excitement in her voice, she says in a loving tone, "Sam, darling, wake up. It's time for breakfast. I have some good news."

"What is it, Marie?" I respond in a low, hesitant voice as I prop myself up on an elbow while still waking up from a restful night.

"You're being given daily furloughs to travel into Paris over the next week. The best news. I'm your guide!"

I forget I'm wounded, and thankfully Marie stops me from trying to lift myself out of bed. Since my wounding in the Argonne, I've been confined to beds and wards. I need to get out and feel like a human being again. The excitement over this news is elating, and questions flow.

"When can we go? What paperwork do I need? What about a uniform? I can't go around Paris without wearing one. Regulations require it. What's the weather like outside? Where should we go first? Can we go to the Louvre? What about the Eiffel Tower, Notre-Dame?"

Marie places a finger on my mouth, telling me to hush. "Oh, so many questions, my love." I've become a little boy again with so many questions. "First, let's eat breakfast, clean you up and then get your uniform. How does that sound?"

"I'm ready. I need to get out of this place. Let's eat. Then it's off to see the supply sergeant for my uniform.

Marie settles me down and gives me a copy of the latest Stars and Stripes newspaper to read while she goes for my breakfast and furlough papers. I watch her walk away and fade from my view. Turning my attention to the newspaper, two stories pique my interest.

∽

SERGEANT STUBBY

Sergeant Stubby, the hero dog of the Great War, saved men from mustard gas, once caught a German by his pants, served in seventeen battles, and helped locate wounded men. Stubby served with the 102nd Infantry Regiment in the trenches. On February 5, 1918, he entered combat and was under constant fire, day and night. In April 1918, during a raid to take Seicheprey, Stubby was wounded in the foreleg by a German grenade. He was sent to the rear for convalescence, and, as he had done on the front, he improved morale. When he recovered from his wounds, Stubby returned to the trenches. This hero dog learned to warn his unit of gas attacks and locate wounded soldiers. Since he could hear the whine of incoming artillery shells before humans could, he became very adept at alerting his unit when to duck for cover. Following the retaking of Chateau-Thierry by the Americans, women of the town made Stubby a chamois coat upon which his many medals were pinned. He was later injured again, in the chest and leg, by a grenade. He ultimately had two wound stripes. With the Armistice, Stubby was retired from active duty and assumed his rightful place in history.

SPANISH FLU

A devastating second wave of the Spanish Flu hit American shores in August as returning soldiers infected with the disease spread it to the general population. Particularly vulnerable were the densely crowded cities of the United States. Without an approved treatment plan, it fell to local mayors and health officials to improvise plans to safeguard citizens. With pressure to appear patriotic during wartime and a censored media downplaying the disease's spread, many made tragic decisions. For example, the city of Philadelphia's response was too little, too late. The director of Public Health and Charities for the city insisted mounting fatalities were not the "Spanish Flu" but instead just the regular flu. So, on September 28, the city went forward with a Liberty Loan parade attended by tens of thousands of Philadelphians. This event resulted in spreading the disease like wildfire. In just ten days, over 1,000 Philadelphians were dead, with another 200,000 sick. Only then did the city close saloons and theaters.

THE LAST ARTICLE INTRIGUES ME, and when Marie returns with breakfast, I pepper her with questions.

"Marie, what is this Spanish Flu? All we've heard was there was an influenza outbreak in some camps and sections on the front-line trenches. When men got sick, they were sent back if they had a severe case, and for those with mild symptoms, they were just given some rest. According to the Stars and Stripes article, it's damn serious!"

While feeding me, she leans in close and responds almost in a whisper. "It is serious. We have had many men come through here who have the flu. We keep them in separate wards and do what we can for them."

She sits back up, pauses, looks around, and once satisfied no one is listening, leans down again, and continues. "This flu is highly contagious and can be very severe. Doctors believe this current wave was created in the trenches due to the closeness and unsanitary conditions of the soldiers. I had a light case before you arrived in Verdun. As you've noticed, we all wear heavy face masks all day when working. It is required for everyone, the doctors, nurses, medics, orderlies, and litter bearers."

"I just thought you were required to wear the masks while on duty. Damn, I had no idea. My god, what else do we have to contend with over here? The brutality and horrific nature of this man-made war, and now a deadly virus, and we can't defend ourselves against it. What else awaits us if we ever return home?"

PARIS FURLOUGHS

Marie gently places the last spoon full of oatmeal in my mouth, wipes the spillage with a napkin, and stands up. Looking down at me with a broad smile spreading across her face, she simply responds, "Enough. You'll be fine. Let's get your uniform, get you ready, and head out into the city. I know a wonderful little restaurant where we can go for your first meal in Paris."

"What's it called?" As if I would know anything about it or any other restaurant in this city.

In her beautiful French accent, she responds, "The Restaurant Procope. It was originally the Café Procope, considered one of the oldest Cafes in Paris, dating back to 1686. It was the hub of the artistic and literary community in 18th and 19th century Paris. Marie Antoinette and Napoleon Bonaparte frequented the restaurant. The original café closed in 1872 and became the Restaurant Procope."

"Sounds interesting. Is the food good? What about their wine?" The look on Marie's face told me all I needed to know. Those are not questions you ask when in Paris, the city of fine cuisine. Mistake noted.

Marie takes me to the Quartermasters location, where I'm provided with a new uniform. Although my right leg is healing well, and I can get around on it, I still use a crutch under my right arm. It's more of a precaution, as I do not want to injure my leg again.

I was measured earlier, and my new uniform was fitted with authorized insignias and First Sergeant stripes, three up and two down. I'm surprised to discover that it's close to my size and fits rather nicely. It consists of a blouse coat, trousers, leggings, brown boots, and a campaign hat. While I'm dressing, Marie excuses herself to go change into appropriate clothing to visit the city and instructs me to wait here until she returns. Upon her return, I'm stunned by how attractive she really is in her French dress and fashionable hat. This is the first time I've seen her without her Red Cross nurse uniform. She walks up to me, and I impulsively pull her to me. We embrace and kiss passionately to the delight of other soldiers who witness this display of affection.

Our afternoon begins with a stroll outside the school. Then a short taxi ride to the restaurant, where we enjoy a wonderful meal of soup du jour, duck cassoulet, sauteed spinach, flatbread, a selection of cheeses, and wine. We spend the rest of our day together, savoring the Parisian lifestyle.

Over the next several days, we spend our time together visiting iconic locations around Paris. Our first stop was The Musee du Louvre. Although it is not open to the general public, Marie's father was able to arrange special tours for us over a two-day period. The Louvre had been shut down early in 1918 when two large shells from a German howitzer exploded in its gardens. We viewed many of its beautiful treasures and works of art during our tours. At times, I found the museum over-whelming and was simultaneously amazed at the collection of Roman, Greek, and Egyptian artifacts spanning over two thou-sand years of Western civilization. I thought the Mona Lisa by Leonardo da Vinci would have been larger and maybe not so dark. Marie enlightened me that it isn't the size of the painting, but its history and the mysteries surrounding it, which is its real treasure.

On the third day, we visited Notre-Dame Cathedral. Marie mentioned that ground was broken here back in 1163, and two centuries later, in 1345, worshipers began participating in Mass. Standing in front of the cathedral and looking up at its facade, it struck me that I was standing where people for over 600 years would have stood and admired this cathedral. Walking through the interior, I was awestruck by the soaring Gothic arches and beautiful stained-glass windows. Marie, who has visited the cathedral many times over the years, acted as my tour guide— what an experience with Marie by my side. I felt at total peace within the walls of the cathedral. At one point, while sitting in the nave, the solace, serenity, and peacefulness of it all hit me hard. I was overcome with emotion thinking of all the men I saw die and those I killed. If I carry these memories with me into Notre-Dame, a place of worship with the feeling of God's presence surrounding me, can I ever rid myself of these demons?

The next day was gorgeous. We visited the Eiffel Tower, which only took two years, two months, and five days to build and opened to the public on May 15, 1889, when the World's Fair began. You can see the tower from miles away. As we walked up to the tower, I was amazed by its massive structure and height. I've never seen anything like it before. Holding Marie close to me, we rode its elevator to the top. Stepping out onto the third level and into a strong cold wind, we gazed upon a sweeping view of the city below. I pulled Marie close to me as we bundled up to stay warm and slowly walked around the small platform while Marie pointed out many iconic locations. We enjoyed lunch on the first level at the Brébant, which is considered a chic restaurant, and then took in the views from this level. On more than one occasion, we embraced each other and showed our affection. I was told it's a natural and spontaneous reaction that many experience when visiting the tower here in Paris.

During our many trips around Paris, we always found some time most every day to spend at Montmartre enjoying the views from the highest hill in Paris. From this hilltop, standing on the steps of the Sacre-Coeur Basilica, I express my undying love for Marie. Here, I got down on one knee, held her hands in mine, and asked her to marry me. Although I had asked her earlier in a moment of spontaneity, this was the place I had intended to ask for her hand in marriage. When asked, she responded with a passionate embrace and loving kiss. "Oui! Yes, my love. My dearest Sam. I'm yours for all of time."

Paris truly is the "City of Love." I begin to feel alive again and hope this will start me on the road to recovery from the terrible nightmares which occur with regularity.

J'adore Paris!

24

NEW ASSIGNMENT

MILITARY AWARDS

With the end of November approaching, I'm informed of several events affecting me personally. My recovery is progressing rapidly, and I'll be retained in Paris through December until I make a full recovery. With the doctor's release, I should be reassigned to another unit starting the first of next year. Sometime during December, I'm to be awarded several medals for various actions on the battlefield. They'll be presented by General Douglas McArthur and French General Ferdinand Foch. Marie will remain in Paris with the 57th Field Hospital until the end of the year, at which time she'll be released from duty. Captain Glazebrook has been assigned as the new CO of the 1st Battalion of the 165th Infantry Regiment of the Rainbow Division. Sergeant Henry Miller is his new First Sergeant. The 165th Regiment has been assigned occupation duty in Remagen, Germany. They are scheduled to return to America in April 1919.

For the remainder of my stay at the hospital, I've been

assigned to a smaller, more private room with three other men awaiting release. We are considered healthy enough to manage on our own.

REUNITED-CAPTAIN GLAZEBROOK AND SERGEANT MILLER

Marie is on duty today, so I'm on my way to the Café de la Paix, near The Musee du Louvre, to meet up with Captain Glazebrook and Henry. We haven't seen each other since I was wounded and evacuated. I'm looking forward to reuniting, sharing stories, and drinking French wine.

Approaching the café, I see them waiting for me, and I pick up my pace. I'm no longer dependent on crutches, but still, I have a slight limp in my step. Closing the distance, we exchange customary hand salutes and shake hands, Captain Glazebrook slaps me on the back, and then Henry grabs me with his usual bear hug.

"Not too hard, Henry. I'm still a little sore in the chest." My face must show discomfort as I strain to keep from wincing in pain. He immediately releases me, steps back, and continues to shake my hand. It's good to see these two men again. The last time we were together was on top of Côte de Châtillon with Germans trying to kill us.

"Sam, damn, I'm sorry, I should have known." He says in a low, sheepish voice but with a huge grin on his face.

Captain Glazebrook directs us toward an outside table and motions for a waiter to bring three glasses of wine.

"Sam, you look good. That little limp you have, is it permanent or just temporary? Have they been treating you well? How do you feel?"

"Thanks, Captain, I'm doing well, and yes, they've been good to me. My thigh is almost healed. According to the doctors, I should be able to get around without limping very soon. It's great to see both of you again. I miss the fellows in the company but not the action. I'm just thankful it's over, and none of us must go back on the line."

The waiter places three glasses of wine on the table and informs us it's on the house. We thank him and, while standing, raise our glasses in a salute to the men we served with and those we lost. The café is full of other men in French, English, and American military uniforms, as well as many Parisians. Seeing us toast, several people near us stand up and raise their glasses of wine as they join us. In a spontaneous gesture of goodwill, unity, and comradeship between our countries, everyone stands and looks to Captain Glazebrook to make another toast. In a moment of emotional solidarity, he raises his glass and speaks.

"To all the men who fought, those that died, and those who suffer from their wounds. To those who gave us victory, we salute them and shall never forget them. I offer this toast." He raises his glass as everyone joins him. He immediately follows up with, "Vive la France!"

There are few dry eyes in the café. I'm sure many of us are reflecting on our own experiences, which brought us here, together, at this moment in time. Cheers and hugs erupt throughout the café. I wish Marie were here to see this. Clearly, Captain Glazebrook is intelligent, sophisticated, well-spoken, and politically astute. He will go far in life when he returns home.

The café patrons settle back into their chairs and resume conversations. We continue with ours as Captain Glazebrook enlightens Henry and me on the Rainbow Division's future assignment in Germany. He tells us that some American troops have already entered Germany and are viewed as more of a curiosity to the German people than a conquering foe. They have found Germany to be clean, unscarred by the war, full of food, and filled with charming frauleins and hospitable people. In many cases, shortly after the troops billeted in, they found themselves in local bars and restaurants, making the acquaintance of local girls. The relationships that will grow out of these interactions and fraternization may be the biggest challenge. When the division arrives in Remagen, their main tasks will be supervising and reporting on the conditions of the city. This will include maintaining law and order, arrests, food supplies for the population, or other matters of concern for civilian administration.

He then turns his attention to me and provides an overview of what will occur on December 1st at the medal awards ceremony. Five men, including myself, will be presented with medals for valor. General McArthur will present the American medals and French General Foch the French medals. The ceremony will be held in the Court of Honor of the Les Invalides in Paris. Les Invalides is a complex of buildings containing museums and monuments, all relating to the military history of France. There is also a hospital and retirement home for war veterans. It is a grand complex with parade grounds that are routinely used for various military award ceremonies.

Until now, I wasn't sure what I was being awarded or for what. He looks directly at me with a sense of purpose and pride.

"Sam, you will be presented with the American Distinguished Service Cross (DSC) for your actions in the second battle of the Marne and a second DSC for your actions in the battle for Cheppy. This is the second-highest award for valor that can be awarded to an American doughboy. You'll also receive two War Wound Ribbons for your wounds sustained at the Marne and the battle for Côte de Châtillon." Looking at me with those intense eyes, he tries to gauge my reaction. I'm not sure what he sees, but I'm at a loss for words. He continues.

"The Legion of Honor is France's highest award for heroism and will be presented to you by the French General Ferdinand

Foch. Foch became the Allied Commander-in-Chief in late March 1918. He is credited with successfully coordinating the French, British and American efforts, which ultimately defeated the Germans. He accepted the German cessation of hostilities and was present at the signing of the Armistice on November 11, 1918. He is the top commander of the Allies."

The captain slides his chair back, stands, extends his hand, and says, "Any questions, Sam?"

I'm stunned and feel like I have just entered a surreal world, another dimension. There were many men out there around me who faced the same dangers, took risks, and helped take our objectives. What makes me so special. I didn't do what I did on the battlefield for medals. I did it for the men around me. We rely on each other; it's not a one-man show. It's an honor to be recognized in this fashion. But I...

Henry shakes me back into reality. I slowly rise from my chair, face the captain, extend my hand, and simply respond. "No questions, sir. I'm honored!"

We shake hands. He steps back, comes to attention, and presents me with a snappy hand salute. This is an honor. NCOs salute officers, not the other way around. When this is done, it's a show of respect well beyond just words. I immediately return his gesture and struggle to keep from showing my inner emotions. I'm deeply moved. Henry stands, grabs my hand, and shakes it vigorously while adding his congratulations.

I'm just another doughboy who did what I was told and to the best of my ability. Nearly every man I served with while part of the Rainbow Division falls into that category. There are very few exceptions. Why I'm receiving these awards is a question beyond my understanding currently. Maybe sometime later in life, this will take on a higher level of significance and meaning to me personally. At this time, I just consider myself very fortunate to have survived this madness and be going home to pursue my life with Marie.

25

AMERICAN WAR BRIDES

NEW FRIENDS AND PLANS

Later that evening, Captain Glazebrook, Henry, and I return to the Field Hospital, where we meet Marie after her shift. This is a pre-planned Parisian evening for all four of us—going out on the town together. Marie is waiting for us when we return. She is stunning as we walk up to her. Her evening outfit showcases her feminine qualities, her smile radiates beauty and confidence, and her grace and style impress both Captain Glazebrook and Henry.

Marie extends her hand to me as I clasp it in mine. Looking at the men with me, she says, "Sam, aren't you going to introduce us?"

I was so into the moment absorbing her beauty that the presence of my comrades escaped me. Looking at her, I make the introductions.

"Captain Glazebrook, I want you to meet my fiancée, Marie Petit."

Glancing at me, then turning to gaze upon Marie, he looks at her with genuine admiration and extends his hand. Marie extends her hand for him to hold while the captain responds eloquently. "Mademoiselle, it's an honor for me and a genuine pleasure to finally meet you. Sam talks about you all the time. I can certainly see why. He is a good man, and the two of you together will make a wonderful couple."

She returns his gaze and says, "Captain Glazebrook, thank you, sir. Sam has spoken many times of you and holds you in the highest regard. I'm happy to make your acquaintance." He responds with a small head bow and releases her hand. Stepping back, he again looks over at me. His warm smile conveys a sense of pride and happiness for me.

He continues in a calm, fatherly manner, "One more thing, you two! From this point forward, I insist you call me by my first name, Charles." Slowly drawing in a breath of air as a smile crosses his face, he says, "Sam, we'll need to keep our military protocol of name and rank when on duty. Understood?"

"Yes, sir, not a problem."

Marie responds eloquently, "Oui, Monsieur Charles Glazebrook."

Looking at Henry, I introduce him to Marie. Henry approaches her, extends his arms out as if to give a bear hug, pulls them back, and smiles. "You're a lady, not one of the boys. I'm very pleased to meet you. I don't know what you see in this bloke, but he's a good man, and he'll make you proud." Henry's quite the gentleman and only extends his hand, taking hers in his and lightly holding it while they exchange pleasantries.

With introductions complete, the four of us head out for a night in Paris. Over the course of the evening, Charles explains to Marie and me the requirements and process for obtaining permission to marry. Marie has another set of requirements to follow when she's ready to immigrate to America. Charles assures us he'll obtain the required documents and resolve any hurdles we encounter along the way. We only need to set a date for our wedding and a timeframe for Marie to join me in the United States.

Marie shares with Charles that we wish to marry before the end of December and would like to do so the day before Christmas in her hometown city of Versailles. She lives in Porchefontaine, a working-class residential neighborhood southeast of Versailles. Her father is a mid-level government bureaucrat working with the French Parliament. She also shares with Charles that we visited her parents earlier in the week and obtained permission for her to marry me and move to America. Armed with this information, Charles assures Marie and me that he will take care of what needs to be done. Feeling confident in our immediate future, we continue celebrating well into the early morning hours of the next day. This is Paris. The lights are back on, the war is over, and hordes of Parisians are celebrating throughout the city.

MEDAL CEREMONY

It's December 1st. The weather is cooperating. The day is clear, cold, and sunny. I'm standing at attention in the middle of the Court of Honor at the Les Invalides. Two Companies from my battalion are standing in military formation in their dress uniforms behind me. Captain Glazebrook is standing in front of them, commanding the unit, and to his side is Henry. A company of French infantrymen is standing at attention in their dress uniforms to the right of the American unit. A French military band is playing The Star-Spangled Banner after playing La Marseillaise, the French anthem. Around the courtyard, separated by rope lines, are many civilian dignitaries and Marie and her family. What a glorious sight. It's a very proud moment for me.

After the American Anthem, General McArthur steps in front of me, and with his aide assisting, he pins a DSC on my uniform dress coat, chest high. He then pins a second DSC, followed by two War Ribbons to my dress coat. In a deep, authoritative, and calm voice, he says. "First Sergeant McCormick, the United States of America is proud of you. I'm proud of you. You epitomize the best of our countrymen. Your deeds on the battlefields of history will be remembered, never forgotten. Well done, son! If there is anything I can ever do for you, First Sergeant, just reach out to me."

"Yes, sir, thank you, sir!"

He shakes my hand, steps back, and renders me a snappy hand salute.—which I return. He is replaced by the French General Foch, who steps forward and to my front. Assisted by his aide, he places the French Legion of Honor on my dress coat. Moving closer, he puts his hands on my shoulders and pulls me toward him, kissing my right and left cheeks.

Stepping back, he says, "Sergeant McCormick, les François personnes vous remercient. The French people thank you!" He presents me with a hand salute, I respond, and he returns to his position next to General McArthur.

Following the ceremony, we adjourn to a Reception Hall inside Les Invalides, where I am joined by Marie, her family, Captain Glazebrook, and Henry. After introductions, our group mingles and socializes with the other guests well into the afternoon. Immediately after the awards ceremony concluded on the field, I never saw the Generals again. They moved on to socialize within their own circle of friends, associates, and power players, each in pursuit of their personal goals and objectives.

OUR WEDDING

True to his word, Captain Charles Glazebrook, with the help of an unknown benefactor, rumored to be General McArthur, arranged everything for Marie and me. We are married in the early afternoon on December twenty-third in a small church near her home, followed by a reception held at her parents' home that lasts well into the evening. Those present are Captain Glazebrook—my best man, Henry—my groomsman, several men from my infantry company, and Marie's family and friends. The wedding is well attended, beautifully performed in French, and very lovely. Several of Marie's attractive single French lady friends are present. The fellows from my company waste no time during the reception making their acquaintances.

When the evening ends, Charles pulls me aside and informs me I'm being sent home sometime in January. I'll be receiving an honorable discharge from the United States Army effective the first of January. When I ask how he did it, he simply shrugs and says, "Consider it a gift from several friends and admirers."

Marie's immigration to the United States was also approved. She will join me by the end of February after spending some time here in Paris at a holding camp. This information adds a beautiful ending to our reception party and is a great gift. The war is over, and everyone just wants to go home and get on with their lives. With the uncertainty surrounding everyone's future over here, this could not have come at a better time. I consider us both very fortunate and look forward to our time together before we must part again, albeit for a short time.

After much hugging, kissing, shaking hands, and saying our goodbyes to everyone, we walk through a line of people throwing flower petals. At the end of the line, we are whisked into a Parisian taxi by Henry, who managed to sneak a kiss from my new bride before she settled into the cab. We travel to Montmartre for our honeymoon at the Hotel des Arts-Montmartre. Checking in just after midnight, we retire to our room on the top floor. The room has a large window, which, when open, provides a beautiful view looking out over parts of the city bathed in lights. It has been a beautiful day and evening, and the best was yet to come. I hang a "do not disturb" sign on our door and close and lock it.

OUR HONEYMOON

While enjoying our view, we begin caressing each other, followed by passionate kissing. We have never truly been alone before this night to explore the depths of our love for each other. I remove my uniform jacket, tie, and shirt and throw them over a chair. With Marie's help, I slowly disrobe her while gazing upon the full beauty of her naked body. Marie, silhouetted in front of the window with city lights shining in the background, is angelic in her beauty. This is a moment I have been dreaming about since we first met. With Marie's help, I make short order of the rest of my army uniform. Here we stand, our naked bodies fully embracing and caressing each other slowly as our sexual desires blossom from within. Our heartbeats increase, our loins ache, our bodies begin to quiver, and our breathing heightens. I pick Marie up, carry her into the bedroom, slowly place her on the bed, and lay down next to her. Our marriage is consummated as we make passionate love well into the early morning hours of Christmas Eve Day. After a light breakfast just before noon, we venture outside and begin our first full day as Mr. and Mrs. Samuel McCormick.

For three more days at Montmartre, we immerse ourselves in the cancan and cabaret nightlife, enjoy fine foods and wine at local restaurants, coffee and pastries at sidewalk cafes, and the bohemian artists practicing their craft. Our late evenings are devoted to making love well into the early morning hours of each succeeding day. Marie is a beautiful woman with stunning features. When coupled with her lovely green eyes, long dark hair, and intoxicating French accent, she becomes irresistible to me.

I'm a very lucky man and look forward to sharing the rest of my life with Marie.

HOLDING CAMPS

The American Expeditionary Force command structure discovered very quickly after the war ended those marriages between American soldiers and European women, mostly French, some British and Belgium, and surprisingly some Germans, were deemed controversial. In America, President Woodrow Wilson expressed his concern these marriages could reflect poorly on the AEF's image. American families, particularly mothers, were concerned that loose and immoral French women would take advantage of their innocent and inexperienced doughboys while in France.

The French people and their government took offense to this view of French women and feared their daughters would be abused and abandoned by American soldiers. After taking under advisement all the concerns expressed by both countries, General Pershing issued regulations regarding the requirements for American soldiers seeking to marry European women. Once the regulations were in place, the AEF was faced with the issue of transporting war brides and any children they may have to America. Three holding camps were established in France to accommodate and process war brides and their children.

United States citizenship laws allow foreign-born wives of American servicemen to become American citizens by marriage. These camps are structured to help prepare war brides to live in

America, and they can be challenging for the women. They are subject to morning inspections of their living quarters which are very similar to soldiers' experience during their military training. Physical examinations are performed routinely to ensure they are free of venereal diseases. Classes in the English language, American geography, American laws, customs, history, and cooking are offered. The French could probably teach the Americans a thing or two when it comes to food and cooking.

When deemed ready and the required documents and transportation have been arranged, war brides are transported to the United States on ocean liners or troop transport ships. These are often referred to as bridal ships or honeymoon detachments. In their own way, these women are as brave as the men they married. They're leaving their homes for a country whose manners, customs, language, way of life, and thoughts are different and strange to them. It takes courage, resolve, confidence, trust, and love for the men they married.

26

GOING HOME

Since our marriage, Marie and I have been living with her parents and enjoying our time together. They are both wonderful people, and I have come to appreciate how much Marie owes her personality and character to her parents. They have done a terrific job of raising a fine daughter. I can only hope we do the same with any children we may bring into the world.

The week I've been waiting for has arrived. I'm preparing to ship out and return home. Marie has been assigned to a holding camp near her home and will report there by week's end. Henry received good news, he's being released from the military and will be headed home within a few weeks. He must first turn over his duties to a new First Sergeant who recently transferred from the States. Charles, Henry, and I exchanged addresses and will maintain contact with each other.

Captain Glazebrook will be returning to the United States when his unit is relieved of its assignment in Remagen. They should be going home at the end of April 1919. He'll return to his position as an investment banker in New York with JP Morgan &

Co., managing accounts related to United States Steel Companies. Henry is returning to Canton, Ohio, and resuming his job with Republic Steel. He made it very clear that if I wanted to go into the steel business and move to the Canton area, he would secure me a job with the company. They're both good men, good friends, and fellows I can count on when needed as they can me.

On the day of my departure, January 22, 1919, Marie, her parents, and I sit drinking coffee at the Paris train station, waiting for me to board the train to Brest, France. I'm sailing back to the United States on board the U.S.S. Mercury, an old German ship, which has been serving as an American troop transport. The vessel will depart from Brest Harbor, sail to New York City, and from there, I'll take a train home. Marie and I both struggle to contain our emotions about my departure, and it's not easy. Marie is concerned that I may regret marrying her when I return home without her. That's a tough one. I've been doing my best to assure her that it simply won't happen. Looking into her eyes and holding her close to me, I say in a low, compassionate, loving, and caring voice. "Marie, darling, before the war, when my life was just working, cards, some drinking, and occasionally dating local women, I didn't give any thought to settling down someday. I've met several women over the years and was happy to call them friends. I never felt the desire or urge to share a table with any of them for the rest of my life. Not until I met you!"

She looks into my eyes as tears begin to swell in hers. I continue, "That's not the trenches, loneliness, or lack of female companionship speaking. It's you! You're the one! There is no one else I want to share my life with but you. Just you. I can't envision my life without you in it. If it took this war and the Huns to bring us together, then so be it. I love you and will love you for the rest of my life."

Marie responds, pulls me closer to her as we embrace and

kiss passionately. We're oblivious to the people around us. We're in our own universe, just the two of us. Marie has that effect on me. Her father must separate us when the last call to board the train is announced. Separating, I hug her parents, climb up on the steps to the train car as it pulls out of the station, and stand there until I can no longer see them.

My trip home begins.

27

WELCOME HOME DOUGHBOY

THE SHIP

There are several doughboys on the train going to Brest Harbor for transport home. Arriving at 4:00 a.m. in the city of Brest, we are hustled off the train, lined up in formations, and marched to waiting trucks. From there, we are driven to the harbor. At the pier, we disembark the trucks and find ourselves staring up at our ship, the USS Mercury, silhouetted against the morning sky. Not very impressive. The ship looks like it's been at sea a very long time and could use a massive overhaul. What a contrast, an old rusting, grimy-looking ship tied up at the dock and a beautiful sunrise peeking over the bay behind it. I just hope it is seaworthy.

While onboard the ship and sailing back to the States, I write an ongoing letter to Marie about my trip home. When I arrive in Wellsville, Ohio, I'll send it to her in care of the holding company to which she has been assigned in France.

～

Dearest Marie,

I trust this letter will find you in good spirits and doing well when you receive it. Instead of writing you a letter every day, I've decided to write one long letter treating it more like a diary. When I get back home to Wellsville, I will mail this letter to you. Since we'll be at sea for fourteen days, with no mail service, it won't matter anyway.

I'll write down my thoughts and observations as they occur during my trip home. They should, hopefully, give you an idea of what transpired on my way back to the States. I believe the biggest issue most of us will be dealing with is "boredom." Our daily routine can't be that different and exciting.

Well, here it goes.

We arrived in the city of Brest at four in the morning and were immediately placed on trucks and driven to the pier next to our ship, the USS Mercury. It didn't take them long to get us organized and onboard. I was placed in a large troop bay with two hundred Texans headed home as a unit. Since I'm a First Sergeant, they allowed me to pick out a bunk in the NCO section of the bay. Of course, I chose a lower bunk in a relatively secluded area.

I've made friends with many of these men. They're a good bunch, and I like them. But they are certainly a rowdy bunch. I would have thought that after all the fighting we did in France, they would just want to relax, sleep, and be left alone. That is not the case. They like to drink, play cards, particularly Texas Hold'em, and occasionally they fight. I regularly join some of them in friendly games of poker, and they share their liquor with me. I don't know how they got the liquor on board, but American soldiers can be very resourceful when challenged and inspired. Although I haven't witnessed any fighting, I have it from reliable sources that some money exchanged hands a few times when fistfights broke out, and the fellows placed bets on who will remain standing.

Most of our trip back to the States has been over calm seas. However, we occasionally run into some rough weather, which causes our ship to pitch and rock severely. I find it very difficult to hold down my food and never seem to get used to it. I believe they call it "seasickness." After this long sea trip, I vow never again to step foot on another ship going out to sea.

This ship is old, rusty beyond belief. It needs extensive overhauling, equipment constantly breaks down or doesn't function well, and is overflowing with doughboys. We must eat in shifts and take turns on the open decks to get some fresh air, sunshine, and exercise. Our living conditions in the troop bays are cramped. It smells of oil, unbathed men, smoke, overflowing heads (Navy toilets), and vomit from men getting seasick when the ship is in bad weather. There are no portholes on most of the troop decks, which doesn't help with ventilation. We eat, sleep, and spend much of our time in these bay areas where the air is stale, foul-smelling, and just plain offensive. It isn't as bad as life in the trenches, but it certainly isn't pleasant.

The food is not bad, but it does not compare with your French cuisine. Thanks to you, I'm just a little spoiled and picky now when it comes to food and wine. God, I miss you. I love you very much.

Our return home is at hand, and we have sighted land. As we sail closer to the shoreline of America, the fellows pour out from their sleeping bays and crowd the decks of the ship. There must be over a thousand men on the open decks of this ship as they take over every available spot from which to view our return. Sailing by the Statue of Liberty sends thrills through the hearts of many of the men. We know we are home!

We have finally docked at Pier Number 4 in Hoboken and

have been transferred to the SS Washington, which ferried us over to Long Island City. We were then transferred by trucks to a nearby military camp. There were no masses of people waiting to greet us, no parades, just stateside soldiers herding us around for processing. Most of the men on the ship are returning as units, such as the Texans with whom I quartered. These units are being transported home together by train, with their departures being staggered to promote efficiency. Men such as I, who are returning home with discharge papers and not part of a unit, are set up in a holding company area. Here we wait on travel arrangements to be completed for a train trip to our home cities.

I remained overnight in the camp and was taken to the train station early this morning. I'm now on the train headed home to Wellsville. It's been a long two-week journey to get to this point, but I'm close; it's almost over. I'll stop now and mail this to you from home.

I miss you greatly and long to be with you again. Your smile, your love, your beautiful features, your lovely voice, and most of all, just being with you and sharing every moment together is what I live for.

Je t'aime, Marie!

Yours always, Sam

∾

WELLSVILLE RECEPTION

A WEEK BEFORE LEAVING FRANCE, I sent a telegram to William Butler, the owner of K.T.&K. Pottery Company. Before I left for France, he agreed to watch over my home, rent it out to suitable families in my absence, and guarantee my old job back when I returned. After I departed for France, the communication between William and me grew more distant and ceased altogether months ago. In my telegram, I let him know I was returning home and should be in Wellsville by the 15th of February and would appreciate it if he would ensure my house was vacant and ready for me to move in. I never received a response from him and don't know what to expect when I arrive.

The train pulls into Wellsville around noon. There is a heavy snowfall in progress, and the platform is covered in several inches of slushy white snow with some visible patches of ice. Very few people are outside, and those that are, move quickly to get out of the weather. Carrying my duffle bag full of souvenirs from France, I step off the train onto the platform and make my way to the terminal. I must be careful not to slip for fear of hurting my right leg. The limp is gone, but I still tend to favor my leg. Covering the distance to the door slowly, I enter the terminal as if I were walking through a German minefield. It's warm, the smell of burning coal hangs in the air, and a wisp of hot java catches my attention. There are very few people inside, none of whom I recognize. Since my parents are gone, and I have no relatives living in this country, I'm on my own. I was hoping William or one of his two sons would be here to greet me and give me a lift to the house. I guess not. Welcome home, doughboy!

After taking a moment to have some java, I catch a taxi ride to my house. I have no key, and no one with a house key met me at the train station. Pulling up to the front of my home, memories come flowing out as I recall happier times being raised here by my parents. It's a modest two-story, three-bedroom, wooden-framed house painted white. White was a popular color at the time, maybe because it was cheap and there was plenty to go around. It was also my dad's favorite color. He even had the curb painted white in front of the house. I instruct the taxi driver to wait for me to ensure I can enter my home.

Walking over the snow-covered sidewalk and up the steps to

the porch, I'm struck by what I see. The place is in a state of total disrepair and looks abused. The paint is chipping off the front porch walls. The windows are cracked, and the main door is loose on its hinges. Since I don't have the key and it's locked, I can't get in the house. Peering inside through the two main windows on the porch, my heart sinks with despair. The place is a mess. Furniture looks broken and worn out, the walls need repainting, and garbage is stacked up in several corners of the two rooms I can see. This infuriates me. Rage begins to overtake me. I storm off the porch and walk around the house, checking to see what other damage may have been inflicted. Approaching the back porch, I find the door locked and the two back windows cracked. Peering into the kitchen, I see the same pathetic conditions that were in the front. I've seen enough. Furious, I return to the taxi and instruct the driver to take me to the Pottery Company.

I don't know the driver, but I make an inquiry in a stern, authoritative voice.

"Have you been here long, and do you have any idea who has been living in my house?"

He says, "I've been here for about six months and am still learning my way around town. As to your home, I've been told it has been rented out several times to transit people working at the Pottery Company for short periods of time. They came and then went! Many of them."

"Damn! Get me to the Pottery as quickly as you can."

Pulling up to the main gate, I pay the driver, grab my bag, cautiously make my way to the main office, and enter. Once inside, I place my bag in a corner and head directly for William Butler's office. My mind is racing. Building within me is a growing rage I'm struggling to contain. I'm not sure what will happen when I see him. This is not 'no man's land" that I'm in, and he's not a Hun trying to kill me, but it sure feels like I've been taken advantage of and violated. That does not sit well with me.

Removing my overcoat to display my uniform and the medals pinned to it, I throw it on a chair, blast past the secretary and enter his office, slamming the door behind me. He's sitting there enjoying a cigar when the door slams shut. Startled, he looks up, sees rage in my eyes, and his relaxed mood instantly changes to fear as his facial expression becomes one of momentary panic. He's an old man who looks like he has one foot in the grave, overweight, sloven in his appearance, his breathing is labored, and he struggles to move around in his chair, probably suffering from severe arthritis.

Relax, I'm not here to kill anyone! But you're going to tell me what the hell has been going on in my home during my absence.

Closing the distance to his desk, I stop and stare down at him. An intense feeling of anger is boiling up within me as I struggle to keep it under control. I almost feel sorry for him. He looks like he is about to have a stroke. In a loud, irate, matter-of-fact voice, I confront him.

"Mr. Butler, you remember me? I'm the son of a former senior manager for your company who was a loyal employee. I was one of your low-level laborers who was hoping to follow in my father's footsteps."

I pause and give him a chance to react. He just stares at me with a look of fear in his eyes. With no response, I continue. "You and I had an agreement, I thought, for you to manage my property while I was gone. I just came from there, and it's a mess. I understand you've been running people through there as temporary help for your factory. That's not what I had in mind when I entrusted you with my family home."

He finally regains some sense of presence and responds meekly. "Sam, I didn't expect you back so soon and planned to clean the place up."

"Not good enough, William. I trusted you, and you took advantage of me! What about my job here? Is it still being held for me, or was that just more empty words?"

He takes his time responding as he looks at my uniform with the medals and my First Sergeant stripes. He's slowly coming to the realization that I'm no longer the boy he knew. I've become a man, fully capable of taking matters into my own hands. His response is measured and delivered slowly in a calm, low voice.

"Sam, while you were gone, things back here were not particularly easy for us. We had to run our factory and look for workers wherever we could find them. Now, with the war over and men returning in droves, we have more men wanting to work than there are jobs. I'm afraid it will be some time before we have an opening. Given the circumstances, it could be tough for you to find a job for some time."

Responding curtly, "I'll take that as a no!"

He does not respond, and I detect a smirk spreading across his face. Stepping back from his desk, my eyes staring fiercely into his, I give him an ultimatum.

"Mr. Butler, you will see to it over the next three weeks that my home is fully restored to its original condition and new furniture is delivered and set up. This will be done to my satisfaction! If not, you will not believe the pressure I can bring down on you, your family, and this company. Trust me. You don't want to go there! Do we understand each other? A simple yes or no will do."

The smirk is gone, his eyes show concern, and he simply nods and says, "Yes!"

Walking out of his office, I run into his two sons, who had been summoned by the secretary. They're about my age—with medium builds, both are well dressed and groomed. They're used to living a good, comfortable life, and I'm sure they missed out on an opportunity to serve their country. Looking past me and into their dad's office, they see he's not been harmed. They stop, step back out of my way and allow me to pass.

As I pass him, the youngest son blurts out in a sarcastic voice, "You're damn lucky you didn't hurt my dad. Oh, and Sam, we sure appreciate you letting us use your house as a barracks for our transit workers while you were defending France."

I stop abruptly, turn to face him, and stare directly into his eyes with an intense hatred showing in mine. I respond with my command voice and in a loud, gruff manner. "Don't you two assholes try my patience today, for if you do, you will regret it!"

Neither son speaks as the smirks on their faces slowly fade away, and fear shows through. The younger son who spoke is visibly shaken as he steps back further and averts eye contact with me. The older son just looks at me like a deer would when caught at night in the headlights of a rapidly approaching car. I continue, "I'll be seeing one or both of you fellows later as your company is repairing my home over the next couple of weeks."

I turn and continue without incident to the building's front entrance. Gathering up my overcoat and duffle bag, I ask the receptionist to call me a taxi. On my way home, I have the taxi driver stop at the post office where I mail my letter to Marie.

HOME REPAIRS AND NEW OPPORTUNITIES

I spend my first two days home cleaning a bedroom to make it suitable enough to sleep in, fixing the upstairs bathroom to use its amenities, and repairing the kitchen so I can store and cook some food.

Mr. Butler delegates to his older son the responsibility of repairing and restoring my family home to its original condition. The younger son has an insufferable attitude, and it would be a bad idea to send him. For the next three weeks, the older son oversees the installation of new appliances, bathroom fixtures, plumbing, and a coal heating system. The house is repainted on the inside, wallpaper replaced where appropriate, and hardwood floors cleaned and resurfaced. When completed, new furniture is delivered to my home. Because we're still in the middle of a harsh winter, I agree to have a team return in the spring to complete any exterior repairs and painting they can't finish now.

During this time, I make inquiries around town seeking employment opportunities and quickly learn there are none. While over four million American men were serving in Europe, jobs in this country were filled by anyone they could hire. Women found opportunities in the workforce, foreign labor was brought into some locations, and younger boys and girls were pressed into service for many unskilled labor jobs. In essence, the workforce was staffed and maintained during our absence. Now with all the men returning home, competition for jobs is tight. Many individuals hired during the war are now skilled at their jobs and do not wish to be replaced. Why would management want to do so? There is no cost-benefit to having returning soldiers, unskilled in many cases, replacing workers who have some experience and training in their current jobs thanks to the war.

Jobs are available in various sectors of the economy and regions around the country. However, Wellsville is not one of them. I'm being forced to look for other opportunities in other areas. Many of the men returning will find similar disruptions in their lives as they try to assimilate back into American society and find decent jobs. I resolve to expand my search to industries with a future regardless of their location. I prefer to remain in Ohio since this is my home state. While I was in Europe, I had my monthly pay forwarded to my local bank in Wellsville for safe-keeping. I should have enough to live on until my situation stabilizes.

As the end of February approaches, I receive a telegraph from

Henry. It is good news, and it could not have come at a better time.

Sam, you old bloke. How are you? I'm back home in Canton. Next Monday, I start working at my old job in the steel mill. If you're looking for work and don't mind the heat, I'm sure you could get a job here. They're looking for good men. Let's get together, Henry.

IN FEBRUARY, a list of Wellsville, Ohio boys who served with the American Expeditionary Force in Europe was published and circulated in the community. There are 366 names listed. Neither one of Mr. Butler's sons are on the list. Those who died are identified. Among them are three of my closest friends. The loss of my parents and closest friends and the memories this hometown holds for me make it impossible to stay here and try to settle back into the community. My nightmares have resumed, and my respiratory and digestive health issues are acting up again. There is not much medical care available here. It's time for me to move on and pursue opportunities in another location, preferably one with suitable medical facilities. Marie is coming to America soon, and with her by my side, I believe our future will be bright and hold many joyous moments for us.

It's time to move on.

28

REPUBLIC IRON AND STEEL COMPANY

MEETING THE FAMILY

Last night we had another winter storm blow through, which deposited a foot of fresh snow. The view from my train car is magnificent as we travel through beautiful Ohio countryside covered in glistening snow. I've always enjoyed the winter months when heavy snows cover everything. The world looks pure, peaceful, and innocent. It's a moment in time that feels like I need a clean slate and can start over, change direction, move forward, and pursue my dreams.

Having taken up Henry on his offer, I'm going to Canton. Enjoying the view while drinking hot coffee, I feel relaxed and rested as the train rocks back and forth, bumps up and down, and clunks over the rails toward our destination of East Canton. There's a certain rhythm to these sounds, which I find comforting while reflecting on my situation. I'm a newly married man with no job, no opportunities in Wellsville, and a restored family home that is debt-free. Unfortunately, there is very little demand for housing in Wellsville, and trying to sell my house will present a challenge.

Marie wrote in her last letter that she sails for America on the first of March and should arrive in New York City by mid-March. Time is short. I need to pursue opportunities and make decisions. My priority is to secure a job with a future, settle into a small community, build friendships, and establish a future for Marie and me.

How hard can that be?

Arriving at the small depot in East Canton, I find Henry standing under the outside shelter waiting for me when I step off the train. Carrying a small travel bag over my shoulder and being careful not to slip, I make my way over to him.

"Henry, damn, I almost didn't recognize you without your muddy uniform and combat gear. It's great to see a friendly face. You're looking fit."

Waiting for it, here it comes. The "Henry" bear hug. Thank goodness I'm healed. He closes the distance, wraps his big arms around my shoulders, and gives me a bear hug that only Henry can give. Releasing me from his bear hug, we shake hands as he takes the travel bag from my shoulder and slings it over his.

"Sam, you're looking good yourself. I'm glad you could make the trip. I'm really looking forward to catching up with you and hearing all about Marie." He turns to leave the station and says, "Follow me and be careful out here. It's slippery."

"Thanks, Henry."

I follow him through the depot, which is not crowded since it's a Sunday afternoon, out the front entrance, and over to a 1916 Ford Model T automobile. The Model T has been a great success story right from the beginning. Henry Ford said it best when describing his vehicle: "I will build a motor car for the great multitude. It will be large enough for the family but small enough for the individual to care for and run. It will be constructed of the best materials by the best men that can be hired, after the simplest designs that modern engineering can devise. But it will be so low in price that no man making a good salary will be unable to own one and enjoy with his family the blessing of hours of pleasure in God's great open spaces."

The weather is cold and damp, and a strong wind is blowing. Henry's Tin Lizzie does have a top, but the sides are open and exposed to the elements. Henry mentions the car belonged to his father, who purchased it before America entered the war. His dad gave it to him when he returned home. After my parents were killed on the Lusitania, I inherited everything, including a Model T. Before going off to war and not knowing what the future held for me, I sold it.

The weather is very uncomfortable. Sitting in an open passenger compartment puts us at the mercy of mother nature and her elements. Since leaving France and the war behind me, I resolved not to be uncomfortable again because of mother nature's unpleasant weather. I'm done with sleeping in the mud, rain, snow, and merciless cold. It's dry clothes, a warm home, and clean sheets for me.

The distance to his parents' home is just a few miles, and we cover it quickly. Their house is a modest two-story wooden and brick structure with two fireplaces, one on each end of the house. There is a massive front porch with two suspended swings hanging from the ceiling. Their home sits on a large piece of land with several large hardwood trees that are dormant for the winter. They appear to be red oaks, beech, and possibly some maple trees, all common to Ohio. Henry drives his car up their driveway, parks in a large garage, and turns off the ignition. He grabs my bag and says, "Follow me." We walk briskly up the sidewalk to the front porch being careful not to slip. Following Henry inside, I enter a warm, cozy, and inviting home. Henry drops my bag next to the staircase leading up to the second floor and leads me into the dining room, where his parents are enjoying a cup of coffee. Steam rises slowly from their cups, and the aroma smells enticing. They stand as Henry introduces me. "Mom, Dad, this is our Company First Sergeant Sam McCormick. He's one of the reasons I'm alive and here today with you."

First, they glance over at their son, then look at me as their eyes glaze over and become misty. Standing there, as if frozen in time, their facial expressions radiate sincere admiration and a warmth I haven't felt since my parents' death. It's very touching, and I'm not sure how to respond. As I extend my hand, Mrs. Miller steps forward, hugs me, and Mr. Miller joins her. We stand there. No words are exchanged; only a feeling of love transcends words and permeates the room. I wasn't expecting this, but it's gratifying.

Stepping back from them, I look over at Henry and his parents. "Mr. and Mrs. Miller, your son is much too modest and generous with his praise. The same could be said of Henry being the reason why I'm here with you today."

He and I look at each other, nod approval, and Henry follows up with another one of his bear hugs. After he release me, his father guides us into their living room next to the fireplace. While we warm ourselves, he leaves the room and returns with a tray holding four glasses, a bottle of Irish whiskey, and a cup of steaming hot coffee for me. I guess he saw my reaction to their drinking coffee when we entered the dining room. He sets the tray on a coffee table, pours some whiskey into each glass, hands them out, and raises his glass in a toast. "To you two fine men, your comrades who came home and those you lost on the battle-fields of France."

We raise our glasses, tap them together, and drink them down. His father is an elegant, well-spoken man, and his toast hit home with me. I fight back the tears, as does Henry. After our toast, Mr. Miller invites me to take a chair as he pours me another whiskey. First, I drink some coffee and then switch back to the whiskey. After everyone is settled in, we enjoy each other's company sipping whiskey well into the evening and sharing stories. They are fine people, and I look forward to spending time with them in the future.

THE INTERVIEW

Monday morning dawns early. Henry and I are driving to the mill to meet the manager and his two assistants. I'm being interviewed and given a tour of the steel mill. During breakfast, Henry shared with me that the manager is retiring in a few years and will be replaced by one of his two direct reports. Kirk Snyder, the senior assistant, by date employed, and Otis Wells. They both hold similar positions of responsibility and authority. Henry chose not to talk to me about either man before the interviews. He prefers I form my own opinions of them. Henry did share that the competition between the two men to secure the mill manager position was the best unkept secret at the mill.

Pulling into the parking area of the mill, I'm struck by the large number of cars. Obviously, there are a considerable number of men working here. When I comment to Henry about the number of cars and men who must work here, he replies that is just some of them. Many walk to work or ride with a friend. The mill has three eight-hour shifts working Monday to Friday and sometimes on Saturday to meet a shipment order. They are currently the largest employer in Canton.

Entering the mill's administrative building, Henry leads me to the manager's office, where I'm introduced to his administrative secretary. She is an elderly lady, well dressed and outwardly friendly. She directs me to a seat with a smile on her face that appears to be saying. I know something you don't. Henry shakes my hand and says with an air of confidence and a little mischief.

"Sam, you old bloke, you'll do fine in there. Just be yourself. I think you might have a shot at being hired."

"Thanks, Henry. I really appreciate this!"

"Not a problem. I've got to go to work now, or the mill manager might fire me. I'll see you after my shift ends. Enjoy your day." He turns, heads for the door, and, walking out with his back turned to me, gestures with a thumbs up for good luck.

The door opens to the manager's office, and out steps Henry's father, Mr. Miller. He's the mill manager. With a smile on his face and a slight grin, he says in a father-to-son manner. "Good morning, Sam. I trust you slept well and had plenty to eat for breakfast?"

The look of surprise on my face must be a giveaway as I regain my senses and respond. "Yes, sir, I did. You and your family have been most gracious."

"Come on in, Sam, let's talk about the steel business."

Mr. Miller is also a pipe smoker, and for over an hour, we enjoy each other's company as we smoke our pipes, drink coffee, and talk about the steel industry. About mid-morning, he takes me to meet Otis Wells, who's a short, stocky fellow. He is low-key, well-mannered, and personable, and I feel very comfortable being around him. Otis is in his mid-thirties and has been in the steel business for fifteen years, having worked his way up through the ranks. We spend the rest of the morning touring mill areas for which he's responsible and meeting his supervisors. I enjoy our time together and feel good about my chances of being hired. After lunch, he takes me to meet Kirk Snyder for the afternoon portion of my visit.

After being introduced to him and invited into his office, my day implodes. Kirk is in his mid-thirties, has an intimidating presence, is well dressed, immaculate in his appearance, and speaks in an authoritative, overbearing manner. He steps behind his desk, sits down, places his feet on the desk, pulls out a cigar from his suit jacket, and lights it. I'm not offered a seat, but I take one anyway. I'm not impressed and have no patience for this kind of treatment.

As I sit down, he blurts out, "So tell me, Sam, what do you know about the steel business? What is your experience, training, and qualifications for employment in our industry?"

That's a mouth full, and before I can respond, he continues in the same manner. "Don't tell me you can shoot rifles, fire machine guns, or throw grenades. I won't be impressed. The fact that you served in the war and are highly decorated doesn't impress me in the least."

Standing up slowly, staring directly into his eyes as mine glaze over with an intensity not displayed since my days in the trenches, I shot back. "Well, Kirk, it seems to me that working in a steel mill involves many men working together as a team to complete their daily assignments. They don't use rifles, machine guns, or grenades, but they must work together as a unit. These units need to be led by foremen and supervisors who are capable and look after their men. When I acquire the skills needed for my assigned jobs, I will be a valuable member of this mill. If I attain a leadership role, the men will work with me and meet their work quotas in a timely manner!"

He is stunned by my response and manner of delivery. It's evident; he's not used to being talked down to like that. He's shaken and tries to recover the initiative. Before he has a chance to speak, I turn to leave and make one more comment. "Kirk, if you're the best they have in this steel mill, I'm not inclined to work for you. Enjoy the rest of your afternoon."

He stands up and tries to clear his throat, but nothing comes out. I walk out of his office, slam the door behind me and head for the receptionist at the front entrance to the building. Approaching the receptionist, I ask her to please call me a taxi. Regaining my senses and feeling good about my response to

Kirk, I stay just inside the building, enjoying its warmth. While waiting for a taxi, I take out my pipe and tobacco pouch, pack some tobacco into the pipe, and light it. When the taxi arrives, I head back to Henry's house.

What an asshole! I'll probably not be hired for a job at this mill. I find it hard to believe he works there. Welcome home, doughboy!

THE OFFER

Later that evening, sitting around the dinner table with the Millers, we discuss the day's events. Mr. Miller is sincerely apologetic for Kirk's behavior and comments. He goes to great lengths to explain that other managers and supervisors in the mill do not share his attitude and views. Kirk's parents are quite wealthy and used their influence to keep him out of the draft and going off to war. They own a portion of the mill and are prominent in the Canton community. Henry explains that Otis is the man he and his father hope will become the new manager when his father retires. The Millers own a portion of the mill themselves and believe the other owners will follow the recommendation of Mr. Miller when the time comes to select his replacement.

Over a glass of Irish whiskey after dinner, I'm told by Mr. Miller, they're offering me a position with the steel mill. If I accept the offer, I'll be assigned to areas that Mr. Otis Wells is responsible for managing. While in training, Henry will be my mentor, and I'll start in the hot section as a boilermaker. These are the men who lay out, fabricate, assemble, erect, and make repairs for all types of structural, boiler, and plate work. Henry mentioned there are several men working in the mill who served in the military before the war and many who served in France. He's confident I'll fit in well and become a valued member of the mill.

When I ask Henry why he didn't say anything about Kirk to

me earlier, he responds. "I wanted you to deal with him in your own way. Several men in the mill have difficulty working with or for Kirk. He has an overbearing personality. Those who initially stand up to him fare better during their employment with the mill. I knew you wouldn't take any guff from him, so I was counting on that Irish temper of yours to jump down his throat."

I'm very impressed by Mr. Miller and the opportunity he is giving me to join the company and learn about the steel business. I know Henry to be a man of honor and integrity. I see where he got it from—his parents. The Millers are good people, and I'm taken in by their warmth, hospitality, and kindness toward me. I accept My Miller's offer.

COMING TOGETHER

Over the next several days, Henry and I spend time together reminiscing about our time in France and the men with whom we served. On a few evenings, we attend boxing matches in Canton. We see K.O. Christner, a heavyweight contender, Al Walther, and Pat Peronie, both light heavyweight contenders, fight in local boxing arenas. Henry hasn't lost his passion for boxing but has not stepped back into the ring since returning home. He won't admit it, but I believe he's lost the combative instinct it takes to be competitive in the ring. After what we've been through, who can fault him?

During the day, Henry loans me his car to travel to Louisville, a small community just a few miles from the steel mill and East Canton. There are two men living there who work for the mill. Both men are veterans and good friends with Henry and Mr. Miller. John served as an enlisted man with Mr. Miller, who was a major in the Spanish American War of 1898. Richard was an infantryman who fought in the Philippine-American War of

1899-1902. Both men offered their help finding a house for Marie and me to rent or purchase.

John and Richard introduce me to a builder who has just finished constructing a new house in Louisville. After seeing the house, the builder and I agree on a price and sign a contract. He agrees to rent us this home until I sell my house in Wellsville. The new home for Marie and me is a two-story wooden structure with a basement, covered front porch, and coal heated system. It sits on a quarter-acre lot on Mercier Street, a few blocks from downtown Louisville. My employment at the steel mill begins on the first of April. This gives me time to relocate my belongings, place my house in Wellsville on the market, and hope it sells quickly. I need to purchase a car and make plans for a trip to New York to meet Marie and bring her home. It's going to be a busy month. The good news is everything seems to be falling into place.

John and Richard are good men. We established a rapport immediately, probably due to our shared experiences while in the military. Our service dates are separated by several years. However, the hardships we endured transcend time, making for an enduring bond of brotherhood. I like these men. They have been very helpful and good to me. Without asking, they take it upon themselves to introduce me around Louisville to other veterans and community leaders. I have found a new home.

Veterans helping Veterans, welcome home!

29

WILL IT EVER END?

We're 200 yards from the Huns' listening post, and the moon is bright. We bend over and stay low to the ground as we walk quietly down a small dirt road running diagonally across the front into the Huns' line. Our squad of doughboys makes our way closer to the enemy. There is a stream to our front which we must cross. Approaching the stream, we see that boards placed over the spot chosen to cross have fallen into the stream. We go another 30 yards paralleling the stream until we find a spot where our squad can cross over to the other side. This spot has boards placed over the stream that we can use. We stop, listen, and drop down on the muddy ground as flares pop above and light everything up. As the flares burn out, we continue forward, crawling slowly over the boards on hands and knees.

No one has seen us to this point. We crawl through a line of wire. For about fifty yards, there is dead flat weed-land with a few shell holes. We slowly crawl forward, head down, propelling ourselves by toes and forearms, body, and legs flat on the ground, like a snake.

Approaching the Huns' front listing post, we can just barely see dark shadows and hear the Huns' sergeant. He has a bad cold. The *squad of doughboys flanks out to the left and right, forming a firing line. When set and on command, we throw grenades and open fire with our rifles. Screams and cries of pain pierce the night as the Huns are caught by surprise. It's over, and all goes silent. Turning to head back to our trench, we are caught in a horrific crossfire of German machine guns. The noise is deafening as the men are being slaughtered and cry out. Sergeant, I'm hit! Help me! Help me! Sergeant, I don't want to die! Mom! Mom!*

I'm jolted awake. My body is trembling. I'm sweating profusely, my breathing is labored and heavy, my heart races. My god, I'm back in France. I look frantically around my room for a place to hide from German machine gunners. It's another dream. They seem so real. Will they ever end? Can I ever really return home and feel safe from the war?

30

MARIE COMES TO AMERICA

LEAVING LOUISVILLE

Waking up early this morning from another nightmare, I'm sitting at my kitchen table drinking coffee and nibbling on some toast. It's March 14th, and tomorrow Marie's ship is due to dock by 9:00 a.m. at the Port of New York. According to her latest telegram, she is sailing on the USS President Grant that left Liverpool, England, with 800 war brides. My bag is packed. I have my train ticket to Manhattan, two return tickets for Marie and me, and a room for two nights at The Plaza. I'm told it is a very nice place, having opened its doors in 1907. It is just across the street from the south side of Central Park.

While waiting on my ride, I reflect on the previous two weeks, which have been a whirlwind of activity and very hectic. With the help of Henry, John, and Richard, all my material possessions have been moved here to our new home on Mercier Street. The house looks great and is ready for Marie to add her touch to the place. The house in Wellsville is on the market, and I may have a buyer. Trying to find a car to buy is a tough nut to crack. There is a severe shortage of automobiles available to purchase because of two factors. First, automobile factories must convert back to making cars in mass quantities. Their production lines were turning out war equipment for the last eighteen months. Second, the number of returning doughboys looking for vehicles has created a huge demand for them. Everybody wants one.

A significant issue for me is where do I turn for help with my nightmares and health issues. Many of the doughboys returning home have digestive and respiratory problems from our exposure to poor living conditions, tainted water supplies, diseases, and gas attacks. Civilian doctors are not experienced in these matters, and I fear health issues will plague other returning veterans and me for years to come. However, I must believe we will be dealt with humanely, professionally, with a sense of purpose, commitment, and in a timely manner by the medical community. For now, I'm solely focused on going to New York, meeting Marie, and bringing her back to Louisville and her new home.

A knock at the front door refocuses my attention. There I see John peering through the window. He's here to take me to the train station in East Canton. Opening the door, he steps in and extends his hand to me. "Sam, you ready? The weather's a mess out there. The roads are iced over in many areas, but I'll get you to the train station."

Extending my hand and shaking his, I respond. "John, I really appreciate your doing this for me. It's been a long time since I've been with Marie. I feel like a kid waiting for Christmas morning to get here. Let's go."

"Not a problem. I've been there myself. It won't be long now." John responds in a sympathetic and mischievous manner as he grabs my bag and heads out the door.

Looking back around the main room of the house, satisfying myself everything is in order, I close and lock the front door. There is light snow blowing, and the ground is still covered in about six inches of the white fluff. Being careful not to slip as we walk to his car, I'm relieved to see he's installed canvas siding around the vehicle to protect us from the blowing snow. The trip to the depot is short and uneventful, and the train is running on time. It will be departing within minutes.

John walks over with me to the train car, hands me my bag, and we shake hands. "Have a good trip, Sam. We're all looking forward to meeting your Marie. Take care of yourself. We'll see you in a few days."

Looking down at John from the train car platform, I respond. "Thanks, John. See you then." The train jerks forward as it pulls out of the depot. I hurry inside the car, find a comfortable seat next to a window, and settle in for the day-long trip to Manhattan, New York.

TRAIN TO MANHATTAN

It's late in the afternoon as I work my way back from the dining car to my seat, having just finished a light meal of meatloaf, mashed potatoes, and green peas. I sit down, get comfortable, and once again light my pipe. The porter has given me a New York newspaper dated March 13, 1919, to enjoy for the remaining few hours of my trip. The front-page story is about the Spanish Flu epidemic, which has swept the country and is now on the decline. It's a long article with considerable information and updates about the flu. One small section of the article interests me the most, summarizing New York City's approach to dealing with the epidemic.

~

NOVEMBER 1918 WAS a time for hope and renewal for New York City. Although influenza continued to circulate for several more months, the end of the epidemic was in sight, and New Yorkers began to piece their lives back together. For New York City to arrive at this point was a challenge. There was no established Federal Government agency, nor were there guidelines to follow on managing an epidemic. New York City has fared well compared to other major cities.

The New York City health department immediately worked to isolate cases coming from ships landing at the port. They organized several advisory panels and committees and cooperated with volunteer organizations to allocate resources, recruit and direct nurses, and relieve the suffering of the ill and their families.

Unlike other major cities, New York did not issue school closure orders. They remained open. New York health officials believed that the most crucial method of disease control was within the public school system with the city's young population. Other notable strategies were staggered business hours to avoid rush-hour crowding, and more than 150 emergency health centers were established to coordinate home care and case reporting. Those who became sick were cared for in hospitals, at home, gymnasiums, and armories.

New York City relied on a mixture of mandatory and voluntary measures to curb the spread of the disease. It increased its capacities for disease surveillance, case counting, and recording valuable information. This was accomplished through physician reporting, health inspections, and massive public health education campaigns. Every effort was made to distance New Yorkers from one another. These efforts significantly contributed to New York City's rebound from the Spanish Flu.

∾

THIS ARTICLE EASES my concerns and gives me more confidence that the possibility of Marie or me contracting the Spanish Flu while in Manhattan is very small. As I scroll through the newspaper, another article on the last page catches my eye.

Mr. Edward House, an American diplomat, and advisor to President Wilson, will leave Paris soon. Having been present at the Peace Conference negotiations since the outset, he recently voiced some of his concerns. "I'll be leaving Paris soon but with conflicting emotions. While there is much to praise, there remains much to regret. It is easy to say what should have been done but difficult to have found a way to do it. I tend to agree with those who claim the treaty (in process) is poor and will only encumber Europe in infinite difficulties with efforts to enforce it. But I would also reply that empires cannot be destroyed and new states raised upon their ruins without disturbance. To create new boundaries is to create new troubles. The one follows the other. I would have preferred a different approach, but I doubt that one was ever possible. The ingredients required for such peace were simply not present. You may ask, what are some of those ingredients? Trust, empathy, compassion, understanding of what caused the war and why. Just to list a few."

FOR SOME TIME NOW, the news has not been encouraging about the treaty that is being negotiated between the Allied Powers and the Central Powers in Paris. There has been much talk about how boundaries are being redrawn, attempted land grabs by the Allies, excessive punitive damages, and a host of other issues. If an advisor to the President is frustrated with the process, then it can't be good.

My God, have we fought for nothing? Are these men in Paris sowing the seeds for another world war, potentially bigger, deadlier, and more destructive than the one we just fought?

I lay the newspaper down, lean my head back against the seat and look out the window at the snow-covered landscape. What a beautiful sight as the sun begins to set and glistens off the snow. I marvel at its beauty. The land is pristine and unscarred by years of war. There are no trenches, "no man's land," or destroyed homes and buildings. There are only beautiful fields covered in snow. Trees dot the landscape in their dormant state. Farms and towns are populated with people who go about their daily lives. Cars and trucks drive over undamaged roads. There is no concern given to being shelled, gassed, bombed, or shot. I hope war never comes to America.

THE PLAZA

Arriving in Manhattan last night, I was amazed at the number of people in this city. The pace they sustain will challenge any visitor. During my check-in, there was a problem with my room. I had reserved the bridal suite, but they gave it to someone else. After some discussion, I was given a suite near the top of The Plaza with a terrific view of Central Park. The Plaza is a beautiful hotel with exquisite charm and is impeccably maintained. The lobby, restaurants, bars, and my room are built with craftsmanship rarely seen in many parts of our country. This hotel reminds me of some of the buildings I visited while in Paris with their interior and exterior architectural features and lavish interior furnishings.

It's now mid-morning, and I'm waiting for Marie to exit from the terminal holding area in the Port of New York, where the war brides are being processed. I don't have to wait long—here she comes. What a beautiful, graceful woman. Men standing around me waiting for their brides to exit through the door turn their attention to her. Their looks of envy don't go unnoticed. She is a head-turner, and I'm one very fortunate man. She is still looking for me as I move out of the crowd toward her. Our eyes meet, and we swiftly close the distance between us. Dropping her bag and throwing her arms around me, we embrace tightly and kiss passionately. We are oblivious to the men staring and comments directed our way by many around us. "She's beautiful." What a figure, wow!" "Lucky guy!" "Where did you find her, doughboy?" Their teasing continues until we separate and move swiftly out of the terminal to a waiting taxi.

Riding back to The Plaza, Marie begins our conversation. "Sam, how I've missed you. Our time away from each other seemed like an eternity. We're together now. I never want us to be apart again."

I can't resist her and pull her close to me in mid-sentence, embrace her tightly and kiss her passionately. After she recovers, with longing, she looks into my yearning eyes and responds with a bit of mischief in her voice. "Sam, darling, how far is it to the hotel?"

Sensing her desire for me and I for her, I lean forward and say to the driver in a low-key authoritative voice. "Step on it; there's an extra twenty in it for you!" He accelerates. The forward momentum throws me back into my seat. The drive there is a blur of streets and people. I could've sworn he would hit someone as he weaved in and around groups of people walking and other taxis competing for road advantage. Our driver made excellent time covering the remaining distance to the hotel while inflicting no casualties or damage to other vehicles. I presented him with an extra twenty for his demonstration of exceptional driving skills and performance behind the wheel. Not to mention that he didn't hurt anyone. Welcome to New York.

Although it's only been seven weeks since we were last together, it seems like an eternity. Finally, we are back together again in America, and our first night is heaven on earth. We order concierge room service, enjoy the view from our room looking out over Central Park covered in light new snow and make passionate love well into the morning hours. We approach our future with hope, optimism, and undying love for each other.

31

SETTLING IN - 1919

With Marie by my side at our new home in Louisville, we set about establishing a comfortable life for ourselves. We're fortunate that my family home in Wellsville sold quickly. The Pottery Company purchased it for cash and is using the house as a rental property for supervisors they employ at the factory. I guess old man Butler had a momentary feeling of remorse for his treatment of me and believed he owed me more than just a house repair. The cash came in handy as Marie finished decorating and furnishing our home. I used some of the money to purchase a used 1918 Model T Ford.

When Marie wasn't spending her time decorating our home, she was meeting and socializing with other ladies in town. She has become active in social circles and is well received within the community. Some American families were against our boys dating and marrying French women while serving in Europe. However, Marie has been accepted in this town and has proven herself quite persuasive when it comes to what she wants and believes is right. I am committed to the steel mill and have worked long hours of overtime to learn the types of laborers and the tasks required of them. Jobs such as pipefitters, machinists, welders, blacksmiths, millwrights (maintain all mechanical equipment in assigned work areas), bricklayers, motor inspectors (maintain all electrical equipment in designated work areas), and conductors (direct movement of train cars for freight dispatches) all play vital roles in a steel mill operation. In some respects, a mill organization is structured similarly to an army division, with its various units and command hierarchy.

Working with Otis Wells is an absolute pleasure, and I learn a great deal about the business from him. Kirk Snyder is a constant menace as he routinely checks on me and constantly berates my performance and those of the men I'm assigned to supervise. Comments like, "Sam, you're just not a steel man!" "Why don't you move on to another line of work?" "Do you really think you're doing a good job?" "Your work here simply does not meet our quality standards." "Your workers are not meeting their quotas." "You have a lazy bunch working for you. Have them get the lead out!" He doesn't care for me, and I fear that he and I will have a serious falling out someday. For now, I deal with it and just ignore him. After all, we're not in the trenches of France, so I can't shoot him. If he's chosen to replace Mr. Miller when he retires, I'm convinced there will be a severe decline in morale, esprit de corps, and operational efficiency. Without a doubt, production here at the Republic Iron and Steel Company will suffer.

Henry and I have taken up playing poker once a month on Saturday nights above the fire station in downtown Louisville. We usually have between six and eight men, all former doughboys, and we play cards well into the early morning hours. Occasionally we drink a little bootleg liquor. Often our conversations drift off into our post-war dilemmas, frustrations, fears, and remembrance of buddies we left behind in France.

We were generally greeted with a hero's welcome when we first returned home. Parades and flag-waving were the order of the day for many of the returning troops that were sent home right after the Armistice. Those of us who stayed in Europe as occupying troops and returned later were generally ignored and treated as if we had never left the States. Most of us only received a few weeks' wages after returning home from war and continue to struggle as we try to re-adapt to everyday life.

For many veterans, there is an even more terrifying prospect: Prohibition. After fighting the Germans, American troops returned home to find that our country outlawed drinking alcohol. Many of us consider that a ludicrous law and have difficulty accepting it. I, for one, enjoy a good drink and find that it helps me deal with haunting memories of fighting in the trenches and my nightmares. Several veterans believe, as I do, and feel that not being able to buy liquor legally makes it harder for us to cope with our demons. So now we have become lawbreakers trying to keep our demons in check. Like so many Americans, we've found ways to get around the law.

Social attitudes toward returning veterans are also complicated. No one doubts the bravery of those who made it back, but the nation's mourning for those who didn't survive causes some problems for those who survived. Because our war dead are revered so much, people often speak of "the nation's best men being lost to war." This attitude implies that those of us who managed to return home are somehow less important or less brave than our fallen comrades. For many of us who experienced the horror of war directly, there is nothing we want more than to forget the events we witnessed. Unfortunately, mourning nations are obsessed with reliving and honoring the past. We honor the past and the men we left behind as much as the next American, but we simply ask that they not forget those of us who made it home. This attitude toward returning

veterans is proving tough to accept and deal with for many
of us.

Millions of men have returned from the war to their homes,
families, and friends. Many are handling the transition well and,
against all odds, are managing to assimilate slowly back into
civilian life. However, many of these men still find themselves
alone in a crowd. No one has yet defined the nature of combat
fatigue. What is it? How does it affect men? What can the
medical profession do for these men? There is little psychological
help available, nor are there established treatment centers to
help us readjust back into society. Some soldiers back from the
front simply saw too much; experienced too many horrors to go
quietly back into the tranquility of civilian life. The collection of
symptoms known as "shell shock" is common; however, barely
commented on in public life. It's not effectively being dealt with
among the veterans suffering from nightmares, depression, or
other manifestations of mental anguish.

Civilian doctors do not understand our physical wounds,
such as respiratory issues from exposure to gas attacks and
severe digestive problems from long periods in the trenches.
Treatment for these issues locally is limited and not very effective. Some facilities in the country are making strides in this area,
but unless you live near them, seeking their help is not currently
an option for many veterans.

Many of us believe it's a national disgrace that the government sent our generation off to fight a war, and the politicians
failed to foresee that many of us would come home wounded
and sick. Across the country, Americans see the grim cost of the
fighting in Europe. Many doughboys returned without arms and
legs. Many more are blind, deaf, or mentally ill. Our battle scars
tell the story of massive, pounding artillery and warfare mecha-
nized at unheard-of levels. Chemical warfare, used extensively,
left many doughboys with gas-seared lungs and struggling to

breathe. Prolonged and chronic illnesses will forever hamper the lives of hundreds of thousands of us returning home from the horror of rat-filled disease-ridden trenches.

This is the world in which Henry, Art, I, and our fellow veterans live. We have found talking with our fellow countrymen and women, who were not there, is extremely difficult and not productive. In most cases, there's just a feeling of apathy and no empathy for us or what we struggle with in our daily lives. Nevertheless, we go forward-facing each new day, doing our best to adjust and assimilate back into our American society.

32

ART AND THE CLEVELAND INDIANS - 1920

THE VISIT

"The bloody war is over! It's over! No more slaughter, no more maiming, no more mud and blood, no more killing and disemboweling of horses and mules. No more of those hopeless dawns, with the rain chilling the spirits, no more crouching in inadequate dugouts scooped out of trench walls, no more dodging snipers' bullets, no more of that terrible shell fire. No more shoveling up bits of men's bodies and dumping them into sandbags." Art blurts out in a loud, angry, and emotional manner as he gulps down his shot glass of Irish whiskey. The two of us have been sitting on the front porch of my home in Louisville, reminiscing and enjoying some Irish whiskey.

Art was on another one of his rambling diatribes about the war. He's been visiting Marie and me at our home in Louisville for the last two days. We haven't seen each other since we left France. Although we correspond regularly, we were unable to come together until we set up this visit. Art lives with his parents in Cleveland and doesn't have a woman in his life. He believes his disabilities make it difficult to establish any female relationships. He's having difficulty adjusting to society, accepting his war wound disabilities, and working around them. He suffers from bouts of depression and nightmares and lacks confidence in himself. His right arm was shattered, and he has multiple scars and limited mobility. To hide his scars, he only wears long sleeve shirts. Art can still hold a baseball bat and swing it with both arms but has little power or finesse in his swing. His baseball career as a player ended with his wounds in France, and it has been a tough pill for him to swallow.

While growing up, everyone always said Art would be a professional baseball player someday. It was said so often that Art had come to believe it himself without really thinking about it. When he first picked up a baseball bat, he became hooked on the game. He was a natural and progressed from playing baseball in the streets and open spaces around his neighborhood to playing on high school teams. After finishing school, he bounced around minor league teams until the Cleveland Indians picked him up. Impressed with the young man, they gave him a contract. Over the years, they were not disappointed in the man from Cleveland, the greatest power hitter to play for them.

The Cleveland Indians had not forgotten him when he returned from the war. Most major league baseball teams have two full-time coaches but employing additional coaches for pitching or batting is rare. Art was offered and accepted a full-time position with the Cleveland Indians as a batting coach at the start of the 1920 season. He is considered by many in the game to be one of the best power hitters to have played for Cleveland. They wanted him to mentor their young players. By all accounts, he's performed above expectations and helped the Indians win the American League pennant. It's the 20th season in their franchise history, and they'll be playing in their first

World Series against the Brooklyn Dodgers. Also known inter-
changeably as the Robins, in reference to their manager, Wilbert
Robinson.

"Hey Art, relax, buddy! You're right. The war is over. We're
home. We don't have to deal with all that. It's history. You need
to get on with your life." I pause and then continue. "You're the
Cleveland Indians' batting coach, and you helped the Indians
win the American League pennant. Hell, Art, you're going to the
World Series."

Responding in a melancholy manner, "Yeah, you're right,
Sam. I'm just not going as a player; the war took that opportunity away from me."

Looking intently at Art and with an understanding concern
for his feelings, I respond. "We both know there are a lot of men
out there who would love the opportunity to be in the World
Series as a coach or player. But they're not going! You are. So,
lighten up and enjoy the experience!"

Art is just about to speak when Marie steps onto the porch
carrying a tray with three glasses of lemonade and a half-empty
bottle of Irish whiskey. It may be prohibition, but we always
manage to have a little Irish whiskey in the house.

With her calm, reassuring voice and accompanying French
accent, Marie says, "How are you gentlemen doing out here?
Would you care for some more whiskey and lemonade?"

Her presence lightens the mood as she serves each of us and
takes a seat next to me.

"Merci beaucoup, Marie!" Art says as he raises his shot glass
to her. Reaching over and taking the whiskey bottle from her
tray, he refills his glass and mine. She responds, "De rien, you are
welcome, Art." Cuddling up next to me, she continues. "So,
gentlemen, what's on the schedule for tonight and tomorrow?
When do you have to return to Cleveland for the Series, Art?"

I respond, "Marie, darling, it's Saturday night, and our

monthly poker game is tonight. Art is joining us at the fire station. We'll be a little late getting home, but much earlier than usual since Art must return to Cleveland tomorrow morning."

Art interjects, "Marie, I've really enjoyed my stay here with you and Sam. It's been relaxing and very pleasant. I needed these few days to get ready for the World Series. It's going to be a tough one, but I think we have a chance."

He pauses, takes a breath as a big smile spreads across his face, and continues. "Sam, Marie, I've been given three seats right behind our dugout for game seven. I want you to join me for the game—if we get that far in the series. We're playing a nine-game series, and the first team to win five games wins it. If we must play game seven, it will be the last one in our ballpark. If there's no winner after game seven, we go back to Brooklyn to play game eight and nine if needed to end the World Series. At the poker game tonight, I'm asking Henry to join us. I could use the support of close friends. I want all of you to share in the game experience, and hopefully, we'll win."

Until now, Art hadn't said anything about this, and we're both surprised and delighted by his invitation to the game. Tickets for any of the home games in this World Series in Cleveland are very difficult, if not impossible, to obtain. Marie jumps up and gives him a big hug as I stand up and join them. Art is clearly moved by our response to his generous offer to join him for game seven. Now, all we need is for there to be a game seven.

THE GATHERING

Later that evening, Art and I—joined by Henry—walk up to the second floor of the fire station to meet the usual group of former doughboys for an evening of poker playing. Walking up the stairs, turning the corner, and entering the large room with its big round table in the middle, we are met by a crowd of men from the community. The room has a warm, welcoming feeling with the aroma of lingering tobacco smoke. It's a relaxing setting for men to gather, bond, and just enjoy each other's companionship. There are older, worn-out couches strewn about the room, ashtrays everywhere, a small kitchen sink, a cupboard holding a few cups and dishes, a large coffee pot, and a fan for those hot summer evenings. Everything a group of men might need to sustain them as they play cards well into the morning hours.

It looks like the word got out about Art being here tonight. These fellows are not here to play cards; they want to meet and talk baseball with Art. Even Otis and Kirk from the steel mill are among the crowd gathered. I don't believe I'll get any poker playing in tonight, but this could be an interesting evening. Some fellows brought in bootleg liquor which we'll drink very cautiously. After all, we are in City Hall, which is a two-story building in the center of Louisville. Located in the building are the mayor's office, his staff, the city police department, and the fire department.

Art's outgoing personality and showmanship slowly emerge as he realizes these men have come to see him. A big grin crosses his face as he works the room shaking hands and introducing himself. With one noticeable exception, the men present respond to him and act like boys who are meeting their favorite baseball player for the first time. Even Babe Ruth would be envious of the reception Art is receiving. Last year's baseball season saw record-breaking attendance, and Babe Ruth's home runs for the Boston Red Sox made him a baseball sensation. His reputation continued to grow during the 1920 baseball season elevating him to national prominence. Everyone knows who Babe Ruth is, and every kid wants to be like him when they grow up. Art is not Babe Ruth, but he is a legend among Cleveland Indian fans.

Art is peppered with questions as he moves around. "What's

it like to coach the Cleveland Indians?" "Who's your favorite hitter on the team?" "Any future Babe Ruths in your batting line-up?" "What's your chances against the Brooklyn Dodgers?" "What are your team's strengths and weaknesses?" "Do you have any tickets I can buy?" The latter question is most prevalent. And so, it goes as Art does his best to answer their questions and enjoy the moment.

As the evening progresses, the men break out into smaller groups and engage in general conversations. Art has several men around him. All are former doughboys, and they are sharing stories about their difficulties trying to readjust to civilian life. When I walk up to check on Art, he is speaking in a relaxed, somewhat melancholy manner to the group.

"Fellows, it's been a difficult transition for me. I realize I'm very fortunate to have been hired on by the Cleveland Indians, but it's only a seasonal job. None of the players or coaches are on an annual paycheck or guaranteed a place on the team for the next season. The Indians have been a godsend for me. Before I was hired, I couldn't find a job. My disabilities always seem to get in the way."

Several of the men around him show their agreement with head nods and supporting comments. "Yeah, me too!" "It's tough, no doubt about it." "I've been trying to get a regular job, but they keep telling me I'm not qualified for anything." Several fellows respond, "Me too!"

Art interjects a comment, "It seems to me like the men who didn't have to go off to war and stayed home have done much better than those of us who went."

Out of nowhere, a drunk Kirk steps in and throws a sucker punch at Art, hitting him in the face and knocking him to the ground. Standing over him and looking down at Art, Kirk blurts out. "I take exception to that comment. Just because I didn't go doesn't make me a coward!"

Art is furious and looks up at Kirk as he tries to get up. "Who the hell are you?" Kirk draws back to throw another punch. Before he has a chance to deliver the blow, Henry steps in between them. With a burning hatred seething from within him, Henry stares directly into Kirk's eyes and says, "Try that again, Kirk, and I'll send your head right through that wall. Got it?"

Kirk is momentarily stunned. Fear spreads across his face. He begins trembling as he slowly steps back from Henry. Before Henry can follow through with his threat, several men forcibly escort Kirk out of the room. Otis, some of the other fellows, and I help Art up and place him in a chair. He's had a few drinks himself and is alright, other than a bloody lip. He's furious and lets loose with some profanity and threats of retaliation against Kirk. We manage to calm him down with another shot of bootleg liquor.

With the evening coming to an early end, Henry, Otis, and I walk Art back to my house. He must leave early in the morning for Cleveland and needs rest for the trip home.

THE WORLD SERIES

Art returned to Cleveland, reported to the Cleveland Indians for the World Series, and has been very successful with his coaching responsibilities. His batting proteges are performing magnificently and are contributing to the Indians' dominance over the Robins. Marie and I have been following the games on our radio and in local newspapers. We're on the eve of the seventh and last game to be played in Cleveland. I'm sitting on the front porch, enjoying my pipe, and reading the sports page of The Louisville Herald newspaper, which is covering the World Series.

～

"The Brooklyn Robins are on the brink of elimination in the 1920 World Series. They are down four games to two against our Cleveland Indians. Their offense has been absent for the entire Series, scoring only eight runs in the first six games. Since the Series moved to Cleveland three games ago, their bats have gone silent. It's a rude awakening for a club that averaged over four runs a game during the regular season. Yet Brooklyn skipper Wilbert Robinson is still optimistic after his team lost a 1-0 decision in game six of the best five-of-nine Series. "Beat? I should say we're not," said Robby. "We haven't been hitting, and that's the only trouble. We're going out there tomorrow and smash into those Indians so hard they'll wish they'd never seen a World Series, and when we get back to Brooklyn, Cleveland won't have a chance. I'll pitch either Rube Marquard or Burleigh Grimes, and either one of them can stop Cleveland." The Robin's manager is confident in his team's abilities to make a comeback on the throwing arms of his strongest pitchers. But the Indian's hitters are on fire, and under the careful eye and coaching of Arthur Wilson, they are a power to be reckoned with—no doubt about it."

MARIE STEPS OUT on the porch and says, "Sam dear, come on inside. It's time for dinner. We must get up before sunrise to start our day tomorrow. We need to turn in early tonight. It's a big day tomorrow." I stand up, empty my pipe, walk over to Marie, place my left arm around her waist, and walk into the house as I respond, "Yes, dear."

GAME DAY

It's early morning on Tuesday, October 12, 1920, game seven, the day of the 1920 World Series. Like a boy on Christmas morning, I spring out of bed and go about dressing and preparing for our train trip to Cleveland. Marie woke up earlier and has been preparing herself for the big day. My giddiness is only surpassed by her cool, calm, and collected manner. You would think we were just going out for an afternoon picnic. I know she's thrilled for Art and enjoying every minute, but her demeanor certainly hides it well.

It's only the World Series, what's that? What's all the fuss about?

After a cup of hot java and a biscuit, we step out on the porch to a cool, clear early morning sky. The sun has yet to make an appearance, as the dew on the ground can attest. We take our Model T to the train station in Canton, where we meet Henry on the station platform. He's all dressed up in his Sunday best and eager to start our day.

He walks up to us, gives Marie a little hug, then extends his hand to me as we shake. "Good morning, Marie, Sam. It's going to be a lovely day. Sam, I would give you a hug, but I don't want to mess up my Sunday best. You both ready?" We nod yes, and he says, "Well, let's go watch our Indians clobber the Robins."

With excitement in my voice and a matter-of-fact tone, I respond. "You're right, Henry. It's going to be a good day."

Marie says calmly, "We'll prevail, no worries. You two boys need to be on your best behavior and be good sports about winning the Series today. Don't be too hard on the Robins. They're a good team and well-coached. They could prove to be tough, and it may just be a rough day for us."

Both Henry and I step back a little from Marie, look quizzically at her, and wonder—*"Where did she acquire this baseball knowledge all of a sudden?"*

Looking at Marie with a smile on my face and pride, I respond. "Marie dear, I wasn't aware you've been following the Series that closely." Henry just stands there with a look of surprise.

Marie flashes a look of defiance as she looks back and forth between Henry and me. She reacts in a calm, soft manner and, with a heavy French accent, says, "What? You think this is just a game for boys?"

Our banter back and forth is interrupted when the conductor yells, "All aboard, next stop Cleveland and game seven of the World Series!"

Our train trip to Cleveland is uneventful and pleasant. We enjoy each other's company and sip coffee with a light breakfast served at our seats. Arriving in Cleveland, it's late morning as we step off the train to a warm, sunny autumn day. After a leisurely walk to League Park, we arrive to find that a circus atmosphere has consumed the stadium and surrounding area. The crowd is thirsty for a world title and for it to happen here on our home turf. The biggest crowd of the Series, 27,525, is pushing through the turnstiles in hopes of seeing history. There are souvenir vendors everywhere selling pennant flags, ball caps, Indian dolls, and any number of contrived items to pass off as souvenirs of the big event. They are joined by ticket sellers and scalpers, food vendors, and hordes of people who just want to be around the stadium to enjoy the moment and say they were here today.

We have been told that interspersed within the crowds assembled around the park are several undercover police officers looking for scalpers. Just prior to game one of this World Series, Rube Marquard, one of the starting pitchers for the Robins, was arrested at the Hotel Winton in Cleveland by a detective. It was there that the baseball star was alleged to have offered six tickets for World Series games in Cleveland for $350.00. Once the policeman heard the offer, he swore out a warrant for an arrest.

The matter drew considerable attention in the press. After the 1919 World Series and the Chicago Black Sox throwing the Series to the Cincinnati Reds in a gambling fix, the baseball world and fans didn't want any more improprieties. Professional baseball and the men who play are considered national heroes and looked up to, especially by young boys. It is our national sport, and many boys dream about growing up and playing in the World Series someday. Had this scalping incident happened a few years earlier, it may not have received the attention it did. Unfortunately, Rube Marquard's attempt at scalping tickets came across as just another ballplayer chasing money in an underhanded way. To protect the image of the game and its players, added security measures have been instituted for today's game.

Art had instructed us to go to their team's private gate entrance and ask for Frank. It takes us some time to work our way around through the crowds, but we find the gate and meet up with Frank. He's well-rounded in the belly, jovial, and a very accommodating fellow. He lets us in, much to the amazement of the crowd standing around the gate waiting to see their favorite Cleveland Indian players. I'm sure they're wondering, 'Who are these people?' Arriving at the Indians' locker room, Frank asks Marie to please wait outside for a few minutes while we go in and find Art. Marie understands and takes a seat near the entrance. Her look is one of understanding, but at the same time, it conveys the message very clearly, 'don't be in there long.' I get the message.

Once inside, we find Art talking to some of the players and a whirlwind of activity as they suit up and get ready to take the field for some practice. Art greets us and shuffles us through the locker room quickly. There's no time to meet any of the players right now. As we hurry past them, several greet us with smiles, and some welcome us to their locker room. I'm sure my face has the look of a young boy who's walking among his heroes and can't quite believe his good fortune. I'm a kid again; what an experience!

Exiting the locker room, Art sees Marie, walks over to her, and gives her a big hug. "Welcome to my world, Marie!"

"Merci, Art."

We slowly catch up to him as both Henry, and I, are still in the moment, gazing back at the players as the door closes behind us. Some activities in life just bring out the boy in a man. To me, this is one of them.

Art guides us out onto the playing field. This is my first time on a professional baseball field. This is the first professional game I've ever attended. The smell of fresh-cut grass, the baselines marked in heavy white chalk, the clear blue sky above, the sounds of activity emanating from all around the ballpark, and its sheer size, are a sensory delight. Standing there gawking at our surroundings, Art gives us a visual tour of the stadium, pointing out different aspects of the structure and field layout.

We're still ninety minutes to game time, but the ballpark is rapidly filling up. Art guides us over to their dugout and up a few steps to our seats. We are right behind the dugout. While seated, we can lean forward and place our arms on the dugout or lean back in our seats and place our feet on the dugout roof. These are great seats. It's time for Art to go back to work as he bids us farewell. He smiles, gives us a thumbs-up, and disappears into the dugout on his way back to the locker room.

Settling into our seats, Henry calls over a food vendor and places an order. Since it is a ballpark, we are limited to hotdogs, peanuts, cracker jacks, and bottled soda. While enjoying our ballpark cuisine, as Marie refers to it, we watch the Indians take the field to warm up. The crowd behind us goes wild with excitement as the Indians come out of the dugout to take the field. Elmer Smith—who was presented with an automobile and a diamond pin for his heroics in game five, when he hit a grand slam in the Indians' 8-1 victory—emerges from the dugout. The crowd starts chanting, "Elmer, Elmer, Elmer!" He momentarily stops, turns to face the crowd, tips his hat, and then runs onto the field.

With pre-game practice completed, announcements over, and playing of the "The Star-Spangled Banner" performed, game seven is now set to start on time at 1:55 p.m.

A tradition was set in motion during the first World Series afternoon game between the Chicago Cubs and the Red Sox back in 1918 at Comisky Park. During the seventh-inning stretch, as the crowd of spectators stood up to take their afternoon stretch, the band broke into strains of "The Star-Spangled Banner."

The fans took notice as the ball players turned quickly about, faced the music, and removed their caps. Jackie Thomas, on leave from the U.S. Navy, was at attention. He stood erect, with his eyes set on the American flag waving on top of the flagpole in right field. At first, some in the crowd began to sing, they were joined by more, and when the final notes were played, the crowd went wild with enthusiasm. American patriotism was on full display as the minds of many of these baseball fans were on the war.

Following this patriotic outburst at the 1918 World Series, the singing of "The Star-Spangled Banner" at the beginning of baseball games began to spread across the country. I wonder if it will become a regular feature?

The Indians take the field as the Robins get the first crack at batting. The roar of the crowd is deafening, and trying to talk with Marie or Henry is out of the question. We're caught up in the moment and join the yelling and cheering for our team. The umpire steps behind the plate and motions for the crowd to settle in and the players to take their positions. When satisfied, he yells, "Play ball!"

The first three innings go by quickly, with neither team scoring a run. We're in the fourth inning when our third baseman gets a base hit just past the Robins' second baseman. Our next batter hits the ball into right field for a single, moving our man to third base. The next batter flies out to left field, and our man on third base holds his position. The next man up is our catcher. There is some discussion on the mound between the Robins' pitcher, catcher, and coach. They resume their positions. The pitch is thrown, and our batter lets it fly by him. Cleveland puts on the double steal, but the catcher reads their play all the way. Instead of firing to second base, he throws it back to his pitcher to hold our man on third. But their pitcher seeing our man standing well off the bag, wheels around and throws to his third baseman. But the throw goes wild, and our player easily scores the first run of the game. The crowd in the stands erupt with excitement, cheering, yelling, and throwing confetti into the air. It takes some time for the crowd to settle back down before the umpires can resume play.

It's the bottom of the fifth inning, and our left fielder hits a single and makes it to first base. With a wild pitch to the next batter, our man on first base steals second base. The crowd is yelling with anticipation as they sense another run in the offing. Our batter digs his feet into home plate, crouches down, plants himself, and waits for the next pitch. It's down the middle. He makes a picture-perfect swing and smashes the ball, hitting the sweet spot of his bat. Even over the noise, you can hear the crack of his bat as the ball gains altitude and heads out to right field. He gets a triple, and we score another run.

It's the top of the seventh inning, and Brooklyn is coming to life as they threaten to score. The score is Cleveland 2 and the Robins 0. The Robins have two of their players on base, but they also have two outs. The crowd is subdued as the pitcher winds up and throws his pitch. The batter swings and hits the ball down the third baseline. Our man makes an incredible catch and throws him out at first. The inning is saved. The crowd comes to life again. We are close, so close.

In the bottom of the seventh inning, we score another run and go on to hold Brooklyn to no runs through the top of the ninth inning. The World Series is ours. Our pitcher, Stan Coveleski, only needed ninety pitches to win the game, 3-0. Cleveland Indian fans swarm onto Dunn Field to congratulate our heroes. We see Art for the first time since the game started as he emerges from the dugout and motions for us to join him on the field. Our celebrating begins on the field and carries well into the night as we join Art and some of the Cleveland Indian players for a night on the town.

BACK TO WORK

Our first day back at the steel mill for Henry and me begins on a bad note. We are greeted by Kirk, who accuses us of taking time off from work without permission. He definitely has it in for both of us and views this as an opportunity to improve his chances of becoming the next steel mill manager when Mr. Miller retires.

Accuse the son and discredit the father.

Maybe Kirk should have done his homework since we did have approval from our manager for time off to attend the World Series. His accusations fall on deaf ears, and we resume our daily duties as supervisors. However, I'm sure we haven't heard the last of him. I believe a chain of events has been set in motion that will ultimately lead to a confrontation with Kirk.

33

SEAN-OUR SON - 1929

BACKGROUND

It's Saturday morning, November 2, 1929. Marie, Sean, and I are driving to Myers Lake Park in North Canton for our workers' annual Republic Iron and Steel Company outing. It's a beautiful fall day with clear skies and a light cool breeze. In the early 1900s, George Sinclair, owner of Myers Lake Park, opened with the first roller coaster, and by 1926 the park had several amusement rides and a ballroom for big bands. The location is perfect for today's outing. It should be a welcome distraction from work for the men, a pleasant afternoon for our wives, and an entertaining and fun-filled day for our children. We could all use this opportunity to slow down, relax and take our minds off recent events.

Our son Sean was born on November 3, 1921, and tomorrow we'll be celebrating his eighth birthday. He is our only child, and due to complications at birth, Marie is no longer able to conceive. It was difficult for both of us to accept at first, but we have managed to move on. Sean is our whole life, we both adore him, and Marie dotes over him. He is a typical boy, always inquisitive, impulsive, active, and challenging. At his young age, he already displays a desire to be challenged and has a high tolerance for risk-taking, much to his mother's dismay. Sean has many of his mother's traits. He's an avid reader, speaks fluent French, and is very caring and respectful toward other people. He's a good-looking boy who hasn't gone unnoticed by the young girls in his classes. In keeping with his adventuresome spirit, he has developed a love of airplanes and dreams of becoming a pilot.

Located on the east side of Louisville is a grass airfield with two old barns serving as airplane hangars. The tiny airfield is built on a plateau providing a panoramic view of Louisville and the surrounding countryside. Sean spends some of his time there listening to stories by former WWI pilots who live in town and have taken a liking to him. None of them are barnstormers, but occasionally barnstormers fly into our airfield for a day or two. At the end of WWI, many trained pilots were out of work and itching to fly again. The military had a surplus of aircraft, mostly "Jenny" biplanes, which they sold to former aviators and civilians for a fraction of their original cost. These former pilots' boredom and bravery, combined with access to inexpensive planes, led to the rise of barnstorming as a widely popular source of entertainment across the country. Barnstorming earned its name from these pilots who would land their light planes in fields and use local barns as venues for their impromptu airshows. Charles Lindbergh was a barnstormer in his early days as an aviator and flew under the name of "Daredevil Lindbergh."

Several barnstormers are flying in later today and will spend the night at our airfield. Tomorrow afternoon they will give rides and perform a barnstorming air show. Sean's only birthday request is to go up in one of their biplanes and fly around looking down on our town. I've arranged such a flight for him tomorrow.

LARRY A. FREELAND

Marie, on the other hand, is not very happy with me for doing so and has expressed her opinions quite eloquently to me in private. But, being a wise mother, she realizes that Sean, even at his young age, is destined to become an aviator later in life. With some trepidation and after considerable soul searching, we both agreed to send him up into the sky tomorrow and see what happens. Later tonight, after dinner, we'll tell him about his flying excursion scheduled for tomorrow. Hopefully, he'll sleep well, but Marie and I both have our doubts. He's going to be one excited young man after he's told.

On the drive over to Meyers Lake, my thoughts are on the steel mill and what's happening with the stock market and its possible impact on our lives. Henry and I are now foremen at the mill and report to Otis. When Mr. Miller retired last summer, Kirk was elevated to his position and is now the steel mill manager, and Otis reports to him as the number two manager. Henry's father wanted to retire several years earlier, but some members of the board, fearing Kirk's ascension to his position, continually pressured Mr. Miller to stay on. With his health deteriorating, he had to retire. At that time, there was considerable debate and disagreement among the board members about Kirk's appointment to the position of mill manager. Kirk's father has considerable influence in the community and with the board, and his insistence that Kirk be elevated to mill manager prevailed.

Unfortunately for both father and son, Kirk's performance has been marginal, which hasn't gone unnoticed by the board, the community, and the mill workers. He is a tyrant who flaunts his power over the workers openly, demonstrating no managerial or leadership skills. The steel mill's productivity, performance, and profitability have continued a downward spiral since he assumed control.

The Republic Iron and Steel Company had one strike in the

fall of last year, shortly after Kirk assumed control of the company. When he was appointed mill manager, he immediately froze all wages, increased the workweek by several hours, increased work quotas considerably, and generally cut back on expenses associated with mill safety. Accidents increased. The mill workers requested but were denied the opportunity to negotiate shorter work hours, better wages, increased safety measures, bargaining rights, and union recognition. This resulted in most of our workers going on strike.

Neither Henry nor I could prevent them from going on strike, and we quietly supported their efforts. Kirk tried to bring in strikebreakers, but his attempts failed when the community supported the strikers, and the board of directors agreed with Henry and me that it was not a good idea. The board forced Kirk to reinstate mill policies that were in place when he assumed managing control over the mill. Although the strike lasted only a few days, tempers ran hot, the workers' morale plummeted, and production suffered for months. Many of our workers are WWI veterans, and their battle cry became, "We are on the firing line once again, and we are going over the top as we did in 1918. We are as determined to lick the steel barons and Kaisers of this country as we were to lick the German Kaiser!"

It's taken Henry and me many months to soothe over the anger and frustrations built up by Kirk's actions after he assumed control. We have been challenged every step of the way by Kirk and the two assistants he recently hired to keep him informed of activities within the mill. Today's annual event will hopefully continue to move us forward in re-establishing some goodwill with our mill workers. I personally believe we are in for a long bout of worker unrest and strikes until unions are welcomed into the steel industry and can play a role in improving our workers' lives.

Adding to our troubles—there has been considerable

economic chaos in the last few weeks as the stock market has sustained multiple sell-offs. On October 24th, Black Thursday, the New York Stock Exchange lost 11% of its value. On October 28th, Black Monday, it lost 12.8% of its value. On October 29th, Black Tuesday, 16 million shares were traded on the Exchange with billions of dollars lost, wiping out thousands of investors. The next day panic selling reached its peak, with some stocks having no buyers at any price. The combined losses on the Exchange amounted to 23% for just these two days.

Most of our workforce does not own any stock, including me. Unfortunately, you don't have to be a stockholder to feel the pain and economic hardships that have already started to spread across the country. The crash of the New York Stock Exchange is setting off widespread panic and disruptions in our social fiber and economy, which I fear will have significant and long-term implications.

THE STEEL MILL EVENT

Arriving at Myers Lake and seeing all the parked cars and people flowing into our picnic pavilion, I refocus on the tasks at hand today. In the backseat, Sean is overcome with excitement looking out at all the rides. He yells out, "Dad, can we go on the roller coaster first as soon as you park? I want to ride it as many times as I can. Okay, Dad?"

Turning to look at his face, full of youthful excitement, I want so badly to say yes, but my mill duties beckon first. Marie saves the moment and responds. "Sean, dear, let's allow your father to park the Tin Lizzy so we can go to the pavilion and help set up for the picnic today. There will be plenty of time to go on the roller coaster and the other rides later today."

Being a good son, Sean responds dutifully but with disappointment reflected on his face and in his voice. "Yes, mother.

But will I have to wait a long time?" Marie responds, "No, dear, I promise, you'll be able to ride all you want before the day is over." Sean's face lightens up, and all is well for the moment.

The day progresses with everyone having a good time and enjoying each other's company. Sean rides the roller coaster many times, once with me, then with Marie, and follows up with several more trips with some of his friends. He's undoubtedly enjoying his day. After our picnic lunch, Kirk informed Otis, Henry, and me that he was going to speak to the employees at three this afternoon and wanted us on stage with him. He did not indicate why or what he was planning to say or do.

It's three o'clock, and Otis, Henry, and I are on the stage waiting for Kirk. As I Look out over the crowd, there must be at least a thousand people here today. That constitutes almost our entire workforce and their families. By the smiles on their faces, it appears we may have made some progress with reducing tensions within our crew. Kirk walks up from behind the stage, passes us without saying a word, and swaggers up to the podium.

What a jerk. What is he going to try now?

He stops at the podium, adjusts the microphone, steps back, and looks out over the crowd. As he does, he says nothing but moves his head up and down as if agreeing with what he sees before him. He steps forward and speaks into the microphone. "Ladies and gentlemen, please give me your attention." He steps back again, allowing the crowd to settle down and give him their attention.

Continuing to scan the crowd, he slowly approaches the podium once more. As the crowd of workers and their families before him quiet down, he speaks. "Thank you, thank you. I hope everyone has been enjoying themselves today." Pausing, he looks out over the crowd and nods his head up and down, looking for a response. There are some comments and light applause. He is not a popular man, and their lack of enthusiasm for him shows.

Kirk's facial expression morphs from a fake smile to a slight smirk, almost contemptuous for the men and women standing before him. Disregarding their lackluster response, he continues in an authoritative, matter-of-fact manner. "As you are aware, these last few weeks have seen considerable chaos and losses on the New York Stock Exchange. This will have serious consequences across our country and the economy. My managers standing here with me today, and the board of directors have given serious thought to what may happen to our industry and you, our workers. We have decided to act now to help mitigate any serious consequences in the future."

Kirk has worked himself into a mild frenzy as he looks around at the crowd before him, trying to gauge their reactions. Until now, they have been unresponsive and shown little interest in him. That is about to change. They look up at him with an intensity bordering on hatred. They know he will try anything, and from their facial expressions, it's apparent they anticipate his next comments will not be good for them.

Standing behind him on the stage, I'm stunned. No one has confided in me about what I just heard. Looking over at Henry and Otis and seeing the expressions on their faces, they obviously haven't either.

What the hell is this guy doing?

Kirk's body language and facial expressions convey that he's enjoying himself. His arms are flailing around. He speaks in high pitches, almost screaming at times as he launches into a verbal tirade. He attacks our workers for not supporting him in the past and wanting to unionize. He believes management is in complete control now, given what is transpiring on Wall Street and across the country. He tells us things will be changing. Longer working hours, less pay, higher quotas, and fewer benefits. Within the steel industry and this steel mill, "his" steel mill, workers will comply with management edicts or lose their jobs. The crowd before us is stunned into silence. Kirk finishes and turns to leave the stage as the crowd starts to "boo and hiss" at him. The crowd grows louder. Kirk hastens off the stage and toward a group of police officers standing near us. Otis, Henry, and I are as surprised and stunned by Kirk's comments and attitude as the rest of the people present here today. We look at each other in total disbelief. I feel frozen in place, I want to move, but my body won't move.

What now? It seems like my life just flashed before my eyes. This man has just set in motion the possible demise of our mill and the livelihoods of many of our workers, including mine. Here we go again with this egomaniac!

A rage slowly builds within me while I struggle to control it. Do something, anything! Every fiber in my body wants to beat the hell out of Kirk, but the better angels on my shoulders restrain my impulse. I slowly and deliberately step forward to the podium. Grasping the microphone, I calmly speak, trying to quiet the crowd and restore some order. They respond and give me their attention. "My fellow workers and family members, hear me clearly! Otis, Henry, and I were not aware of any of what we just heard here today from Kirk. I stand before you now and can assure you; we are just as concerned as all of you. We will pursue this with the board of directors and evaluate what just happened and why. I promise you we will do our best to influence the board to restrain Kirk from following through on anything he said here today!"

Looking out over the crowd of men, women, and children staring up at me, I give them a moment to digest what I just said. Otis and Henry step forward and join me, one on each side, as they motion for me to continue.

"This is not what we had planned for our program here

today. I think it best if we all go about enjoying the rest of our day together with our families and friends. We have the park for the remainder of the day, so I implore you to take advantage of all it offers. The members of management you see standing before you need your cooperation, support, and patience. We will work this out with the directors. Thank you for your understanding!"

With my last comment, I walk off the stage heading straight for Kirk and his assembled wall of police officers acting as body-guards. Otis and Henry fall in behind me. Approaching Kirk, I'm verging on uncontrolled physical retribution against him for his sheer arrogance and contempt for his fellow workers and their families. This man doesn't deserve to be in the position to which he has been elevated by his father. He's a damn disgrace.

As I approach Kirk with my arms ready to take a swing at him, Henry pushes past me and lands a right hook on Kirk's jaw, sending him flying backward hitting the ground hard. Henry is outraged, and the look in his eyes sends the message, don't mess with me. No one wants to get in his way, including the police officers present, who just stand there. Kirk is slow to get up as he looks at Henry while massaging his swollen jaw. He wants to say something but remains silent. He's smarter than I give him credit for because if he further enrages Henry, there is no telling what might happen next. I step between Kirk and Henry as I pull Henry back to avoid another confrontation.

Our day ends with everyone heading home for a depressing evening on a day that started out as a great company outing and picnic.

SEAN GOES FLYING

Sunday dawns early in our house. Sean is up, dressed, has eaten breakfast, and waits patiently for me to finish my coffee and biscuits so we can drive up to the airfield. His big day has arrived. He's eight and going flying for the first time in his life. Marie has chosen to stay home and let her boys go out for some father-son time together.

The drive to the airfield only takes a few minutes. Sean has been hanging his head out the side of the Tin Lizzy like a puppy going for an open-air car ride. As we pull up next to the hanger, several men from the community, who are pilots, greet him. "Good morning, Sean. Great day to go flying." "Are you ready for your big day, Sean?" "You'll do great!" One of the men steps out of the crowd and says as he holds something out to Sean. "Remember to buckle up good when you get in the cockpit seat. Here, you'll need these. Keep them. They're for you." He gives Sean a leather flying cap and goggles.

Sean takes the flying cap and goggles from the pilot and tries to slip them on with some difficulty. The pilot kneels and helps him place them on while adjusting them for his head and face. Sean extends his hand and says, "Thank you, sir. I appreciate this very much!" The pilot just nods, stands up, and pats him on the shoulders.

There are three barnstormers present, and one of them walks up to Sean. "Good morning, Sean. I'm Roscoe Turner. I understand you would like to go flying today." Turner created a well-known barnstorming act during the early 1920s named the "Roscoe Turner Flying Circus." Roscoe had just participated in the Bendix Trophy Contest and the Thompson Trophy Race. The Bendix was a nonstop cross-country flight contest from Los Angeles to Cleveland. Turner made a good showing, finishing third. Then, a few days later, he flew in the Thompson Trophy Contest in Cleveland, a 100-mile, closed-circuit, "free-for-all" around a series of pylons while flying at top speeds. One of my war buddies, who was a pilot in France and a friend of Roscoe, asked him to stop by here on his way back to Los Angeles as a personal favor to him and my son.

Sean has heard of Roscoe, and his excitement shows through when a big smile spreads across his face. Sean responds as he extends his hand. "Yes, sir! I would love to go flying with you." Only eight years old and always the gentleman. Marie has taught him well. They both make me proud.

Roscoe, apparently a man of few words, places his arm on Sean's shoulder and leads him over to his Jenny biplane. He helps Sean into the front seat, ensures he's strapped in carefully and gives him a few safety instructions. Tapping Sean on the head when he's ready, Roscoe climbs into his pilot seat and straps in. With the help of one of his barnstorming pilots, they fire up the engine. With the Jenny ready, Roscoe increases the power as they roll down the grass field, gaining airspeed. Roscoe pulls back on the flight stick, and gradually his biplane lifts off the ground. Slowly, the Jenny gains altitude as Roscoe and Sean climb toward the heavens above. My son is flying.

The other fellows present and I have taken seats in one of the small bleachers set up for the air show this afternoon and watch Roscoe take Sean through a series of flying maneuvers. He puts on a dazzling display of spirals, barrel rolls, loops, steep dives, slow climbs while spiraling up, followed by slow spiraling descents, and the sideslip, a basic WWI fighter maneuver. After an hour in the air, Roscoe lands, taxis up to where we are, shuts off the engine and climbs out of the cockpit. He helps Sean to unstrap and climb out. Removing their flight caps as they walk toward us, the two of them act like they are best friends just back from an adventure.

Seeing me, Sean runs over, gives me a big hug, and, stepping back, says in a confident and strong voice. "Dad, I'm going to be a pilot when I get older. Not just any pilot, but one of the best."

Roscoe walks over and shakes my hand as he says, "Sam, you

have a terrific son. He's a natural up there in the sky. I let him take over the controls and do some of the flying. He's unbelievable."

I respond, "Thanks, Roscoe. You've made him a very happy boy. We both appreciate your taking him flying this morning. I think he's hooked." Roscoe pats Sean on the shoulder, gives me a short salute, turns, and we part company as he rejoins the other barnstormers to prepare for this afternoon.

The other fellows take turns congratulating Sean and welcoming him into the world of aviation. With the morning slipping away, we say our goodbyes until this afternoon, and Sean and I head home. Marie is waiting on us to return so we can attend church, have lunch, and attend the airshow as a family later today. I have no idea how Marie will react when she sees our son and his enthusiastic response to flying. You can see it in his eyes and the swagger he's just developed.

I've got my hands full now!

During dinner this evening, all Sean talked about was his first flight and the airshow. He was mesmerized by what Roscoe and the other barnstormers were able to do with their biplanes. If I had any doubts about his desire to be a pilot, they vanished today. I'm truly happy for him, and I'm sure my expressions of support and encouragement were demonstrated to him and his mother. Marie sat silently through dinner, listening to her son and watching the two of us interacting. As so many times before, I could not discern her true feelings about Sean flying.

Later in the evening, after dinner, we ask Sean to retire to his room for the night. He's had a full day and needs his rest. With Sean down for the evening, Marie and I cozy up on our sofa by the fire while sipping some Irish whiskey as we talk through some of the weekend's events. Marie snuggles up next to me and, in her soft, sweet, but conceding voice, says, "Sam, Sean is only eight years old. How can he and you be so sure he's going to grow up to fly?"

"Marie, I'm not sure, but watching him today and seeing him up there flying and running over to me shortly after he landed, I think he's hooked on it. Roscoe, who is one of the best barnstormers and rapidly becoming one of the top aerial racers, believes he's a natural. The fellows in the community who know him and are pilots believe as I do. It's in his blood."

Marie looks into my eyes and says softly, "If it's to be, so be it!"

The topic briefly turns to the steel mill and Kirk's asinine performance on Saturday. Marie finishes her drink and says, "Sam, what are you, Henry, and Otis going to do about Kirk's threats to the mill workers on Saturday? He can't be serious, can he? Surely the board of directors aren't behind this foolishness and won't support him, will they?"

I finish my whiskey and respond in a calm, melancholy manner. "Marie, except for his father and maybe a few other directors, I don't think the rest are involved in any way with this idiot. He and his dad see an opportunity developing in our country right now. They want to exploit it for their own ambitions. I'll work with Otis and Henry to try and convince enough directors to intercede and overrule his father. They need to stand up, take back control of the company and do what's right for our workers."

Marie interjects, "What do you mean by an opportunity developing they want to exploit?"

"I believe we're headed for some long-term serious issues and disruptions to our economy, which will hurt many people across this country in the process. Jobs will become scarce, hard to find or keep, and management will try to rule over their workers. Time will tell, but the cards are starting to stack up against the average American worker and his family."

Marie asks, "What are you going to do about it?"

"Whatever I can to keep the steel mill open, men employed, and get that idiot Kirk fired from managing the mill."

There is nothing else I can say. I pour a little more whiskey into our glasses and pull Marie closer to me as we enjoy the moment together. Sitting in silence, with only the crackling sounds of the dying logs in the fire, we drift off momentarily into our own thoughts.

With everything that is happening in this country today, I'm not very optimistic about being able to work with the board of directors to accomplish much of anything. I believe they are obsessed with being in control and protecting their own wealth. They share a similar mindset with business titans across the country who are not receptive to sharing control over their Companies or their wealth. We are headed into rough times as workers come together to organize unions in their factories and mills. Their efforts to organize and confront company titans, senior management, and controlling stockholders will undoubtedly be met with considerable resistance. There are storm clouds gathering, and before they clear out, I'm afraid many people across this country will suffer dearly.

As the last embers from the fire dwindle out, we get up, turn off the lights and work our way upstairs to the bedroom. It's been a long weekend, and our future looks challenging. I just want to put it all out of my mind for now and relive our Paris honeymoon. Holding Marie close to me as I lead her into the bedroom, she turns to me with longing in her eyes and stares deeply into my eyes as if searching my soul for a response. Her message is clear as she softly says, "I love you! I'm yours!"

34

BONUS ARMY MARCH OF 1932

"If the Army must be called out to make war on unarmed
citizens, this is no longer America."

Washington Daily News

MORNING JULY 28, 1932

Several years pass, and I'm sitting with Art and many
other World War I veterans, eating a light breakfast of
biscuits and drinking some java. We are at one of several
encampments housing thousands of World War I veterans and
some family members from across the country who converged
on Washington D.C. about three months ago. These veterans are
demanding their grievances, needs, and appeals for help be
heard. With very few resources, they set up encampments on the
mudflats of the Anacostia River, a tributary of the Potomac River,
which soon became a large shantytown where the inhabitants
live in squalor.

The men I'm with are all seated around a small table

outside of a mess hall tent set up in this large veteran encampment. It's a steamy morning, and I've been here for three days. Art reached out to me last week and wanted Henry and me to join him here for support and witness a historical event. I agreed to come, but Henry had married his high school sweetheart, Melanie, a few days earlier and was still on his honeymoon. They had been dating for many years following Henry's return from France. Although he cared for her very much, Henry was always hesitant to commit to marriage. He preferred to remain single and occasionally dated other women. Entering marriage was a big step for both. Henry wasn't going to do anything to jeopardize their marriage, particularly their first week. He didn't make the trip. *Henry has always been a wise man.*

When these camps were first set up, it seemed like order might be maintained. The organizers set up their encampments along military lines, announced that there would be "no panhandling, no drinking, no radicalism," and that the marchers were simply "going to stay until the veterans' bill is passed." The government also did its part, as Washington Police Superintendent Pelham D. Glassford treated his fellow veterans with considerable respect and care. But by the end of June, the movement has swelled to more than 20,000 tired, hungry, and frustrated men. Now, conflict seems inevitable as most of the men here are dejected, frustrated, and increasingly desperate for some help from their government. They are tired of all the broken promises.

Not until this morning had I heard Art speak so openly about his love of baseball and his fondest memories of playing the game he loved. It is clear, the game was his whole life, and the war took that away from him. Now, he's an angry, bitter, and sad man who no longer has a job as the Cleveland Indians batting coach. He helped the Indians win the 1920 World Series by mentoring the team's young players, some of whom still play for the Indians and consider him a legend.

Art has struggled over the years with alcoholism which eventually caught up with him, and he lost his Cleveland Indians coaching position. The Cleveland Indians owners and general manager worked with him trying to salvage his position with the ballclub but to no avail. His demons were too great, and his performance deteriorated to the point where he had to be released in 1926. Living at home with his parents, unemployed, and with no prospects of finding a job, he has looked elsewhere for support and help. He has been drawn to other veterans and has become involved with veteran groups demanding more benefits and recognition for their service and war wound disabilities.

While quietly sipping his java and reading a copy of the Washington Daily News, Art has moved away from the assembled group. One of the fellows looks over his way and yells at him. "Art, what the hell are you reading that can possibly be so interesting? Why don't you share it with the rest of us?"

Art looks up from reading, glances over at the man, and responds jokingly, "I think it's a little over your head!" A few fellows laugh, and Art continues. "It's certainly nothing we haven't heard before and already know. You would think our elected officials could resolve our grievances and demands for some respect. But here we sit, waiting, going nowhere with no end in sight. When will the public rise and say enough is enough? Help our veterans!"

That generates several grunts, some light laughter, and comments like, "Are you kidding? No one cares!" "We're yesterday's news. The depression is front and center now!" "Congress and the President don't give a flip about us!" And so, it goes. I interject with, "Say, Art, why don't you read us a few paragraphs and enlighten the group here?"

He stands up, looks over at the group as a smile crosses his face, and begins reading from the newspaper. "Well, fellows, here it goes. The World War Adjusted Compensation Act of 1924, passed by the United States Congress, awarded World War I veterans' bonuses in the form of certificates. Each qualified veteran's certificate has a face value equal to the soldier's promised payment with compound interest. However, veterans cannot redeem them until 1945. Many veterans have been out of work since the beginning of the Great Depression."

Art looks around, gauging his audience's reaction, and then continues reading in a more commanding voice.

"Large numbers of veterans organized and referred to themselves collectively as the "Bonus Expeditionary Force," the BEF. They derived this title from the name of World War I's "American Expeditionary Forces." The media refers to them as the "Bonus Army" or "Bonus Marchers." Their principal demand is straightforward and simple. Congress should authorize and provide an immediate cash payment of their certificates."

Becoming more agitated as anger wells up from within, Art takes a moment to regain some composure, then continues reading. "They are led by a former World War I sergeant, Walter Waters of Oregon. The so-called BEF set out for the nation's capital and came from all over the country. Hitching rides, hopping trains, and hiking finally brought the Bonus Army, about 15,000 strong, into the capital in June 1932. Although President Hoover refused to address them, the veterans did find an audience with a congressional delegation. Soon a debate began in Congress over whether to meet the demonstrators' demands. As deliberations continued, the Bonus Army built a shantytown across the Potomac River in Anacostia Flats. The marchers were encouraged when the House of Representatives passed the Patman Veterans Bill on June 15, despite President Hoover's vow to veto it. But on June 17, the bill was defeated in the Senate, and

tempers began to flare on both sides. Most of the veterans deject-
edly returned home. But several thousand remain in the capital
with their families. Many have nowhere else to go."

Art abruptly stops and starts pacing as he rips the newspaper
to shreds. The group of veterans looks on as his rage is on full
display. A shot rings out in the distance, and several more follow.
The group goes silent. Some stand up and look around as men
from every direction start running toward the sound of the
gunfire. Our group takes flight and follows the sound of shooting
off in the distance near the encampment's northern perimeter.

Approaching the location where we heard the shots fired, we
come upon a scene of utter chaos where Washington D.C. police
officers and veterans are fighting in large numbers. The police
are clubbing the veterans and knocking many to the ground. The
veterans tear into them with their fists, sticks, and clubs, and
some are throwing bricks. It's not trench warfare like we fought
in France, but we've come upon a surreal scene where Americans
are viciously fighting each other. Men are being knocked to the
ground and getting clubbed over the head as blood flows from
their wounds. Several men are taking heavy blows to their
bodies, sending them screaming to the ground in pain.

The D.C police seem to have the upper hand, but more
veterans are pouring into the area, joining in on the melee.
Without a moment's hesitation, our group rushes into the fight.
Suddenly I'm pushed violently from behind and try to save
myself from falling as the pavement shoots out from under me. I
hit the ground hard, landing on my stomach. Out of nowhere, a
foot comes up from the pavement and kicks me in the face. Blood
flows from my mouth and nose. Two police officers fly past me,
airborne, slamming into the pavement just to my front as I
struggle to get up.

Art sent them flying and saved me from further beatings. He
reaches down and pulls me up by the collar. "Are you alright,

Sam? This is quite a brawl we have going here. These bastards are showing us no respect or mercy. They're just beating the hell out of any one of us they can."

Looking at Art, I manage to nod my head in agreement. "Thanks, Art." As I do, two more police officers try to take Art down. Big mistake! Even though he's a man with one bum arm, he knocks them both down to the pavement with a club he is carrying. They lie there motionless. Our group forms a defensive circle and engages anyone who attacks us. Art seems to relish the fight, along with some of the other fellows. I believe their frustrations have reached a peak, and their patience has waned.

I'm still trying to assess the extent of my injuries when three police officers come at me. We may all be Americans, but this madness is unjustified, and I'm livid. Closing in on me, swinging their clubs wildly, I take evasive action using my military training and send all three to the ground. Two stay down, one tries to get up, and I flatten him with a knee to the face. He's out cold. I feel guilt and shame as I look down at the men I just knocked out.

What is this madness? Why has it come to this? How can men from the same country, those that serve it as law enforcement officers and those who fought for the country in WWI, fight like this? How does this end?

More police officers are flooding the area. Art, the group of veterans we are with, and I retreat from there and head for a first aid tent. We're all bruised, bleeding from being hit, and some are limping from the beating we took at the hands of the police. We stop at the first aid station we come upon. It is overcrowded with wounded veterans being treated and those waiting their turn to be helped.

We join them and wait our turn.

AFTERNOON JULY 28, 1932

Art and I are sitting under a tree near the first aid tent, talking with the men in our group. We're being attended by medics while trying to relax and digest what we've been subjected to by our fellow countrymen. Sitting here lamenting, a veteran in partial uniform with the rank of Captain walks up to us and introduces himself.

"Gentlemen, I'm Charles Glazebrook, formerly a captain in the Rainbow Division." The man's accent is very familiar. Looking up and seeing his facial features as they come into focus, I recognize him immediately. As Charles looks down on the men around him, he focuses on Art and me. As he does, a huge smile crosses his face, and he walks over to us. Both Art and I stand up and extend our hands. Art steps forward first and gives Charles a big hug, releases him, and they shake hands. I move forward and give Charles a long hug. Stepping back from each other, we shake hands and comment on each other's appearance. We have aged some with a hint of gray hair, but we're both in excellent physical condition. "Damn, Captain, it's great to see you. It's been a long time."

"It has been, Sam. Why don't you introduce me around to our fellow veterans?"

"Sure, Captain. Fellows, this is Charles Glazebrook. He was our Commanding Officer in France. He's a good man, and I would serve with him anytime, anywhere."

With that comment, the other fellows take turns introducing themselves and shaking his hand. Introductions completed, we take a seat, and I ask Charles to tell us what he knows about the situation. Our group settles in. I light up my pipe, Art puts some chewing tobacco in his mouth, and most of the other fellows light up a cigarette. Charles tells us he is part of a group of former officers who are fanning out around the encampments to share what they know about our situation and gauge the conditions and attitudes of the veterans still here.

Charles shares what he knows. He speaks in a controlled, authoritative, and matter-of-fact manner. "Fellows, earlier in the week, with the army preparing to step in at any moment, Police Superintendent Glassford was ordered to begin evacuating several buildings on Pennsylvania Avenue, using force if necessary. This morning, U.S. Attorney General Mitchell ordered the veterans removed from all government property. When the Washington D. C. police began their clearing operation, they met with resistance. Veterans fought back, throwing bricks and refusing to move. The police shot at the protesters, and two veterans were severely wounded. They are not expected to survive. President Hoover has ordered the Secretary of War to surround the affected area and clear it without delay."

Charles pauses, takes out a cigarette, lights it, and continues. "Army Chief of Staff General Douglas MacArthur has been ordered to clear the BEF out, and he commands a contingent of infantry and cavalry, supported by five tanks. The Bonus Army marchers, our wives, and children are to be driven out, and the shelters taken down. To make matters worse, if that's even possible, it seems General MacArthur is convinced that the march is a communist conspiracy to undermine the government of the United States. But that is simply not the case. There may be a few communist sympathizers scattered among us, but if anything, most of the men seem to be vehemently anti-Communist."

He stops and pulls a clipping of an article from his pocket. "I'm going to read this from yesterday's paper written by a journalist and eyewitness, Joseph C. Harsch." Charles unfolds the clipping and reads it to us. "This is not a revolutionary situation. This is a bunch of people in great distress wanting help. These are simply veterans from World War I who are out of luck, out of money, and want to get their bonuses. They need the money now, not in 1945."

We've been listening intently to Charles, and the look on his face is one of dire concern and apprehension. I ask him, "Charles, what do you think will happen next, and what should we do?"

He responds. "Sam, I think the army will be unleashed on us before sunset, and it could get violent. They are amassing quite a force of soldiers, and with MacArthur and Patton, who commands the cavalry unit, in charge, you can bet they will follow their orders. They're both military men to the core, regardless of how they may feel about us and our cause."

With a somber, almost pleading voice, I respond. "What about approaching the authorities and attempting to calm the situation down. It seems to me we should be able to make some progress through talking?" Several of the fellows nod their agreement and respond with, "Sounds like a good idea to me."

Charles looks around at the men present and then at me. "Sam, we have been trying, but no one in authority at the Federal level or military hierarchy, nor in Washington D.C. law enforcement will meet with us. They have all been stonewalling us since the Senate failed to pass the House bill. That bill would have helped our situation. I think it best that you men break camp as soon as possible and leave the area. Particularly if you have any family members with you."

Charles then stands up and asks Art and me to follow him. We join him as he bids farewell to the other men and wishes them good luck.

Away from the other fellows, Charles shakes our hands, gives us each a hug, and bids farewell for now. "Sam, Art, it's terrific to see you men again. When this is over, we need to hook up for a meal, play catch-up and spend some time together. For now, take care and be careful."

We part company as Art and I walk back to his tent, and

Charles fades into the distance as he heads for the command tent. That is where the central organizers are located and where he'll report what he's seen and heard.

EVENING JULY 28, 1932

Major General Douglas MacArthur watches as a battalion of steel-helmeted soldiers align themselves in a straight four-column formation, bayonets affixed to rifles. He nods his head in satisfaction. Discipline is essential in the military. Up ahead, Major George Patton kicks his heels against his mount, and the big horse rears forward to signal a line of cavalry. The riders draw their sabers, and the animals step out in unison, hooves smacking loudly on the street. Five Renault tanks lurch behind them. These seven-ton relics from World War I are presumably just for show. However, they leave little doubt as to the seriousness of the moment. On cue, at about 4:30 p.m. on July 28, 1932, the infantry begins a slow, steady march forward. Completing the surreal atmosphere, a machine gun unit dismounts their trucks and sets up their weapons. These weapons of war had a devastating effect on troops attacking across "no man's land" in France. To deploy them here and now in front of these veterans is a deplorable act of indifference and unbridled disrespect for the men gathered here today.

This is no parade, although hundreds of curious office workers have interrupted their daily routines to crowd the sidewalk or hang out of windows along Pennsylvania Avenue between the White House and the Capitol to see what will happen. Up ahead, a group of weary veterans, many dressed in rags and ill-fitting, faded uniforms, wait in anticipation amid our sorry camp of tents and structures made from clapboard and sheets of tin covered in tar paper. Some loiter in the street. We heard something was afoot and expected it after what happened earlier. Now, a murmur rises from the camp crowd. At first, we think the troops are marching in our honor. Many of us cheer them until Patton orders the cavalry to charge, an action which prompts many veterans to yell, "Shame! Shame!" Seeing the army's menacing approach, we are momentarily stunned, disbelieving.

Recovering our senses, a few of the men curse and send bottles and bricks flying toward the troops, ineffective weapons against so formidable a force. The missiles shatter with the impact on the hard pavement or bounce off the flanks of horses and soldiers. Undaunted, the roughly 600 troops maintain their discipline with tight-lipped determination.

Some of the veterans have already begun running from the oncoming soldiery, but angry packs hold their ground, defiantly wielding clubs, and iron bars, yelling profanities. An officer signals, and the infantry halts to don masks and toss gas grenades. Forming into two assault waves, they continue their push. Clouds of stinging, gray fumes float through the air, forcing most of us unarmed veterans to flee the area.

After the cavalry charge, the infantry, with fixed bayonets and deploying a vomiting gas agent, enter the smaller camps, evicting veterans, families, and camp followers. The veterans, with their families, flee across the Anacostia River to their largest camp.

Next comes the most controversial moment in this whole affair, a moment that directly involves General MacArthur. Secretary of War Hurley has twice sent orders to MacArthur indicating that the President, worried that the government reaction might look overly harsh, does not wish the army to pursue the Bonus Marchers across the bridge into their main encampment on the other side of the Anacostia River. But MacArthur responds, "I'm too busy and don't want to be bothered by people coming down and pretending to bring orders." He sends his men across the bridge anyway, after pausing to allow as many people as possible to evacuate. A fire soon erupts in the camp. While it's not clear which side started the blaze, the sight of the great fire will surely become an iconic image of the Bonus Expeditionary Force movement and the Bonus Marchers.

During this last encounter at the main camp, tragedy befalls our group of veterans. Having been chased back across the river, we take refuge in an area near the back of the encampment and form what we called a battle line in France. We've taken enough intimidation, violence, and brutality directed at us with no regard for our well-being by our own army. The very army we served proudly with in France is now beating us mercilessly and treating us like criminals. Our battle line is three rows deep with about fifty men per row. We are a rag-tag-looking bunch dressed in torn and patched clothes, with scarves over our noses and mouth to help mitigate the gas. Many of us have made crude shields out of discarded metal and wood. Several men have wooden clubs and heavy metal pipes for defensive purposes. We have no guns or knives and are not looking for trouble.

But enough is enough, leave us alone, and we will depart the area in the morning.

Apparently, it is not to be. We see soldiers in their battle line moving methodically through the encampment and closing in on us. They are wearing gas masks. Several of the soldiers are throwing gas canisters as they move forward. They hit anyone in their way with rifle thrusts and blows to the head with the wooden stock of their rifles. Many veterans are hurt and fall to the ground bleeding. The soldiers just move over them and onto the next group. As they approach us, we don't wait for them to hit the first line of us. We advance at a quick run and engage them with our clubs and pipes. At first, they are stunned and don't know what to do as we knock several to the ground. They quickly rally behind their officers and continue moving forward. All be it at a much slower and cautious pace.

Art, who has been by my side the whole time, and I are immersed in the skirmish. We use our own clubs and shields to dish out some punishment on the soldiers attacking us. Art takes on several soldiers and knocks them to the ground before he is clubbed over the head viciously by one, then another soldier. I move to his defense, but not before he takes another heavy blow to the head and falls lifeless to the ground. I'm enraged and attack all three of the soldiers who clubbed him. I send two to the ground withering in pain from striking them hard with my club. The third soldier thrusts his rifle and bayonet at my chest, but I manage to perry his thrust and club him hard on the back of the helmet. He falls to the ground, shakes violently, and goes lifeless. I feel nothing for him, no remorse, no regret, only concern for Art, who I fear is mortally wounded by all the blows they gave him. Looking around at the scene before me, I can almost imagine we were Spartans at the Battle of Thermopylae, fighting off the hordes of Persians.

I'm knocked to the ground from behind by some soldiers who keep pushing forward. It isn't a severe blow, and I manage to crawl over to Art. He is still breathing, but it's shallow, his head is bleeding severely, and he's not responsive to my physical and verbal gestures. Two other veterans witness his plight, move over to me, and the three of us manage to carry him from the field and out of harm's way. Looking for a first aid station, we find an army unit near us that has set up a medical triage station. There are army soldiers and veterans lying on the ground around the station with various wounds, some serious, others superficial.

We carry Art up to one of the attending medics and plead with him to help Art. At first, he is reluctant but checks out Art's situation and immediately directs us to place him on a makeshift table. He calls over one of the army doctors, who proceeds to check him out more closely. It is not good. They do their best to stabilize him and then place him in an ambulance for transport to the nearest hospital. I insist on accompanying him and bid farewell to the other veterans with whom I've spent the last few days.

Arriving at the hospital, Art is taken into the emergency room, and I'm directed to a waiting room where I'm told they will keep me informed. While waiting, my adrenaline rush slowly wears off, and my heart rate and breathing return to normal. As I begin to relax, the full extent of my exhaustion and various cuts and bruises come into focus. The soldiers really did a number on many of us, including me. In a nutshell, I'm a mess but will survive. The jury is out on Art. He took a hell of a beating. I don't want to lose a close friend, especially in this manner. What a tragedy for all involved. To serve your country honorably and then be killed by your own army just for standing up for your rights, demanding some respect and appreciation, and seeking what has been promised you by the very government you served faithfully.

My thoughts drift off as I think of Marie and Sean. They didn't want me to come here, and in retrospect, maybe I shouldn't have. But our cause is just, and the outcome is disgraceful. Many of us will have to live with what happened here these last 24 hours for the rest of our lives. I don't know how I feel about it now. As time passes and the full ramifications of what transpired here become known, maybe I'll figure it out. For now, I just want to go home, see my family, and move on with my life. Unlike Art and so many of the veterans participating in the BEF, I have a good, steady, decent job with some stability in my life. I could have made a case for not being here and just stayed home away from this madness. But I'm not made that way. The veterans of World War I deserve better, and I will do what I can, going forward, to help make it so.

MORNING JULY 29, 1932

I'm awakened by an orderly shaking my shoulder. It's early morning, and a bright sun rises in the east and shines through the waiting room window. Slowly waking from a light sleep, I find myself looking up into the faces of an orderly and a distraught medic. From their expressions, I sense the news is not good. The medic speaks in a low, compassionate voice. "Is your name Sam?"

"Yes. Who are you? How is Art?"

"My name is John. I've been sent out here to inform you about your friend Art. I'm afraid he didn't make it. He was severely beaten about the head and neck. There was nothing the medical staff could do for him. He passed away an hour ago, having never regained consciousness. We are all very sorry."

I'm tired, drained of emotion, and numb to the news. I didn't think he would survive the beating, but it still comes as a shock. Art was a good man, a loyal friend, and one hell of a soldier. He did not deserve to die at the hands of other American soldiers. I stand up, look at the medic and respond. "Thanks. Art is from Cleveland; he was a professional baseball player for the Cleveland Indians and a highly decorated doughboy from WWI. I'll be taking his body home. When can you release him? Who do I need to talk with, and how do I go about getting this done?"

They take me to an Army medical captain who handles the arrangements. The next thirty-six hours are one big blur. I manage to get myself cleaned, secure some decent clothes, have a warm meal, and inform the other veterans in our group about the death of Art. I then accompany Art's body back home to Cleveland and his waiting parents.

Bringing Art's lifeless body back to his parents and trying to explain to them what happened has to be one of the most difficult moments in my life. I'm not sure how to explain to them the senselessness of it all, particularly the loss of Art, their son, at the hands of our own soldiers. It is an emotional visit, and I don't believe I provided them with much solace over the loss of their son. All I can do is offer my thoughts and prayers and grieve with Art's family. I've lost a great friend in a senseless act of violence where nothing was gained.

This country had better wake up! You can't treat the military men who fight and come home wounded the way you have the veterans of World War I. How do you expect to staff the military with good men when we are forced to stand up to our own countrymen and defend our way of life? Wake up, America, think this through!

It's late when I arrive home. Marie is waiting for me at the top of the steps on our porch. I walk up to her, embrace her tightly and let my pent-up emotions flow out. Tears stream down my face as we stand there in a tight embrace, and Marie caresses the back of my neck while whispering into my ear. "I love you; I love you."

AFTERMATH

It was a messy affair for everyone. Patton, a man who revered duty, had mixed emotions, calling it a "most distasteful form of service." Still, he commended both sides. "It speaks volumes for the high character of the men that not a shot was fired. In justice to the marchers, had they really wanted to start something, they had a great chance here but refrained." To his dismay, the routed marchers included Joseph Angelo. A man who 14 years earlier had helped save the wounded Patton's life by pulling him into a foxhole until they were rescued by Art, some other doughboys, and me.

In the aftermath of the violence on July 28, 1932, two veterans lost their lives from being shot by the police during the assault, and an eleven-week-old baby died from what was believed to be a gas-related illness. In addition, an eight-year-old boy was partially blinded by gas, several police officers were injured, and two had their skulls fractured. It was estimated that up to a thousand veterans suffered gas-related injuries, with several sustaining beatings from clubs, rifle butts, and sabers. Some of the veterans later died from severe beatings they received during these violent encounters.

Although many Americans applauded the government's action as an unfortunate but necessary move to maintain law and order, most of the press was less sympathetic. "Flames rose high over the desolate Anacostia flats at midnight tonight," read the first sentence of the New York Times account, "and a pitiful stream of refugee veterans of the World War walked out of their homes for the past several months, not knowing where to go from here."

35

THE LITTLE STEEL STRIKE OF 1937

THE MEMORIAL DAY MASSACRE OF 1937

It's Sunday, May 30, 1937, Memorial Day. Henry and I have joined many Republic steelworkers and their families gathered at a park just a few blocks from the front gate of their mill located on Chicago's Southeast side. The atmosphere is festive as they prepare to march on their mill. There are many women and children in the group. Two days earlier, these workers went on strike against Ohio-based Republic Steel for better treatment, wages, and working conditions. Republic Steel owns the mill located here in Chicago's Southeast Side.

Henry and I are the two senior managers at our mill in Canton, which is owned by Republic Steel. We were asked by representatives for the workers of the Chicago mill to join them in a show of support. We arrived yesterday by train to support these workers with their grievances and demands. Our mill has experienced similar protests and has been threatened with strikes. We hope to gain some insight into how this strike is progressing and maybe learn something from their experiences.

As the two of us stand here looking out over the crowd around us, I wonder what is going through their minds as I momentarily drift off into my own thoughts.

How did it come to this? Why must workers have to confront owners and management just to be treated fairly? Will we ever reach an understanding and appreciation for what constitutes fair treatment of workers by owners and management? Some of the main points of a news article I read back home before we left to come here still linger on with me.

In the late nineteenth and early twentieth centuries, factory workers in the United States faced low wages, almost no benefits, poor, and in many cases, unsafe working conditions. This situation affects American workers employed in most industries and companies, including the steel industry. Workers at the Republic Steel Company, Youngstown Sheet and Tube Company, and several other smaller Ohio steel companies started going on sit-down strikes in May of this year. These steel companies collectively have become known as "Little Steel."

Historically when workers went on strike, they would leave the factory and join picket lines. Factory owners and managers would hire "scab" laborers to cross the picket lines and continue production. Scabbing refers to workers willing to accept terms that union workers have rejected, and they interfere with the strike action in progress. This practice makes it difficult for striking workers to obtain their demands. To gain an advantage and force management to negotiate with them, workers adopted the sit-down strike. Using this tactic, workers quit working but still occupied their places within the factory. This process meant factory owners could not send in additional workers to continue the job. They are reluctant to use private security forces or other strikebreakers to enter their factories and intimidate the striking workers. Factory owners fear this approach could result in the destruction of plant property. They can and often do hire security forces to protect their factories from the outside and prevent entrance to them by their workers.

Little Steel company strikes are pitting steelworkers, represented by the Congress of Industrial Organizations (CIO), a federation of unions that organize workers, against the owners and management of their steel companies. The strikes at Little Steel companies did not start immediately. It was generally expected that owners of Little Steel companies would follow U.S. Steel, referred to as "Big Steel," and sign a deal with the CIO. On March 30, 1937, the CIO proposed an agreement to Little Steel companies similar to the agreement that U.S. Steel had accepted. The proposal sought an eight-hour workday, a forty-hour workweek, overtime pay, a minimum wage, paid vacations, health and safety standards, seniority, and procedures for resolving grievances—reasonable requests that would help create a better working environment for steelworkers.

Rather than sign, Little Steel Company representatives held meetings, debated, and delayed while they prepared for actual battle. Owners and management of many Little Steel companies stockpiled weapons and gas, hired private police, donated weapons to official law enforcement, and encouraged them to hire more deputies. They also installed searchlights and barbed wire, built up supplies of food and bedding, and fired hundreds of workers who were demanding that they be allowed to unionize.

So here we are today, standing with the steelworkers from this Southside of Chicago steel mill.

Henry places his hand on my shoulder and asks, "What are you thinking about, Sam? You seem distant and lost in your thoughts."

Henry's action refocuses my attention to the moment at hand as I respond. "I was just thinking about how we got to this point and wondering what all these people here today are thinking about?"

Gazing out over the crowd, Henry responds. "There sure are a lot of them. Do you remember what one of the steelworkers we met earlier today from Youngstown Sheet and Tube told us?"

Before I can answer him, he continues. "He said that Chicago Republic Steel was scabbing. So, they came up here to South Chicago with truckloads of people, working-class people, to show their support and solidarity for the unionization of this factory—I guess that rather sums it up!"

Chicago Republic Steel mill has long anticipated this strike and fortified their factory. There are loyal employees stationed around the clock inside and outside the factory. There is a stockpile of munitions, including poison gas.

On this Memorial Day, approximately 250 city police and twenty to thirty private police form a defensive perimeter around the plant. They are armed with revolvers, nightsticks, blackjacks, and hatchet handles.

Because of the large number of protesters here today, the police have cut the crowd off a block away from the mill by creating a line of officers blocking access to the gate. With no access to the mill, more and more angry protesters have begun to crowd in front of the line of officers. They're arguing with the officers to let them pass and continue their planned march. As the protesters and police argue, the conversations become more heated, and pending violence is in the air.

Henry and I begin roaming through the throngs of protesters observing their actions and that of the police. My observations convince me there will be a major confrontation very shortly. Looking over at Henry, I convey my concern in a calm, loud voice. "Henry, this doesn't look good to me. We need to step back from the crowd. What do you think?"

He responds, "I agree. Let's get the hell out of here now. It's looking bad. The cops are itching for a fight, and they're well-armed."

I nod in agreement. We move far back from the crowd and take up a position on a little knoll. From here, we have a good view of unfolding events well out to our front. Henry and I have been together since France. We've seen more than our share of violence and are no strangers to it. But the violence, disrespect, and mistreatment of workers, many of whom are veterans, that I've witnessed since returning home from France is concerning. Kirk is still the top manager of our steel mill in Canton. He systematically degrades our employees, threatens them, and calls in scabs to stop strike attempts. Neither Henry nor I have any control over company policies, yet we are continually called upon to resolve worker issues. Without the power to change policies, there is little we can accomplish. We both fear our mill is headed for a major showdown with Kirk and some of the directors.

The Bonus March of 1932 resulted in the death of our good friend, Art, at the hands of our own soldiers. The doughboys of World War I who participated in that tragedy only wanted what had been promised them. For demanding that our government live up to its promises, we were set upon with a vengeance. Art, who now rests peacefully in his hometown cemetery with a veteran's marker over his grave, died standing up for what was right and just.

In 1936, Congress finally acted and overrode President Roosevelt's veto of the World War Adjusted Compensation Act and paid the veterans their bonuses nine years early. It came too late for many doughboys who served and participated in the Bonus March in 1932. Art and many other doughboys died of war-related injuries and health issues before bonuses were finally paid. Delaying bonus payments for over two decades, punishing those who participated in the Bonus March, and then finally attempting to make it right eighteen years after the war ended is a tragedy and travesty of justice!

Once again, here in Chicago, I believe we will witness another tragedy. Americans will be subjected to violence at the hands of other Americans just for standing up and demanding a safe work environment, some of the same benefits as management, and a decent wage. Many of these men here today are World War I veterans, some are former Bonus Marchers, and all have seen their share of violence over the years.

Why must we resort to these tactics simply to provide a decent standard of living for ourselves and our families? Where is the empathy, understanding, and courage to do what is just for the men and women who work for company owners?

From our vantage point, we see crowds pushing forward on the police lines trying to get to the mill's main gate. As they move forward, some protesters in the back of the mass of people, start throwing stones, sticks, and whatever else they can find. Several police officers are hit, and many panic and open fire on the crowd of men, women, and children. Then it starts. Scores of club-wielding police set upon a peaceful crowd. They move through the crowd beating people, throwing gas canisters, and firing their weapons. The police rampage goes unabated while senior police officers watch from the sidelines. What a despicable act of indifference and a total lack of disciplined leadership on their part! They must be getting paid to look the other way by the mill's management.

Our instincts take over as Henry, and I rush out onto the field, where hundreds of protesters are scattered on the ground. Many have been severely beaten, and several have gunshot wounds. Some are not moving and appear dead. The first man I approach, lying on the ground, looks up at me and pleads for help. "Help me, please. I've been shot in the legs. I can't get up."

I reach down, sit him up and check out his wounds. "You're

okay, buddy! Your wounds don't look too bad. I'll get you over to that knoll where you should be safe."

He grasps my hand as I pull him up. His facial expression is one of appreciation as he responds to me. "Thank you! I thought they were going to kill me. I was in the war and fought in France, but I never heard so many bullets as those coppers fired. Women and children were screaming all over the place. They were like a herd of panic-stricken cattle. I ran till they got me. I saw one woman shot down, and a policeman dragged her away." Taking a moment to catch his breath, he continues, "What the hell is wrong with them?"

While helping him traverse the ground over to the safety of the knoll, Henry comes up next to me, carrying a woman in his arms who has been severely beaten and is unconscious.

Henry is mad, and he has that look in his eyes we used to get when we were fighting Huns in the trenches. He's full of rage, and his face reflects it as he yells in an angry and emotional voice. "My god, what is going on here? They're beating, shooting, and gassing women and children. My god!"

We reach the safety of the knoll and place our wounded people on the ground. We do what we can to make them comfortable. The woman regains consciousness but has been severely beaten. As we help her and the wounded man, other protesters trickle in carrying wounded men, women, and children. In a matter of minutes, a basic triage station is set up. We're not in France, but damn if there isn't a familiar sight and sound to it all.

Some of the protesters were medics in France during the war and are now helping the wounded. For the next hour, Henry and I move back and forth, recovering wounded protesters from the field where they were beaten and shot. The police do nothing to help us, but neither do they interfere with our efforts, as many former doughboys have taken to helping the wounded. From the look on our faces, it's clear we will not accept any more of their punishment.

By the end of the afternoon, working together as a team, we manage to move all the wounded to various hospitals for medical attention. Noticeably absent from our efforts to do so was any cooperation from Chicago police officers. They focused on their own men and left us to fend for ourselves.

Henry and I retire that evening with a clear picture of what we can expect should any strikes occur at our mill. We resolve to go back home and do what we can to prevent a similar incident from happening to us.

There is only one problem, Kirk!

THE DAY AFTER

It's late Monday morning, and we are headed back home on the train to Canton. Not having eaten since last night, Henry and I decide to have an early lunch. On our way to the dining car, a porter hands me a current newspaper from Chicago. The newspaper's headlines catch my attention immediately. After being seated and provided some hot coffee by the waiter, I read the article intently.

The incident on Memorial Day is already being called the Memorial Day Massacre of 1937. Of the twenty-three people killed or seriously injured in the Memorial Day Massacre identifiable as steelworkers, eighteen were married, eight were at least forty years old, and several were World War I veterans. Middle-aged family men were not the only victims of the Memorial Day Massacre: an eleven-year-old boy was shot in the ankle, a baby was wounded in the arm, and two women were shot in the legs.

Four demonstrators died of gunshot wounds on or near the

scene, and six others were severely wounded and not expected to survive their injuries. Another thirty demonstrators were shot, and sixty others were injured, for a total of around one hundred significant victims. Thirty-five police were injured, but none of their injuries were severe.

There were notable examples of police misbehavior in the treatment of pro-union demonstrators. Although the police brought ambulances for their men, they did little to aid grievously wounded participants and didn't bother to use their stretchers to carry the injured. One shooting victim probably died when the police removed him from a Red Cross van— clearly marked— that was trying to take him to a hospital. They were observed removing his tourniquet and placing him with several other people into a patrol wagon while he continued to lose considerable blood from an artery wound.

A young lady named Elena was walking near the front of the group when Chicago's finest opened fire with tear gas and pistols. In a telephone interview from her home with this newspaper, she stated: "I started to run and fell. Several others stumbled on top of me. It wasn't very comfortable. But it may have saved my life. And it certainly kept me from being beaten with those riot sticks the cops were using." She continued: "By the time I came up for air, the worst was over. It was unbelievable what I saw! The place looked like a battlefield. I looked around to see a policeman holding his gun against my back. Get off the field, he ordered, or I'll shoot you."

Immediately after the incident, Republic Steel's public relations team sent out multiple reports justifying the actions of the Chicago police force. With both local police forces and the National Guard supporting Little Steel, the situation can only deteriorate for strikers after the events of the Memorial Day Massacre. That event turned what seemed to be a peaceful strike of picketing and a rally march into what could become several months of arrests, beatings, and more deaths across the Midwest and Northeast. It is certain that more conflicts will emerge between Little Steel Companies and CIO union protesters.

FINISHING THE ARTICLE, I place the newspaper on the table and let out a long sigh of despair. It is unintentional, but it catches the attention of Henry, who looks at me directly and intently. "What's that all about, Sam?"

"This is some article, Henry. I knew a lot of people were hurt yesterday, but the level of carnage is hard to comprehend. The viciousness of the Chicago police officers who attacked the strikers and their families is appalling."

Looking out the dining car window at the passing landscape, Henry responds forebodingly. "Sam, I believe we'll experience the same very shortly. That fool Kirk has created a powder keg at the mill. Hiring all those thugs to protect himself and the mill facilities is a beast waiting to be unleashed on our workforce."

"I agree, but what can we do about it? After Kirk fired Otis last month with many directors supporting him, I believe we have little or no leverage left. Like you, I think we're headed for big trouble and very soon."

Henry nods his agreement. I close with, "Henry, let's meet early in the morning in your office. We need to take a position and confront Kirk. We must avoid a confrontation between our workers and management. I will reach out to Charles Glazebrook and see if he can help us defuse the situation."

Henry responds enthusiastically. "That's a great idea. With Charles handling U.S. Steel's accounts as the Senior Investment Banker with JP Morgan & Company, maybe, just maybe, he can help us." Taking a moment to look out at the passing countryside, he continues. "Are you going to reach out to him tonight?"

"Yes, when we get home, I'll give him a call and see what he suggests. Charles is a good man. If anyone can help us, he's the one."

Henry says, "I agree."

Looking back at me with a broad smile on his face, he continues. "Sam, Melanie, and I haven't shared this with anyone yet, not even my parents. I want you to be the first to know—we're going to be parents."

That catches me off guard. Impulsively, I leap from my chair as Henry stands up; I give him a bear hug. "That's terrific, Henry. Congratulations to you both. When is the baby due?"

Henry responds, "In about six months. Sam, Melanie, and I want you and Marie to be our baby's godparents."

I'm moved beyond words as I try to maintain my composure. Henry is also moved. Here we are, two grown men, standing in a dining car, hugging while fighting back the tears. People looking at us must be wondering what all the fuss is about and Henry, seeing their reactions, blurts out, "I'm going to be a father." Several people in the dining car smile, some clap, and many offer their congratulations to him.

We sit back down, settle into our seats, get comfortable and look out the window as rolling hills and pasture lands of the Ohio countryside roll past us. For the first time in several days, I feel relaxed and enjoy the rest of our trip home. It helps that neither Henry nor I pay for another drink while we enjoy a leisurely lunch.

HOME

During dinner, Sean, who is now a senior in high school, shares with me some of what he did while I was in Chicago. His exploits involve baseball and flying. He's on the high school baseball team, plays center field, and is one of their best hitters. His hitting style reminds me of Art. When Sean was a little boy, Art would give him batting lessons while visiting with us. Those lessons must have stuck with him. When it comes to flying, Sean has been going up into the air by himself for some time now, flying solo, as it's called. Since his first flight with Roscoe, the pilots he knows have trained him to the point where he has become a very experienced biplane pilot.

After dinner, Sean retires to his room to do his homework. Marie and I stroll out to the front porch and sit together on the swing. It's a very comfortable evening with a light, cool breeze and a glimmering half-moon hanging low on the horizon. I'm enjoying some Irish whiskey, and Marie sips coffee as I share with her my experiences over the last several days in Chicago. Marie has followed the events on the radio and in newspaper articles, but hearing it from me, an eyewitness to it all, discourages her. She is aware of the situation at our mill and believes, as I do, that a major confrontation is coming. I pull her close to me while sitting on our swing and share my conversation earlier this evening with Charles. He is taking a few days of leave and coming here tomorrow afternoon to help Henry and me at the mill. He'll be staying with us. Marie is delighted and looks forward to seeing him again. Charles holds a special place in her heart because of all he did for both of us back in France.

CONFRONTATION WITH KIRK

Henry and I arrive at the mill early and are in Henry's office discussing a strategy to deal with Kirk. Charles is scheduled to arrive later this afternoon; at which time we'll work out the details of our plan with him. We called a special meeting for 5:00 p.m. with Kirk and the board of directors. Our assistants have notified all concerned. Apparently, Kirk is not happy about this but has no power to stop us. As the two senior managers of the company, we have the prerogative and authority to do so. Smoking my pipe and enjoying some coffee while we talk, Henry's assistant knocks on his door, walks in, and conveys a message from Kirk Snyder.

"Excuse me, sir, but Mr. Snyder's assistant just called, and he wants the both of you to join him in his office immediately."

Henry responds, "Thank you, tell him we'll be right there."

As she exits the office, we both look at each other and smile.

"So, it begins!" Henry says out loud.

I reply, "So it seems. Let's go see what the asshole wants."

Snuffing out my pipe as we walk down the hall to Kirk's office, I have no idea what he'll say. I know we desperately want to convince him to slow down and give the workers a break. If he does not back off, we are on the brink of a Chicago-like incident.

Arriving at his office, his assistant takes us in and closes the door behind us as she leaves the room. Kirk sits at his desk with his feet propped up on it and a big smirk on his face. Standing well back are his two assistants, who he hired years ago and are nothing more than goons/hatchet men who do whatever Kirk tells them. His office is the largest in the mill, has high-end furniture and trappings, and his desk and chair are on a small platform. Those invited into his sanctuary appear smaller when they sit in front of his desk. Kirk believes this configuration commands respect and demonstrates his position of power.

This should be interesting!

Kirk speaks first in an authoritative, derogatory manner. "Gentlemen, I was just informed about your special board of directors meeting for five today. I don't know what you plan to say or do, but this is my mill. You work for me. Whatever I say we're going to do, we will do. Any questions?"

We ignore his rant and stare right past him. He then continues. "How was your trip to Chicago? Did you learn anything that we might be able to use here at the mill? More specifically, any defensive actions or use of force tactics we could employ here?"

He doesn't offer us a seat, nor do we move to take one. I prefer to stand and look down on him as I respond. "No, actually, Kirk, we have some suggestions, which hopefully will help us avert a strike at the mill and avoid violence."

Henry speaks, "Chicago was a disaster for everyone there. No one gained a damn thing."

Kirk cuts us off, stands up, walks around his desk, and sits on one side of it. He takes his time as he grabs a cigar from his humidor, bites off the end, spits it on the floor, and lights the cigar. He takes a long draw on it and blows the smoke our way. We look on in amusement as his two goons stand there in a menacing pose. They remind me of some Huns standing at attention while waiting on their commanding officer to give them an order to dish out some punishment.

Kirk continues. "Here's the deal. I'm bringing in a group of strikebreakers—scabs, I believe the men call them. Tomorrow. They will take over the mill floor and work reduced shifts. Any man who works for us now and doesn't show up tomorrow for work will be fired. Based on previous encounters we've had with our workforce, I'm assuming that most of the men will stay out of the mill and strike."

Observing our body language and facial expressions, he tries to read our reactions to his comments. Seeing none, he continues. "I need to know if you two are with me and will be here tomorrow, or will you support the workers as you have in the past?"

I look at Henry, he looks at me, and we're both struggling to control our emotions and reactions to this idiot. I unload on Kirk first.

"Kirk, you're a damn idiot. If we learned anything in Chicago, it's this! What you're going to do will result in violence. The mill's production and steel quality will suffer, and the men's morale and dedication to the mill will take a severe hit. Do you have any idea of what you're about to set in motion here?"

Henry unloads on him next. "My god, you really are a fool. My father was right. He always said you would be a disaster for this company. Not only no, but hell no! I'm not going to support your foolish actions. I'm with the men and will fight you every step of the way."

Kirk smiles at him with that smirk he has, takes a puff on his cigar, and looks over at me still with that smirk. "What about you, Sam? Where do you stand on this?"

I step forward and get right in his face. "You're a disgrace and one hell of a low-life human being. No way in hell I'll support this madness or you. Clearly, there is no talking any of this through with you." I look over at Henry, then the two goons, and back at Kirk. My blood is running hot. My heart is racing. I have an intense hatred for this man, and I'm sure it emanates from my eyes as I stare into his face. He flinches, moves back in fear, and motions for his two goons to step between us.

"Don't worry, Kirk, I'm not going to kick your sorry ass here today. We're going to challenge your authority with the board of directors later this afternoon. We will be joined by Charles Glazebrook from JP Morgan of New York. In case you haven't heard of him before, he's one of three senior investment bankers in the country that works with U.S. Steel in their handling of union activities and employee relations."

Kirk steps back as his two assistants place themselves between him and me. He looks surprised that we brought in Charles and asks, "How did you manage to get Mr. Glazebrook involved?"

"It's a long story, and you wouldn't understand or appreciate it."

Both Henry and I turn to leave his office. Kirk shouts at us as we leave. "I'm the boss here, don't turn your backs on me. Come back here."

We walk out of his office, and I respond over my shoulder at him. "Go to hell!"

Late that afternoon, Charles arrives by train. We pick him up at the station and drive to the mill. On our way to the mill, we brief Charles on what is happening and how we hope to convince the board of directors to fire Kirk and avert a disaster. He agrees with our approach and offers a few suggestions to strengthen our case.

Arriving at the mill, we head directly for the boardroom, where everyone is gathered and waiting on us when we enter the room. The atmosphere is chilly and hostile. It feels like we're about to take on the Huns in the trenches again. We take a seat at one end of the large, long cherry wood table. After welcoming everyone and extending our appreciation for their attendance, I introduce the board of directors to Charles and touch briefly on his background. They know who he is and how well respected he is throughout the steel industry, especially with Big Steel companies. Henry and I brief the directors on our Chicago experience and express our concerns about what will happen if Kirk is allowed to proceed with his plans to bring in strikebreakers— especially since the workforce isn't currently on strike. They have no immediate plans to do so. Kirk is deliberately setting up a situation where the workforce can't step back. They listen to us intently, with no questions.

The atmosphere in the room hasn't changed when we turn the floor over to Charles. He spends considerable time informing them of what will happen and offers several alternatives to consider. Pursuing these alternatives will help to avert trouble, show good faith with the workforce, and provide them with many benefits and improvements in the workplace that Big Steel has implemented for their workforce. They listen intently and respectfully to Charles.

Finally, I stand up and deliver the final comment to the directors in a calm, deliberate, and matter-of-fact manner. "Gentlemen, it is our opinion that Kirk should be relieved of his duties immediately and asked to resign from the company. If he does not do so, he should be terminated." The room goes completely silent. I don't think anyone was anticipating that statement.

Kirk is present and has shown no interest in what any of us said during the meeting. Apparently, up to this point, he has not been swayed. However, his swift reaction to my comments comes when he stands up and starts shouting at the men present. His father joins him as they try to discredit Charles, Henry, and myself. When a vote is taken to stop Kirk, it's close. Kirk's position prevails for the moment, and they decide to back him.

The special Board meeting ends. There is no doubt now. We are headed for a train wreck; an unmitigated disaster from which the mill may not recover. Time will tell. Charles, Henry, and I leave the Board meeting with a stern warning to the members about what they just voted to support and the disaster which will follow. That night after dinner at my home, the three of us sit on the front porch and consume several shots of Irish whiskey. It's going to be total chaos tomorrow at the mill.

36

REPUBLIC IRON AND STEEL COMPANY STRIKE

RIOT AND TREACHERY

Charles and I awaken early this morning. We enjoy our breakfast of ham, eggs, warm biscuits, and some hot coffee prepared by Marie. This will be a long day, and Marie wanted us to have a good hot breakfast before leaving for the mill. It's the first week of June, and Sean is home on summer break. He joins us at the kitchen table. Looking over at Charles and me, he says in a low, concerned, and quizzical voice.

"Dad, what's going on down at the mill? I heard yesterday afternoon from some of my friends that there is going to be a large demonstration at the mill this morning. They were saying that a bunch of police, thugs, and possibly some National Guard troops will be there to keep the workers out of the plant while strikebreakers go inside and do their work."

Charles and I are both a little surprised by his comments and general knowledge of the situation we face at the mill. I look to Sean. "Well, son, it's like this. Mr. Snyder has created a situation that will probably escalate very quickly before the morning is over. We tried late yesterday afternoon to convince the board of directors to allow us to handle the situation. But they left it in the hands of Mr. Snyder."

Sean asks, "Are you going to lose your job?"

"No, son. But it is going to be a rough day! We'll ultimately prevail."

Marie has quietly listened to our exchange, and now she speaks out. "Sean, dear, don't you worry about your father. He will do the right thing. Hopefully, this will all end quickly and without anyone getting hurt."

Charles finishes his cup of coffee and stands up to leave. "Sam, we better be on our way."

I stand up and nod in agreement gulping down the rest of my coffee. Looking over at Sean, I tell him goodbye for now and not to worry. I'll see him this evening. Marie gets up, comes over to me, and we hold each other closely as she walks Charles and me to the front door. Before opening the door, she gives me a big kiss, "Be careful, Sam. I love you. I'll see you this evening." She then hugs Charles and tells him to watch over me. We leave my house and drive to the mill.

It is the first warm day of summer. Driving up to the mill with the car windows down, we see a large picket line has already been established near the front gate by hundreds of our steelworkers, backed by hundreds of supporters; some dressed in their Sunday best. They face a large contingent of police officers from Canton, several strikebreakers, and thugs standing between them and the entrance to the mill. Inside the fence line is a company of National Guard troops arrayed in what appears to be two lines of about a hundred troops each. They are protecting the mill.

This doesn't look good, and we just got here. Upon parking my car, Charles and I rush over to the group, pushing our way through the crowd. Many people recognize me as we work our way forward. Some shout out their encouragement, tempered with threats and demands. "We just want to be treated fairly." "We don't deserve this!" "Fire Kirk, he's a disgrace!" "Down with the directors!" "We want Sam and Henry to manage the mill. We can work with them." "We want fair wages, more benefits, and time off."

So it goes as Charles and I reach the front of the group closest to the main gate and look across at the line of men blocking our entrance to the mill. Threats and insults are yelled across the picket line at the police, strikebreakers, and thugs. They, in turn, respond with their own insults and threats. The situation is rapidly deteriorating, and at any moment, violence could erupt. Charles and I are yelling over the crowd of people nearest us and trying to get their attention. It's not working. From behind, Henry taps me on the shoulder and pulls Charles and me over to him. He yells to us, trying to be heard above the noise of the crowd.

"Sam, it's useless. They're not willing to listen—neither side. Kirk has fired up the goons he's brought in, and they have been taunting every steelworker they see. The police are not attempting to quiet them down and, in fact, appear to be encouraging them."

Charles interjects, "Should we try and move your steelworkers and supporters back further to put more space between the two groups?"

I respond, "Let's give it a try."

The three of us fan out about twenty feet from each other and start to move the people in front of us backward. Some of the steelworkers see what we're doing and assist in the effort. As we gain some advantage with the crowd and they start to move back, the line of police and strikebreakers starts moving forward. Our attempt to increase the distance between the two groups is not working.

That damn Kirk! He and I will come to blows before this day ends.

We have as many steelworkers and supporters here today as there are police, strikebreakers, and thugs. Since we can't increase the distance between the two opposing lines, I go looking for someone in charge. I find the police commander who is reading from a document using a megaphone at one end of the police line.

In a calm and authoritative manner, he speaks to the crowd in front of him. "I ask you in the name of the people of the State of Ohio to disperse." He looks out over the crowd in front of him and repeats his message. "Again, I ask you in the name of the people of the State of Ohio to disperse." He then drops the paper to his side with a flourish and gives no verbal commands.

When he lowers the paper, all hell breaks loose. Bullets and gas start flying everywhere. Then the clubbing begins. The entire line of police, thugs, and strikebreakers descend on the steelworkers and their supporters with a vengeance. In seconds, the scene changes from two large groups facing each other and shouting insults and threats, into a battlefield. We're being attacked by an army of gun-toting, stick-wielding cops, strikebreakers, and thugs. Steel men and some women are being severely beaten, many temporarily blinded by tear gas, and some are shot.

I can't believe what I'm witnessing. It's Chicago all over again, only here at my mill. I work my way through the battling crowd toward Henry and Charles, who are just off to my right. Along with several steel men, they are battling a horde of police officers and thugs. They are just trying to defend themselves. When I get close to them, shots ring out. Henry, who is standing less than an arm's length from me, is shot in the back three times and falls to the ground mortally wounded. Standing a few feet from him are Kirk's two thugs holding revolvers. Smoke is coming from the barrel of one of the revolvers.

Without hesitating, I attack the thug, wrestle the gun from him, and beat him severally about the head with his own gun. Charles steps in, stopping me from killing him. Kirk's other thug did not fire his weapon and dropped it on the ground. Charles secured both weapons and held one of them on the two thugs.

I kneel next to Henry. There is nothing I can do for him; he is dying. Holding him close to me, he looks up and says in a low fading voice. "Take care of Melanie and my baby...."

His eyes close, and his shallow breathing stops. He is gone. My god, I've lost another dear and close friend. To come this far in life, survive what he has endured, and be killed standing up for his workers. Hatred boils up from within, and rage overpowers me. I stand up, move over to the two thugs, and grab the one who shot Henry. Staring into his eyes intensely and oblivious to the chaos around us, I pull his face close to mine. "Listen to me, you sorry bastard. I have one question. Did Kirk order you to do this?"

Both thugs look scared and are hesitant to talk. I'm impatient. I step back and slam my right fist into the jaw of the thug who killed Henry. He reels back and falls to the ground as blood flows from his mouth and nose. "Answer my damn question, or I'll shoot you myself! Right here, right now!"

This brings a response from both thugs. "Kirk told us to kill both of you."

With their admission, I begin to calm down as my senses detect the level of activity and noise around us is abating quickly. I've been so focused on what just happened that I hadn't noticed the National Guard troops deploying and moving through the throngs of combatants trying to restore order. Looking around the field before me, I see a young boy limping by, bleeding from a bullet wound in his leg. Men and women are scattered over the ground, and many lie there motionless. Some appear dead, others wounded and bleeding from clubbing, gunshot wounds, and severe beatings.

Charles manages to convince the officer in charge of the guard unit, a major, to detain the two thugs for the murder of Henry. He also directs him to get some of his men busy taking care of the wounded. Charles is well connected in Washington DC and within the military hierarchy. The carnage he's witnessed today infuriates him. The National Guard Major knows Charles by reputation and realizes he'll bring down considerable heat and attention to this whole sorry affair. I'm guessing the major decided to cooperate fully to help save his own skin when the inquiries and retributions begin.

Charles and I remove Henry's body from the field and carry him to one of many ambulances that arrive on the scene. We've lost another close friend with whom we served in France and with whom I've worked since returning home. How can this be? Once again, an American doughboy has been killed at the hands of his fellow countrymen. What a travesty of injustice, and the man who caused it sits in his office thinking he's untouchable. Pausing over the body of Henry and saying a silent prayer, I wipe away my tears, regain my composure, and set out to do what I should have done a long time ago. I walk straight through the main gate to the mill and head for Kirk's office. Charles follows me without saying a word.

KIRK'S OFFICE

Walking through the door to Kirk's outer sanctum, his secretary informs me he's busy and can't be disturbed. I just look at her and walk past. Grabbing the door handle to his office, I turn it and swing the door wide open. The door slams against the wall, and to my front sits Kirk. He's smoking a cigar and talking on the phone. With my dramatic entrance, an intensity of purpose seething with deep anger, I walk right to the front of his desk. He drops the phone on his desk and pushes his chair back as if trying to escape from behind his desk. He's shaken, and fear spreads across his face.

I walk around his desk and stand directly over him. He hasn't gotten up from his chair. He is still sitting as if frozen to it. "Kirk, you lousy son-of-a-bitch. Do you really think you're above the law and can order your thugs to kill people?"

Kirk is scared and trembles as he struggles to respond meekly. "I don't know what you're talking about."

I respond. "Oh, really. Your two thugs just admitted that you ordered them to kill Henry and me during the chaos you orchestrated. The National Guard is now detaining them."

"They're lying. Whatever happened, they did it on their own. I had nothing to do with it." He responds once again meekly.

I've had enough of his bullshit and grab his shirt collar, pulling him up to me. I then slam him against the wall. His head snaps back and hits the wooden wall. Hard. He's dazed and afraid. "You're wrong, Sam. I didn't do it. I swear I didn't!"

"I don't believe you." I grab him again and slap him repeatedly across the face until he starts whimpering and slowly responds. "All right, all right, I told them to!"

With his admission, my reaction is swift as I hit him repeatedly with left and right punches to his face and stomach. It's over quickly as he crumbles to the floor, bleeding from the mouth and withering in pain. Charles moves in and stops me from punishing him further.

"Sam, that's enough. The law will take care of this asshole. Trust me. I'll see to it."

Looking down on this miserable excuse for a man, I feel no pity or remorse for him. Nor do I have any joy in what I've done. Charles pulls me back, and I slowly settle down, trying to relax, as the reality of what has taken place this morning overtakes me.

Several National Guard troops come into the office with a captain in charge of them. Charles tells the captain to take control of Kirk, put him with the other two thugs they have in custody, and get him out of our sight now. All three are going to be charged with murder.

AFTERMATH

After the violent encounter between Kirk's armed thugs and enforcers and our steelworkers and their supporters, actions and outcomes occurred swiftly. The board of directors met later that day and fired Kirk, removed his father from the board of directors, and installed me as the new Republic Iron and Steel Company Manager. I hired Charles as a consultant to work with management and our employees to establish a union and improve the work environment for the men and their families.

Kirk and his two thugs were all tried for murder and found guilty. The thug who killed Henry was sentenced to death, and Kirk and his other accomplice were sentenced to prison for their crimes. Although several mill workers and their supporters were hurt that day, some seriously, all recovered from their wounds. Henry was the only person to lose his life; paying a heavy price for what we ultimately gained. I commissioned a sculptor to design and sculpt a life-size figure of Henry in full World War I battle dress with his rifle slung over his shoulder. It stands proudly at the front entrance to our main mill building for all to see as they enter and exit our facility.

The base of the sculpture was inscribed: "Henry Miller, doughboy, husband, father, son, steelman, and a great friend to all who knew him. We owe much to Henry and men like him. Be thankful they walk among us."

37

ANOTHER MCCORMICK GOES TO WAR

WAR CLOUDS

In Europe, under the dictator Adolf Hitler and his Nazi Party, Germany invades Poland on September 1, 1939. This unprovoked aggression pulls France and England back into war with Germany. The Germans then invade France on May 10, 1940, which ends shortly with the surrender of France to Germany. Germany then turned its sights on Great Britain and conducted unremitting and destructive air raids with their Luftwaffe Air Force from July through September 1940. England holds on and fights the Germans alone until Germany invades Russia on June 22, 1941. Fascist Italy, under the dictator Benito Mussolini, invades Ethiopia, annexing it into their East African Colony. Mussolini then invades Albania and, after a brief military campaign, overruns that country and forces its ruler into exile.

In Asia and the Pacific, Japan follows an aggressive and imperialistic expansion policy of gaining access to more territory, raw materials, oil, and regional dominance. From 1931 to 1937, China and Japan skirmish in small, localized engagements, which they call "incidents." On July 7, 1937, a dispute between Japanese and Chinese troops in Peking escalates into a full-scale invasion, and war between the two countries ensues. This full-scale war between the Chinese and the Empire of Japan is regarded as the beginning of the war in Asia. An alliance eventually forms between Germany, Japan, and Italy, and they refer to themselves as the Axis Powers. Here in our country, we have an official policy of neutrality and have stayed out of these conflicts so far. This has not been easy as both Germany and Japan have tested our patience many times with small, unprovoked attacks on our merchant ships and citizens living and traveling abroad in the areas they control.

Congress passes the Selective Training and Service Act of 1940 on September 16, 1940, which establishes the first peacetime conscription in United States history. Shortly after the Act passes, Marie is asked to serve on the Selective Service Board of Stark County, which includes Louisville. This is quite an honor, as no woman has previously served on earlier boards of this nature. Her official duties in this capacity keep her busy many days during the week.

Outside of her board duties, Marie maintains an active social calendar within our community. She still finds time to give freely of herself to Sean and me. She's always doting over Sean, constantly worrying about him, yet beaming with pride at his accomplishments and development into the fine young man he has become. I believe she has loved me since the day we first laid eyes on each other back in France at the field hospital. Our love for each other has only grown stronger since that day.

Melanie gave birth to a healthy boy whom she named Henry Jr., our godson. Marie dotes over him just as she does with our son. We're both very proud to be Henry Jr.'s godparents and consider him our second son.

As for myself, I stay busy at the steel mill as manager of the company. After the steel strike in 1937, I was elevated by the board to run the company and turn it around. It has not been easy, but with the help and support of many good men at the mill, we have come a long way. With the guidance and support of my close friend Charles Glazebrook working as a consultant for the company, we set the standard for other Little Steel companies to emulate.

While recovering from my wounds in France after the war, doctors told me my respiratory and digestive systems would deteriorate as I grew older. This was from being gassed, eating inferior—sometimes bordering on abysmal—food, poor sanitary conditions, and tainted water. They were right. They have. Most doughboys suffer from the same maladies. Over the years, I've learned to cope with the consequences of serving in France with little assistance from our own government. France provided more medical facilities and assistance to their soldiers following the war than are available here in America. Many doughboys believe our country should have emulated the French in this regard. We haven't. Generally, we as veterans have been left on our own to seek out medical attention concerning our lingering post-war issues. As war clouds gather again and we move closer to another war, I can only hope they do a better job with the next generation of veterans.

DECEMBER 7, 1941

Today is beautiful, with clear skies and a mild chill in the air. We are just finishing our lunch, having returned home earlier from church this Sunday, December 7, 1941. Sean came home last night from Ohio State University, where he is a senior majoring in Mechanical Engineering with a minor in Russian History. He is a cadet in the U.S. Army Reserve Officer Training Corps and the

Civilian Pilot Training Program (CPTP). This program began in 1939 under the sponsorship of the Civil Aeronautics Administration with the stated purpose of fostering private flying. However, it's well known that the CPTP has assumed major importance alongside the Army, Navy, and Coast Guard in our National Defense Organization. The United States has been slowly, ever so slowly, preparing for another war.

Sitting around our kitchen table enjoying some coffee, Marie and I listen to Sean share some stories about his most recent college and pilot training experiences. He is athletic and handsome, standing at just over six feet with dark wavy hair, green penetrating eyes, and a muscular build. He has grown into a very mature, level-headed, and well-mannered young man. He inspires confidence and exhibits leadership potential. His many friends enjoy his company and covet his friendship. Marie and I are very proud of him and feel blessed to be his parents and play a role in his life.

In a calm, mature, low-key manner, Sean conveys his latest flight experiences. "I love what I'm doing in the pilot training program. Those of us in the senior program have come a long way as a group and individually. We finished our Primary Pilot Training earlier this year. We accumulated sixty hours of flight time flying old Stearman biplanes. To me, it was like riding a bicycle. Thanks to all the pilots up at our grass airfield here in Louisville, I managed to accumulate a lot of flying time before entering the CPTP program. This certainly helped me, and I found myself helping other fellows get the hang of it."

Sean takes a moment and looks at his mother and me for a reaction. Maire looks at him with a mother's love radiating from her smiling face. "Sean, dear, was it dangerous? What kind of flying did they teach you? Were the planes you flew in good condition?"

Responding, "Well, mother, it wasn't dangerous, and the

planes were well maintained. As for flying, they taught basic stuff to get us up in the air and back down again without killing ourselves. They wanted to weed out any fellows who weren't comfortable with or couldn't adjust to the physical and mental challenges of flying."

Marie is beaming with pride, but I see fear in her eyes for Sean as she strains to hide it from him. Looking over at Sean, I inquire of him. "Sean, what kind of training came next, and how was it?"

"Well, Dad, next came what they call Basic Pilot Training. We just finished that in mid-November. I accumulated seventy-five flight hours in a single-engine monoplane. The monoplane has a single main wing. Unlike the biplanes, which have two main wings stacked one above the other. Our monoplanes are a little faster, and the airframe can handle a little more stress."

"What does that mean?" I ask.

"We can do more aerobatics with them and faster, steeper dives. But not much more than a good biplane. In this phase of our training, we were taught how to fly in formation, fly by instruments, fly at night, and fly for long distances."

"How did that go, son? Just curious. Has everyone that started the training program with you stayed in the program?"

Sean responds in a more subdued, low-key manner. "We've lost three cadets due to accidents in training so far, and two others dropped out early. They just couldn't get comfortable with being up there in the clouds. It seems that some fellows are just born to fly and others, not so much. Just about anyone can learn the basics of flying, but if you're training to fly in combat, you better be sure!"

Marie and I are both intrigued by what he is telling us, and she asks another question. "Sean, what comes next in your training?"

"It's called Advanced Pilot Training. This is where we select either single-engine for fighters, or multi-engine for bombers, to continue our pilot training. We'll fly about eighty hours in this phase and receive our pilot's wings upon graduation. We should start this phase sometime in late January next year."

Sean's excitement about flying and training with his fellow cadets is conveyed through his responses and the smile on his face. Once again, I'm convinced he was born to fly. Sean looks at both of us with those penetrating green eyes and smiles as he realizes we're totally engrossed in what he is telling us.

Continuing, "Our last phase of training is called Transition Pilot Training. This is where we transition into the actual fighter or bomber that we will fly when we finish the program. I understand we'll then spend at least two more months training for potential combat duty."

I look at Sean and ask, "What do you want to fly, son, fighters or bombers?"

Sean responds without hesitating. "I'm going into bombers. I'm hoping to be assigned to B-17s, Flying Fortresses. They are the newest heavy bombers and will surely see a lot of action should we go to war."

With Sean's last comment, reality sets in for Marie. Sean is training for war. Her facial expression changes to one of concern and fear. Some tears form in her eyes and slowly trickle down onto her cheeks. Using her blouse sleeves, Marie wipes them from her face trying to hide them from Sean.

Our conversation is interrupted by heavy knocking on the front door. I go to the door and find John and Karen, our next-door neighbors, standing there. They both look distressed, scared, and mad. I open the door and invite them in. John speaks in an emotional and outraged tone.

"Sam, have you heard the news over the radio?"

"What news? We've been enjoying conversations with Sean and haven't been listening to the radio. What's going on?"

"There's news of a 'sneak attack' being broadcast across the country on radio bulletins."

I'm joined by Sean and Marie, who walk up to me as I respond to John. "What are you talking about?"

"The Japanese are bombing our naval base at Pearl Harbor in Honolulu, Hawaii. They have hundreds of planes attacking military installations and our ships. Initial reports aren't good. Many ships have been sunk and others badly damaged. There are multiple casualties!"

Marie puts her arm around my waist as I pull her close to my side. We're both stunned by the news and struggle to control our emotions as we comprehend what we just heard. Sean comes up behind us, places his arms over our shoulders, and pulls us all close together. He speaks slowly, softly, and almost hauntingly. "Mother, Father, it looks like it's my turn to go off to war."

Those words send a chill up my spine. I fear it will reawaken within me the nightmares from my days in the trenches and crossing over "no man's land" in France. Those nightmares have slowly waned over the years as memories faded into the recesses of my mind. With Sean going off to war, how can I keep these memories dormant, knowing that he will experience the horrors and trauma of war for himself? While he is gone, I will live every day until he returns, fearing for his safety.

My god, we were told that World War I was "The War to End all Wars," and some of us believed it. It may sound extraordinarily naïve, but I think one had to believe it. The mud, blood, and brutality only made sense if it were the last time civilized man would ever have to suffer through it. I wanted to believe that men on all sides of that war would rise as one and kick any politician in the teeth who even mentioned the possibility of another war. I cannot believe anyone who has been through it could ever allow it to happen again. Yet here we are, about to open the door to hell and go at it again!

EPILOGUE

On the morning of December 7, 1941, the Japanese launched a surprise attack on Pearl Harbor at 7:48 a.m. Pacific Time, and rained death and destruction down on United States Navy and Army personnel. The base was attacked by 353 Imperial Japanese aircraft in two waves, launched from six aircraft carriers. All eight of the United States Navy battleships docked in the harbor that fateful morning suffered considerable damage. Four were sunk—all but the USS Arizona were later raised. Six were returned to service and went on to fight in the war.

Many of the men serving on the USS Arizona were still in their bunks or just preparing for the day when it all came to a sudden and traumatic end. A Japanese bomb hit the main deck of the USS Arizona. It penetrated several decks down to an ammunition magazine, which exploded violently, taking the lives of 1,177 officers and crew members.

The day after the attack, President Roosevelt delivered his Day of Infamy speech to a joint session of Congress in which he called for a formal declaration of war on Japan. Congress approved his request less than an hour later. On December 11, Germany and Italy declared war on the United States. Congress issued a declaration of war against Germany and Italy later that same day. Thus, began World War Two, which would far exceed the deaths and suffering experienced in World War One.

In *The Son*, book 2 of the *Legacy of Honor* trilogy, Sean finishes college, is commissioned a 2nd Lieutenant, and completes his pilot training in 1943. He's sent to England to fly B-17s with the 8th Army Air Force, the "Mighty Eighth." The readers share first-hand experience of Sean's harrowing bombing missions over Europe in which he and his fellow aircrew comrades experience horrific aerial combat, and meet historical figures while serving in the Korea War, Cold War, Cuban Missile Crisis, and Vietnam War. His three sons continue the family's military legacy in book 3.

In Book 3, *The Descendants,* readers follow Sean's three sons as they serve in the military, participate in armed conflicts, and interact with historical figures in historical events. In Vietnam, Alan serves as the Commanding Officer of an Infantry Company with the 101st Airborne Division. Lee is commissioned an ensign in the U.S. Navy, completes Navy flight school, and is assigned to fly helicopters. Scott begins college, is drafted into the military in 1971 and is stationed in South Korea as an Infantryman. He'll go on to serve in Iran and Afghanistan. Their varied lives and encounters will make even the most jaded reader appreciate their service and sacrifice.

The *Legacy of Honor* trilogy chronicles the gripping saga of an American military family as its members experience life, love, and combat over one hundred years of uniquely different cultures and world events and warfare.

You won't want to miss reading all three books in this remarkable *Legacy of Honor* series.

ACKNOWLEDGMENTS

Telling this story has been another exceptional and rewarding writing experience for me. Growing up around my grandfather, who was a doughboy in World War I, and many of his friends who also served in France during the war, I often overheard some of their stories. As a young boy, my grandfather took me with him many times to his Saturday night poker games on the second floor of the fire station in the small town of Louisville, Ohio. He and his buddies, all former doughboys, would play cards, smoke their pipes, and have a few drinks. As the night progressed into early morning, they would occasionally start talking about some of their shared war experiences and frustrations following the war. They always thought I had fallen asleep on the fire station couch, which wasn't always the case. As I grew up and experienced war for myself, I often reflected on those times and found I could better appreciate their stories.

My grandfather only shared two stories with me personally over the years; both were light and humorous. In fact, he shared them many times over the years when we were together. What little I learned about his war exploits came from his friends and my father, his son, later in life. Although they've long since passed, I wish to thank my grandfather and those men for their shared stories and the inspiration they gave me to write this book.

I wish to thank my wife, Linda, for all her support, encouragement, and understanding as I endeavored to write this novel.

It was another journey we traveled together to arrive at the stage where my book was published. Linda served as my first editor and helped make it a better manuscript for submission to my publisher. Thank you!

A special thank you to Frank Eastland of Publish Authority, who accepted my manuscript for submission and subsequent publication. His professionalism, guidance, and support are very much appreciated. Working with him and his staff during the publication process improved my submitted manuscript greatly.

Also with Publish Authority, to Bob and Nancy Laning, my editors, and Raeghan Rebstock, my book cover design lead, thank you for everything. It was a real pleasure to work with each of you on the publication of this novel.

The combined efforts of the staff of Publish Authority have resulted in my second novel, *Legacy of Hono: The Patriarch*. This is book one in the trilogy titled *Legacy of Honor*. I look forward to working with Publish Authority on books two and three.

My sincere thanks to those members of my family and friends who provided me with their technical support, encouragement, and comments during the writing, editing, and ultimate publication of my novel. A special thank you to Kathy Cretney for her input during the drafting of my manuscript.

To you who read my novel, I say a special thank you. I hope and trust you found your reading experience insightful, educational, and enlightening.

ABOUT THE AUTHOR

Larry Freeland was born in Canton, Ohio, and comes from a long line of military veterans. His father was an officer in the Army Air Corps/United States Air Force whose career spanned thirty years and included World War II through the early stages of the Vietnam War. His grandfather was a doughboy in World War I, and his two brothers were both war veterans, having served in multiple conflicts that our country has been involved in following the Vietnam War.

After graduating from high school at Ramey Air Force Base in Puerto Rico, he attended the University of South Florida in Tampa, Florida. After graduating in June 1968, he entered the U.S. Army and served one tour in Vietnam with the 101st Airborne Division as an infantry officer and a CH-47 helicopter pilot.

Upon release from active duty in 1973, Larry returned to civilian life and pursued a career in the financial industry. After retiring from banking in 2001, he worked as an independent financial consultant for three years in the Atlanta area. He then worked as an instructor for six years with Lanier Technical College in their Management and Leadership Development Program.

Larry is now retired and lives in North Georgia with his wife Linda, a retired schoolteacher. They enjoy traveling together around the country, going on cruises, and visiting historical places in Europe. They are both fans of LeMans racing and drive their Corvette to some annual races held in the United States. They stay involved in various activities, most notably those associated with the Cystic Fibrosis Foundation and Veterans-related organizations.

For more information about the author, visit his website at www.LarryFreeland.com

And visit him on social media via
Linkedin.com/in/larry-freeland-8b8618204
Facebook.com/LarryFreeland.author
Instagram.com/larryfreeland_author